D1504668

The mysterious rifle bullet

did little damage to the world's largest building, and few of the 27,000 employees roaming the 17 miles of corridors would ever know about it. The high-powered slug smashed the window of the Chemical and Biological Warfare Officer, but was it meant for him? Or for an incoming VIP helicopter? Or for whom?

Lee Frost, head of Pentagon security, had to know. A man scarred by many battles and burdened by many doubts and griefs, he was still a tenacious investigator, and he was determined to run down the truth no matter where it led him.

So Colonel Frost began to probe and question throughout the bureaucratic labyrinth of the military complex, upward toward the levels of command and outward, into the halls of Congress and the Executive offices, and at last outside, into the rolling streets of a city inflaming itself to violence.

A daring, controversial novel in the tradition of **Fail Safe** and **Seven Days in May**, PENTAGON is the first authentic, inside look into the world's most awesome concentration of power and influence, and how that power may be used—and abused—in a moment of crisis.

ABOUT THE AUTHOR

HANK SEARLS, an Annapolis graduate, spent ten years as a regular officer and two years as a civilian in the defense industry. In World War II and Korea he served as a deck-officer, a public-information specialist, a combat-cameraman, and a naval aviator. He is a combat veteran of the South Pacific, the Philippine Sea, Iwo Jima, and Okinawa. As a Navy combat-cameraman he served with the Marines during Korea and ranged the Far East from Bangkok to Manila. He was in Saigon during the French Foreign Legion campaigns in Viet Nam and in Tokyo during the Communist riots of 1951. He was a regular officer when the Defense Department was born, observed its adolescence, and resigned his commission as it reached maturity. He worked in the Southern California defense industry until he quit to begin his first novel, *The Big X*. His other major novels are: *The Crowded Sky, The Pilgrim Project, Hero Ship,* and *Pentagon*.

He is married, with three children. He and his wife live aboard their 40-foot ketch, cruising the Pacific and the Caribbean.

PENTAGON

A NOVEL BY

Hank Searls

WARNER

PAPERBACK LIBRARY
NEW YORK

WARNER PAPERBACK LIBRARY EDITION

First Printing: September, 1972

Copyright © 1971 by Hank Searls

All rights reserved under International and Pan American Conventions.

Author's Note:
The Pentagon changes very little, for it is too big to change. The people in it change very little, for there are too many of them. My ten-year term among them as a regular officer and my two years in the defense industry may have forced some of them into this book in the flesh. Their presence, while mostly coincidental and unintended, is welcome and gratifying.
—HANK SEARLS

This Warner Paperback Library Edition is published by arrangement with Bernard Geis Associates, Inc.

Warner Paperback Library is a division of Warner Books, Inc., 315 Park Avenue South, New York, N.Y. 10010.

To my wife, for Everything

Boswell: "Yet, Sir, I think that common soldiers are worse thought of than other men in the same rank of life; such as labourers."
Johnson: ". . . A common soldier, too, generally eats more than he can pay for. But when a common soldier is civil in his quarters, his red coat procures him a measure of respect."

BOSWELL, *Life of Johnson,* 1776

"You are . . . entering an Army that has borne the brunt of a lonely and difficult war, far from home and in the face of open and hostile lack of support from a minority of our citizens."

SPIRO AGNEW, Graduation Address, United States Military Academy, 1970

Who represents my body in Pentagon? Who spends billions for war manufacture? Who levies the majority to exult unwilling in Bomb Roar? Brainwash! Mind-fear! Governor's language!

ALLEN GINSBERG, *Pentagon Exorcism,* 1968

Phase I

OPERATION FICKLE-FINGER

Chapter One

The act of the rifleman who last August slammed a slug through a Pentagon window was never reported in the established press and has remained practically unsung by that of the Washington underground. Among the reasons for the veil are faint communications, journalistic lethargy, and compartmentalized bureaucracy. Power in the Pentagon traditionally welcomes a vacuum around such news and would not dream of filling it.

But most of all, the shot was simply lost in the brutal size of the place. From the air the Pentagon is so vast that it seems one-dimensional—the successful geometric effort of a Gargantuan child to scratch a series of five-sided polygons one within the other in the grass beside a muddy stream. Seen from the ground, though, it actually turns out to be five stories high and to loom quite massively between the Potomac River and Arlington National Cemetery. Thirty years ago its architect was asked to assure a Senate committee that the building would not obstruct the view of Washington "when one is in the Arlington Cemetery, on the high ground." The architect replied that it wouldn't, but he was apparently referring to the dead, for, though the slopes of Arlington finally rise to challenge it, still the Pentagon dominates those rows of graves from which it can be glimpsed between the trees.

It is the world's largest office building. It would displace a dozen city blocks in downtown Washington. Each of its five faces is three football fields long: to orbit the outer of its concentric rings you must walk a mile.

Twenty-seven thousand people work there, ingesting 30,000 cups of coffee and 30 tons of food daily and emitting 3 million gallons of sewage and 13 tons of wastepaper every eight hours. Although the place has more than one phone per capita, makes 90,000 internal and external calls a day, and has 15 miles of pneumatic tube for messages, as well as 5,000 intercoms, the structure is so enormous that news travels slowly along its seventeen miles of corridor. Some news, if those who would prevent its circulation are lucky, travels not at all.

So the high-velocity round that tore last August 3rd from a row of graves halfway up the eastern slope of Arlington passed almost unnoticed. It whispered over the heliport tower on the lawn by South Parking and crashed through the fourth-floor window of the Army's gentle, benign, and ranking Chemical and Biological Warfare Officer. Since the general was out to lunch (and the office itself had become invisible on the week the President had elegantly washed the nation's hands of chemical and biological warfare), the slug was allowed by Public Affairs officers to penetrate the consciousness of the Pentagon hardly at all. Most reporters in the Pentagon Press Room —only two stories and two corridors away—heard of it only much later.

Outside the Pentagon's walls the general citizenry was spared the item entirely. Even the radical "Street Community" of Dupont Circle would never have heard of it had it not appeared mysteriously in a jumbled issue of Washington's *Underground Clarion*. It was read by acid-heads and speed-freaks hawking the paper around the Circle: they could not have cared less. In the Friend's Meeting House on Florida Avenue (thought by the Pentagon to be the first stop on the Underground Railway to Quebec) and at the Peace League on Decatur Place, it was digested with some attention, and in the brownstone communes along Q Street with still more, but at all these places with only the faintest hope that it was true.

Ignored or not, the bullet is the only message ever known to have been delivered from a grave in Arlington to the Pentagon. Army Counterintelligence inside the building acknowledged it and set to work.

Holding the fine old Springfield rifle at the balance, with his fingers wrapped in a handkerchief in case there were prints, he watched his two sergeants and the potbellied FBI man sweating to remove the back seat from the FBI

12

agent's car. Standing coatless, lean, and in cool slacks in the shade of the oaks, he was still too warm on the cemetery slope. He smelled rain to come and caught a whiff of the Potomac, evoking the Mekong River. A gnat tickled his ear. He brushed at it, longing to be back in his air-conditioned office, but the Pentagon was infinitely distant through the leaves above the graves.

When the three men had placed the car-cushion on the cemetery road between his own Army sedan and the agent's Plymouth, he laid the weapon on the seat like an accident victim. He watched for a moment as the FBI man began to dust the scope and breech, found him competent, and left the three. Tall, lank, and limping slightly, he began to traverse the grassy hill, for the second time, along the row of identical headstones toward the private's grave by which they had found the gun. He stayed intent upon the terrain until his knee began to hurt from being too long in graveyard dampness. When this distracted him he deliberately paused until he could return his attention to the well-clipped turf, not wanting to miss a glove dropped in the rush to get away or a pair of dark glasses or even the footprint of a man scrambling to get back to a waiting car.

The grave at which the weapon had been found (near the long florist's box in which the rifleman had apparently carried it) overlooked the Pentagon. The name cut into the stone was in GI letters, standard issue. It read: "Pvt. Paul Krause, U.S. Army, 1908–1939." That was all. Most of the nearby graves had company, battalion, and regiment inscribed, but perhaps Krause had reached Arlington via a casual company or Walter Reed Hospital or the District Stockade and no one had bothered to identify him by outfit.

He studied the surrounding markers: Lemmon, McNally, Jorgensen, Lister, two Joneses, and a Schultz, all buried the same year. He doubted that he had really known any of the men who lay around him now, but he knew them anyway: whining alcoholic regulars snuggled tightly into Army routine, rarely married, refusing responsibility, drunk on pass and argumentative in barracks, obsequious to their lieutenant and hating his guts, unedu-

13

cated but close-knit. Even on the tail-end of the Depression, thirty years ago when they had been buried, while men still clung to the service for security, the Army had not got twenty-one dollars worth of man for twenty-one dollars a month, but there had been regulars like those who lay here who had later fought on Bataan and on New Guinea beaches and died as well or better than the bright volunteers and draftees of '41, and at a greater cost to the Japs. To slither up a coral cliff under fire required no brains, only fear of not looking well in the eyes of the only friends you had.

Nineteen thirty-nine had not been a vintage year for Arlington, but the dead in this area could not all have been flotsam. There must have been married men and fathers seeded in the rows around him. Now that he was away from his own agents and the FBI man he could let his mind range without distraction, and he wondered if there was a tie between the nearby graves and the shot at the seat of the mighty. He played with the notion that some demented relative had simply fired in blind anger at the Pentagon after decades of brooding. Perhaps the rifleman had been a dead soldier's psychotic son brought up to believe that his father had been somehow wronged by the Army or his mother cheated of a pension. He even toyed with the intriguing image of a little old widow of sixty, herself blasting away with her husband's old piece at the limestone colossus below.

He passed his hand along the top of Krause's streaked headstone. All of the markers in the area were exactly alike, for in 1939 no Service family had the money to improve on the government's gravestone. Krause's had a chip in its top, but the notch was as weathered as its face and the chunk must have been knocked off when the marker was placed, or perhaps hit by a tread on one of the cemetery's dirty-yellow Ford gravedigging scoops. One machine had clanked back from lunch with its crew while he was looking for the weapon, and now it was gnawing out a grave by the wall a hundred yards away.

He strolled down the slope to the excavator. He signaled the operator, a gnarled Negro in a straw hat, to stop the scoop. There was a final metallic screech and the gaping

14

jaws hung swinging over the grave. He questioned the driver and the two black "assistants" who watched him. At the presumed time of the firing they had been—or said they had been—sitting in the ampitheater behind the Tomb of the Unknown Soldier, eating their lunches and watching the tourists. They had heard no shots at all. He asked the operator how deep he had got before lunch and the black replied: "Four, five feet."

The accent was deep Virginia but there was no "sir" on the end of it, a mark of the times and of the Negro's conviction, since he was in civvies, that he was a plain-clothes cop. While the three blacks stared at him impassively, he skirted the grave, now six feet deep. Down the hill, bordering the stone wall, similar mounds arose. Despite what he had heard of Arlington being finally and irrevocably filled, there was apparently always room for a few more.

He squatted by a new mound and squinted through the oaks towering further down the hill. The Pentagon was visible and even more closely in range than from Krause's grave, although from here trees blocked the window the slug had holed, and blocked, too, the heliport tower on the lawn. He moved to the fieldstone wall, only four feet high and perfectly scalable, and peered across at the quiet road by the Navy Annex.

He drew his first conclusion. Given the absence of the gravedigging personnel, anyone who didn't care which Pentagon window he hit would have left his car on the Annex road outside the low stone wall. He himself would have fired from behind a newly dug mound, slipped over the fieldstone, and been gone without exposing himself for more than a few seconds. Instead, the rifleman had hazarded fifty feet of open terrain between the point at which the gun had been found and the winding cemetery drive at which he must have parked his car, and then had risked the possibility that the sound of his rifle had closed Arlington's lower gates.

He decided that the rifleman had been firing at something definite that could not be hit from here. He returned to Krause's grave. He studied the ground again, this time looking for the divot the rifle would have made had it

15

been tossed, say, from another row. There was no mark, not even an imprint to show that it had been simply dropped. It weighed, he had learned nearly thirty years ago, precisely nine-and-a-half pounds, more with the scope on it, and it would have left a deep depression in the damp, grassy sod. So the sniper, despite what must have been an impulse to drop it and flee, had instead laid it down carefully. To treat it gently even when in haste could have been a military inhibition ingrained on parade grounds and drill fields: "All right! Who dropped the fucking piece?"

But he put the deduction aside and watched his men and the tubby FBI agent, carrying the rifle, moving toward him along the row. He noticed that Sergeant Liebholtz, a slim young agent with feral ears and foxy eyes, was searching the ground; his other sergeant, Maxon, broad-faced and wide-eyed as always when excited, had his head down studying his clipboard. Maxon, always on display when he thought he was being watched, probably thought that fiddling with his notes made him look efficient. The FBI man handed Lee Frost the rifle.

"Nothing, Colonel. We even dusted the empty brass. Nothing on the florist box, either. He must have worn gloves."

Lee Frost nodded and took the weapon. It was stamped with the symbol of the Rock Island Arsenal. Its serial was only a few hundred numbers from the one issued him as a recruit and etched forever into his brain. You never forgot your first woman or your first rifle, they said. At least twenty-five years old, this gun must be, and in mint-perfect shape. He longed to keep the weapon: maybe he could. He opened the bolt. Then, grasping the muzzle, he swung the stock in an arc toward the sun and peered up the barrel. The grooves were deeply etched, the lands were sharp. It could not have had more than a hundred rounds pumped through it.

Perhaps the rifleman was an ex-Marine. There were old-time jarheads who swore by the Springfield's accuracy, still carrying it into battle with their personal gear. In Korea he had shared a ridge near Chorwon with the Fifth Marines. Their colonel, for sport, had each morning been

16

helicoptered with his scope-mounted Springfield to their forward O.P. There he would lie half the day waiting for a shot at 1,200 yards across a ravine (and finally scored, too, on a Gook hanging out his laundry at the bunker door).

Rifle in hand, Lee Frost studied the Pentagon. The rifleman, expert or not, had only actually hit the window once, but from the empty brass they had found by the grave they knew he had fired three times. He wondered where the other two rounds had flown, and wondered, too, why the Honor Guard at the Tomb had reported only one shot.

"You get hold of that sentry, Liebholtz?" he asked. Liebholtz reported that the silly bastard had headed for his barracks at Fort Myer the moment he had been relieved; his platoon leader was bringing him back. There being no further reason to delay, Lee Frost tried the rifle's sling for size and found that he could easily fit his arm into the loop but that the strap was set too tightly. The rifleman had apparently had a good set of biceps but short arms. No matter how Lee struggled, he could not fit. The FBI agent observed his efforts: "Maybe he was just more, you know, supple?"

"Younger?" suggested Lee Frost.

"*You* said it, Colonel," the agent smiled. "I didn't."

He found that he didn't like the FBI man at all, but tried not to show it. "I'm forty-six," he said mildly, "and I've had a strenuous life." He glanced at the agent's rubbery pot and thought: And stayed in a hell of a lot better shape than you. What's your excuse? But he decided that he might need the FBI's good will in the matter of liberating the rifle, and so kept silent, gritted his teeth against the pain in his knee, and sank to a cross-legged sitting position behind the grave. He left the sling off his arm and rested the piece on Krause's headstone. Before he was ready to sight, he heard a car door slam and looked up. A glossy black second lieutenant in iron-starched khakis and a private in gleaming full dress braced above him. They saluted in unison, with the extra flick of Honor Guards.

"The Colonel wanted to see my duty-sentry, sir?" the lieutenant asked. "This is Private Rasmussen."

"I had the post from twelve to thirteen hundred hours," the private volunteered. He was a blond youth with vacant eyes. His shoulders were back like a West Point plebe's. The twin yellow stripes down his dress trousers were not even creased, and only a tiny stain at his collar showed that he had begun to sweat.

"A whole hour? At ease; you must be exhausted."

The boy did not crack a smile. He snapped into a position of parade rest just as stiff as his stance at attention. Lee Frost asked if he had looked at his watch when he heard the firing.

"No, sir," the private said, almost proudly. "I just kept walking my post."

"That's very military of you."

The young man flushed. "Well, sir, at first I figured maybe I'd heard a blank."

"A *blank,* for Christ's sake?"

"A firing squad, sir. Funeral near Kennedy's grave," interposed the lieutenant. "Tell the Colonel, Rasmussen."

"I thought one of the guys on the burial detail, like, you know, missed the last salvo? And then fucked-up and fired anyway?"

"President Kennedy's grave," Lee Frost pointed out, "is a quarter of a mile away! In the opposite direction."

"They echo, Colonel," volunteered the lieutenant. Lee Frost looked at him silently. Not ROTC or OCS, he judged, but West Point, Negro or not. His eye fell on a massive class ring, sure enough. He had apparently learned the motto "loyalty up and down": what he needed now was a fast lesson in staying out of the way. The lieutenant read his mind: "You can't really tell," he said lamely, "up there on the Tomb."

"Jesus," breathed Lee, "I'm glad it wasn't an ambush. How many shots?"

"Just one, sir," said the private.

They had found two empty cases on the grass and one in the breech. Since the sentry had heard only one shot, the rifleman must have synchronized the other two reports with the salvos from the firing squad.

"How many firing squads do you have here a day?" he asked the lieutenant.

"All day long, sir. We try to discourage it. Navy Annex doesn't like the noise, and the men have to clean the rifles, but the next of kin always wants the whole *enchilada*."

"That's a damn shame, having to clean the rifles," Lee Frost remarked. He remembered serving on a burial detail in the Presidio a million years ago, with an old sergeant mumbling the ancient chant that gunners intoned to space the salvos: *"If I wasn't a gunner I wouldn't be here . . . Fire! If I wasn't a gunner I wouldn't be here . . . Fire!"* but he wanted to find out if the young lieutenant knew it too, grasping for a tie between the old days and the new: he was always doing that now; he didn't know why.

"How long between salvos?"

"Three seconds, sir."

And three salvos total. Less than ten seconds to fire, from the first to the last salvo. Not impossible, perhaps, even if the man had waited until he heard the first volley before removing the gun from its florist's box.

He told Maxon to get the private's statement in writing and returned his attention to the rifle. He had deliberately avoided reading the range set on the scope, not wanting the sniper's judgment to influence his own. Now, sitting behind the headstone, he let his eye rove over the silent ranks below: companies of white markers, battalions, regiments, a whole division drawn up as if waiting to vault the fieldstone wall and assault the Pentagon beyond. He let his vision drift to the manicured fields around the structure and finally up the western wall. The building was so enormous that it seemed much closer than it was until you noticed how tiny were the windows and antlike the cars in South Parking. The windows were a good gauge: when you could see them clearly, and distinguish the molding, the range was five hundred yards; when detail was lost, a thousand. He looked up at the lieutenant.

"Nine-fifty," he announced. "What do you figure?"

The officer squinted at the building. "Colonel, I never shot at over five hundred yards in my life."

Sergeant Liebholtz was grinning. "That must have gone

19

out with puttees," he ventured, "begging the Colonel's pardon."

"OK, you smart shit," murmured Lee Frost, "what's the windage?"

There was hardly a whisper of breeze, but Liebholtz touched a finger to his tongue, held it up professionally, and ventured: "Two left?"

Lee Frost shook his head. "Stick to Counterintelligence. Stay out of the line. OK?"

"Yes, sir," Liebholtz agreed. "I was going to volunteer for one more tour in Nam, but since the Colonel puts it that way, I'll stay."

Lee Frost squinted at the sniper's range-setting, having to hold the rifle almost at arm's length to read it. The sight was set at zero windage and 930 yards, almost precisely his own estimate. He was dealing with an expert, not some clown who had picked up the fine piece by luck and mail-order and shot it half-a-dozen times in the local dump. Of course, both he and the sniper could be wrong. He told Liebholtz to measure the range on a topo when they got back.

At last he put the weapon back on the headstone, and his cheek to the stock. The Springfield felt good. He had not sighted one in years. It even smelled right, of linseed oil and sweat. He put his eye to the scope. The Pentagon leaped at him from behind the crosshairs, clear and sharp, so that now he knew that the sniper was as far-sighted as himself, for he had warned the agent not to disturb the focus.

He raised the scope to the fourth floor of the western face, sliding it along the row of windows from the northwest point of the giant prism. He stopped at the window from which they had draped General Greenberg's green conference-table cover for want of a better marker. At twelve-power magnification with the Lyman scope, he could easily see the cracks radiating from a tiny dot in the upper-right-hand corner of the pane and the triangular hole from which had been knocked the shard of glass he had seen inside. He searched with the scope for a pit in the limestone wall to show where the other slugs had flown, sweeping first around the general's window and then around adjoining ones.

He had moved the field of view to the green-coppered roof above the general's office when he heard an echoing volley somewhere behind him: another funeral. Quickly he dropped the crosshairs back to the general's window, worked the bolt, held his breath, and waited for the second salvo. He tried to squeeze off in rhythm with it, but his cocking-piece snapped loudly a good half-second after the echo of the firing squad. If he had been a sniper trying to hide his fire, it would have sounded in his ear like a German Eighty-eight. He recocked the piece and on the last volley jerked it off in rhythm, so that he hardly heard the slap of his own firing pin, but he knew that if the rifle had been loaded he would have flinched in anticipation of the kick. He doubted that he would have hit the window at all. A dusty vision intruded, of a gross, half-Cherokee sergeant on the Benning range, probably long dead and possibly buried in the rows around him: "*Squeeze* it, Frost, like yuh mothuh's tit! Yuh jerk yuh prick, but yuh *squeeze* yuh trigger!"

If the sniper had succeeded in putting a slug through a given window while jerking the trigger to stay in time with the firing squad, the sniper was a better shot than he. Not liking to admit that, he decided that the shooter had pulled high—perhaps overshot the roof, even—on the first two rounds, diagnosed the problem, then recklessly, when the firing squad had stopped, properly squeezed off a third round.

He was about to lower the rifle when he heard a helicopter. He looked up from the scope. A big Huey was thrashing down the Potomac, nose low, tail high, and moving very fast. It reared over the glassed heliport tower on the lawn by the western face, shuddered like a horse reined in, plummeted, at the last moment thumped still in midair, a few feet above the pad, and touched down gently. It had passed between his firing position and the green-marked window. He returned his eye to the scope and centered the crosshairs on the helicopter door. A Pakistani colonel and an Air Force general clambered down the steps, the colonel holding his turban against the rotor blast. Lee followed them with the scope as they passed the glassed heliport tower and entered the building after a Gaston-Alphonse act at the glass swinging door.

"Liebholtz," he decided suddenly, "when we get back, get the incoming-outgoing log from the heliport tower. See if they have a passenger manifest. I want to know everybody who came or left by chopper between twelve and one."

"Yes sir. But sir?"

"Yeah?"

"If the guy was trying to knock down a chopper, and trying to synchronize with a firing squad at the same time, how would he know the squad would be firing just as it landed?"

He handed Liebholtz the rifle and stood up stiffly. He asked Liebholtz if he had ever heard of *serendipity:* Liebholtz had not. OK, Liebholtz, suppose the guy had come over to knock off somebody special, the Secretary of Defense, say, arriving by helicopter, and got here to find out there was a military funeral going on and it'd cover the sound of the shot, so he's trying to stay in rhythm with the salvos and he jerks off and misses the helicopter, only the Secretary has canceled out and isn't in the chopper anyway, he's visiting the office the bullet hit, and the slug misses him only just barely, so he dies of a heart attack anyway, that's serendipity, OK?

"The Colonel is putting me on," Liebholtz said sadly. "Putting me on again."

The young black lieutenant stared: "Colonel? Did somebody try to kill the *Secretary?*"

"Why do you ask, my friend?"

"My men'll be curious."

"Well, let me tell you something, Lieutenant. This is a military secret. You can warn your boy here, and also his corporal of the guard, that if we hear any rumors about this from Arlington Hall or Fort Myer—and believe me, we will if there are any—you're going to be down there in my office explaining just how it leaked out. Is that clear?"

"Yes sir," said the lieutenant stiffly. "By your leave, then, sir?"

"The reason," Lee Frost added more softly, "is if any-

22

body finds out how easy it is to take a shot at that Palace of Fallacy and then get away from the cemetery police and your Honor Guard, then the whole goddamn hill will be alive with snipers. In fact," he added, "I might be one of them."

The lieutenant saluted and left. Lee Frost took a last look at the scene of the crime and followed his men back to his Army sedan. The G-man stammered and threatened when Lee told him he was keeping the rifle, even when Lee assured him he would lock the evidence in an Army vault. Lee finally suggested that he ask his Director to write a memo to the Secretary of the Army, in triplicate. The agent retreated, growling that he would do just that, and Lee Frost climbed into the sedan and settled back. He had been at the Pentagon for just over a year, but he learned fast.

Sergeant Maxon, easing the sedan along the winding cemetery roads like a high-school student trying to prove his carworthiness, paused at the Arlington gate while Lee Frost leaned forward and confirmed that the guard there had heard no shot. Maxon crept north to join the Pentagon's nearest tentacle at Memorial Avenue. "For Christ's sake," protested Lee, "drive it or leave it!" Liebholtz in front giggled. Maxon stiffened: "Yes *sir!*" They rocked south onto Jeff Davis Highway and the building leaped toward them. It dominated them all the way. A year before, with the dismal orders in his dispatch case, Lee Frost had arrived in Washington and peered at the Pentagon from the window of a DC-8 at ten thousand feet. Whether from his altitude or attitude, it had struck him as a penal colony for ants. As head of Pentagon Counterintelligence, responsible for its defense and security, he had taken custody of its deepest secrets and most trivial inanities and none of them had changed his mind.

Now the place grew before his eyes as Maxon paralleled the Potomac. Lee shrank correspondingly. He had once measured the Pentagon with a pair of dividers on the aerial photo on his office wall and had found that the National Capitol, dome and all, would fit side-by-side with the State Department within its walls. (A fact of symbolic significance, he imagined. He had mentioned it that night to his wife, who saw nothing ironic in it at all; of course it was big—didn't 27,000 people have to work there?) Now, as they passed the Mall Entrance and swung the sedan into a privileged row of vehicles dripping with fender-flags, he felt more like a Pfc. than a senior colonel ready for his stars.

He looked up with distaste at the lofty columns that dwarfed them as they moved toward the steps of the River Entrance. After a year at the Pentagon, he still considered himself a fighting man. From a combat officer's point of view, Pentagonians, military or civilian, were fascinating. He sometimes sympathized with them, for they were lately much maligned. Compared to bureaucrats in State, Interior, or the Budget, Frost considered them an energetic if untalented breed, galvanized by astronomical funds, unlimited manpower, and infinite opportunity. Given (or sometimes achieving) war, insurrection, or national emergency, they were capable of long hours of unpaid overtime fighting it (fighting it, unfortunately, from here). To their optimism, zeal, and remote ubiquity, he knew that he owed the deaths, in Vietnam, Cambodia, and Laos, of some of his closest friends, and, he sometimes suspected, that of his only son.

With his son's death he had lost any real ambition for stars, but he still served the memory of an older, smaller service. If he retired from the Army he had nowhere else to go, and whether he liked the place or not, the monolith was here for good, looming between the Capitol it claimed to protect and the cemetery it had almost filled.

Carrying the rifle at the trail, he mounted the steps, passed between the tall pillars, and spent five minutes trying to get the weapon signed past a General Services Administration civilian guard who recognized him, saluted him, worked for him, but had never had an unconcealed weapon to deal with before. Lee finally left the gun and the problem with Liebholtz and headed for General Greenberg's office with Maxon to dig out the slug in the general's wall. Passing the golden area near the Joint Chiefs of Staff country he saw that their special tri-Service guard, resplendent in natty gray uniforms, was forming outside the National Military Command Center. His responsibility for

Pentagon security did not extend to them, thank God: he had lost his taste for mirrored shoes and jeweler's rouge somewhere between Okinawa and the A Shau Valley. He had decided that it would not be long before the United States had its own Coldstream Guards. The White House Police had taken to ceremonial uniforms and had looked like aging Liechtenstein border policemen until public opinion had forced them to abandon their shiny new hats. Even the British were said to be laughing, but the virus was not dead; he wondered how long it would be before tourists were gaping at shakoed warriors changing the guard on the President's lawn.

He entered Greenberg's outer office and went to work.

Chapter Two

In the men's room nearest General Greenberg's office, Specialist Fourth Class Marty Lumpert, U.S. Army, pretended to wash his hands while Dewey Dupays, Private, USMC, voided triumphantly in the urinal a few feet away. They could not talk until a civil servant next to Dewey gave up and disappeared. When he did, Dewey lowered his belt, tucked in his razor-creased Marine shirt, zipped his fly, stepped to the basin, and squirted soap onto his palms. "You ever notice," he observed, "how many white cats they can't piss next to a nigger?"

"How would I notice?" Marty wanted to know. He had been waiting for Dewey for half an hour, sweating it, and the stumpy Negro was so cool, so relaxed, that despite his own elation he began to wonder if they had picked a psycho to fire the shot. *"Was everything OK?"* he murmured urgently.

"You tell *me,*" Dewey grinned. "Did I discommode the Establishment?"

"You might say, Dewey," Marty muttered, "you discommoded the Establishment." Despite his irritation at the long delay, he could not restrain his admiration. He grasped the chunky Negro's arm; it was as solid as oak. "Beautiful! Right on! With one shot!"

"It wasn't one shot."

"What do you mean?"

"Three." Dupays was sorry about that. He had driven into Arlington, as planned, with the Springfield in the long-stemmed florist's box on the seat of the car. He had passed a military cortege, and then he had got too fancy. With any luck, he had decided, he could use the firing squad to cover his shot. He drove on down the eastern slope. It was empty, not even a widow in black. So he knew that today was the day (after the three previous scare-offs). He took

26

the flower box to the grave they had chosen, counted the seven fourth-floor windows north to south, saw Marty moving the Venetian blind up and down, up and down, until precisely 12:30, gave Marty thirty seconds to vacate the general's empty office, removed gun from box, waited until the firing squad had begun. Some mother in a chopper came humping down the river to the heliport and almost fouled the range: nevertheless he had jerked off two rounds in rhythm with the firing squad's last two volleys. (You can't hardly place a pattern for shit, that range, les- sen you *squeeze* it off, and suppose you do squeeze it off, you're going to miss the beat of those salvos.) His third shot he squeezed nice and easy—it sounded like a cannon in the silence. Then he had put down the piece and split. He didn't know where those first two rounds went: high, most likely.

"Into the river?" Marty begged. "Christ, Dewey, they couldn't carry all the way to the city, would they?"

Dewey smiled and said softly: "Sure, they most likely did." He chuckled, rapped Marty's soft paunch a little too hard, winked, and left. Marty, envisioning two dead chil- dren holed neatly in their temples, returned shakily to his desk in General Greenberg's outer office. Ethel Langlois was still busy rising to the occasion, and if you did not notice her trembling hands she seemed quite calm. She had been absent, of course, when the shot was fired, having her hair fixed in the basement arcade during lunch-hour (still too dedicated after twenty years to do it on govern- ment time). The hair was perfect, not one gray strand dis- placed—a well-preserved old bat, juices probably still flowing, a real woman for Ben Franklin. To prove that she was unshaken, she was trying to change the ribbon in her typewriter.

"Marty!" she exclaimed. "Where have you been?"

"Smoking pot," said Marty. He produced a pack of Pall Malls. "Here, mother, have a joint."

"They *want* you in there! That Colonel's back!" Marty straightened his tie reluctantly. An hour before, he had sat at his desk in the outer office, awaiting Dewey's shot. When he heard the window crash he had stalled for an eternity, finally gathered his courage, glanced into the gen-

27

eral's empty office to check the damage, and called Security to tell them excitedly that someone was shooting at the building. The lanky colonel with the reflective gray eyes had arrived within moments, it had seemed. With the colonel had come two men, apparently Counterintelligence agents in civvies, one dumpy and excited, the other lean and cool, like the colonel. Marty had hoped for high confusion. Instead, the colonel had simply grabbed a roll of Scotch tape, handed one of his agents one end, and irreverently mounted the general's desk to sight along it while the agent held his end at the hole in the wall and the other the roll at the hole in the pane. Then the colonel, announcing that the shot had come from the eastern slope of Arlington National Cemetery, had phoned to shut down the Arlington gates. Departing, he had paused only to glance at the inglorious crossed laboratory retorts of the Chemical Warfare Corps on the general's mahogany nameplate. "What's his post?"

"Director of Sanitary Doctrine, Plans, and Programs, for the Army Chief of Staff, sir," recited Marty.

"I don't mean his *buzz* title; what's this office *do?*"

Like a high-school virgin forced to repeat a dirty word, Marty had murmured: "Director of Chemical and Biological Warfare, sir."

"That's nice." The colonel thought it over. "You better keep a lid on this. Anyone calls, reporters or anybody, you don't know *anything,* understand?"

"Yes sir," Marty said bleakly. The truth dawned: the shot meant to be heard around the world would apparently need press-agentry to escape from the office itself. The colonel had left, moving so fast that Marty began to fear for Dewey's safety behind the cemetery gates.

Now Marty cinched his tie. OK, Dewey had escaped, and Marty was ready for the next phase of the inquisition if the colonel was. The clear gray eyes couldn't really read his own. He was a poor liar, he talked too much when trapped, but he had weapons he had used from childhood to put people on: round, weak eyes, chubby face, a hesitation in speech that could make him seem downright stupid. He pulled out his pocket comb, leaned over Ethel to see the mirror on her desk. His hair was too damn long; he should have cut it before this bit. His eyes looked frightened behind the thick glasses, and they should not be; his cheeks should not be flushed. He must not let worry over Dewey's two wild shots blow his cool; the odds were they had landed harmlessly in the river.

The intercom on Ethel's desk crackled: "Marty back, damn it, Ethel?" The general's voice was uncharacteristically impatient. Marty braced himself and opened the door.

Lee Frost, staring out the window at Arlington National while Maxon chipped with chisel and mallet at the bullethole in the plaster wall, wheeled as the boy walked in. Lumpert, a dumpy, pallid young man, with two rosy spots on his cheeks showing excitement, stared at him owlishly. He was as unsoldierly a soldier as Lee had seen in years: hair too long, belt too low, a nervous sack of khaki stuffed with lard, the image of the fat boy in *Pickwick Papers*. The poor bastard was still shaking from the sniper's shot, which he must have considered a brush with death. There was something about him that begged forebearance, but habit forced Lee into a bluff.

"Lumpert, why'd you wait so long before you reported that shot?"

For a moment he thought that Lumpert would collapse where he stood. His mouth opened and nothing came out; he licked his lips and turned to General Greenberg, who frowned at Lee and glanced at his clerk sympathetically.

"Settle down, Marty," the general said. Greenberg had a high forehead, and his nose curved downward to almost touch a small chin and delicate mouth, as if the lower part of his face had been pinched toward the upper. He was a compassionate man, a square peg in a round hole. The small, wet mouth was mobile. The lips went in and out when the general was thinking, turned down lugubriously when he frowned, soared too high when he grinned, and he was a nervous grinner. He had remarkably even, pearly teeth. He was as uncomfortable now as a father with an awkward son. "I'm sure he reported it as soon as he heard it, Colonel."

Lumpert finally found words of his own: he had indeed reported the shot right away; well, that is, he had looked into the office, seen the smashed window and the hole in the wall, and run into the hallway to look for a security guard; no, that wasn't right. *First* he had come into the office and spotted the damage and looked out the window, only he had dropped his glasses when he heard the window crash, and couldn't remember where, so he had to, you know, find *them*—

"He has bad eyes," interjected the general.

"His glasses didn't break," observed Lee.

"No sir," said Lumpert, "they don't, very easy."

"So you found them?"

"Under my chair."

"And then what?"

"I went back to the window again to see who'd fired."

"You went to the window again?" Lee wondered what kind of an idiot would present himself as a target twice. "Did you just go over and look out, or what?"

"As I recall," Lumpert said, "I kind of crawled over on my hands and knees, and, like, you know, peeked over the sill. That took a little time too, I guess, and *then* I reported it."

Lee Frost had been in Intelligence and CID and Counterintelligence since he had torn up his knee on the Inchon drop, almost twenty years before. He had interrogated in the two decades perhaps five hundred men, in Korea (including his own father), on Army posts in Germany, in Nam, here in the Pentagon: enemy prisoners, double-agents, sticky-fingered club directors. Lumpert was unique, out-of-focus. Lee suspected that he was more complex than he appeared. He was evading something, too. Perhaps he'd been afraid of drawing another shot and had not looked out at all and now was simply ashamed to admit he had not. It didn't matter. *Not* looking even made a certain cautious sense. Anyway, the kid was obviously no security threat or he wouldn't be in so sensitive a billet. It was no use embarrassing him in front of his boss by breaking him down; besides, the general would blow his stack if he got too hard. "Did General Greenberg ever get any kook-calls, any threats that you didn't want to bother him with?"

General Morris Greenberg's active lips flew into a smile. "Colonel, I can't conceive of this shot having been directed at me. If some anti-CBW freak took it into his head to try to knock me off, how would he find out where I worked? It's not listed in the directory under any title he could evaluate. And why do it here? Why not my quarters? I'm probably the only officer in the Army without a gun in the house."

Chip Bolen, Major, U.S. Air Force, knocked and entered. He was a handsome Public Affairs Officer with command-pilot wings. He radiated quiet integrity, especially in uniform: in civvies, without his campaign ribbons and the DFC, he lost something in translation and became a little loud. There were 200 "Public Affairs" officers like him in the Pentagon and another 6,000 in the field. They typed press releases, lectured Kiwanis Clubs, ghost-wrote speeches for admirals, and arranged Boy-Scout tours of military bases. A Pentagon Navy Public Affairs lieutenant, resident amateur novelist, tapped out pseudonymous fiction on government time, trying for another *Fail-Safe* in reverse, with the Soviet Navy as heavies. Public Affairs (for field trips to local dignitaries, free lecturers to civic groups, and the salaries of Chip Bolen and his mates) charged its civilian targets forty-seven million dollars a year to influence them, and the advertising departments of tax-supported military industries spent millions more in billings that fell more obscurely on the prey. Lee supposed that their efforts were necessary to obscure the fact that the average American head of a family of four, whose government spent four times as much on his military establishment as on educating his children, worked for three full weeks a year to support the Pentagon and spent six months' food budget for a year's military protection.

Chip Bolen was neither novelist nor speechwriter, but he was impossible to doubt when his blue eyes looked into yours. Lee had long ago decided that it was his open face that had got him his job as a Public Affairs Officer.

"I made a sweep through the Press Room, General," Bolen said, "and there's not a ripple. The only man there is Howard Chaplee of UPI. If he hasn't heard of it by now,

31

I don't see how he will. It's dangerous, he's got lots of sources, but I guess we can try to sit on it."

General Greenberg became agitated. Slapping his desk every fourth word, he said that indeed they *would* try; they had better damn well *succeed;* he'd already called the Secretary of the Army *personally* and the *Secretary* agreed; anything that drew attention to the Chemical Corps today was *dynamite.* For Lee, he spelled out the reasons: the public had accepted the President's assurance, virtually true, that U.S. chemical warfare was now entirely *defensive;* the President's disavowal of first-use of chemical weapons and his promises that Pine Bluff would be denuded of biological stockpiles had *emasculated* the peaceniks. But any reporter or free-lance hack who wanted to make a fast buck, with a little investigating, could blow the *whistle;* the Chemical Corps, which had often enough been forced underground before, would survive if left alone, but if anyone rocked the boat now, would have egg all over its face. The anti-war demonstrators would be back in gas masks again on the Capitol steps; the whole *shooting* match, CBW-speaking, would start *over.*

Lee Frost considered the whole sham ridiculous, biological warfare a more remote threat even than nuclear, and gas warfare self-defeating. His job was to solve the mystery of the invisible sniper, not to pass judgment on the general's unhappy specialty, which men in and out of uniform had been deriding for years. But the anti-CBW people had been demonstrating on the Mall when he first took over Building Security and caused him and Bolen more trouble, with their following of TV and press photographers, than all the other demonstrators combined. He hated the thought of their taking the streets again with their dismal chants, gas masks, and death's heads.

Maxon, attacking the wall doggedly, had finally reached the bullet. Soft-nosed and completely out of shape, it was flattened to a stubby cylinder. If it had been steel-jacketed military-issue, it would have gone on through. He jiggled it thoughtfully and turned to Marty, watching his reaction: "Son, if that plaster had been an inch thinner, you might just have got your brains splattered all over that reception room."

32

Lumpert looked suitably frightened. Sergeant Liebholtz phoned for Lee from the heliport tower. He had been studying the arrivals in the log. The only chopper that had landed between 1230 and 1315 hours had been bringing in an Israeli buying commission to a meeting in the Brass Ring. "International Logistics Negotiations Officer, sir."

"You look at the bird?" Lee asked softly.

"Not a scratch on it, sir," Liebholtz said, and read him the passenger manifest: two Israeli lieutenant-colonels, a major, and a captain, all with exotic names. Lee hung up, moved to the shattered window, gazed at the cemetery slope, looked down at the heliport tower. Behind the blue-tinted window of its control room he could see Liebholtz leaving the phone. He asked the general if arriving helicopters bothered him.

"No, I'm used to them."

"I'm going to follow up a lead, General; I'll let you know what develops." He suggested that the hole in the wall be hidden with a picture in case there were visitors, and Chip Bolen offered a painting from the gallery outside Public Affairs. Lee slipped the battered slug into his pocket and left for the International Logistics Negotiations Office.

Marty Lumpert hurried down the corridor. Instead of going directly to Public Affairs for the painting, he stepped into a pay phone and dialed a booth in Washington off Dupont Circle for Red Handlemann, who treated his *Underground Clarion* phones as tapped, and seemed to spend half his time hovering near the booth and the other half in a futile search for a bug in his editorial office. The receiver came off at a half ring. Handlemann answered, as always, simply: "Yes?"

"Check off Phase I," Marty said cryptically. "The fickle finger has struck."

"No *shit!*" Handlemann cried, elatedly. The shot was his baby, conceived when Marty had mentioned Greenberg's real job. The peace rally, scheduled when Communist infiltration of the cease-fire line stopped scheduled withdrawals from Vietnam, was only two Saturdays away, and anything they could do this week to discredit the Pentagon would help to draw a crowd. To show that despite Presidential lies CBW was still alive and well would be a master stroke. Handlemann had wanted Dewey (or said he wanted him) to shoot at the office when the general was in. "Not kill him, maybe, just give him a new asshole." Marty had laughed that one off, but agreed reluctantly to set up a shot at the empty room. Now Handlemann, who had stayed well out of the planning, sounded positively triumphant. "I told you, Marty! All you had to do was *do* it!" As an afterthought he added: "Deadeye get away?"

"Clean. But they've bottled it up. You have an exclusive, Red! Your readers are about to be uniquely enlightened. All six of them."

"Damn it," muttered Handlemann. "I told you we should have—skip it."

"Should have what, Red? Hit him?"

"I said skip it. Look, it's a couple of columns, anyway, even into the empty office! I mean, Christ, the Pentagon? Get those news-service apes in there! You got to get it on the wire!"

"No way," Marty refused. "If *I* leak it, there's a Counterintelligence Colonel on this that'd have me in front of a firing squad in ten minutes." He thought for a moment, trying to recall the reporter's name: Chaple? Chaplee! "Hey, look! Do you subscribe to UPI or just steal their shit?"

"Subscribe."

"Call the Pentagon Press Room. Tell their guy—Howard Chaplee's his name—you want to check out a rumor that somebody shot at the Chief of Chemical and Biological Warfare. No! Hold it!" To give him anything but the room number would be a finger pointing directly to himself. "Just tell him the office: 4E5424. Nobody's supposed to know what we do there. He'll have to smell that out himself, or I can make a slip, maybe, when he gets there. I'll let him in the General's office, like by mistake, if I can. The bullethole in the wall is going to be under a painting, but I'll try to leave some glass on the rug and there's warm air coming in through the window. So get him going."

"I got you, Clausewitz," said Handlemann.

34

Marty left the booth and moved on a radial corridor toward the center of the Pentagon. The building was a giant spiderweb with ten strands radiating from the inner court to the outermost of the five-sided symmetrical polygons or "rings." If you were an insect trapped in the net, you soon learned that against all instinct the shortest distance between two points on the outer rings was to head for the innermost, find the proper radial strand, and proceed back along it to the office you wanted.

Near Public Affairs he moved along a gallery of heroic paintings. He finally selected, as appropriate to Chemical Warfare, a tank with immaculate GIs crouched behind it, spewing flame at a Nazi pillbox. He cleared the loan with the Combat Art Section of Public Affairs and receipted for it in triplicate with a WAC major whose girdle hurt. He hung it in General Greenberg's office and sat at his desk to wait for Chaplee of UPI, hoping that Handlemann was right and that they had not risked so much for nothing. Now that the pressure had eased, his mouth was dry, his hand damp, and his legs were beginning to shake.

Handlemann's energy had galvanized him at first, but now, though he wouldn't admit it, the tall redhead scared him half to death.

Chapter Three

Bull Collins, World War II ace and now Aerodyne-LA's Washington representative, stood in the after-lunch river of human traffic channeling out of the subterranean vestibule of the Pentagon Officers' Athletic Center. He was still puzzled by an invitation from Admiral Niles Strickland to play squash. Immovable, he split the crowd like a beefy, affable boulder in a stream while the admiral signed him in as a guest. As he waited, his meat-red face, flushed from too much whiskey for too many years, would break into a grin or fold into a wink as Air Force and Naval Air officers flowed by. His memory for names and faces was sharp with use, and enough of his wild fame as a Marine fighter-pilot remained so that those he favored were pleased.

Admiral Niles Strickland had reserved his favorite court, and Bull, now that he had nothing to gain by letting Strickland win, waxed him fifteen-six, fifteen-eight, and fifteen-three. They retired as in the old days to the steam room, a massage by Ono, and the showers. Drying down, Admiral Strickland, who was as spare and wiry as he had been when he graduated from the Academy, surveyed Collins' immense belly. "I never could figure how you move it around that fast on the court."

"It doesn't take any more work to win than to lose," Collins said, "and I like to win."

They retired for a brew to a table in the Center's mess. Bull noticed that Strickland, as aristocratic as ever, was visibly nervous. Bull sipped his beer, musing. Years before, Aerodyne-LA in California and General Dynamics in Fort Worth had been neck-and-neck with Boeing, headquartered in Seattle, in a three-way race for the only contract in sight, the TFX-F111 tactical fighter. Admiral Strickland, one of three Navy members on the Air Force

Council, had favored Bull's own company because its lighter, shorter design promised better carrier-compatibility. The admiral was talking early retirement. Bull, presuming on the brotherhood of the golden-winged, had indelicately offered Strickland a job at Aerodyne—Director of Military Sales, at sixty thousand, cheap enough to sew up the vote but probably exceeding Strickland's wildest hopes.

Bull had been too brutal. The admiral saw himself as an officer and gentleman first, a Naval aviator second. Having achieved flag rank, he conceived of himself as a guardian of the public interest. His face had frozen. Had he been half Bull's size, he had claimed, he would have tossed him from his office. From that day to this they had never spoken, although finally over the years the admiral had relaxed so far as to nod when they met in a corridor.

It had all been quite unnecessary: Strickland had voted right anyway, on merit, for Aerodyne. The battle had seemed won at first. For once, the Navy and the Air Force even agreed. Aerodyne and Boeing, with better designs, had outscored General Dynamics on the Council's point-system. The Council recommended either as prime contractor to the Chief of Naval Operations and the Air Force Chief of Staff. Both approved. From thence the recommendation floated upward to McNamara. Once it was safely out of the Air Force Council, Bull had enplaned for Montego Bay with a ten-thousand-dollar company bonus for having reached the finals, taking along the wife of an Army doctor whose husband was otherwise engaged with an "advisory group" on the Plain of Jars. They stayed at Try-All at a thousand dollars a week. One morning as Bull lay on his sunripened belly tracing obscenities with his forefinger on the Army wife's thigh, an enormous black barboy had handed him a cable from Los Angeles: OUR BID AND BOEINGS SHOT DOWN BY BROTHER MAC. RETURN IMMEDIATELY. President Kennedy, it turned out, had political commitments to a Chicago politician closely allied to a financier with large General Dynamics holdings. McNamara, angry anyway at over-runs inconceivable in the auto industry and prodded by a Deputy Defense Secretary who had once acted as outside counsel to General Dynamics,

37

suddenly became convinced that Aerodyne's and Boeing's sugared cost-estimates were even more treacherous than those from Fort Worth. A little muscle, probably unnecessary in view of the horsepower already available, from Vice-President Johnson, Governor Connally of Texas, and the undeniable fact that Navy Secretary Korth's Fort Worth bank made loans to General Dynamics, had finished Aerodyne and Boeing. McNamara had overriden the military chiefs and pulled the rug out from under Bull, Aerodyne, Boeing, and all the military experts: General Dynamics had the contract, sure enough.

Bull had shrugged it off. He had learned over Guadalcanal that some prey was simply fated to escape. Besides, everyone knew now that General Dynamics had blown the F-111. Seven General Dynamics employees and subcontractors had been indicted for substituting new serial numbers on government-rejected longerons—*longerons,* no less, the main structural members of the fuselage—surprising Bull not in the least, but leading some of his younger Air Force friends to wonder just what values of the free-enterprise system they were flying to protect. The Navy, as Strickland had predicted, had found the plane unmanageable on carriers. The Air Force had grounded it, ungrounded it, grounded it again. Bull hoped that Aerodyne-LA's turn would come next week when he and General Dynamics submitted competing proposals on the ill-fated plane's successor, the AFX.

Boeing in Seattle, Aerodyne's former companion in misery, was not even playing, for it was still recovering from another Presidential screwing on the Air Force B-1 "Advanced Manned Strategic Aircraft." Despite Boeing's greater experience in the bomber field, they had lost it. With a California President and six per cent unemployment in the Golden State, the contract had been awarded, just prior to Congressional elections, to North American Rockwell in Los Angeles. The down payment had been one billion dollars. Forty-five thousand hysterically happy Los Angeles aircraft workers had toasted their President, movie-actor Governor, and song-and-dance Senator (the last having leaked the news prematurely, on a Thursday before the stock market closed). They had rewarded their

Governor, if not the Senator, three months later with their votes. There would be Scotch in the cupboards of Los Angeles for eight years while engineers in Seattle lined up for unemployment checks. No one in Congress listened to Washington State legislators who cried that North American had spent two billion dollars and ten years on the last bomber contract trying to build the B-70 Valkyrie and that of the two B-70s that had been built, one rested in the Air Force Museum in Dayton while the other had collided with a photo-plane taking publicity pictures and crashed in the desert.

No one had told Congress that United States superiority in strategic bombers was already a healthy four to one, or that the new Soviet bomber that had triggered the whole B-1 project had a range of only 2,500 miles. Bull Collins approved the deception in principle. What the assholes on the Hill didn't know wouldn't hurt them. It gave him a large problem, though, on the new AFX. To coax another major contract to Los Angeles would be just that much harder. People at General Dynamics in Texas voted too, and elections were not far off. General Dynamics had an ace in reserve, besides—a deal with Congressman Ab Dennes of the Armed Services Committee. Bull had smelled it out last week and now he knew that he needed all the help he could get. Bull wished he had let the admiral win on the squash court, and wished he could approach him again with a job offer, more delicately.

"What's on your mind, Niles?" he asked. He had often wondered why Strickland had decided after all not to retire. There had been plenty of jobs then. Even now, after the cutbacks, there were 2,100 retired admirals, generals, and colonels still floating in and out of the Pentagon for the top one hundred defense contractors. Maybe Strickland had stuck around for a shot at CNO.

The admiral was silent for a long while. He was a silver-haired man with a lean jaw. He had a Boston accent and firm lips and a trace of Groton in his voice. Bull wondered what family financial disaster in the Thirties had forced him to Annapolis rather than Harvard Law. In the days before the insult, Bull had visited his home in Arlington, found evidence of elegance, and assumed that his wife had money. Strickland looked fifteen years older now.

"Bull, I want to retire. Can you do anything for me?"

"Jesus, Niles, you know how things are now! Why'd you wait so long?"

"You know damn well why! Did you think I was a god-damn Peruvian general or something? If you *can* offer me a job, I'm disqualifying myself from voting on the AFX. So you should know that."

Apparently he was under strain, for Bull had never heard him curse before. Stiffly he told Strickland that he had respected his decision years before, whatever had caused it. It hadn't really been a bribe. When Bull offered a bribe, he would know it, he said, but he appreciated his honesty now on the AFX. (He didn't, really: for the admiral's vote, he'd have tried to get him a vice-presidency.) "Oh, shit, Niles, why go into it? You know who's got that job now! And there's nothing else I know of."

"I don't mean at the sixty thousand . . ."

"Jesus, I *hope* not!"

"Thirty-five?"

"You must make twenty-five now."

"Twenty-seven. It's not enough."

Bull looked at him carefully. "Why not?"

Strickland reddened. "I asked for a job, not a budget analysis. You say there's nothing at Aerodyne, I believe you. All right, that's it!"

He had swallowed an immense amount of pride even to ask. Bull was sure that he had been to Lockheed, Mc-Donnell-Douglas, every manufacturer in the defense industry before him. Maybe he smelled a contract for Aerodyne on the AFX and had decided that if he joined the team he could learn to live with the old affront, but why didn't he simply retire and fish instead? Strickland had presumably lived on Service pay all his life. Gambling? Drinking? A mistress? Or a bad investment? "Niles, how is Aerodyne today?" Bull asked abruptly.

"Down an eighth," mumbled Strickland, caught unawares. Bull hid a smile. He would give odds that the moment the secret vote in the Air Force Council had been counted years ago, Strickland had hocked the family

40

jewels, phoned his stockbroker, bought every share of Aerodyne he could swing on margin, and sat back to await the rain of wealth. When Aerodyne, on the news of Mc-Namara's "decision," had dropped out of sight, he had been caught. He had probably been trying to hang on for years, needing half his admiral's pay to keep up with the interest.

"Down an eighth?" Bull mused. "Thanks."

Strickland looked up, suddenly alert. "Why'd you ask me? It's your company."

"Just thought you might be following it," Bull said mildly.

"Well I do," the admiral said. "Among others." He hesitated. "Considering the competition next week, what would be the effect on Aerodyne stock of news that the Air Force was pushing Sid Ellsworth to unload as many of those goddamn F-111s as he can, surplus? Just as quick as he can?"

Alert, Bull thought it over carefully. Ellsworth, the Pentagon's international arms salesman, headed the International Logistics Negotiations Section. What "surplus" he wanted to sell, he sold. If the price was right, fine; if not, he sold it anyway. "Well," Bull decided finally, "it would be *favorable* to us in terms of public relations. We labeled the F-111 as a dog. If the Service has given up and is trying to unload them on some cowboy air force in South America, say, or in Southeast Asia—"

"What about the Israeli Air Force? Are they 'cowboys'?"

"The Israelis?" Bull demanded, astonished. Israeli pilots were too experienced to accept the F-111; procurement in Tel Aviv was too cagey to get caught on another West German Starfighter deal. And the trouble was, everybody knew it: the sale of F-111s to Israel would be a vote of confidence for General Dynamics, one that Bull would find it difficult to overcome in the weeks ahead. He had planned to use the F-111 failure next week against Fort Worth, but if somebody knowledgeable loved their beast, it was a pat on the back for General Dynamics and a kick in Aerodyne's teeth. If it was the Israelis who wanted it, it might be fatal. "Why would the Israelis buy them? I'd rather fly Spads!"

41

"They *are* buying them," Strickland said firmly, "if nobody rocks the boats."

"Jesus! How much Aerodyne stock *do* you hold? Confidentially?"

The admiral, tight-lipped, answered that he was not here to discuss his portfolio, but simply to ask about a job.

"Well, let me tell you something, Niles," Bull warned softly. "If the Jews *want* F-111s, and word gets out that they do, that stock you're holding—"

"I didn't say I was holding any stock. And word won't get out. It's top secret."

Strickland was not stupid, and he had good sources, but after fifteen years in the Pentagon, Bull had feelers out that few military or Naval men could match. "It will be leaked," he assured the admiral, "out of Ab Dennes' committee."

"By whom?"

"Dennes," promised Bull.

Most military and Naval men feared the Chairman of the House Armed Services Committee, some fawned on him, but most (and Bull was sure that the admiral was one of them) disliked him personally. At least Strickland didn't defend him. "Why?"

"He'll be in General Dynamics' corner next week," Bull announced.

"What's he care about Fort Worth?"

"Nothing. But they've promised to give that Dixieland band he represents every damn subcontract they'll need on the AFX. He's all primed and ready to go. *They've* got Dennes and all we've got to use against them is *their* last screwed-up bird. If we let that son-of-a-bitch Ellsworth start selling them to the hottest pilots in the world, when Dennes leaks *that,* we're dead!"

The admiral smiled thinly. "I don't think he'll leak it."

"You overestimate his respect for security, Admiral."

"No. You overestimate the selling price. And the reason they're buying them. What do you think the F-111's worth?"

"Nothing," Bull answered promptly. "I wouldn't climb into one."

The admiral smiled again. "You couldn't, Ace. Check your waistline."

"I get around on a squash court," Bull pointed out.

"Seriously, how much per plane? Surplus, but no combat time?"

"Seriously?" Bull's mind raced, and a gleam of hope appeared at the end of the tunnel. A *real* discount could do it. A fire sale on the F-111 would cause a virtual Congressional revolt. Even if Congress went along with a giveaway, if the press smelled it out they would shoot General Dynamics down in flames for good. Fort Worth had promised to deliver to the Pentagon 1,700 F-111s for six and one half billion dollars. Actually, in the smoke of failure, when the plane had fallen on its ass, the Pentagon had settled for anly 550 planes and *raised* the total ante to seven and one half billion, so that General Dynamics had got a billion bucks more for making only one-third the aircraft. If the public learned that planes that cost 13 million each and were supposed to have a useful life of fifteen years were six years later being sold for, say three or four million, *somebody* in Congress would howl, that was for damn sure, and what a perfect time!

"Admiral," he said conservatively, "I'd hate to be Ellsworth, *or* SecDef, *or* the President, if it got out that they sold them for under three million each."

Strickland looked satisfied. "How's a half a million grab you?"

Bull sat bolt upright. *"What?"*

"One-half million each. Delivered in Tel Aviv by U.S. Reserve pilots."

It still smelled. The Israelis were not using their dollars to buy junk. Bull's eyes narrowed. "Who are the Israelis selling them to?"

Strickland looked at him with new respect. "The Greeks."

"How much?"

"Two million each."

"And then Israel buys more Phantoms?"

"Could be, Bull."

"Are you sure?"

The admiral shrugged. "It might be worth checking."

43

"How many planes? *When?*"

Strickland was suddenly tight-lipped, either unsure of his facts or afraid he had gone too far. He suggested that Bull sniff around for himself.

Bull finished his beer. He knew just where to begin.

Chapter Four

The tanned young civil servant behind the massive desk in the innermost office of the International Logistics Negotiations Section irritated Colonel Lee Frost at sight. Lee sank into a leather chair and watched him inspect the battered slug. He wondered how Ellsworth had traveled so far so fast. The office was in "Status Row" over the River Entrance. The heavy drapes behind the desk were open to frame the Washington Monument and the Capitol dome behind. But Ellsworth seemed to need no such props. He had, despite his youth, an air of having been there forever. He took off his horn-rimmed glasses, blew on them, and swiveled his chair to survey the view, his reward for what must have been a whole career of bureaucratic triumphs. He turned back and tossed the bullet across the desk.

"That's simply incredible, Colonel. I can't believe it!"

"We'd better believe it, Mr. Ellsworth," Lee Frost said, "until we find out differently." With twenty-nine years in the Service, he was outranked, and disliked it: Ellsworth, as chief arms salesman for the Pentagon, was a Deputy Under-Secretary of Defense. On any military post he would command the honors of a general officer; when he traveled civilian airlines on government TR, he would fly first-class as a brigadier would; at the Air Force target shoot at Tyndall Field he would be entitled to his own sprightly girl-guide dressed in Lincoln green, and a chauffeured car. (Lee had gone once and found himself in an ancient bus full of similarly degraded colonels.) On a visit to Vietnam, Ellsworth would cause all the Security headaches of a U.S. Senator. He was obviously too young to have fought in Korea and Lee wondered whether he had ever heard a shot fired in anger.

Waiting for the head of the Israeli delegation to join

them, Lee contemplated other trappings of success. Ellsworth's wife and two smiling daughters regarded Daddy gratefully from a silver frame on his desk. Charts covered the wall. Whether or not he knew the butt of a rifle from the muzzle, he apparently knew how to sell them. Lee had done a paper on the international arms business at War College, and he knew how the office worked. Ellsworth headed four teams of international drummers. He had a "Red Team," responsible for arms sales to Canada, the Far East, Scandinavia, France, and most of NATO. His "White Team" sold planes and tanks to West Germany; his "Blue Team" to Latin Ameria, Italy, Spain, and the Benelux countries; and his "Gray Team" peddled surplus and not-so-surplus arms to the United Kingdom, Switzerland, Austria, and the Middle East. He was Chairman of the Committee on Military Exports, composed of representatives from United Aircraft, North American Aviation, Bendix, Chrysler, Lockheed, Northrup, Boeing, General Electric, General Dynamics, McDonnell-Douglas, Raytheon, International Tel and Tel, FMC Corporation, Avco, IBM, American Machine and Foundry, and Philco. On the committee sat members, too, from First National City Bank, Chase Manhattan Bank, Riggs National Bank, and the Morgan Guaranty Trust Company.

He made less than thirty thousand dollars a year, but he and his forty-one assistants, spurred by bureaucratic ambitions, concern for the balance of payments, or perhaps even loyalty to the U.S. taxpayer, sold two billion dollars' worth of U.S.-manufactured arms annually, to developed and under-developed countries, arranging terms if necessary through Chase Manhattan, Riggs, First National City, or Morgan Guaranty. Once Lee, serving in Thailand with the Military Advisory Group, had requested an exhibit for a U.S. trade fair in Bangkok, expecting, at most, an XM19 dart-rifle or a demonstration grenade launcher. Instead he had received a Sherman tank and a dozen mortars, followed by a salesman from Ellsworth. Military sales were supposed to have been taken from the Pentagon's control by the Foreign Aid Program, but there was no visible sign of change. A half-million dollars a year in hidden defense funds were still allotted to this office for sales promotion. Ellsworth claimed that the jobs of half a million American workers depended on military sales abroad, and that a dollar per employee was not much to spend on marketing when you considered the gross. The extravagance, Lee had noted in his War College paper (which had not been popular with the faculty) lay in the fact that a plane or a tank you sold to a foreign army had to be replaced at greater cost to your own, a truth not lost on United Aircraft, North American, Bendix, Chrysler, or the other members of the board.

On Ellsworth's desk a red light flashed and a throaty voice oozed from the intercom: "Mr. Ellsworth? Lieutenant-Colonel Sharett back to see you, sir."

"Send him in."

A slim, languid Israeli Air Force officer rambled through the door. He had twinkling brown eyes and a cheerful, British carelessness. Lee Frost sensed a combat man. No, the Israeli said, the delegation had received no threats; they had heard of no prowlers around their Embassy quarters; just what, precisely, was the trouble?

"Chaim," Ellsworth said, "The Colonel thinks somebody tried to shoot down your helicopter this afternoon."

Sharett shot Ellsworth an odd look, and then retired to a comfortable leather chair at the side of the desk. Lee told him of the three shells at the Arlington graveside and the shattered Pentagon window, not mentioning whose.

"Well, you should look for an Arab, shouldn't you? We're over here, after all, to purchase military equipment."

"What equipment?" Lee Frost demanded.

"Just a second," Ellsworth cut in. "If you have to be specific, Frost, I think we'd want to establish a need-to-know."

Lee Frost flushed. "Mr. Ellsworth, I'm trying to find out if anybody took a shot at these gentlemen! Isn't that need-enough-to-know?"

"I don't see why you need to know the exact military items, or sums involved, or terms of delivery, do you?"

"Maybe not," Lee admitted tersely, "since *I* won't be

47

involved if it's actually an Arab plot; the FBI will. But assuming it's not, how do I jar the motive loose?"

Ellsworth shrugged. "Get cleared for it. I report to the Secretary of Defense, as you know. It's up to him. In the meanwhile," he added, "I think we get the message. You don't advise their traveling by helicopter any more."

Lee didn't, and he promised to help Ellsworth provide an automobile convoy for the commission. Even if foreign intrigue was beyond his own scope as Chief Pentagon Security Officer, he could do that much.

"Which brings up another matter," Ellsworth put in swiftly. "Is there any necessity to broadcast this attempt?"

"It's already got a lid on it," Lee said briefly. "I hope."

"Really?" mused Ellsworth. "I wonder why?"

Chemical-biological warfare was as far from Ellsworth's province as foreign arms sales from Lee's own. "Why don't you establish," Lee suggested, "a need-to-know?"

As he crossed the golden carpet in Ellsworth's reception room he noticed a broad, beefy man in civvies massaging the receptionist's neck while she typed. He smiled at Lee and started for the inner office. Lee had seen the face somewhere, but it was not until he glimpsed a tiny replica of the Congressional Medal on his lapel that the man's more youthful image came to him, last seen twenty-five years ago in a helmet and goggles in a *Stars and Stripes* delivered to him in a company CP on Okinawa. Some flying ace, but he had forgotten the name.

"Who was that?" he asked the girl. She was a big redhead, packed neatly. Her lips were moist and she looked as if she were about to burst from her clothes. There were crowsfeet at her eyes and a trace of age at her neck, too. Past forty but ripe, she evaluated him with a long, languorous glance.

"Bull Collins. Aerodyne rep. Dirty old man."

"Young enough to paw the merchandise, though."

"Old Marines never die, Colonel," she smiled. "They just feel away." She had longing brown eyes like a cow ready for milking, and they seemed to add: *What about old soldiers?*

He headed back for General Greenberg's office. Sexually, Jenny had frozen when their son was killed. If his balls began to explode before his wife thawed, at least he knew where to look.

Chapter Five

Lee Frost found Bolen from Public Affairs and General Greenberg in worried conference, and Marty Lumpert, on his hands and knees, feeling for glass on the carpet beneath the window. They had pulled down the Venetian blind to hide the hole. Lee suggested to the general that he had better get out of the line of fire if he ever heard that there was another chopper coming in with Israeli officers aboard.

"Was that it?" breathed the general.

"Apparently."

"It's a better premise than anybody taking a shot at *me,* anyway," Greenberg said. "Since I don't even exist."

Lee looked around the office. Lumpert seemed to have found the last of the glass on the rug, and an oil painting of a flame-belching tank was effectively covering the scar in the wall. Presumably the windowpane could be replaced without too many questions tomorrow by Maintenance; in a few weeks the general could call for a plasterer. "Well, sir, I guess you're home free."

"Not exactly, Lee," said Chip Bolen. It seemed that someone had called Chaplee of UPI in the Press Room with a rumor that a shot had landed in a Pentagon office, and given the room number. The reporter, busy rewording an official release from the Army Materiel Command, had believed Bolen's denial but asked him to double-check. Now it was time to report back.

"Who the hell called him?" demanded Lee.

"He wouldn't say," said Bolen. "But I'll ask again." He picked up the phone on the general's desk and dialed. Lee noticed that Marty Lumpert paused in his search for glass. He wished that Bolen would wait until the young man left. The image of an intrepid Birdman was about

50

to be tarnished, and youth in uniform needed all the images it could get.

"Chappy?" Bolen asked. "Well, look, Chappy. I'm down
here, like you said, Room 4E5424? It's just another office,
Chappy, Director of Sanitary Doctrine, Plans, and Programs for the Chief of Staff, and there's no security involved, but there *is* a conference going on." He paused.
"Frankly, nothing. *Zilch,* Chappy: no shot, no bullet, no
broken window. Where'd you *get* that crap, anyway?"
Bolen had donned his sincerest smile for the telephone.
The smile froze for an instant, and then melted again.
"Well, that figures. . . . *Those* Commie bastards! Not at
all, Chappy. That's what I'm here for."

Lumpert was watching him wide-eyed. Suddenly, as if
aware of Lee's scrutiny, he began to search again for
slivers. Bolen replaced the phone. "Somebody from the
Underground Clarion phoned him," he said tensely. "He
won't say who. With a query."

"What's the *Underground Clarion?*" General Greenberg wanted to know.

"A New Left paper," Lee Frost murmured, "down on
Q Street. Edited, or not edited, depending on how you
look at it, by a guy named Handlemann." He was puzzled.
"Now who the hell told them?"

"That Honor Guard sentry that didn't report the shot?"
suggested Bolen.

Lee's impression had been that the Arlington sentry
couldn't follow a comic book; let alone the exotica of radical journalism, and that he had probably never heard of
the *Underground Clarion,* but he reserved judgment. The
chubby FBI agent, angry at his keeping the rifle, may have
leaked it, or Lumpert, or the general's receptionist outside, but all were unlikely: you did not look for radicals
in the FBI or the Chemical Warfare Corps. The leak may
have come from the sentry's black lieutenant. Probably
not, since he was a West Pointer; still, today you never
know. There were the gravediggers, too, who might have
seen more than they admitted, and the sentry's corporal
of the guard, and anybody the sentry might have talked
to back in his barracks. To try to check out even the military personnel seemed impossible. The poison of dissent

ran deep in the Army's veins and everyone knew it, although in the Pentagon the feeling was that if you didn't talk about it maybe it would go away.

"They won't *print* it?" begged General Greenberg.

"Not UPI," said Bolen. "Not now. But the goddamn *Clarion* will print anything."

Lee watched Lumpert get to his feet. A glaze of sweat glistened on his forehead. He dropped the last shard of glass into the general's wastebasket, saluted, and moved self-consciously to the door: Private Sad Sack come alive. The damp strands at the nape of his neck were so long they curled. The general was probably so deep in nerve gas and anthrax that he hadn't noticed his clerk's haircut in months.

"Gentlemen," said Greenberg, "you have to stop them! They *can't* print it! Call the FBI again!"

Chip Bolen shook his head: there was no way, no way at all. You could *talk* to the established press, but those underground bastards would love to have the Department of Defense call the FBI in on them. They'd absorb it like a blotter, and print every word of the interrogation. It was better to let it strictly alone; in fact, it was all they could do.

Lee moved to the window, studied the slope of Arlington, dropped his gaze to a jeep near the heliport. Behind the wheel was his sergeant, Liebholtz, searching the face of the building with binoculars for the two other bulletholes. Liebholtz saw him in the window and lifted a hand languidly. Lee nodded and turned back. "Look, General," he said, "I don't see why your office would be mentioned, under any name. Nobody in Arlington was told the round landed in Chemical and Biological Warfare, or even 'Sanitary Doctrine, Plans, and Programs.' "

"You sure, Lee?" Bolen asked.

Yes, he was sure. Bolen, trying to soothe Greenberg, grasped the guarantee like a life preserver. Even if the *Clarion* did print the item, it was just an unconfirmed rumor that somebody shot at an undisclosed Pentagon window; nobody but a bunch of filthy hippies believed anything they read in Handlemann's sheet anyway. If the other wire services picked it up from the *Clarion,* so what? He'd already denied it.

Leaving Bolen to placate the general, Lee headed for the Pentagon roof. Outside the door he passed Lumpert standing at a coffee-machine, clumsily searching for coins in his pocket. Lee slipped in a dime for each of them, noting that someone had slapped a sticker on the machine demanding cheaper Pentagon coffee; even tame Pentagon employees were having their mini-rebellion.

Shakily, looking as if he would like to flee, Lumpert took his coffee. Lee looked into his owlish eyes. They regarded him with dread, as if he were still scared from the shot. Or scared of having lied?

"You didn't really look out that window, did you, son?"

"Oh, yes sir."

"I wouldn't have."

"I did."

Still lying, if not about that, about something. "You ever read that *Underground Clarion?"*

"No sir."

"The Olive Greensheet?" Lee asked suddenly. It was an incendiary Serviceman's sheet, published by GIs and prohibited on military bases, but Lee's assistant, Major Homer Troy, had found copies recently in Pentagon men's rooms.

"The what, sir?"

"Never mind," Lee crumpled his empty cup and threw it into a trash can. "See you later."

At 1620 hours, Sergeant Freddy Liebholtz, sitting in the jeep in West Parking, spotted a bulletbole in the mortar between two limestone blocks twenty feet above General Greenberg's window. Fifteen minutes later, his partner, Maxon, on the roof, discovered a bright new crease in the aged copper sheathing. Lee decided, on inspecting it, that one of the three slugs had ricocheted into the Potomac or perhaps into the private boats nestling on the farther shore at the Columbia Island boatbasin.

The pattern of the shots showed dispersal in elevation and practically none in azimuth. It still seemed likely that the marksman hàd ben trying to lead a descending helicopter, so in his basement office Lee called the FBI-military liaison section and asked the Department of Justice to continue on the case. If the shot had really been fired by an Arab agent, a civilian agency would have more latitude than he. The FBI liaison man he talked to was not Potbelly, but had heard about the rifle, and reminded him that they might want it for future ballistic tests. Lee, perversely, told him to take it up with Lee's own boss, General Lucius Hardy, the Chief of Army Intelligence.

Now that in approved bureaucratic style he had passed the buck to the FBI, he could concentrate on the source of the leak to the *Underground Clarion*. He dictated a memo to Central Files, requesting security packets on the sentry who had heard the shot, the Honor Guard lieutenant, the general's receptionist, Mrs. Langlois, and the general's clerk, Lumpert. Finally he called Fort Holabird, outside Baltimore, where he had gone to Army Intelligence School. There the Counterintelligence Analysis Division maintained a computer named "Gloria Hallelujah." In its memory banks lay all that Army Counterintelligence agents had ferreted out on 5,000 civilian activists and such anti-militarists as Mrs. Martin Luther King, Julian Bond, Angela Davis, and Arlo Guthrie. Lee gave his authorizing code number to the girl who tended Gloria and requested a print-out on every member of the staff of the *Underground Clarion* and a run on Marty Lumpert, too. Gloria's inputs were kept quietly current, despite recent Counterintelligence manpower cuts inspired by Congress and the courts.

Isolated in his office, he could hear the rumble of buses departing from the Concourse above. His civilian security chief poked his head in and said goodnight; so did Thelma, his mousy secretary. Reluctantly, he dictated a report on the shot, and the leak, to General Picket Aspen, the waspish, ambitious Director of the Pentagon's Civil Disturbance Center. He hoped he could keep Aspen out of the act, but he had learned that any move of his own that dealt with a radical paper was bound to stir up the general and that to ignore him would only cause trouble.

When there was no more excuse to delay, he went through the pile of routine paperwork on his desk. He forgave a small security violation in Army's Plans and Logistics and scanned the daily compilation of graffiti collected by Major Homer Troy, whom he had months before shunted out of the office in pursuit of a mysterious pervert marring Pentagon toilet stalls.

Finally he put the Springfield rifle in the office safe and walked through the tunnel to the Officers' Athletic Center. Passing above a line of handball courts, he heard the slap of rubber soles and looked down at General Scorchy Blain, Chief of the Army Chaplains Corps. The padre was volleying with himself, white hair flying and face cherry-red. Lee hesitated. Scorchy, "Battling Pastor of Hill 880," was a man whose history, promising much, lost all in the telling. Lee, who had a low threshold of boredom, avoided him when possible. Scorchy had been a good Texas-league pitcher (and a shouting Baptist preacher off-season) before Korea had shown him the true path to glory. Despite his athletic career, he was no competition on the court. Years of on-and-off alcoholism had slowed him and made him clumsy as well. But he had just lost his wife, Beth (Heaven-bless-her), and the poor old bastard looked so lonely that Lee called down and challenged him. He changed clothes and they played a disjointed three games: Scorchy kept forgetting the score and ramming until Lee pled an aching knee and suggested a drink. They showered and sat down in the lounge. The general, virtuously, declined a beer for a Coke (which meant that he was on the wagon again, and would engender a new batch of Scorchy-stories when he fell off, his entertainment value having won him his post in the first place). He regarded Lee paternally and hitched his chair closer.

"Going to send you down something tomorrow," he drawled. "I hope it don't rile you any, and I think you'll like the idea."

Whatever it was, a schedule of Pentagon church services or a request that Lee address the Chaplains Corps on the Pentagon narcotic problem, Lee didn't want it. Cautiously, he asked for details.

"Well, we've had a difficulty in the Corps," said the general.

"Haven't we all," Lee said quickly. "Never been so busy in my life. You wouldn't believe—"

"I do believe, I *do!* My career's built on it!" This was a Scorchy-joke and Lee smiled dutifully. "No," said Blain, "what I'm sending you is what you might call a form letter. Only yours won't be exactly a form letter." He paused for effect. "Because *yours* will be signed by the President."

"My *what* will be signed by the President?"

"We had this problem, Corps-wise. Came from lack of contact with civilians, really. Now, of course, the President hasn't got time to sign them all, even with things winding down over there, and we can't fool people with a Xerox, we found that out. But we got a chaplain's clerk, Lee, you wouldn't believe it, the way he can copy signatures; hate to tell you where he learned it. He's a convert. To Catholicism, of course, but even so, a true miracle, his salvation, if you believe in miracles. Where was I?"

"You got a forger," said Lee.

"Did time for it," admitted Scorchy. "Anyway, he signs them."

"Signs what?" Lee asked helplessly.

"The letters. The *KIA* letters. To the families of the bereaved! Now, I imagine you and Jenny got a telegram. Isn't a letter nicer? Edged in black?"

"Edged in black?" murmured Lee, studying the cherry face for some trace of insanity or even dark humor. He found none. "Jesus Christ, General, he's been *dead* for a year!"

"Just the same, you're entitled. And yours will *be* signed, the real thing, suitable for framing."

"General," swallowed Lee, rising, "I'm late. I have to go."

Scorchy smiled benignly. "Sure, Lee. Get home to Jenny, good home-cooked dinner. Beth, Heaven-bless-her, used to worry, *I* know."

There were tears in the old bastard's eyes, and Lee almost asked him along, but not quite. He thanked him for the game, pled earnestly that he give the Presidential letter to the next Army colonel who lost a son, and left the Pentagon.

His car was parked next to his Army sedan at the River Entrance. Fishing for his key, he looked up at the dark mass of the building. A few lighted windows stared balefully. A blue-uniformed GSA guard stepped to the giant doors, looked out at the deepening twilight, yawned, and returned inside. A bearded young man in sandals, blue jeans, and fringed leather jacket, last survivor of the April demonstrations, slowly patrolled the entrance at the two-hundred-foot distance Lee had specified after Congress had passed the Pentagon Anti-Demonstration Law. On his shoulder, carelessly, he bore a picket-sign: A NUCLEAR WAR WOULD RUIN YOUR CHILD'S NEXT BIRTHDAY: *Work for Peace, not the Pentagon.* He smiled and Lee nodded. God knew what, if anything, the kid did for a living, but he was there twice a day, morning and evening, to meet Pentagonians coming and going. Each night he laid his sign in the bushes by Jeff Davis Highway and no one ever bothered it. Lee supposed that one day he would drift away like the rest.

He lent color to the place, and Lee felt that he would almost miss him when he was gone.

Chapter Six

Lee Frost's alarm began to croak hoarsely at 6:45. Jenny had arisen before him, which meant that she had not slept, or that she had awakened dreaming of Rick. He could hear her puttering about the breakfast nook, looking for something to eat, always something to eat. A cup of coffee would not do, or even a glass of milk. She needed doughnuts, apparently, coffeecake, anything sweet to replace the vision of their son grinning, or angry, or sad; to add another layer of fat over the wound. It had taken him almost a month to gain back the weight he had lost the week they had heard, but she had been able to eat, gluttonously, the day after. Grotesque, monstrous. Her doctor at Walter Reed, much as Lee disliked him, was right. It was slow suicide.

He was dressed by the time she returned to the bedroom. He brushed her cheek lightly with his lips, and she grinned. The folds of fat, when she smiled, very nearly buried her eyes, which were emerald and enormously beautiful and should not have been hidden at all. On the bureau stood their wedding picture, shot on the West Point chapel steps; he a captain in full dress, she slim and lovely, the swell of Rick not showing yet. A different woman altogether, now, where even a year ago she had been simply the same girl grown twenty years older. Today the picture reminded him of a before-and-after ad for a diet food.

"I put on some toast for you," she said, handing him the morning paper. She climbed back into her bed; the springs groaned. She flicked on her bedside lamp and took up Shirer's *Rise and Fall,* her summer's project. Quickly he scanned *The Washington Post,* looking for news of the shot at the seat of the mighty. There was none, so Bolen's boy-scout honesty had succeeded again. All at once his eye fell on another item. The peace rally scheduled for next Saturday at the Washington Monument had been retargeted by the Rally Committee as another Pentagon march. The Department of Justice, citing the Pentagon Demonstration Act, was trying to block the change, denying the marchers a permit over Arlington Memorial Bridge. But that, he knew, was simply a horse-trading position from which Justice might be blasted when the time came, and stupid, too, for the refusal would have all the effect on the Peace League of a hotfoot on an angry drunk. Lee would be in the midst of it again, arguing, bargaining, pleading, threatening. Jesus, it was unfair, too much to ask him to deal again with those who had been so close to Rick. He would simply have to get the job delegated, somehow, or he would crack wide apart.

The toast clicked up and he munched it as he moved to the dinette window. From here you could see a portion of Arlington Cemetery, and watch the morning Pentagon traffic inching down Columbia Pike. You could see, looming always in the distance, the Pentagon itself. He hated living within sight of it; it was enough to have to worry about fire, pornography, theft, rape, and sabotage in the damn place twenty-four hours a day (enough even to have to work there at all) without awakening to find it staring at you every morning. He had seen no choice but to live here: General Lucius Hardy, Chief of Army Intelligence, had found them the apartment and insisted. Luscious Lucius was a dedicated officer but an ambitious and wary bureaucrat. Dealing from power, the general had stolen the Pentagon Security Office—the billet he coveted for Lee—from the Washington Military District, only to face the prospect of losing it in turn to General Picket Aspen's Civil Disturbance Center. "Lee, I found you a place to live where you can run down there quick. Suppose they have a surprise demonstration on the weekend, and you lived halfway to Richmond; time you got to the Pentagon, you'd find Picket had swiped Building Security and all you'd have left would be the janitors."

Now he was trapped between the building and home. Each night, postponing the silent evenings of TV with Jenny, dreading the constant *click-thunk* of the refrigerator door as she searched for something to nibble on, he would make paperwork and play handball and wander the guardposts in the Pentagon basement for hours. He hated to come home at night but hated equally to leave for the Pentagon in the morning.

Jenny heard the front door closing after him. For a while she tried to immerse herself in Shirer's intricate study. They had served in Germany when Rick was little, and, isolated as always, had learned nothing of the country. She tried to concentrate, but when she found herself rereading a paragraph for the third time, she laid down the book. He hadn't kissed her when he left, or had he? No. But he had earlier, when she had returned to the bedroom after starting his toast and coffee. Toast and coffee was no breakfast for a man who worked as he did; that was how he stayed so damn trim. He didn't eat enough, and would rather race around a Pentagon handball court than come home to dinner on time, while she had nothing to do all day but dust a one-bedroom apartment and market for two. His eating habits explained *how* he stayed in shape, but there was another question—*why,* and for whom—and that she couldn't face. She wondered how long a forty-six-year-old man who looked forty could do without sex.

She slipped from the bed and padded into the living room. She glanced at Rick, who was staring at her from the mantel as if startled by the rolls of fat, or angry at her doubts about his father. She tried to shame herself from what she was about to do with a long look at the wedding picture beside Rick's. She had been so beautiful, then, and arrogant, some people thought. Now the few who saw her must feel only pity, and the arrogance, though still there, was obviously a front. They could poke a thumb through it anytime they wanted, knowing that if she lost Lee she would collapse like a pricked balloon.

Against her will she moved into the kitchen. Danish coffeecake lay hidden in a cupboard (not in the breadbox, where he might spot it) and she never touched it until he left. At the last moment she whirled and left. Today she would not eat at all, just a salad, maybe, at lunch, until dinner when Lee returned.

She looked at Rick's picture to see if he approved. He was impassive. She had a quick vision: he was studying her from the crazy Japanese crib they had got him when they had the quarters at Washington Heights in Toyko. His first words had been Japanese, learned from the maids. He had picked up languages easily; Japanese first and German and French, and now it was all wasted.

She moved suddenly back into the kitchen, found the coffeecake and buttered it. Her hands shook with anticipation. She sat at the dinette table, stared at the Pentagon, and found it as malevolent a presence to her now as it seemed to be to Lee. He would be getting to work, entering). But what about the rest of the day? She envisioned a there (or was there? No, he *couldn't*, not that little nothing. But what about the rest of the day? She envisioned a corps of civil-service secretaries, GS-3s and 4s, Army WACs, and Navy WAVEs drooling as he passed. He had this thing for women, and didn't even seem to know it, or sense their heads turning as he moved by.

The coffeecake had only whetted her appetite. She finished with two slices of toast and returned to her bed and Shirer.

Bull Collins, Aerodyne representative, awakened with a champagne mouth, throbbing temples, and Ellsworth's redheaded secretary at the Marriott Twin Bridges Motor Hotel. The Marriott squatted halfway between the concrete plateau of the Pentagon and the great plain of Washington National Airport. It was a vast village of luxurious cubicles, with brightly painted doors to disguise their sameness, expanding from a central hotel area. Some of its guests at this time of year were tourists. To Bull, summer mornings were misery. Children generated spontaneously like pollywogs in the central swimming pool (which in winter was an ice rink, and quiet). The thump of the diving board pounded his ears, car doors clunked, and babies cried and mothers screamed in rage. (Once the little bastards had awakened him, he was doomed, for

61

punctuating it all, every thirty seconds as the daylight airline schedules took hold, a plane whistled over on final for National Airport and there was no longer any chance of shutting out the vision of his competitors from General Dynamics swarming into the coffeeshop and restaurant, attaché cases filled with proposals, awake and ready for the day's assault on the Brass.)

He turned on his side and was not pleased. Sherry—he had forgotten her last name—had borne the night poorly. The full red hair was tangled, she had crowsfeet at her eyes, which he had never noticed, her neck was creased more deeply than he remembered, and damned if she hadn't proved to snore. He had better beat her to the can; she'd be an hour repairing the damage. There was another jet due over any moment and if it woke her up, plain courtesy would require him to let her in first, and his bladder was bursting. Besides, he had last-minute birddogging to do on the AFX proposal before he left for California to polish it up with the engineers. He had an appointment with Admiral Strickland at Fleet Procurement at 1100 and with a Tactical Air Command colonel from the Air Force Evaluation Team at noon.

He lurched for the bathroom, potbellied and hungover. He would have to get Strickland or somebody back on a squash court again today; he was turning into a real slob. Emerging, he found Sherry still asleep and went through her pocketbook on the bureau. He found her ID. Her last name was Pace, and she was not thirty-five, as she had hinted, but forty-two. That was all right, no sacrifice was too great for Aerodyne, and besides, snorer or not, she was a good lay. The ID picture had been taken some years before, which figured. No one as stupid as she rose to GS-6 under a prick like Ellsworth unless she had plenty of seniority. He wondered if Ellsworth himself was screwing her. Unlikely, a young stud like that could do better. Besides, with Ellsworth's opportunities to travel he'd be an idiot to fool around so close to home.

He allowed himself a Machiavellian vision of the Air Force Association Convention next month at the Statler. He knew that Ellsworth would be there, and that he had a pretty wife and two little girls. Aerodyne would have a suite and if he could hire some doll, a real chippy from Baltimore, maybe, and get Ellsworth drunk and into the sack with her, even snap a picture . . .

He dismissed the whole idea. He had been seeing too many spy movies, or something. All he needed was the facts, just the facts, Ma'am, on the Israeli purchase, and a word to Fulbright or Weintraub, the radical young Jewish dove on the House Armed Services Committee, would be enough. Another jet screeched over. Bull took out his razor, banged the medicine cabinet closed, coughed loudly, plugged it in by the bureau mirror a few feet from the woman's head, and set it snarling across his cheeks.

"Oh, God," Sherry moaned, running her tongue around her mouth. "Champagne?"

He turned off the razor. "Nothing but the best, Sherry-san. Get your ass in gear, honey, if you want to sell your boss's aireyplanes."

"Aireyplanes?"

"To the Greeks, via the Jews. Forty F-111s?"

"Forty F— Oh, that? I could care less. It's a hundred and fifty, anyway, isn't it? What time is it?"

Bull hid his shock. "Nine-oh-seven," he said, starting the razor again, "and the john's all yours."

A hundred-fifty was too many. Nobody would ever believe him, journalist or Congressman. He did not really believe it himself. Still, she should know; she had been typing out the memo while he massaged her neck yesterday. Had it not been for the goddamn Army colonel in civvies—Chief of Security, Frost was his name—he would have had time to read the whole thing. By bribery, stealth, or the fading power of his well-hung organ, it was a memo he had somehow better get before he left for California.

Lee Frost began to look for the leak to the *Underground Clarion*. He sat at his desk and checked the first of the pile of security files he had been delivered. It was the dossier on Ethel Langlois, General Greenberg's receptionist. She turned out to be a long-time Pentagon employee, widow of a World War II fighter-pilot. He scanned the Service record of the black lieutenant at Arlington.

His West Point background proved nothing perhaps (one recent graduate having resigned as a conscientious objector and some 5,000 Service-Academy alumni having just formed an anti-war group), but still, the old-school tie somehow eliminated him as a prime suspect in Lee's mind. He glanced at the file of the sentry, who had no record of any sort of political activity and very little record of anything. Then he turned to the 201 file on Martin Lumpert, Specialist Fourth Class, U.S. Army: *Cleared Secret 2/4/70, Chemical Research and Development Labs, Edgewood Arsenal, Maryland. Cleared Top Secret 4/11/70, Biological Warfare Center, Fort Detrick, Maryland: Affirmed Pentagon 5/12/70. See supporting annex . . .* He leafed through the papers. A Counterintelligence agent had once interviewed Lumpert's high-school chemistry teacher and his principal: *"Dedicated to academic work . . . especially motivated by the life sciences . . . President Chemistry Club . . . school paper photographer . . . popular with teachers . . ."* His recorded IQ was 142. Amazed, Lee leafed to the front of the file to check the photo again. It was Lumpert, all right, staring glassily into the camera, the tip of his head touching the five-foot-six line in the background, his Service number across his chest like a prisoner. Not Service number, social-security number, nowadays: Orwell's *1984* was closer than Lee cared to think. Lee flipped back to Lumpert's academic file. Jesus, the kid had actually had three years at U.C. Berkeley before he had dropped out for six months and apparently been caught in the draft. The three years were heavily weighted with chemistry and physics, in which he had starred. If he had been a student radical, Fort Holabird would have coughed it up. But no mention of subversive activity on the record, just a bright and eager scholar.

The chemistry explained why Lumpert was the personal clerk of the Chief of Chemical and Biological Warfare, but it put him even more out of focus, unless he had had a recent lobotomy or scrambled his brains on acid. Lee sat back, thinking. Lumpert had gone to U.C. Berkeley, and Berkeley was Berkeley, and he had acted more stupidly yesterday than the record showed he should have. Although he was unmarried, his 201 showed that he had lived out of barracks for over a month. His hair was too long. There was no telling what influences he had run into since his last security review.

Lee called Fort Holabird and asked for surveillance on him. Holabird complained, pleading shortages, but finally gave in. They would probably use student-agents and the students would quite possibly blow their cover and Lumpert would go crying to General Greenberg and the general would land on Lee with both feet, but it was worth the risk. Lumpert was his best suspect, and in a sensitive spot. He told Holabird to have the assigned agents report to him tomorrow for background. He turned to his mail.

On the top of his basket was a letter from the Reverend C. E. Scott of the Peace League on Decatur Place. Lee scanned it with distaste: *"My dear Colonel: As you may have read by now, or developed from other sources"* —paranoia in a clerical collar; so far as Lee knew they had never had an agent at the League— *"our plans for the Washington Monument Peace Rally have been changed to include a candlelight procession from the Monument to the Pentagon, somewhat to my distress. I wonder if you could meet again with me here to insure that we enjoy the same peaceful state of affairs as last spring. . . ."*

"Shit!" exploded Lee. He took the letter directly to his boss, General Hardy, a tall, toothy officer with a placid smile but a stubborn streak. He listened to Lee's plea, grinning. "Delegate it? I can't let you delegate it! What the hell, Lee, they like you! Anyway, they don't *hate* you. You *know* all those fuzzy bastards!"

"General, there's too much to do internally, right here. . . ."

"How true, how true! Have you discovered who writes dirty words in the toilet stalls?"

"Come on, Lucius. I didn't ask for this damn tour!"

Luscious Lucius smiled benignly: "You find out who grew the pot in the Central Court? Who runs numbers in the basement? I mean, *important* stuff like that?"

"Damn it, it all takes attention. This—"

"Give this your attention, too, Lee." Hardy was

amused. He didn't know that the Peace League was full of young men who had known Rick and would only remind him of his son, that when he saw Handlemann of the *Underground Clarion* and the kid started bleeding about Rick, Lee would want to kick his teeth down his throat. Hardy didn't dream that the Reverend Scott himself would know that Rick was dead and would probably bray like the ass he was. "This guy's a minister!" Lee protested. "Why can't he deal with the Chief of Chaplains?"

"Because Scorchy would buck it to Aspen, and Aspen would want to machine-gun them on the Mall."

There was no out, short of telling him of his real reasons, and even that, if he could bring himself to do it, might not work. To Luscious Lucius, when his empire was at stake, the job came first.

"All right," Lee said stiffly. He picked up Scott's letter. "Shall I even *show* it to Aspen?"

"You have to. So he knows we're carrying the ball. But Lee?"

"Don't let him steal it, right?" Lee asked sardonically.

"That's right," General Hardy grinned. "We'll make a general of you yet."

Chapter Seven

It had taken Congressman Cyrus Weintraub all morning to worm his way into the hearings off the Army War Room. When an obsequious but still-reluctant lieutenant-colonel from the Army's Congressional Liaison Office finally got him properly cleared, Weintraub, a cadaverous young man with frizzled hair and heavy-lidded, sleepy eyes, settled into a first-row seat. Within five minutes his presence had stopped the proceedings.

His entry into the Court of Inquiry had been discreet enough so that few members even glanced his way. The Army had placed its investigation wisely: anyone attending had first to be cleared through the War Room, effectively eliminating press, families of the "Parties" (a euphemism for the "accused"), and very nearly having eliminated Congressman Weintraub himself. (Passing through the War Room, he had noted that even his own unheralded coming had closed the huge green curtains on the world map set at one end and that the men who handled the computers and the teletypes behind the great glass panes at the other end were taking time out for coffee and a smoke.)

A real Star Chamber, he decided. Two lieutenant-colonels, two bird-colonels, and a grandfatherly brigadier sat at a kidney-shaped table on a raised dais in the hearing room. The three Fort Meade Army privates under investigation sat at a table before them, with their counsel, all of whom were Judge Advocate General officers. Weintraub was the only civilian in the audience; everyone else was a captain or above, and wore the starred-and-striped shield of the JAG Corps or the sphinx of Intelligence. As he watched, one of the privates was asked to take the stand. It was his own constituent.

Private Hackle (who had written the letter that brought

him) was a petulant, hot-eyed young man. He admitted that he wrote for *The Olive Greensheet,* and that it was not a paper popular with Army Brass, but he confessed almost nothing else except his membership in MDM—Movement for a Democratic Military. He denied any attempt to encourage mutiny, desertion, or contempt for authority. When the rotund, unhappy judge advocate who was examining him had exhausted his list of questions, the boy asked to make a statement. Despite the objection of Hackle's own counsel, a captain, the brigadier nodded and Hackle said: "Instead of trying to stick *us* for digging out dirt, why don't you try to get at the facts? We're talking about murder, rape, and a massacre; you're talking about 'solicitation to commit sedition.' What the hell—"

Hackle's counsel jumped to his feet: "Sir, Hackle doesn't mean—"

"Strike that. This inquiry will take no notice of his contempt, this time. But ask your charge to watch it, Captain!"

It was a short session for Weintraub. Someone in the Liaison Office had finally reached Ab Dennes, House Armed Services Chairman, and the sergeant-at-arms moved stiffly to deposit a note in front of the general. The general glanced at Cy, flushed, nodded politely, tapped his gavel, and adjourned until 1300 hours the next day. As everyone shuffled out, Weintraub moved swiftly to Hackle's side. "I'm Cy Weintraub. I got your letter."

The boy's eyes widened. "Jesus, Congressman! I never thought I'd see you here!" Hackle introduced him to his counsel, who quickly ran down the facts. It was the three who were in trouble, not the Army. Of the supposed witnesses to a massacre the three alleged to have been uncovered, they had produced not one Vietnam returnee, now that the chips were down.

"Why not?" asked Weintraub.

"We promised to protect them. OK, now we're protecting them. They were armed, all but one. If you're carrying a gun, how do you prove you didn't fire? Hell, maybe some of them *did* fire."

"So the Army's hanging Hackle *et al,*" Weintraub asked the captain incredulously, "instead?"

The officer colored. "Well, JAG holds that they dreamed it up for copy for *The Olive Greensheet.*"

"Nobody *dreamed* it up," Hackle said. "The rumors are all around. I just *wrote* them up, is all."

"Congressman," the captain protested, "we charged the *Superintendent of West Point* for concealing facts of Mylai! Do you think the Army'd try to hide this?"

"With a lawyer like you," Hackle snapped bitterly, "who needs a prosecutor?"

"I'd be glad to recommend cilivian counsel," the captain flared.

"They'll hang me anyway. Why pay a lawyer?"

Cy Weintraub motioned the officer to leave, and said: "What about the man who wasn't armed? You promised him anything?"

"No sir. But I don't want him here."

"Why, if he wasn't armed?"

"He'd deny it. He's a lifer, Army all the way. Met him at the Gas House, outside Edgewood Arsenal. He was gassed, all right, or he wouldn't have told me anything."

"Maybe he'll tell a Congressman."

"Not if you gave him sodium pentathol!"

"Let me try, Hackle," begged Weintraub. He hoped that his own motives were more humanitarian than political, but either way, he wanted the massacre aired if Hackle was right. "What was his name? Why wasn't he armed?"

"You won't believe this," Hackle said softly, "but he was shooting Army movies."

"Movies?"

"Too much?" Hackle asked sadly. " 'Don't cut, Cecil, the poor devils are dying.' "

The lieutenant-colonel from the Liaison Office presented himself. "Congressman Dennes would like you to phone him, sir, at your convenience."

"Thanks for telling him I was here," Weintraub said grimly. Daddy was calling, and it would not be a happy session, "at his convenience" or not. "Hackle," he said firmly, "I want that cameraman's name. And I want it now!"

Hackle studied him for a moment. "All right, sir," he

decided. "Alioto. Tony Alioto, Spec One. Shooting training films at the Chemical Warfare Center now. He'll swear he never heard of Ban Doc—that's where it was—or me, and then you'll think I was lying."

"And you won't be any worse off than now, right?" He decided to call his chairman immediately, rather than to wait. The less head of steam the old bastard worked up, the better. Dennes did not like junior committee members operating singly in the Pentagon. In fact he did not like his most junior member at all, and it looked as if poor Hackle was going to need all the Congressional help he could get.

Bull Collins, somewhat to his surprise, found it as easy to purloin the F-111 memo as if he had been a trained Soviet spy. He gallantly escorted Sherry to her office, pretended to remember a series of calls he must make, and stalled. He talked for twenty minutes into a dead phone on her desk, while he watched her open her safe (trying unsuccessfully to read the numbers). She took out the memo she had begun the day before and loaded her dictating machine with a tape. He heard Ellsworth's dry voice crackling in her earphones behind the ripple of speeding keys. Head throbbing, he dialed again and pretended to talk to his secretary in the Aerodyne office, then to an imaginary Air Force procurement officer. Finally he began an affable and fictitious conversation with a Deputy Secretary of the Navy, who, for all he knew, was out inspecting the Fleet. When Sherry was finished, she proofread the work in the typewriter, placed it in her out-basket, and typed three short letters, which she dropped in the basket on top of the memo. Finally she took off her earphones and rubbed her eyes. "With the head you must have," she marveled, "I don't understand how you can be so goddamned talkative!"

He looked down at her miserably. "Have to," he whispered, hand over the phone's mouthpiece. "Coffee, please?" He fished in his pocket and handed her a quarter. She nodded and left the office. Quickly he covered his thumb and forefinger with Scotch tape from her desk,

70

to avoid prints, and slipped the memo from her basket: T-O-P S-E-C-R-E-T: TERMS, SPECIFICATIONS, AND DATES OF DELIVERY OF F-111 AIRCRAFT TO ISRAELI PURCHASING COMMISSION, SUMMARY OF. He eased the sheets, copies and all, into his dispatch case and was hanging up the phone when she returned. He gulped the coffee. "I may take you to lunch."

"That's nice," she said wearily. "Hurry back."

He went to the Aerodyne liaison office in the C Ring. He stuck more tabs of Scotch tape on his other fingers and Xeroxed two facsimiles of the memo. Laboriously, he typed up a plain envelope addressed to The Honorable Cyrus Weintraub, M.C., at the House Office Building. Handling the Xeroxed sheets carefully, he inserted one copy, kept one, and mailed the envelope at the Pentagon post office. Then he hurried back to Ellsworth's office.

The reception room was empty. On Sherry's desk was a note: "Bull: If you *do* come back, sorry about lunch. Gone home to die." She had probably delivered the morning work to her boss before she fled. If anyone had already missed the memo, the place would have been in an uproar. On the other hand, he could not imagine how to return the original. Her safe was closed. On its dial hung the standard green cardboard signed, "LOCKED," as required by Security. Her outgoing-basket was empty. He supposed he should try to slip the memo into Ellsworth's basket in the inner office, but that was impossible; he could hear him talking on his phone behind the door. Bull was jumpy and scared. It was time to get out.

He finally dropped the document into Sherry's outbasket as if she had forgotten it. He covered it feebly from immediate view with a blank sheet of typewriter paper. When she found it tomorrow she would wonder how she had overlooked it there, but maybe she would blame it on her hangover, and her own neck was stuck out, so she would certainly not ask questions.

Bull left, sweating mightily. He made his appointment with Admiral Strickland on time, and probed for last-minute hints as to what might be added to Aerodyne's AFX proposal to gild the lily. It was a waste of time, for the admiral was tight as a drum today and would say

71

nothing and Bull saw no reason to tell even him that he had learned the number of F-111s involved in the Israeli-Greek purchase. He strolled to the office of the Tactical Air Command representative on the Air Force Evaluation Team. There he gained an impression from a relaxed, pipe-smoking colonel with a fighter-pilot moustache that if Aerodyne made a minor cockpit change to incorporate a Hughes Fire Control System, it would be looked on with favor by the team.

"With seven days to go, Colonel?" asked Bull, to make sure he would appreciate the difficulties.

The Colonel expressed indifference: "It's just something that came up. General Dynamics hasn't asked, so of course I haven't suggested it to them."

So the colonel wanted Aerodyne's design to win: a good sign. The whole picture aroused Bill's competitive blood. It was like prying an exam question out of a professor before a final. The colonel was new and perhaps hadn't learned his Armed Forces Procurement Regulations, or was napping, or dazzled perhaps by Bull's score in World War II. Or maybe the colonel had something else in mind, and lacked Admiral Strickland's compunctions. It was worth remembering. Bull called Aerodyne in Los Angeles and talked to Hound Dog Cassell, AFX Proposal Manager, who was slated to become Project Manager if the company won. Hound Dog was ordinarily unflappable, rock-steady in unfailing pessimism, but the late change Bull suggested cracked him open.

"OK, Bull," he spat, "get your fat ass out here and break it to them yourself. Me, I'm getting drunk."

Bull smiled and hung up. Hound Dog would not get drunk. Instead, he would assemble his team in the hangar set aside for the AFX proposal. Half of them had been living there for weeks, on cots and in sleeping bags on the cement floor. Design engineers, program planners, product-assurance men, cost analysts, contract administrators, draftsmen, tech-writers, artists, animators for the sales movies would be getting the word within moments, and by the time Bull arrived would be back at their boards and desks, pouchy-eyed, punchy, bitter, and devoutly praying for success.

72

As for Bull, he stopped at the Windjammer Bar in the Mariott and barely made the Redeye Special out of Dulles International. He settled back in First Class, martini in hand, and eyed his favorite stewardess. She had been "stewing" for ten years, lived by LA airport in Manhattan Beach, and except for a tendency to expect and accept expensive gifts (and to shriek too loudly at climax) she would be a perfectly tolerable bed-partner for the next two days, if he ever got to bed.

He did not know whether it was the stewardess or the morning's work, but he had not felt so good since he had caught his first Mitsubishi bomber over Guadalcanal and sent it tumbling and twirling into Iron Bottom Sound.

Lee Frost flashed his Special Security badge at the sentry outside the subterranean domain of General Picket Aspen, hidden under the Pentagon Mall. He waited for the inner guard to check his image on a closed-circuit TV screen. A buzz signified that he was recognized and he opened the door.

The Pentagon Civil Disturbance Planning and Operations Center had been built after the Pentagon riots of 1967. It was hardly smaller than the Army War Room, and the whole area was dominated by a transparent map of the United States, forty feet wide and twenty feet tall, center stage. Most of the graphics on the map were automatic, computer-fed, but in dim recesses behind the map were men on platforms, too, trained to print backwards in grease-pencil if computer circuits failed.

Facing the map was a long console and a row of black-leather swivel-chairs, now empty. The center chair had its own computer-display, in case Aspen had private questions to ask it. In time of major civil disturbance the general's post would be here, flanked by his staff. Before him would twinkle the "Whole Picture" of forces available to put down insurrection: Southern Command; First, Third, Fourth, Fifth, and Sixth Armies; Maneuver Area Commands; and the Separate Infantry Brigades. The headquarters of each of the fifty National Guard Brigades and the Automatic Voice Network codes of their commanders

73

pulsed on the map in purple and each U.S. Marshal's office glowed in orange.

Lee, crossing the room, glanced up at the display. The hidden computer digested everything: a riot call in Mobile, current air temperature in Cleveland or Detroit, a Black Panther bust in Oakland. On the map this morning, civil hotspots from Berkeley to Harlem were calm and glowing steady-green, but if the computer grew worried, it would turn them to amber and then to flashing red. Neatly numbered pink circles showed respectively where Jane Fonda, William Kunstler, Abbie Hoffman, Rennie Davis, and Reverend Abernathy had spent the night, and the location and date of their next speaking engagements. The computer was unprejudiced, though, as any liberal Congressman could see: similar circles, grease-penciled in black, spotted the map with Robert Welch of the John Birch Society, a few of the more audible officers of the American Nazi Party, and even the Army's own General Edwin Walker.

General Picket Aspen used a glassed-in cubicle as an office, the better to watch his favorite view. Aspen, tense and harried as always, beckoned him in. To prove that his problems justified the strain, he handed Lee a random TWX from California's 40th National Guard Brigade requesting a firming-up of the Riot-Suppression Procedure for U.C. Santa Barbara, where students were gathering again in the streets of Isla Vista in protest over the firing of a professor of *Oceanography,* if you could imagine that. "See, there it goes."

Lee peered through the glass at the general's immense pinball machine: sure enough, Santa Barbara had begun to wink at him in amber. "Heating up," said the general, tightly. He had a pale, dead-center gaze; his thin hair was receding. He was a tiny but implacable roadblock between Democracy-and-the-Bloodiest-Fucking-Revolution-You'll-Ever-See. His dedication was supreme; his staff grew by bounds; he knew his job and without a moment's hesitation could tell you how many troops could be mustered in Memphis, and, very nearly, how many hours of riot-training each platoon had had.

He was devoted to the Constitution, and if he regretted

the Supreme Court's interference with those who would "Preserve Life, Liberty, and Property," he certainly advocated ultimate civilian control "When Things Get Stabilized Again." He considered *Seven Days in May* a traitorous satire, Kremlin-inspired. *Doctor Strangelove* should have been burned, reel by reel. He had never forgiven Eisenhower, senile or not, for his parting stab-in-the-back of the military-industrial complex. ("What's *that?*" Aspen would demand. "Show me a conspiracy between industry and the military and I'll show you a far-sighted officer and a businessman with vision.") The liberal magazine articles Marine Commandant David Shoup had written after retirement he would have deemed treasonable, but "Everybody Knew Poor Dave Had Gone Insane."

Lee handed him back the TWX from Santa Barbara. The general filed it carefully. Then Aspen picked up a flimsy of the report Lee had dictated on yesterday's rifle shot. "Instead of sanitizing this, goddamn it, why didn't you make a general release on it? Let people know what we have to put up with around here. Picketing, longhairs yelling, scaring the women! And now they're *shooting* at us!"

Lee explained that the shot may have had nothing to do with the radical Left, and that neither Ellsworth of International Logistics nor Greenberg of CBW wanted to release the news. Then he gave him the letter from The Reverend Scott of the Peace League, expecting another explosion, but there was none. Aspen merely looked up, spearing him with the pale-blue eyes. "Are you going to meet with him?"

"I have to, don't I?"

"It depends," the general murmured. "It all depends."

"Well, we worked it out together last time and nobody got a scratch."

"Last time," General Aspen said mildly, "there was no law against unauthorized demonstrations at the Pentagon."

Lee suggested that the whole purpose of the march was to provoke a confrontation with the Army, and that it would be stupid to oblige, and that neither the law itself nor Justice's refusal of a marching permit over Memorial Bridge was going to deter the demonstrators. To try to invoke the new federal statute would be to play into the hands of the marchers, and to close the Arlington Memorial span as the Justice Department proposed was to simply divert the demonstrators and invite a traffic jam on the Roosevelt, George Mason, and Rochambeau bridges.

"Why don't you let them start across Arlington Memorial and cut them off fore-and-aft?" Aspen suggested. "They'll be in violation the minute they step on the bridge. I'll get a couple of Old Guard companies from the Third Infantry for the District side and a company from the 80th Army Reserve Division for the Virginia side and a hundred U.S. Marshals for arrests."

Lee suggested as politely as he could that sixty thousand or so demonstrators trapped screaming on Memorial Bridge would at least be an interesting study in animal behavior, and wondered whether the general would provide a concentration camp for the survivors, if any. They would need Naval units, too, to pluck out of the Potomac those lucky enough to get thrown off the span. The general never lost his frosty smile. He remarked that, after all, no one was actually *required* to demonstrate against flag and country, and he, unlike Lee and his boss Luscious Lucius, found it difficult to worry about the fate of those who did.

"In that case, sir," Lee asked, "why don't we just load them on the bridge and blow it up?"

The smile remained. "Lucius Hardy tells me," Aspen said softly, "that you're the fair-haired boy in the Intelligence Corps. And you've had a bad blow: I know about your son. But someday, Colonel, you're going to shoot off your mouth once too often. And you're going to get scalped. Remember that, will you?"

"Yes sir," Lee said. He saluted and left for Hippieville and The Reverend Doctor Scott.

Chapter Eight

Three miles north of the Pentagon, across the Potomac near the heart of the nation's capital, lies an enemy village. The hub of the village (or Street Community, as its citizens call it) is Dupont Circle, a small, verdant park named for a departed admiral of an earlier civil war. In the center of the Circle squats a fountain. Around it all day gather heads, pushers, and what used to be called flower-children. Young foreign clerks from nearby embassies bring bag lunches on bright days to eat on the benches and stare at the freaks. Sometimes the budding diplomats score on pot or on the hungry, strung-out young girls who orbit the place.

The indigenous population is in constant motion, drifting in and out on various errands or because there is nothing else to do. There are a dozen regulars: Ju-ju, a tubby butch-lesbian and her sixteen-year-old girlfriend, an angel-faced Ambassador's daughter who arrives on a shiny green bike; Black Michael, an ex-Satan Slave with an enormous belly, who girds himself in chains; two pimply comrades named Mutt and Jeff, in Aussie hats and scraggy cavalry moustaches—Mutt is a high school dropout with a fancy IQ, Jeff is the stepson of an Army lifer. They are in the newspaper business. Mutt sells *The Quicksilver Times* while Jeff hawks the *Underground Clarion*. Since the Circle is federal property, vending is forbidden, and their actual transactions must take place across the street.

The Circle is mostly peaceful. On sunny afternoons it looks like a medieval fair, but that is deceptive. Those who spend their days there are often hungry and jumpy. The tranquility and gentle ambiance will be broken by a screaming trip on acid. A head is burned, or thinks he is, by a friend, and will chase him, knife flashing, into the traffic on Massachusetts. Someone tries to steal a black's chick and there is a high-pitched argument and a flurry of action. Patrol cars converge, but all at once the actors are gone and no one is left but a confused government worker passing the fountain or a tourist with his camera. When the fuzz clears out and the heads drift back, there is much soul-searching and shaking of curling locks, for it is generally agreed that violence is stupid and that there are enough pigs around to break your skull without Street People fighting among themselves.

Narcotics are legal tender in the Circle, but conspicuous onsite consumption is discouraged. A group may blow a cautious joint around a guitarist on the lawn, but a U.S. Park policeman in gorgeous blue-and-gold, walkie-talkie crackling, inhibits anything stronger. He knows everyone, from the chubby Negro photographer flashing pornographic pictures, to Fallopian Philip Your Fine Feathered Friend, a cretinous dwarf who runs for an abortionist. The Park pig is not really unpopular. Studiously, he sees nothing; he must after all return tomorrow and tomorrow and tomorrow and the precinct car may be a long way off.

Everyone carries his own stash in a fringed leather bag, easy to cast adrift, but actual sales are never made here. The place is thought to swarm with federal and District narcs, FBI agents checking draft cards, and Army Counterintelligence agents looking for deserters. There is a local legend that even the old man who exposes himself to the girls at dusk is a CIA agent. So the Circle is a place to meet a friend; from it you retire to an alley or coffeehouse. It is the village green and the Wall Street of the Community, too, but the brokerage houses are a greasy pizzeria, the GI coffeehouse called Street Folk, the Anchor Bar, or a nearby doorway.

Dupont Circle is no Hyde Park. No one makes radical speeches. Enemy outposts stud the area. The svelte Dupont Plaza Hotel overlooks it and the mammoth Sheraton is just a few blocks away. Even the plush little antique shops and arts-and-crafts outlets around the Circle, though depending on the tourists the hippies attract, are hostile. Only the Street Folk coffeehouse actually welcomes the Dupont Circle regulars, who shoplift when necessary. So a sort of symbiosis has set in, and to politicize in the Circle would disturb the ecology.

The political backbone of the Community is the line of brownstone communal pads on Q Street. Here the Community leaders live (avoiding the freaks of Dupont Circle except when necessary to score on dope). In one ancient and shabby house is Switchboard (the answering service that dispenses free advice on everything from abortion to bail). Further up the tree-lined street in another commune are those who publish *The Quicksilver Times;* in another live the pre-med dropouts and their girls who work at the Free Clinic. Almost every shabby dwelling houses a rock group, a health-food cooperative, a contemplative Indian sect, or a fraternity of COs working out their military service in the burned-out ghetto's hospitals. There is much traffic down Q Street to Florida Avenue and the Friends' Meeting House and to the Peace League on Decatur Place, and to George Washington University Library and American U.

Lee Frost parked on Q and New Hampshire and strolled two blocks to Dupont Circle, where he bought the *Underground Clarion* and sat on a bench to read the bad news. Handlémann had done the lone rifleman proud: the item was page one, center, with a black band around it: ATTACK ON THE GENERALS? *Sources close to the Pentagon reported yesterday that a shot was fired at the building from Arlington National Cemetery, near the tomb of the Unknown Soldier. (Right on, hey?) It actually entered an unidentified office on the western side. Department of Defense officials later denied that any shot had been fired at all. (Par for the course.) No details were available.*

Well, he had handled it with his usual objectivity. "An unidentified office," seemed to take the general's clerk Lumpert off the hook, but he might be just one step ahead of everybody, stupid as he seemed. He looked at his watch and found that he had time to read up on Handlemann's version of the coming peace rally before seeing the Reverend.

"Colonel?" Red Handlemann, tall, wolfish, and moustached, stood above him. "Can I sit down?"

Handlemann had grown spookier and more gaunt. His hair was longer and his red-veined eyes more sunken. When first Lee Frost had met him he had been Rick's roommate at George Washington, a gangly, rawboned sophomore, straight enough to be playing varsity basketball. His path, and Rick's, had split further and further from athletics. The two had been unlike but inseparable.

"OK, Red," Lee said, reluctantly, "sit." His own voice had a hollow ring. The kid sagged to the bench, roughened boots stretched before him. Finally he looked into Lee's face. "Colonel, about Rick? Now, what the hell can I say?"

"I'd prefer you not to say anything."

"Right, as long as you know how I feel. A real ache. Physical!"

"I believe you." Lee jabbed a thumb at the story. "I just read your big beat."

"I'm sorry we didn't believe the denial."

"That's par for the course, as you say. Who called you?"

"Che Guevara," Handlemann grinned. "Where'd it hit?"

"I wonder why you're so sure anything hit at all?" Lee speculated.

"I'm not all *that* sure," Handlemann said quickly. "Just a rumor."

He seemed uncomfortable; that was interesting. "When'd the call come in?" asked Lee.

"I don't know. I'll ask our medium."

Lee got up. "OK, Red. You're a great newspaperman. You should string for Tass."

Handlemann smiled sardonically, but his eyes were sad. "I *am* sorry about him, you know," he murmured.

"I said I believed you," Lee said impatiently.

"I even wrote an editorial, once."

"In this goddamn rag? I can see it now: *His blood is in the hands of the White House and the Pentagon, those motherfuckers!*"

Handlemann stared into the distance. "It was mostly about a dog we found, when you were still in Nam."

"A *dog?*" He arose, crumpled the paper, and tossed it into a park trash container. "For Christ's sake, spare me *that!* You were a good bet as a journalist once. Rick read me some of your stuff in the *Hatchet.* Why are you turning out this shit?"

"If somebody doesn't, you assholes down there are going to play around until you blow us all off the face of the earth."

"Well, that's an unhappy prospect," Lee said tersely.

"I think so. So did Rick. Because, Colonel—"

"Yeah?"

"It's our earth too."

Lee looked down at Handlemann. Despite the hollow cheeks he was as fit and healthy as Rick had been. Handlemann, unhappy and bitter, was here; Rick, with everything to live for, was gone. He felt like backhanding the long, shadowed face. All at once he noticed that the eyes were glittering with tears.

Shaking his head helplessly, Lee whirled and strode across the Circle.

In a darkened third-floor room of the brick-fronted house on Q Street where Handlemann lived with most of his *Clarion* staff, Marty Lumpert stood watching film on a clattering Movieola editing machine. The film-editor was First Lieutenant Chris Poma, late of the U.S. Army, presumably most wanted of its 17,000 deserters. The room was cluttered with the projectors and color-wheels of one Ronnie Flieger, who gave light-shows at the Inner Eye in Georgetown. Flieger's unmade bed and a mattress for Poma lay at opposite ends of the room, which smelled of cat urine and of Handlemann's gaunt yellow dog, Cannabis, who slept here. Marty could not understand how Poma, a broadshouldered, applecheeked young Southerner with a shock of golden country hair, could work cooped up all day and then sleep here every night.

Poma sped a sequence through the viewer and stopped on the frame he wanted. The film was work-print, marred with scratches and his editing marks, but the scene was clear enough: a dismal Vietnam landing zone, with infantrymen in flak-vests loading gas canisters into launchers. Marty identified the canisters as vomiting gas and the launchers as E8s. Poma grunted thanks and made a note on the pad beside him.

Downstairs the doorbell rang. Poma tensed. He was jumpier every day. Marty knew that it was more from concern over the fate of his film than for his personal liberty, and that he regretted that penury had caused him to crash in Handlemann's pad to edit it. Poma lit a cigarette, listening as someone below went to the door. He seldom shaved now and a bronze stubble shone on his face. Marty had grown to idolize him, awed by his skill and artistry. Poma had studied drama at Ole Miss, cinematography in the West, and spent his summers in New York working with Warhol until a half-forgotten ROTC commission had caught up with him and he had gone to make Army training films in Vietnam. In the month that Marty had known him he had watched him lose fifteen pounds.

They heard the door three floors below being unlatched, bolt by bolt. Poma dragged at his cigarette. "OK!" someone yelled up the stairs. "Press run, is all. Anybody want to sell papers?"

The voice, Chute's or Tom-Tom's, echoed through the empty house, and no one answered. Poma relaxed, ground out the cigarette, and rolled back the film. "That 4.2 gas shell in the lower right frame. Is that CS or CN?"

"CS," said Marty, squinting. "They were playing for keeps, weren't they?"

"They were playing for keeps," Poma agreed softly, making another note on his pad. Marty's heart began to pound. He knew what was coming in the next scene, dreaded it, had seen it and seen it again. It was simply not fair to have to look at it once again. He glanced at his watch. It was two P.M., he had been here since noon, and he was due back at the Pentagon from his "dental appointment." Silently, he begged Poma for mercy, ashamed to leave. Poma pressed a foot-pedal and the Movieola clacked, into reverse, thank God. The soldiers unloaded the launchers, ran backward toward a waiting helicopter, hopped ridiculously in reverse into its belly.

Its doors closed and it thrashed into the air. Poma reversed the film again and the chopper landed and everyone hopped out. The camera cut to a closeup of the gas shells being passed: everything froze.

"CS for sure?" Poma asked.

"That's right."

"What's the difference between CN and CS?"

"Well, you know how CN works, alpha-chloroacetophenone?"

"Come on, man!"

"*You're* an officer, I'm just a Spec Four."

"But you went to Berkeley, I went to Ole Miss. They-all didn't teach us-all them fancy names."

"Riot gas! Didn't you even have any riots?"

"If we'd had a riot, they'd have used bayonets and bullets, not aplha-horseshitophenone, or whatever."

Marty explained that alpha-chloroacetophenone, or CN, was the lacrimator vulgarly known as tear gas and would make one weep like a baby spurned if one did not leave the immediate area but quick. Did Poma dig? Poma dug.

"The next step would be diphenylchloroarsine, U.S. Army Code DA, and it causes sneezing, coughing, watering of the eyes, headache, followed by violent nausea, acute mental distress, temporary physical disabil—"

"Come on, Marty! What about CS?"

Marty had been watching the film every night for the last three weeks. He had seen it in its entirety perhaps three dozen times, as Poma whittled it down in length, every goddamn inch of it over and over, and he felt his tongue running away as it always did when he was angry or scared, and yet he could not stop it and knew that he would say something stupid and gross to Poma, who had put his life on the line for his footage. He rambled nervously: "I am telling you this, Lieutenant, sir, not to show off but to give you background for your learned narration, which you are writing at such a slow pace that I doubt you will get it done in time for the grand premiere—"

"I'll get it done."

"OK, like I say, DA is bad enough, but *CS* for young

children and other living things is—" Poma's palm slapped down on the viewer. Marty's voice trailed off. "Sorry, Chris."

Poma looked up at him. "Young children and other living things," he mused. "Would you like me to put that in the narration, Marty?"

"No, Chris."

"It fits. It might go pretty good. Handlemann would like it. It has a certain New Left touch. Casual, cool."

"I'm *sorry,* Chris!"

"It's a very funny line, Marty, considering."

"*I've just seen the damn thing one too many times!* Chris, I'm late. I have to go."

"I've seen it," Poma reminded him softly, "once more than you." He flicked off the light and rewound the film. They pulled the rug from a corner and pried up a board beneath it and put the film cans on top of the irreplaceable, pure-gold originals. They nailed down the board, wheeled the Movieola into a closet, and locked the closet door.

"Tonight?" prompted Poma. "Around eight? For the gas-mask sequence?"

Between the landing and the gas-mask sequence there were scenes Marty thought he could not bear again, not tonight, not after standing here for two hours. "Chris," he begged, "let's skip it. You ought to get away from it."

"Sure," Poma said bitterly. "How about taking me out for a cup of coffee at the Street Folk? A beer at the Anchor? Just to rap a little, as you folks put it, blow a joint? With a few other AWOLs and an FBI agent or two? Got an extra draft card?"

"If you *don't* get out," warned Marty, "you'll blow the film. Ease off. You look like hell."

"Sorry, Marty," Poma said. "Eight o'clock, here." He smiled. The smile was becoming rare but had not changed. He tapped Marty's arm and winked: "That's show-biz, boy," he said.

Marty left via a basement window, which opened on an alley, in accordance with Handlemann's latest dictum to him: "In and out the rear." Handlemann's nervousness was becoming obsessive, in all except the matter of the film. There, the danger of harboring Poma and even losing the footage in a random raid seemed outweighed by the risk of his losing control of the massacre's release if the film were edited elsewhere.

A strange man, and growing stranger, reflected Marty. He cut across a well-worn path over a neighbor's garden, climbed a fence, and surfaced on P Street Northwest. He went back to the Pentagon, hoping the general had not missed him.

Lee Frost walked down a quiet street, neatly studded with bright door-knockers and the modest brass plates of MDs. He climbed the stone steps of the First Unitarian Church. Inside, he mounted creaking wooden stairs to the Peace League on the top floor, smelling old varnish, furniture polish, a musty church-odor from the ancient seats below, and sweat from the basement gym.

He stepped into a large room dominated by a poster of Ho Chi Minh. Tables of anti-war literature stretched across the room: giveaways, peace buttons, bumper stickers: POPULATION CONTROL BEGINS AT HOME! JOIN YOUR NATIONAL GUARD! An incredibly beautiful hazel-eyed girl with shimmering bronze hair to her shoulders—God, a face like a petulant angel—was struggling to type a letter on a machine that looked like a prop for a 1920 movie. She was compact and tanned. Her tongue was out and even the tongue seemed beautiful. She would glare at the keyboard, type a few lines, curse, erase, and backspace.

He asked her if Reverend Scott was in. Hardly glancing up, she ripped the paper from the machine, balled it, threw it away, and inclined her head toward a closed door. "He's draft-counseling. Sit down. Or browse around. Buy some books, why don't you?" The office was not air-conditioned, and her efforts had brought a film of sweat to her brow. "You come about the peace march? A reporter, or what are you, some sort of agent?"

"Smile, child," he said. "You'll get frown lines."

She finally looked at him directly and simulated a smile. He saw that her teeth were perfect, and even the fake smile made the clear hazel eyes come alive. "OK?"

she asked, between the teeth. He nodded and she turned back to glower at the machine. "Goddamn thing," she said. "Can't remember its margin, can't even spell. And it's too hot." She blew her hair from her eyes and regarded him with hostility. "If you're an agent, don't just stand there. Leaf through the literature, dirty it up, show some interest."

"What makes you think I'm an agent?"

"Your hair's too short for a professor, you're too hard for a minister. You're an agent, all right, we get so fucking many agents. So buy some books to take back. You can pick up a dozen real Commie classics, just drop a dollar in the jar there, nobody ever checks, and you can charge the home office five bucks when you get there. How about *Anti-Ballistic Missile, Yes or No?* Or *The Silent Weapons,* by Clarke, about CBW, very big this week. Or Chairman Mao? Go on, spring."

"Am I FBI?" Lee wanted to know.

She shrugged: "FBI, CIA, ONI, you see one agent, you've seen them all. What time is it?"

He told her. She studied him for a moment. "You got a car?"

He nodded and she said suddenly: "Could you take me down to my probation officer, when you leave? It's a drag, but I hate the bus and I don't have wheels."

"You sure I won't rape you? I mean, you know, the secret police?"

"I *have* to turn up at the probation office, I don't have to turn up unraped. Well, *can* you?"

"What are you on probation for?"

"Not rape, if that's what's bothering you."

"That's too bad, but I'll take you anyway. Probation for what?"

"Justice Department sit-in, April. You remember?"

He shook his head. "There've been so many."

"So you're not FBI or a federal marshal; you'd remember. You're CIA, I guess. No, you must be that Colonel; we wrote you a letter. OK, don't forget."

She resumed her typing. The young man Scott had been counseling left the inner office. Lee knocked and entered. The Reverend Chuck Estes Scott, D.D, sat in his wheelchair. He was a mild, slow-talking gentleman with a great curling mass of white hair that made him seem older than he was. His heart was in his great basset eyes and you could too easily read it. He made Lee uncomfortable. Lee had found him equally incapable of subterfuge and foresight. They shook hands and Scott briefed him with a street map on the Rally Committee's new plans: a twilight rock-and-roll festival at the base of the Washington Monument, a few speeches—Mrs. King and Spock. Then, the same march route as the last demonstration, a three-mile hike across Arlington Memorial Bridge, and, at the Pentagon by candlelight, an all-night roll call of Vietnam dead.

"That's nice," Lee commented bitterly. "That should help the kids on the cease-fire line."

Scott's huge eyes swam toward him. "I heard about your boy, Colonel."

"Who hasn't? And he was no boy," said Lee. "He was twenty-one."

"Do you want him eliminated from the roll call?"

"Why? He's dead, like the rest of them."

"Some people feel we're *using* their sons, you know."

"They do, and you are. It's street-theater, and poor street-theater. On the other hand, he was a pacifist himself, he might not agree with me, and it's his name, isn't it?" He rolled up the street maps they had marked. "Suppose Justice doesn't waive the Pentagon Demonstration Act? Suppose they don't give you a permit to cross the bridge?"

"Then we'll set up a permanent vigil on the District side. Until we *get* a permit."

"Why'd you retarget this thing? Haven't we caught enough hell?"

Scott looked uncomfortable. "It wasn't really my idea, Colonel. It was the Committee's. But now I agree."

"Handlemann's idea?"

"Yes. But I agree."

"Is he hoping for a riot, or what?"

"I hope not. We'll have plenty of parade marshals, I know that."

Handlemann was an anarchist, but the reverend was

not and most of the Committee seemed moderate. Lee wondered what had suddenly impelled them to lay plans to defy a federal law and to test the Army's temper. When he asked Scott, the minister spun his wheelchair and moved from behind his desk, plainly agitated. He swung his limpid eyes at Lee, considered him sorrowfully, and began finally to speak.

"We heard about another massacre, women and children, by GIs."

"Where?" Lee towered over him. "All right, *where?* Goddamn it, we hear these things all the time, but *where? When?* What are the facts?"

"I can't say."

"I see," snapped Lee. "Listen, how did you feel about *Viet Cong* massacres?"

"Differently," admitted Scott.

"That's what I figured. Why?"

"To start with, I was rooting for the NLF before the cease-fire, and I still am."

"That's granted," Lee said bitterly. "But why?"

"Patriotic reasons."

"Patriotic? My God!"

"It's my country as much as yours. We're not policemen, we're Americans. A defeat will save us a greater lesson later."

"So Viet Cong massacres are OK?"

Scott shook his head. "At least they aren't my fault. I don't pay taxes to hire Viet Cong. I *do* arm GIs, and feed them. I didn't elect the people in Hanoi."

"Nobody did."

"That's not strictly true, but skip it," said Scott. "The Vietnamese can kill their own, and I'm morally no more responsible than I would be for a tribal war in the Congo. But American soldiers are my paid agents. You're damn right I feel differently!"

"The victims of the 'NLF,' as you call them, are just as dead!"

"Colonel, that argument stinks." Scott looked intently into his eyes. "And the sad thing is, I think you know it."

Lee took the street maps, spun on his heel, and slammed out. The girl was waiting in the office, a big handbag slung from her shoulder. She wore blue jeans and a man's shirt, which did not hide her round, tight breasts. She had no waist at all; even the coarse pants could not flaw the curve of her thigh. He felt a great desire for her and knew that he was tense and flushed and wondered if she sensed it. No girl had done this to him for years. Her eyes met his and she smiled again, this time for real.

"OK, child," he said huskily. "Parole board, ho."

"*Probation*," she said softly. "Parole's for criminals." He helped her into his car and she sat just close enough so that he could feel the warmth of her leg on his. Her name was Laurie. They drifted off through traffic and talked easily of the demonstration, of the freaks on the Circle, of Handlemann's intransigence. She was tired of Handlemann's rhetoric but warned Lee not to get her wrong: she was happy working at the League. She had been miserably useless at American U but now she had found her place.

"Has it ever occurred to you, Laurie, that the military establishment is not going away, and you just might be wasting your time?"

"Sure. And then another Mylai pops up or—"

"The orphanage at Phu Thanh?" he prodded, wondering if she had ever heard of the Viet Cong massacre on Highway One.

She admitted that she had. "But Mylai, Phu Thanh, Dachau, Lidice . . . What's the difference? They'll go on until we stop them. There are others you're hiding. Worse."

"Nothing we're hiding." He parked by the District Courthouse. "And nothing worse, I hope."

She looked at him strangely. "Is it possible that you don't know?"

"Don't know *what?*"

"Ban Doc?"

The name had a familiar sound. It was a hamlet, he remembered, near a town called Dong Ap Bia, which had been the target of an obscure operation named Mohawk Sand. "What about Ban Doc?"

"It makes Mylai and Phu Thanh look like nothing. Nothing at all. . . ."

"Bullshit," he exploded. "You've been reading Handlemann's crap again. Every time some discharged supply clerk or an AWOL grunt comes down the pike, he's got his own private horror story and it all gets in that rag without that idiot making the *first effort* to check it out."

"Ordinarily, yes," she agreed. "However . . ." She dug into her massive handbag. She took out a small glossy picture, creased and handled. He stared at a GI in a gas mask with an M-16 leveled at a Vietnamese woman. Her knees were sagging and her eyes white with shock as if she had just taken a slug. To one of her legs clung a child, face buried in her thigh. Perforations at the edge of the print showed that it had been enlarged from the single frame of a movie. "Worse than Mylai?" she asked.

"My God," he breathed. Then common sense took over. "It's a fake!"

"No, Colonel. I've seen other parts of the film."

"Where?" he asked swiftly.

"Forget it," she said, reaching for the print.

"I want that," he said, slipping it into his pocket.

Her eyes blazed and then she relaxed. "All right. There are lots more around."

"It's a goddamn fake!" he said, more violently. "Or why the gas mask?" She got out of the car and closed the door gently. He slid across the seat, looking up at her. "Answer me!" he demanded again. *"Why the gas mask?"*

She looked in through the window, wet her lips with the tip of her tongue, and for a long moment stared into his eyes.

"Because," she murmured finally, "that's how they flushed them out."

Phase II

THE GREAT LIGHT-SHOW

Chapter One

The office of Secretary of Defense Leonard Royce lay on the Outer Ring over the River Entrance, not far from the plaque on Eisenhower Corridor engraved with the general's farewell address (from which his unfortunate reference to the dangers of the military-industrial complex had been deleted). Sometimes as the Secretary sat in his office with the worldwide energy of the Pentagon vibrating around him, he felt infinitely powerful. And then there were days like this one.

Framed dramatically (as he well knew) by the stately window and two flags behind him (one for America, one for the Department of Defense), the Secretary nervously regarded the most important cog in the funding of his country's weaponry, Chairman Ab Dennes of the House Armed Services Committee. Dennes finished reading the Supplemental Defense Budget and looked up from the fine print with bloodshot eyes. "Two suggestions, Leonard. Hide the CBW in Army Research and Development Appropriations, Projected, instead of Field Sanitation. And where's your laser beams?"

"Force Development: eighteen million."

"The Bureau of the Budget will want you to itemize it. You just got to tag that kind of item with 'Research and Development' and stamp it top secret nowadays. The B of B will scream, and leak it, Leonard, and the press will holler 'death-ray' if you buy a dozen flashlights."

"I'll do that," promised Leonard Royce. He looked at the old Navy clock on his wall, rescued from the scrapping of the World War II destroyer he had hated so deeply but whose name he found himself invoking now at every opportunity. One o'clock. He had dreaded this private preview of the Supplemental. He detested Dennes and found him boring. Now, though he had set up luncheon *à deux* in the private dining room off the office, he decided to take him to the General and Flag Officers' Lounge instead. He knew that Dennes enjoyed the military fellowship he thought he found there, and as for himself, he would prefer the distraction of other faces. "Ab," he suggested, "how about lunch?"

"That sounds just about as nice an institution as anythin' I can imagine, Leonard," beamed Dennes. He put down the Supplemental, removed his glasses, and rubbed his black button-eyes. Jowls quivering, he heaved himself from his chair. Together, they moved down the hall to the oak-paneled quiet of the most exclusive military club in the world. They sat at a table by its eastern window, overlooking the Capitol. Dennes downed bourbon and branch water. From a hovering Navy mess steward he ordered "some of that good Gulf red snapper, son." The Secretary, sipping Scotch, had the definite sense that the Congressman would have had corn pone and fatback had it appeared on the menu.

"You know, Leonard," Dennes said, "I got a problem with the Committee."

"I know it. And He knows it." When he referred to the President, the Secretary customarily capitalized the pronoun in his mind: it came out more reverently that way, reminding the Pentagon listeners of the hidden presence across the Potomac. "That kid Weintraub?"

Dennes nodded and poked at his fish. "You *fly* this in from New Orleans?"

"I don't know."

"You could, you know. You ought to. Lake Charles to Bolling, by B-52, one hour. It's all training for 'em."

"What about your problem?"

"My problem turned up in your War Room yesterday. That hearing. Why did Army start that up?"

The Honorable Leonard Royce felt familiar anger at all of the forces rising to pen him in. "Because *The Olive Greensheet* and another fifty filthy rags are getting to the troops. You can bar them from the bases, you can burn them, but you can't stamp them out. So we'll discredit them. Do you know how many GIs will go over the hill today?"

Ab Dennes chewed reflectively, removed a fishbone from his teeth, and placed it carefully in his napkin. "How many?"

"Five hundred."

"Five hundred good, red-blooded American boys," Dennes drawled. "My! Can't hardly *draft* them that fast. But what you going to do if that 'investigation' turns up another Mylai?"

"It won't."

"But if it does?"

"We'd courtmartial those responsible," Royce said virtuously. "Just like Mylai."

"Bull*shit*, Leonard."

"That's what He'd want."

"Mylai happened in a previous Administration. This is your baby."

"Those three GIs, Ab, not one of them has been to Vietnam himself. All their allegations are rumors. Army Intelligence has checked them out. They haven't turned up anything."

Thirteen of the fourteen officers originally charged with Mylai had been Southerners. Dennes had defended them to the bitter end. Now he jabbed at his fish, brought a dripping chunk to his mouth, and said, chewing: "Look, I told Army Congressional Liaison to get that hearing adjourned yesterday. I can't control Weintraub. He's out after MIRV already, wants to bring in some good old boy claims we killed half the babies in the South testing nukes, I can't hardly tell you the stink. I got a goddamn *rebellion* in that Committee, the whole issue of seniority is at stake, and you sit here in this goddamn ivory tower with your West Point soldier-boys trying to paint us into another corner. 'Duty, Honor, Country'? OK, just you don't let them embarrass your old Daddy, or you guys won't get doodlie-squat."

Royce wondered silently whether this was exactly what the Founding Fathers had in mind in the way of Congressional checks-and-balances on the military, but hid his revulsion. In less than a week, if the President decided to go along with the JCS plan to finally win in Vietnam, He might need Dennes for a lot more than a Supplemental

Appropriation. If all went wrong, He might even need his vote against impeachment.

"Maybe," mused Royce, "we *ought* to suspend that hearing entirely, until you get the Supplemental through the House."

"Maybe you ought to," Dennes smiled. He shoved back his chair, asked for a toothpick, and began to dig at his teeth. The Secretary signed the check and, with the quiet courtesy of a Harvard man fallen in with bandits, got rid of his guest.

General Lucius Hardy inspected the glossy print while Lee waited. Lee had known him for almost thirty years. Hardy had become Lee's protector in his plebe year at the Point, the first cadet-officer to "recognize" him and admit him by handshake to equality. Lucius had pleaded and cajoled and threatened for all of the twelve miserable plebe months that Lee, half-wanting to return to his infantry company before the war was ended, had sweated out in an artificial childhood by the Hudson.

When Hardy looked up from the print his expression was unreadable. "Why'd she give it to you?"

"I took it. She said there were more of them."

Hardy's jaw set. "Lovely. What do *you* make of it?"

"It's got to be a phony, doesn't it? With that gas mask? I spent half the night calling around: Hal Minor, Joe Glaston, and General West, they're all just back; nobody's used any gas over there since before the cease-fire."

"You call Greenberg?"

"Sure."

"Why? Why are you *in* it?"

"It could tie into that shot, couldn't it? I didn't mention the picture to him, though. Or any of them."

"I see. And what was *his* reaction?" Hardy seemed guarded. Lee told him that General Greenberg had been shaken, very shaken. Obviously, they had gas in Nam, CN and CS in the storage depots for riots, and Lee suspected DB nerve gas too, as a threat, although Greenberg hadn't cared to admit it. But nobody was supposed to have used even tear gas during Mohawk Sand, which was a reconnaissance-in-force against cease-fire—line infiltrators and which to Lee's knowledge would be the only operation in which anyone would have been walking into Ban Doc.

"Where else did you check?" asked Hardy.

"Editorial Service, Motion Picture Branch, Army Photo Agency, up in 5B272." He pointed to tiny negative numbers which had printed through when the black-and-white enlargement had been made. "First I thought the Cong had forced a POW into a mask and set this up. But this is from *Army* film, color, 16 millimeter, Lucius! Purchased under Army contract!"

"So what's your conclusion? Captured film?"

"No, or they'd have released it themselves. Some Army combat cameraman staged it! Or a news cameraman using Army film. God knows where he got it processed, or where it is now."

"Or where it is now," Hardy mused. He took the print and put it into a drawer. "What would you like to do about this?" he asked, tilting back in his swivel-chair and watching Lee woodenly.

Lee thought of the girl's level eyes, the silken hair, fine golden skin. "I might make another run on the girl." There was something between them, a flow. If he got to know her, she might very well talk to him. The photo had to be exposed as a fake before the thing got out of hand, didn't it? "I guess I'd better talk to her again."

Hardy straightened in his chair. "OK, Lee, I'll tell you what you're *going* to do. First, ask Jenny to start going to the G-2 Wives' Luncheons again. My wife's all shook up about it; she says Jenny just has to get out. Second, are you coming Saturday night?"

"Saturday night?" He remembered, vaguely, an invitation to a party at the Hardys'. An anniversary? Or one of Hardy's classmates retiring, or something? "No, Lucius, she won't go. She doesn't feel well enough—"

"Get her there, damn it!"

"I doubt it, Lucius. About *this,* though—"

"About this, forget it. Forget questioning the girl; take care of the demonstration next week—keeping Picket's sharp little nose out of it—find out who writes dirty on our shithouse walls, see that nobody throws a bomb into Leonard Royce's office—"

"Lucius," Lee said softly, *"I think that picture's a fake. But I also think we've got to check it out."*

"See that nobody throws a bomb into Leonard Royce's office," repeated Hardy, "and tell whoever's running numbers in the basement to either quit or cut you in. OK?"

"Lucius, I'm already in this—"

"No, you're not!" Hardy barked. He got up, all six-feet-four, leaned on his desk and looked deeply into Lee's eyes. "I'm passing it to somebody else. You know nothing about nothing, understand?"

"Why not?" Lee demanded.

"Because I want to see you make general," Hardy said sharply.

"Look," Lee said, "if this *isn't* a fake, if it *is* another massacre, and we don't buck it up to SecDef, you can get just as chewed up in it as I can."

"I've *got* my stars."

"But that picture's floating around on Dupont Circle! And I've got the contacts!"

"And I'm Chief of Intelligence, so it's my job to decide, and your job is to keep this place in one piece, and that's an order."

Lee Frost stiffened and strode from the room. Lucius Hardy watched him go. As the door closed after him, the general lost his nonchalance. Agitated, he moved to a direct line to Army Chief of Staff. Hand on the sky-blue phone, he changed his mind, crossed the room, drew from his office vault a thick sheaf of papers marked ESI—Extra Sensitive Information—bordered in flaming red. It was the Intelligence Annex to "Operation Strangle." In it was contained an estimate of North Vietnamese forces justifying an amphibious landing of ARVIN troops at the demilitarized waist of Vietnam, supported by U.S. air and sea forces (and a U.S. Army and Marine division, after the slopes were well-committed). The JCS had come to hate both the war and the cease-fire, which was rotting the Services from within. There was only one way to save Army, Navy, Air Force, and Marines (and America itself, which had spawned the rot). The Army must win in Vietnam, finally and fully. "Strangle," child of the War Games Agency on D-Ring, was designed to help the bleeding ARVIN forces against infiltrators, now that so many U.S. combat troops had left. In support of the plan, Hardy was scheduled next week to give the most important briefing of his life. He approached it like a military operation. His "Mission" was to convince the President. His "Own Situation" was weak, Pentagon Intelligence being in poor repute since the chopper raid on the empty POW camp. His "Analysis of Enemy Action" discouraged him. (By enemy, he meant the forces of American dissent, for the President would probably be jumpy and in a timorous mood from Saturday's demonstration if the Rally came first; another reason to keep the marchers non-violent.) But his "Own Course of Action" was clear: hard-line threats of Armageddon if the Administration showed softness, and a light at the end of the tunnel if it acted courageously. His personal "Decision" had been to charge ahead, supporting the JCS unequivocally rather than hedging. He had been tempted to hold back, for he was not nearly as sanguine about the probable results as the Chiefs, but the very process of applying the "Estimate of the Situation" to his own briefing problem had hardened his resolve to go for broke and win what might be his last big game for Army.

Having decided, he considered Lee's photo more than an irritation. It was a disaster. To have another Mylai break before the briefing would be a nightmare. For a moment he sat tapping the G-2 Annex to "Strangle." There was almost no one to discuss the problem with unless he wanted to spread the risk of panic. He felt like the carrier of a dread disease. Finally he dialed General Morris Greenberg.

"It's hit the fan, Morrie," Hardy told him. "Can you come on down?"

"What's hit the fan?" Greenberg demanded.

"Poma's film, Ban Doc, women and kids, you name it," said Hardy, and hung up.

Michael O'Hare, Ph.D., ex-South Baltimore newsboy, ex-rookie cop, ex-Second Lieutenant in the Marine Corps, civil-service scientist, had driven from the National Institute of Health in Bethesda to the Pentagon reluctantly, but now that he was in General Morris Greenberg's office he smelled the truth and was glad he had come. He watched the general hang up his phone. Whatever the call had been, it had shaken him. Years ago O'Hare, a rangy young microbiologist with a lean jaw, crooked teeth, and a famously explosive temper, had learned easily to read Greenberg's moods. The general, distracted by the call, nevertheless composed himself. "So where were we, Mike?"

O'Hare shifted in his chair. He had worked for Greenberg at Fort Detrick. Despite the murderous rage he had felt at the Army itself when he left, he and Greenberg had parted friends. But today the general seemed impatient, anxious to get rid of him. The hell with it, and the hell with the rank; he wanted answers. "Where we *were,* General—"

"Not 'General'!" All the lines on Greenberg's face shot up into a smile. "It's 'Morrie,' always, you know that!"

Mike O'Hare had come a long way from a South Baltimore Catholic orphanage to call a general by his first name. "OK, Morrie," he said. "Well, *is* it bubonic plague? And is it epidemic?"

"Slow down! Where'd you hear it, anyway?"

"At the Pathological Congress."

"Who told you?"

"Just a rumor." Not strictly true: a pathologist sent to Vietnam for a TB survey had heard talk of bubonic plague in Da Nang. But there was no use implicating the doctor if the information was classified. "Well, Morrie?"

Greenberg looked miserable. "Why ask *me?*"

"*Why?* Jesus Christ, sir. Can't you *guess* why?"

"Yes," admitted Greenberg. "But why not ask Army Epidemiological Control, or somebody?"

"They deny it."

"Well, then?"

Mike O'Hare got up. He glanced at a tank belching fire at Nazis on the wall: Mother of God, the obscenity of immortalizing flame-throwers on canvas. He turned back to the general. "Sir," he said softly, "I don't buy *anything* the Army tells me. Not any more. Unless it's from you."

Greenberg looked unhappy. "It was terrible, Mike. And we've paid for it."

"That's flattering, but I'd have quit anyway, sooner or later. Now, what *about* Da Nang? Black Death, or a little white lie?"

"The World Health Organization would have figures if—"

"If the Army won't tell *me,* it won't let Saigon tell *them!*"

"That's true," admitted Greenberg. "How many cases?"

"How's forty-five hundred grab you? As of last week?"

The general's eyes fell. And so it was true. Mike O'Hare's palms grew moist. "Are they using it?" he asked quietly. Greenberg didn't answer. Mike leaned across the desk, eyes blazing. *"Are they using my vaccine?"*

"No, Mike," murmured Greenberg. "They aren't."

"In the name of Christ," he exploded hoarsely, "why *not?*"

Greenberg looked as if he were about to cry. "That I can't say. Listen, I have to go."

Mike got up. "I'll be back," he warned. "So think it over, because I'll spread the word, if I have to. So you might as well tell me."

"I'm sorry, Mike, I just can't," said Greenberg. He watched the young scientist go. Suddenly he picked up the desk nameplate with the corps insignia of the crossed retorts. He hurled it blindly at the wall. He slammed through his outer office, ignoring Marty Lumpert, who watched him curiously and then went in and replaced the nameplate on the desk.

Chapter Two

In Lee's outer office, where his agents gathered to spin war stories to his secretary Thelma, he found Sergeant George Maxon in ecstasy. Long before Lee had taken office, Maxon and Liebholtz had entered into a neck-and-neck race on "Spook Patrol," the clandestine round through the Pentagon they alternately made at night. On Spook Patrol they checked vaults and tried drawers, harassed civilian guards, intruded silently into security areas to time the arrival of Air Force armed patrols, tested Navy body sensors in Flag Plot and silent alarms in JCS country. During the two years that they had been at it, Maxon had found only one secret document adrift (counting three points) and three confidential ones (giving him six, at two points each). He trailed Liebholtz, who moved faster, perhaps, or was simply sharper. The prize, given annually by the loser, was a dinner and drinks at the non-com Rocker Club.

But last night Maxon had found a top-secret memo: not simply confidential, or secret, but *top* secret. And to cap his glory, he had found it in Brass Ring, in the outgoing basket of the personal secretary to a Deputy Under-Secretary of Defense. He was marking up his score, wild-eyed and triumphant, when Lee entered. He handed Lee the six-page memo as if it were a contingency of the National War Plan.

"Pat him on the head before he wets his pants, sir?" begged Liebholtz. "I can't hardly stand it."

"Well done, Maxon," said Lee. "As for you, Liebholtz, I hope he orders champagne and caviar." He beamed at Maxon. "Which Deputy Under-Secretary was that?"

Maxon consulted his notebook. "Sidney Ellsworth, Chief of International Logistics Negotiation—"

Lee beamed. "Jesus! I might buy you a dinner myself."

Scanning their trophy, he went into his office. It was unsigned as yet by Ellsworth. It dealt with the Israelis, an F-111 deal; 150 aircraft involved, priced, he noted with astonishment, at half a million each. God, that seemed cheap. He continued on, growing tense. *Waiver of Re-Sale Prohibition: The Government of Israel is authorized to resell the above aircraft at any time after delivery to the Government of Greece, provided only that dollar proceeds of sale are applied to future purchases of F-4 McDonnell Phantom aircraft by said government of Israel.* Dynamite! No wonder Ellsworth had been so touchy with the details. He decided to confront him in his haunt.

His assistant, Major Homer Troy, bustled in. It had been a big night for Maxon and a big morning for Homer: a typist in Navy Financial Management had discovered an obscene message in a stall in a fourth floor, E Ring, corridor seven ladies' room. "Oh, come on, Homer! You got a *woman* pervert too?"

Homer Troy pursed his lips. "It's a man," he said. "A new one."

Homer had twenty-five years' service as a Reserve in the Intelligence Corps. He was a nervous, silver-haired gentleman with full-lidded, defensive eyes. He had latched onto a commission in World War II. He had somehow parlayed the Berlin Crisis, Korea, Vietnam, and a few intermediate emergencies into a full nineteen years in the Army. He lacked a year of active duty for his pension, and Lee had found him wandering endlessly around the Pentagon, carrying useless messages for Lee's predecessor. Providentially, the Mad Poet, soon to be joined by the Mad Artist and finally the Mad Carpenter (who drilled holes between toilet stalls) had given Lee the chance to anoint Homer as Chief of the Pentagon Vice and Obscenity Section and assign him to track down the elusive three, or one, as the case might be. Homer, incredibly, had taken the title seriously (he signed his memos with it). As he often pointed out, he was finally getting his teeth into the problem. But this was the first indication that graffiti had spread to the distaff side.

"How do you know it's a man?"

"I went to the Psychological Warfare people—"

103

"Psychological *Warfare?* Why, for Christ's sake?"

"Because they have psychiatrists up there." He consulted his notebook. " 'Anybody wants a good fuck—' And this is in the *ladies'* restroom, can you imagine how that poor girl felt?—'with a six-inch prick, call NA9-3428.' "

"Did she call?"

"What?"

"Never mind. Did *you* call?"

"No such number."

"You photographed the handwriting?"

"That's the problem. I didn't want to send in an Army photographer—all those women."

"How about after-hours?" Lee asked patiently.

Homer grew red. "Well, I guess we could have."

"Homer, you didn't *erase* it?"

"I couldn't *leave* it," Homer mumbled, "with those girls in and out all day long! Now, reasonably, could I?"

Lee regarded the scarlet tide making its way up his face. "OK, Homer," he sighed. "Next time it happens, will you reasonably call Liebholtz?"

"Yes sir," Major Troy promised, hurt. Back straight, good soldier that he was, he departed, stumbling slightly at the threshold. Thelma sent in the surveillance team he had ordered for Marty Lumpert: two corporals and a young sergeant from Army Intelligence School at Holabird. The corporals were students there and the sergeant had been working College Park outside the University of Maryland. Lee gave them instructions. He wanted a report on Lumpert's activities, nothing else: where he went, what he did with his time, whom he saw. The mission was simply to assess the clerk. "Particularly how bright he is. He may be putting us on. Forget what you'll read in his 201 file—he was a real Phi Bete at Cal—just try to evaluate his intelligence objectively."

The sergeant and the two students left. Lee Frost picked up Ellsworth's top-secret memo. With some relish he climbed the ramps to the Brass Ring.

There was an air of desperation in Ellsworth's outer office. The big sexy redhead with the inviting eyes was frantic. Sweat beaded her forehead, papers were high on her desk, the vault behind her gaped. She had apparently enlisted another secretary to help her search. She herself was close to hysteria, ruffling through one pile of papers and then giving up and turning to another, as though she had been doing it all morning. She looked up, her face so strained that it was hard to remember the provocative leer at all. She tensed, recognizing Lee, and gave a fast, warning glance to the other girl.

"Mr. Ellsworth's busy, Colonel," she mumbled, trying to smile, "but I'll tell him you're here."

"Does he know about the memo?" Lee asked, without preliminaries.

Her eyes widened. "No. How did *you* know?" she asked hoarsely. "Your Spook Patrol?"

"Yes."

She spotted the memo in his hand. "Is that it? My God Colonel, we've torn the place apart."

"So I see." The other girl fled. "Now, what's the story?"

She pleaded her case. She had finished typing the memo before lunch yesterday, put it into her basket, banged out some letters, put them on top, and then asked Ellsworth for the afternoon off because she was not feeling well. Ellsworth had agreed, reluctantly, so she had stuffed the papers into her vault. The memo, she was sure, was among them.

"It spent last night," Lee told her, "unlocked in your basket. Until my agent took it."

"It couldn't have!"

"But it did," he said firmly. "You *could* have left it there, you know. The trouble is, it was hidden under a blank sheet. Mrs. Pace, you were just in too big a hurry to bother putting it in the safe. You ever have a Security violation before?"

"I left a drawer unlocked once. A cleaning woman reported it."

He wondered if she had only told him because she knew it was in her record and that he could check it out. "What did they do?"

"Nothing. My boss took the rap."

"Ellsworth?"

She snorted. "That'll be the day! No, just a poor slob in Installations and Services."

So it had not been in her record, and she had leveled with him anyway. He felt himself sliding into pity. "Damn it," he complained. "I walked through here two days ago and there's some horny Gyrene hanging over your neck, probably reading every word you're typing—"

"Bull Collins? Colonel, he's got the Congressional Medal! He's probably cleared into the National Military Command Center!"

"But he had no need-to-know, did he? Was this the same memo? Top secret?"

"Yes sir," she said hopelessly.

He moved across the room, blindly staring at an oil painting of an old Thor missile on a pad near a Turkish mosque. He had a vision of himself, memo in hand, confronting the supercilious Ellsworth: *"Mr. Ellsworth, much as I hate to do this, I have to forward a report direct to the Secretary of Defense. As you say, you do report only to him, am I right?"*

"Oh, come on, Colonel! After all, it never left the Pentagon!"

"Sorry, Mr. Ellsworth, people saw it who had no need-to-know; me, for instance, and my agent. We can't be too careful, can we?"

He turned back to the woman. The brown eyes were bleak with fear. A tear worked slowly down her pancake makeup, grooving a trench. He rubbed his temples. Everything in the damn Pentagon was overclassified anyway: the Israeli plane deal had probably been anticipated in *Aviation Week* a year ago; jabbing a pin into Ellsworth would be fun, but the hell with it.

He skidded the memo across the desk. "Peace be with you. But watch it." The woman began to sniffle gratefully, so he left.

Marty Lumpert bought two ham sandwiches and two cartons of milk at the wooden snackbar in the center of

106

the Pentagon courtyard arboretum. Balancing them, he joined Dewey Dupays, an ebony Buddha dangling silver sharpshooting badges from his chest. He sat beside him on the bench. Across the yard, between the Southern crabtree and the spreading English yew, by which Security had found the growing hemp, Dewey's granite-faced friend the GSA guard was holding informal court for his numbers customers. It was a lovely Washington day. Marty thought of poor Poma editing film in the smelly house on Q Street and felt guilty. He handed Dewey one sandwich and one carton of milk, for which he received not even a nod. Since his heroic shot, Dewey thanked no one for anything.

"How's your movie coming, man?" Dewey asked. His Marine shoes shone in the bright sunlight. He never seemed to sweat and always made Marty feel like a sack of dough tied in the middle.

"It runs thirty minutes. It's brutal. It's rougher than we thought."

Dewey sucked at his milk through a straw. "They had one of them massacres in the Seventh Marines over there, you know. Son Thang."

"You told me."

"I seen the bodies, afterward," Dewey said, ignoring him. "Man . . ."

"I told you to write it up for Handlemann."

"Shee-it. Our Lieutenant, he hears about me doing that, he'll fairly take my black ass apart. We *done* our part for the press."

"I'll say you did," Marty said uncomfortably. He lit a cigarette. An innocuous young civilian sat down at the end of the bench, adjusted his glasses, and began to read a pamphlet on Defense Department vacation tours to Europe.

"*We*," Dewey smiled. "I like to say 'we.' It was like a *joint* effort, you know?" Dewey was high again, just a little, on pot, but stoned he had only one volume, full-on, and to try to hush him was to tempt disaster. "Joint effort," Dewey repeated for effect. "You ain't laughing, man."

Marty's resolve fled. "Goddamn it," he mumbled between his teeth, "cool it, will you?"

Dewey fumbled in his shirt pocket. "You see it?" He

drew out the item from the *Underground Clarion*. "First page."

"I saw it," muttered Marty. "Now for Christ's sake, put it away!"

Dewey looked hurt. For a long while he stared at distant horizons, smiling. "You know," he said finally, "I think I just might go over the hill, now that job's over, whatever good it done. You and Handlemann, you guys want to send me to Canada, say? How about Sweden, them blonde, fucky chicks?"

"Don't *lean* on me," grated Marty. "It's just as much your battle as ours. So just cool it, is all, will you?"

Dewey flashed him a sudden smile. "Sure, man. No need to get all PO'd at *me*. Hell, you do that and I just might blow the whistle."

Dewey dropped his carton of milk, kicked it under the bench, and headed, weaving slightly, for the entrance closest to the Hall of Heroes. Marty finished his cigarette, ground it out with his heel, and entered the building again, heading for General Greenberg's office. Climbing the ramp inside, he glanced down at the courtyard as he passed an A-Ring window. The civilian, putting away his travel pamphlet, moved down the bench, prodded Marty's cigarette butt with his toe, studied it for a moment, and then moved on. Marty watched him through the window. The man left the courtyard and he saw him no more.

He left the window thoughtfully. The man, curious about Dewey's tone and carriage, might have been an agent looking for a burned-out roach. Marty tried to reject the fear that he was tailing him. For years, at Berkeley and in the Service, he had laughed at those who played at revolution, thinking of their minuscule risk compared, say, to liberal Czech students or a VC cadre in Saigon. Radicals like Handlemann began eventually to see an agent behind every tree and enemies behind every bush. Now, finally committed himself, Marty was becoming as sensitized as any of them, rocketing from bravado to terror, sensing ghosts and hearing footsteps where nothing stirred at all.

He understood it and fought against the syndrome, but nothing seemed to help.

Chapter Three

Lee moved from behind his desk to meet Congressman Cyrus Weintraub, puzzled because he had come to him directly rather than through the Army's Congressional Liaison Office. He was young, Lee observed, and wore his woolly hair too long and his tight pants a little too short. His cheeks were shadowed as if he had not shaved closely enough. He looked as if he would be more at home exhorting a campus crowd than the House Armed Services Committee. Lee wondered what had got him the Committee appointment, and what Ab Dennes had said when he first saw his most junior member. Lee shook hands, called for coffee, and seated the legislator on a leather couch under a detailed plan of the Pentagon.

"Colonel, you investigate compromised classified documents, and all?" He had a New York accent and his heavy-lidded eyes were guarded.

"In the Pentagon, Mr. Weintraub. What's on your mind?"

Weintraub hesitated and then reached into his inside pocket, pulled out a paper, and handed it to Lee. It was a Xerox of Ellsworth's top-secret memo. Lee stared at it and felt his hands go cold.

"Jesus. Where'd you get this?"

"In the morning mail."

"From whom?"

Weintraub didn't know. It had come in a Defense Department envelope, franked, with no return address. He produced the envelope, which Lee noted had a Pentagon postmark.

"Have you read it?" Lee demanded.

"I've copied it. I've transmitted it to Ab Dennes, as a matter of fact."

Lee sagged. If he had properly handled the Security violation this morning, instead of following his stupid sentiments, he would be off the hook, and now there were copies spawned already. He pointed out that it was irresponsible to have made an additional copy of a top-secret document.

"So I'm irresponsible," shrugged Weintraub.

"What's more," Lee said heatedly, "it's a *felony!*"

Weintraub pointed out that it was transmitted, *so far,* only to the Chairman of the House Armed Services Committee, who must have known about the Israeli-Greek deal anyway, or the Pentagon wouldn't have dared to promote it. "I'll take my chances, Colonel. And if Dennes himself doesn't blow the whistle to save his own ass, I may release it to the press myself. Let him try to get me censured."

"But why?"

"I don't believe in selling arms to a Greek military dictatorship, even for the benefit of Israel."

Lee remarked on this new pitch: a Congressman from a Jewish district unafraid of his own constituency. Weintraub smiled, suddenly. He had a warm and gentle smile. "It's not all that idealistic, Colonel. I'm the youngest freshman on the Committee, and I have to use what weapons fall into my hands. This is a nuclear bomb. Dennes went right through the Capitol dome."

And he would go, thought Lee, right through the Pentagon roof when he found out that Lee had known about the possible compromise of this same document and had dropped the matter out of the goodness of his heart. Quickly, he called Liebholtz and sent the memo to fingerprinting. But he had no hope, really. Whoever had mailed it would be a fool to have left prints on it, and even if he had, Weintraub's were probably all over them. "Since you've *further* compromised it," he told the Congressman, "why'd you even bother to bring it to me?"

Weintraub flushed. "So this fell into my lap; all right, I'm using it. That doesn't mean I don't want you to find out who stole it! Suppose it happened with your defense plans for Berlin, or something?" He grinned disarmingly. "Besides, I was coming over here anyway. You're trying one of my constituents in your War Room. Or, you *were,* only the hearings seem to have been canceled since I began to attend."

Lee pointed out that the Army was trying no one, simply investigating allegations by a group of GIs who were making a bad situation worse, and with apparently false allegations, too—no names, dates, places, or witnesses.

"You could find an Army movie cameraman who witnessed a massacre, couldn't you?" asked Weintraub. "If you *wanted* to. Are you sure you do?"

"A movie cameraman?"

The phone was ringing. Lee picked it up. It was General Lucius Hardy. "Lee, goddamn it, what do you know about a top-secret memo, Israeli jets, sales to the Greeks, all that garbage?"

"Not enough," said Lee. "Ellsworth's office sprung a leak."

"Well, get your ass up here to SecDef and tell it to him and Dennes before he cancels out our credit cards. On the double!"

Lee replaced the phone. "That," he told Weintraub, "was my boss, General Hardy. Your nuke just exploded. He's with his boss, Leonard Royce, and your boss, Ab Dennes."

"Ab's not *my* boss, Colonel," said Weintraub, getting up to go. "And don't ever forget it."

"There's an old Service saying, Mr. Weintraub," said Lee, arising. "There are some who think *I* haven't learned it yet, but I've heard it applies to politics. You're young, and maybe you ought to try."

"What's the saying, Colonel?"

"You can't piss up a rope." He opened the door and paused, tempted to probe the hint of the massacre, and apprehensive, too. Failure to report misconduct was "misprision," a courtmartial offense. He might face it already in the matter of the redheaded secretary's violation if Dennes was nasty enough. The less he knew about movies, massacres, or Ban Doc, the better. He was an idiot to pursue it when he had Hardy's orders not to, but he did anyway. "Mr. Weintraub, I'm going to talk to your constituent."

"Hell, he's been talked to. The trouble is, nobody listens to *him!*"

"I'll listen."

"I'll save you the trouble. The cameraman's name is Alioto, Tony Alioto. He talks when he drinks. He's at the Army Chemical Warfare Center, TDY, whatever that is."

"Temporary duty."

"It might be very temporary. If Ab Dennes finds out you're looking for him, he may be in Alaska before you catch him."

"I'll catch him." He promised to let Weintraub know by next Friday what he had learned. He watched him move down the corridor and headed, wearily, for the lions waiting in SecDef's den.

At quitting time, Marty Lumpert dodged through a stream of similar Pentagon minnows shoaling in the basement shopping arcade, heading for the bus concourse. The Pentagon was a self-contained city, in which a man could earn a high-school diploma or a Ph.D., go to church, or watch his stocks on a tickertape, all without leaving the building. The concourse was its Grand Central Station and Fifth Avenue combined. Antiseptic subterranean store windows of concessionaires shone with mannequins, floral arrangements, travel posters. A spy who had forgotten his camera could buy a tiny Minox in the camera shop or if necessary a general's uniform at the tailor's. There was a branch of Woodward & Lothrup's dress shop, Brentano's book store, an employee credit union, two national banks, an airline ticket office, a dispensary, a dental office, an optometrist, a ten-chair barber shop, a beauty parlor, and a pastry shop to tempt sedentary employees already too puffy. There was a dry-cleaning establishment, a haberdasher's, and a jewelry store.

Pentagon merchants sucked two million a year from their captive clientele. Marty ordinarily avoided them as parasites on an animal he already disliked. But today, he remembered, was Sunshine's third birthday and there would be a party for her at Handlemann's pad. He crowded into Walgreen's drugstore and bought her a violet duck with a far-off look in its yellow eyes.

At the departure ramp, reeking of diesel oil and roaring with commercial and military traffic, he bought *The Evening Star* from a stall franchised, like the rest, to a blind veteran. He queued up for his bus, opening the paper in the faint hope that he would find a delayed item on the shot through the general's window. There was none, nor would there be. After three days, Handlemann's idea, intended to be so dramatic a public proof that chemical-biological warfare had survived at the Pentagon, had been defeated by the very size and complexity of the place.

A flushed, tubby young civilian had squeezed into line behind him and now squirmed into the seat beside him on the bus. His armpits were stained, and he smelled of sweat. Marty wished he had taken a seat farther back, since both were lard-butts. Usually shy and easy-going, he put down the paper in irritation when he sensed him eyeing it. The young man, startled, blushed. "Just looking for the Senators-Dodgers score, is all."

Something was wrong with the excuse, but it eluded him. "Help yourself," Marty said testily. He handed him the paper as they rumbled down the ramp. They emerged into golden late-afternoon sunlight, moist with a promise of rain in turreted clouds that hung over the building. Marty watched the Pentagon slide out of sight under the racing elms, hating it more than ever, now that they had bitten the monster's tail as hard as they could and the damn thing had not had the wit to see them or the grace to roar.

By the time they reached Massachusetts Avenue a pelting rain was falling, and he took the paper back from his companion to use for cover in a dash for the house. But after dinner, in Handlemann's kitchen, watching Sunshine stuff brithday cake into her flushed, fat cheeks and listening to the Commune's other children singing, he remembered the civilian on the bus. While Chute, zonked out of his skull, ripped through guitar runs that made "Happy Birthday" sound like the Grateful Dead and Handlemann's flea-hound, Cannabis, tried to sing, he had a chilling thought.

He did not follow baseball, but he knew one thing, even if the chubby young man on the bus did not. The Senators were American League and the Dodgers National. He left the kitchen and went back to the barren, uncarpeted living room. He found the soggy *Star* where he had tossed it onto the table.

The Senators had been rained out of RFK Stadium. Only the Dodgers had played that day, and they had met the Giants in L.A.

Chapter Four

Lee waited, with the Secretary of Defense's phone to his ear, for Leibholtz in Fingerprinting to make his report. He leaned on the desk that had belonged to Black Jack Pershing, who had been Chief of Staff when Lee's father enlisted. ("A bastard, son, but he must have been hung like a bull, the snatch he used to get." A man after Lee's father's heart.) He stared out at the Capitol through the rain-smeared window. Thunder rumbled from across the Potomac. It was dusk. Startlingly, the Capitol dome lit up and the Washington Monument, too; Jefferson Memorial followed, closer and more brilliantly. Great floodlamps would mark them all until dawn. Lightning winked, feeble as a photographer's flash on a floodlit stage. Leibholtz had only bad news. Lee replaced Leonard Royce's phone next to the golden one, direct to the White House, and turned to face the inquisitors seated around the coffeetable: Congressman Ab Dennes, Defense Secretary Royce, and his own embarrassed advocate, General Lucius Hardy.

"Both sets of prints are accounted for," he reported tersely. "One's Weintraub's and the other's Weintraub's secretary's."

"My God, Colonel," drawled Dennes, angrily. "Did *she* read it too?"

"She claims not, Mr. Dennes," sighed Lee. "Just opened it, is all."

"Just opened it, is all," the Congressman repeated slowly. He swished the ice in his drink. Lee had not been offered one, nor for that matter had General Hardy, only Dennes, and it had not seemed to help his mood at all. "Well, Colonel, what step is it you now contemplate?"

"I'll interrogate Mr. Ellsworth, sir," Lee said briefly. He had never before met Dennes personally, but he had watched him often from a distance. The Congressman seldom missed an Army Association meeting or the opportunity to make a speech at a military banquet. When Lee had been in Saigon and Cambodia, it had seemed impossible to go anywhere without stumbling on him.

In Washington there was one Pentagon expert in the care and feeding of Congressmen for every two legislators, but the squad of "Congressional Liaison Officers" that normally tailed Dennes to the field of glory numbered half a dozen. The Pentagon kept 340 Army, Navy, Air Force, and Marine officers full-time in Washington to explain the needs of their respective Services to those who voted the funds. It spent four million dollars annually to channel their efforts. But the Services had found that it was within the sound of distant gunfire that Dennes, at least, was most receptive. You could sell him any program if you dressed him in fatigues and staged the proper operation. It was in flak-vest and helmet that he regretted most moistly that he had missed both of the Great Wars and that he promised most loudly to finish "This One with Honor." To Lee, he had seemed to cover Southeast Asia like a Congressional plague. Nothing Lee had seen in the field had encouraged him to move closer to Dennes, and nothing he saw now changed his mind.

"And what good does it do to interrogate Ellsworth, Colonel?" asked Dennes. "I mean, you talked to his girl; it was her fault. But you found her honesty so appealin' you just decided to drop the whole matter. Very gentlemanly, Colonel. You a West Point man?"

General Hardy flushed. "As a matter of fact, Ab, he is. Why?" The general, though political, was no brown-noser when he felt a subordinate threatened. Lee spoke quickly to cut him off before he angered Dennes. "Congressman, I've admitted a mistake in judgment. On the other hand, it only cost us something like forty minutes, and I've got one man full-blast on the thing at present. If you'll allow me to start on it myself, now . . ."

Dennes simply ignored him and turned to Leonard Royce. What griped his ass, he assured the Secretary, was that if the news had not leaked, the Jews could afford their Phantoms and the Greeks their F-111s, to the ultimate frustration of the goddamn Reds. With a hundred-and-fifty

F-111s sold and out of the country, the U.S. Air Force could have pointed to a regular *airplane* gap to justify a Supplemental Appropriation that everyone in their shop had told him was absolutely essential. The whole aerospace industry would have got a shot in the arm. Instead, the *Pentagon* (not his own Committee, mind you, full of flap-mouthed legislators, but Royce's *own* damn playpen, which in due modesty Dennes had helped equip with burglar alarms, a skillion different kinds of safes, electrostatic body sensors, an army of Security guards, crystal balls, and, for all he knew, electronic chastity belts for the WACs) had sprung a leak, and not the first one either. "And nobody was even fixin' to *do* anything about it until I turned up with a *top-secret* document which my young colleague from Minsk-on-the-Hudson kindly gave me!"

"Now, Ab," said Royce, giving Lee a lazy look of appraisal. "You're awfully rough on Colonel Frost."

"Sorry," said Dennes. "I reckon I might be barking up the wrong tree at that." He assumed the mien of a wiser and saddened man. "This leak could help Aerodyne, out in L.A., and of course that's the President's home town, so I may be doing Colonel Frost an injustice. Maybe there's no way Frost *can* do anything. Maybe the Administration leaked it!"

Royce's face froze and he sat up a little straighter. That, he said, he considered an unwarranted libel, most fitted to previous Administrations. Dennes grinned. He was sorry he had said that. He would simply like to feel that while he was trying to glue the Israeli deal back together in Committee, somebody would find out who was trying to tear it apart here. He had to *know* who had stolen the memo. He needed facts. He couldn't afford to lose a battle to Weintraub in Committee. He'd rather drop the whole Israeli-Greek deal than be vanquished in a fight.

"I understand," said Royce.

"Good," said Dennes, smiling reasonably. "Because supposing your old Daddy loses, you boys will be issuing broomsticks for rifles like in 1939. You-all follow?"

No one answered. Lee heard rain pelting the pane and moved to the window. The drops were blurring the lighted Capitol dome, whipping the Potomac and smearing the

117

dockside lights on Columbia Island. He hoped that he had secured the boat-cover tightly on *Misty* and wished that he had doubled up her lines. "We follow you, Ab," he heard Royce say behind him.

Lee turned back to the men. Dennes drained his glass, wiped his lips, heaved himself from his chair. "Thank you, Leonard," he said. "Colonel, you ought to start checking on Weintraub himself. He don't hold much with Pentagon Security rules, or Pentagon anything else."

"As I said, sir," Lee pointed out, "he brought me the memo himself. It's unlikely that he stole it and then turned himself in."

"On the other hand," Dennes suggested, "he just may be smarter than you think."

Lee didn't answer. When the Congressman had left, he shook his head in disbelief. Disillusioned young ex-Counterintelligence agents had recently testified on a national TV special that they had been assigned to put under surveillance prominent liberal senators, thus very nearly destroying the whole Counterintelligence network and actually bringing it under nominal civilian control until the heat was off. "Does he really think I'd field-check a congressman, after those idiots tried to have McCarthy and Fulbright tailed? They'd hang me from the Capitol flag-pole!"

"It's your show," Hardy suggested. Lee thanked him acidly and left. As the door closed behind him, Royce for the first time lost his equanimity. He slapped the leather armchair with his palm. *"Damn* it, Lucius, how'd that memo get out?"

"Frost will find out if anybody can," promised Hardy.

"He should have started this morning! Why'd he shrug off a thing like that? He's up for general, isn't he?"

"That's why I brought him to the Pentagon, for exposure. He's one of the finest Intelligence officers in the Army. He'll solve it."

"But *when?* Aerospace in the south is dying. General Dynamics has promised Dennes subcontracts at home. If they get a bad press, he's dead. He's scared, and mad. Suppose he's *still* mad if the President opts for 'Strangle'?"

"That could be bad," conceded Hardy.

118

"That could be catastrophic!"

Lucius Hardy agreed and left. The Secretary, he mused, was more excited than he had ever seen him. And he didn't even know about the Ban Doc film. Not yet.

Sidney Ellsworth ran a hand through his full golden hair, yanked off his horn-rimmed glasses, and polished them furiously. He was in a state of shock because Weintraub had seen his memo and angry at having been forced to stay after-hours to wait for Lee. Sitting at his desk in his shirt sleeves, he wrestled for the initiative, attacking since he had no defense.

"Goddamn it, Colonel," he said, "why was I hit from left field! You're her *accomplice* in hiding this from me!"

"Yes," Lee admitted mildly, "I should have cited you this morning; it won't happen again."

"Cited *me*? The *violation* won't happen again. I'm getting rid of her, as of today!"

Lee pointed out politely that even if it turned out that her carelessness was the proximate *cause* of the leak, Ellsworth was Chief of Section: the responsibility was his. Ellsworth flushed angrily. "On paper, maybe. But she's the one with egg on her face. You are too, if you don't mind my saying it."

"I don't mind at all," Lee smiled. He would enjoy working over this glorified shoe-clerk, Deputy Under-Secretary of Defense or not. The game was just beginning. He took out a small black notebook. "Now, can you answer some questions about your standard Security arrangements?"

He began to write. Did Ellsworth dictate his classified memos? Were all classified tapes and voice-belts locked in vaults each time his office was left unattended? How soon were the tapes erased? Were carbon papers used on classified documents burned? What about mimeograph stencils? Who kept the incoming-outgoing log of classified documents?

When he was through Ellsworth's face was damp and his shirt soaked. Through the Pentagon Security Network, Lee contacted Liebholtz, on Spook Patrol, and set him to poking about Ellsworth's office and reception room looking for violations. Liebholtz finally moved Ellsworth from his place and began apologetically to go through his desk drawers, dredging up a confidential dispatch from a Pentagon representative in Rio, misfiled in an unclassified folder, a confidential estimate of Bolivian ammo requirements, and the combination to Ellsworth's safe on the back of his family's photo. By eleven P.M. they had enough deviations from the Holy Book of Pentagon Security Regulations to support a half-dozen charges, exclusive of Maxon's windfall of the preceding night. They had reduced Ellsworth to a very civil servant indeed.

Having politely and without comment exposed the abysmal Security shortcuts of any Pentagon office gone unchecked too long, Lee sent Liebholtz home and went to work on the new Ellsworth.

"Now," he said, "we're both after the same thing. I'm not going to make a stink over these violations, any more than I did this morning, if we can solve the specific problem of who lifted the memo. OK?"

With the back of his hand, Ellsworth wiped sweat from his upper lip. "Anything I can do."

Lee attacked motivation, first: who benefited? Ellsworth shrugged. "The Arabs, obviously, and if they'd shoot at that helicopter in broad daylight, they wouldn't balk at penetrating this office."

"It may not be that simple. And we don't know for sure that the shots were fired at the chopper. Anyway, the FBI's on that tack. So let's see who else could gain if the airplane deal falls on its ass."

Ellsworth thought for a moment. "The liberals. The peaceniks. Greek Communists. Anybody who wants to make us look stupid, or spendthrift. Weintraub, himself."

Lee reminded him that Weintraub, to steal the memo, would have had to know about the deal in the first place, about the memo in the second, and that the girl would have to leave it carelessly exposed in the third.

"OK, Colonel," suggested Ellsworth. "He could have picked up a hint of the deal in Committee, overheard Dennes, maybe, or seen an Israeli officer around, or just guessed. He didn't have to know about the memo; anything to do with the deal would be floating around this office. He's a congressman; nobody'd question him if he came in here—it isn't a Secure Area—"

"You can say that again," smiled Lee.

Ellsworth's jaw tightened. "Anyway, he strolls in here, that damn-fool woman has left the memo lying around, he makes a copy, replaces it, claims he gets the copy in the mail, and blows the whistle."

Lee pointed out that to infer that a Jewish U.S. Congressman would act like a spy from Cairo was a fairly wild conjecture, and that it was even wilder to assume that he had simply lucked-out and found the memo. "It's the least probable of a dozen other possibilities."

"Here's a possibility. What about my goddamn secretary? She's got a son on pot or something, he's in trouble all the time. Maybe she could be had."

Lee, beginning to understand Ellsworth's bureaucratic success, wondered how many squirming bodies he had built it on. But he hid his disgust. "It is a possibility. We'll be running a check on her tomorrow, along with everybody else."

"Including me?" Ellsworth demanded.

"Mr. Ellsworth!" Lee smiled. "You're a Deputy Under-Secretary of Defense. If we can't trust *you*, who can we?"

Maxon was waiting for him in his office. His broad face was shining. He had been moving well and fast and was eager to let Lee know it. He had got a court-order from the Federal District Court in the Pentagon basement in time to enter Ellsworth's secretary's apartment before she returned from work. He had bugged her phone. She had a teen-age kid, who returned home and surprised him at the elevator as he was leaving. (Liebholtz, who had sent him out on the job, hadn't bothered to tell him about *that*, Maxon mentioned pointedly.) But all was well and the bug had checked out and was even now transmitting to a receiver in a panel truck parked across her street. He had presumed in Lee's name to borrow another four agents from Fort Holabird to man the truck. That made, with the three agents tailing Lumpert, seven Counterintelligence men Lee would have to get orders cut for tomorrow, but

Maxon at least was beginning to act on his own initiative, and that was to be encouraged.

"Good man," said Lee. "If she doesn't make any calls tonight, I'll try to flush her out tomorrow. Now get up to Ellsworth's office and tap her office phone, and *his,* and bug their intercom, and then you can have the whole night off."

It was one A.M. by the time Lee left the Pentagon. The squall had passed and the night was cool. Stars glittered over the Capitol and jiggled on the Potomac. Jenny never complained when he was late any more, so instead of turning up Columbia Pike he swung up Mount Vernon Memorial Highway to the marina a quarter-mile from the Pentagon across Boundary Channel, feeling very much in the building's darkened presence all the way.

He nodded at the marina guard and strolled along the lines of sleeping craft. *Misty* was secure and well tarpaulined; Rick would have approved. She groaned sleepily when he stepped aboard. He found a slapping halyard and cleated it. He must try to sail her more often, or sell her. Finally, reluctantly, he drove home.

A parting grumble of thunder rattled the windows of Handlemann's old brownstone house on Q Street. The storm rolled off to the northeast. Marty Lumpert sat in the dark on the bare living-room floor, leaning against the cracked plaster wall with June, sharing a joint. Sunshine sprawled across both their laps, watching the birthday light-show Flieger had arranged for her and the three other children of the commune. The screen was a lazy, crazy montage of warm and weaving animal figures: furry chipmunks and pink-eyed rabbits with quivering nostrils, a Fantasian spilling of golden elephants and purple tigers. At the Inner Eye in Georgetown, Flieger's productions were an erotic blend of pornography and psychedelics, nothing like this at all. But Flieger was a genius, Marty reflected, and thus innocent, and this helped him relate to children. Marty looked up at his pimply hawkface in the light of his projectors (granny glasses glittering with violet highlights and steel-wool hair exploding in rose-tinted violence) and saw that he was grinning with delight at his own work. A genius, Ronnie Flieger was, unsung and mostly unloved, but Marty loved him, and loved Sunshine, loved all of them, even Handlemann at times. June passed him the roach and he inhaled, holding it, and loving that too.

The show ended on a weaving montage of pandas, blended orange and pink and blue on the palette of Flieger's light-filters. Handlemann arose from the floor and flicked on the light. It hung central and unshaded. The glare made Sunshine dig at her eyes. She was exhausted, but she clung giggling to Marty when June tried to get her to follow the rest of the commune children into the dining room, where the young ones slept. (The house was a firetrap. To bed them upstairs would have been criminal. Handlemann, who feared bombings more than fire, claimed that they would be safer above, but for once he had not had his way.)

Marty asked June to let Sunshine stay. Communal living made you a great lover of children. Like a favored uncle, you had all the pleasure of their company and none of the responsibility of the parent. June never asked him for help (nor had she ever asked Handlemann when the two were sleeping together). She would go on photo assignments with the baby riding papoose-style on her back, as if to balance the battered black Nikkon dangling forward with its fearless eye (an extension of her heart and brain), and Sunshine loved it all.

Tom-Tom and Sue, caught by the sudden light, were making love on the couch. Sue, squirming beneath him, squinted and begged someone to turn off the bulb. Handlemann refused: they were going to finally screen Poma's film.

"Oh, no," murmured Marty to June. "Not tonight. Let's sack out."

"I want to see it," said June, who had seen only the few frames she had enlarged in the *Clarion* darkroom.

"I *want* her to see it," said Handlemann. So Marty made June put Sunshine to bed after all, slid the ancient dining-room door closed, and locked it against the children. He braced for the screening, shot down from his high. The work-print was without narration (though a voice track and a sound track would be added to the final prints), so Poma read from his script. His concept was simple. He had been sent to the field to do a training film and a training film it remained, beginning like any other, with a teaser: "Your platoon is ordered to take an objective in which the enemy has been long entrenched. . . . Elements of the enemy have been spotted by aerial reconnaissance near the only available drop-zone. . . . Patrols indicate a bunker complex within the village, and enemy strength at two squads and a weapons detachment." Helicopters thrashed above rolling jungle. Grimfaced infantrymen inside, self-consciously ignoring the camera, checked their clips and their grenades. The landing began, and the narration shifted subtly from standard infantry tactics to the use of irritant gases, and gradually, you began to wonder if it was a military training film at all or a put-on, and all at once the men had forgotten the cameras and the nightmare was on you, and neither Poma's editing marks nor the rough work-print could bring you back to reality or distract you from the horror. Marty had watched the individual scenes dozens of times (awake and in his dreams) but never in any sequential way. Now, caught up in Poma's satirical skill with camera, editing machine, and typewriter, he found himself more shaken than when the first jolting, isolated cuts of the film had turned him on and changed his life. Powerless, he flinched and tensed, grunting at each new shock. Full-screen, you saw much more: trickling blood and trickling tears. You smelled jungle and night-soil and damp paddies and fear. The slithering gas overcame the sweetness of the marijuana writhing in the beam from the projector. Now that the blood had begun, there was no more script, no word from Poma, only the grinding reels and a gasp from Chute as though he had taken a slug in the belly himself. But there remained the sound in your inner ear: a silent howl from a child and the crunch of a gas-shell and the staccato punch of M-16s.

The film ran thirty minutes. When the final scene was played (a long, receding aerial of a deserted village with a lone GI in a gas mask checking bodies on the central road), there was silence in the room. Then June began to cry, distantly and softly. When Marty tried to comfort her, she shrugged him off. Someone turned on the light again and Marty could see her fine-boned model's face all bloated and her eyes squeezed shut. "Bastards!" she choked. "Bastards, bastards, *bastards* . . ."

Sue and Tom-Tom on the couch had separated long before. She had her face to the wall, but now she turned and reached out to Tom-Tom, who sat at her feet, pressing a fist into his palm, over and over; Marty could see his mouth working silently through his glossy beard, cursing steadily. Chute, their gangly, strung-out copyboy, whom Marty had never seen moved to anything but laughter, looked as if he had been clubbed. Ronnie Flieger arose, stared blindly at Poma through his square-cut glasses, threw out a long arm scarred with needle-knots, and hugged his shoulder. He looked deep into his eyes, shook his head. "Chris, you're a genius."

"It's fantastic," breathed Red Handlemann. "How long until we have something we can release?"

"I'm cutting A and B rolls tomorrow," Poma said, without emotion. "And if Marty delivers them to the lab Sunday, they'll give us an answer print next Wednesday—"

"How do you know?" Handlemann demanded.

"I called them."

"Don't use the fucking phone," Handlemann growled. "If you have to talk to the lab, send somebody!"

Poma, red-eyed with fatigue, studied him for a moment. "Handlemann, you're a goddamn paranoid, you know it?"

"All right, but I'm harboring a deserter, and the film's stolen U.S. property. It's no good to us if it's confiscated. So just don't use the phone, is all." He asked if the answer print was what they would release, and Chris told him that it had to be dubbed and narrated.

Handlemann began to pace the living room impatiently. "Like how *long,* Chris?" he exploded. "Without all the bullshit?"

"Conservatively, until the composite print, Monday after next. Without all the bullshit."

"Too long."

"What do you mean 'too long'?" Marty demanded. He had been dedicated to the film since Poma, dirty, jumpy, moving fast and secretly, had contacted the *Underground*

Clarion with the original footage, too hot for Kodak labs to print or even independent studios. Did Handlemann have a processing contact underground? Handlemann hadn't, knowing nothing of movies, but found one: a lab in Washington that processed nudie pictures and advertised them in the *Underground Clarion.* Poma, needing technical advice on gas warfare, had another question: who wrote the anti-chemical warfare items he read in the *Clarion?* One Marty Lumpert, who promptly caught fire, moved into the commune, tasted deliciously of underground activity, and fell in love with Handlemann's girl, June. Well, Handlemann had his paper and his revolution. Marty, incredibly, had the girl. But the film belonged to Poma, and Handlemann had no right to try to drive him faster.

"What's wrong with Monday after next?" Marty insisted. "Who set a deadline?"

Red Handlemann was unused to attack from this corner: "Why do you ask, Clausewitz?"

June squeezed Marty's hand and got up gracefully. She had stopped crying, but her face, with its ever-changing planes and angles, was still soft. He wanted her very much. "Come on, Marty," she murmured. "You've been working too hard on it."

But he was committed now. "*I* haven't been working too hard on it; Chris has." His words began to tumble. "Now, Red, I got to admit that from your Olympian heights as publisher of the capital's only home-owned underground paper, outside of a couple of others, bringing us all the news that's shit to print, you have a certain position in the Community, particularly in this particular household."

"That's good, since I invited you to move in. And since you've been balling my chick ever since."

"Lovely," said June. "Just lovely, Red! Now it turns out you're jealous! All that time I thought you were sleeping with me because you needed a photographer! He's *jealous,* Marty."

"He's a very emotional man," agreed Marty. "He feels deeply about a number of things: puppy-dogs—"

"Lay off Cannabis!" blazed Red. Marty knew that he had a thing about Cannabis, some tie with the past, and

126

tried to rein his tongue. Handlemann, tall and wiry, could probably break him in two. "All right, Red," he said more mildly. "I just want to know if you've changed your plans for this epic."

"Maybe." They had had a long, communal conference about the film when first Poma had arrived. Poma was certain that if it was released raw to the networks, the first film-editor who saw it would recognize the stock-numbers as Army, and the subject matter as secret, and simply phone the Army to come and get it. FCC licenses were at stake. Handlemann had to agree. They had decided to make it into a scathing imitation of a training film and offer it free to art-movie houses, one in Washington, one in Chicago, and one in Los Angeles. "Maybe giving prints to the art-houses is stupid, after all," Handlemann said now.

Flieger had been rewinding the film on the projector. Reaching its end, it began to slap against the body of the machine. Absently, Poma pressed his hand on the whirling reel to stop it. He turned off the projector, moved to the couch, felt for a cigarette, and finally took one from Sue. She lit it for him and he drew on it deeply. Marty had observed that while he never touched pot, he smoked too many cigarettes. He exhaled and said: "Why *not* the art-houses, Red?"

"Suppose *they* panic and turn them in?"

"All three prints? In all three cities? Hell, if one turns it in, there's still the other two."

"At a hundred dollars a print, I don't know if I can still afford three prints," Handlemann began. Subscriptions were off, newsprint up, receipts down, the heads on the Circle who hawked the *Clarion* were burning him.

"I have some bread," offered Tom-Tom.

"Me too," said Marty. "We can raise it. Hell, we *need* three prints."

"But suppose they *all* turn them in?" insisted Handlemann.

"Then we'd still have the original," said Poma, "and we'll make more prints."

"To show where?"

"More art-houses."

127

"Damn it, they're commercial. You think the Army can't get to them?"

"Discothèques," suggested Flieger. "Coffeehouses. Anywhere!"

"Let's get the prints first," Poma said reasonably. "You know damn well the *Clarion* can afford them, Red! The prints first, and then we'll worry."

"By Friday?" urged Handlemann.

Again Marty wondered why he was pressing. The peace rally was Saturday night. Maybe he intended to risk a print to get it on the Friday evening news. The whole nation would presumably explode and even the uncommitted would descend on Washington Saturday like a swarm of hornets. Perhaps the failure of the kick-off, Dewey's shot at the Pentagon, had shaken his self-confidence and he had decided to make doubly sure of a big turnout for the rally. Jesus—Marty felt a shiver in his bowels—a film like this, shown twenty-four hours before a demonstration, could turn it into a riot; it didn't matter how many parade marshals you had. "Wow," he murmured. "I see."

But Handlemann was talking to Poma again: "How about Saturday morning, then?"

Marty relaxed. So a Friday night airing on TV, exciting as it was, was not what Handlemann had in mind. "Next Saturday," Poma was saying, "I can promise."

Marty took June to bed. They shared a room with Tom-Tom and Sue on the third floor next to Poma and Flieger. For a long while June sat in the semi-darkness, arms clasped around her knees, all the fine facial angles blurred for Marty because he had taken off his glasses. Her eyes were dark shadows in the feeble light of a blue neon sign on the decaying Hotel Baghdad across the street. Tom-Tom and Sue were balling again, with a great squeaking of springs, Sue moaning as she always did in climax. The two were insatiable, Sue a maniacal mink. It had embarrassed him for the first few days. Now it aroused him, but June was withdrawn.

"Marty," she whispered finally, "what's happened to people?"

"Everything's turned to shit," he agreed.

128

"That one little girl was younger than Sunshine, and did you see the eyes? What made them *do* it?"

"People will say they were high on hash."

"No hash I ever saw," June muttered. "I want us to have a baby. A boy."

"In this fucking mess? Why? Isn't Sunshine enough?"

"She's not yours. I want a boy. And I don't *know* why."

He told her that if she wanted a boy, they'd have two, three even, and she bent down and kissed his feeble eyes and slithered her body beside him, and they made love gloriously, raucously, and twice, and then again.

Sometime during the night he awakened to Tom-Tom's snoring. He found himself restless and stirring and for some reason the pseudo-baseball-fan on the bus entered his thoughts. Suppose the guy was an agent? And tailed him when he delivered the film to the lab? If it were taken, Poma's whole life went with it, and part of his own.

He decided the doubts were nervousness. The man on the bus had been speaking in a rush, covering his embarrassment at being caught peeking at the paper. No one knew better than Marty how a man's words could tumble when he was covering some minor mortification. June murmured something beside him, half-awake. He began to trace the lines of her face in the blue glow of neon and soon forgot his fears.

For the first time in months, Lee Frost sat across the breakfast table from his wife. Though his office was closed on Saturdays, he had a great deal to do today in Washington, and Jenny, strangely, had got up too. The rumble of country-bound traffic on Columbia Pike had not even started, and yet he found when he had shaved and dressed that the dinette table was set, that his eggs were frying, that Jenny, in the sea-green quilted house-coat that darkened her emerald eyes (and which was the last attractive garment she could still wear, in the house or out) sat with a sparse breakfast of orange juice and toast.

"You were late last night," she commented.

"I didn't know you woke up."

She nibbled on her toast. He knew that she would cheat when he had left, but she always ate quite delicately while he was home. "What kept you?" she asked.

He told her about his session in Ellsworth's office, and that he had stopped to check *Misty* after the storm. She looked at him dubiously, got up, and moved to the kitchen. Scooping his eggs from the skillet, she asked if he wanted to go to the Hardys' party. He was sure that she didn't. "Don't worry," he said. "I told him we wouldn't be there."

She served him and sat down. Her cheeks were flushed from exertion, as if she had just played a set of tennis. They should go tonight, she said; the place would be full of generals. With Royce dubious now and Congressman Ab Dennes aroused against him, Lee might need all the help before the promotion board he could get. He had told her about his poor judgment in the leak in Ellsworth's office and the thought of it angered her again. "Damn it,

130

Lee!" she flashed. "All for some chippy with big baby blues."

"They were brown."

"And she'll never even find out what happened!"

"She'll find out. I'm seeing her this morning."

"Officially?" she asked, avoiding his eyes.

"No, Jenny," he explained patiently, "I've ruined my career for her; now I want the payoff. I'm just going to bang her once, that's all. It won't take long."

She glanced at him narrowly but giggled. "OK. Have fun. When'll you be home?"

He had decided to go to the Peace League, too, to see if he could get a lead on the Ban Doc picture from the worthy Reverend or the girl Laurie. The thought of her excited him and he discovered himself dissembling to Jenny: "Not until around six. I'm going to slap a coat of varnish on *Misty*'s lazarette . . ."

"You never sail any more. Why don't we sell that thing?"

He dabbed his lips and got up. "Maybe that's why I'm getting her ready."

"Or do you just go down there to torture yourself?"

"Let's not talk about torturing ourselves, all right?" he said sharply.

She arose clumsily, clearing the table. Her voice was tight. "You're right, Lee. I'm going to stop. And I *want* us to go tonight."

Lee balanced the prospect of a warm and friendly evening with Intelligence Corps officers he had known for years (and hardly ever saw socially any more) against the alternative of a sterile TV tube, the late news, and bed before midnight with Jenny chewing her nightcap apple and reading the goddamn *Rise and Fall* as her stomach rose and fell beside him. He discovered that he himself really wanted to go. But it would be tough on her. She had seen practically no one since she had put on the weight: from a hundred-twenty pounds to a hundred-eighty, almost, in less than a year. He conjured shocked faces, sidelong glances. Suppose there were friends who actually failed to recognize her? He wondered what she

131

could wear. As if she read his mind, she said: "I could go down to Julius Garfinkel and buy a dress."

"Sure."

Her resolve weakened. "Will I embarrass you?"

To tell her that she hadn't changed that much would be an insult to the beauty she had been. "I couldn't care less. Screw 'em."

She squeezed his hand. "Thanks, Lee. You *don't* give a damn now, do you? You aren't even bucking for promotion."

"Some people think I never did."

She shook her head. "You were always bucking, even when people thought you weren't."

She was right, but he didn't want to discuss the change, which would lead to Rick. Instead he said lightly: "Your father's gone, the pressure's off, I don't *have* to make general any more."

Her father, an old-time Navy football star, had at first accepted Lee (West Point wasn't precisely Annapolis, but at least Lee was a Regular, not a feather-merchant turned war-time lieutenant). Then the old bastard had discovered that Lee's father (although he had been temporarily commissioned under Bradley in World War II) was a master-sergeant in the infantry. Her old man had frozen like the berg he was, but it was too late: the wedding date was set, Jenny was pregnant, and, even if she had not been, would have faced him down. The admiral had lived to see Lee make bird-colonel but died convinced that he was too insubordinate ever to get his stars, and maybe he was right.

"He's still watching," Jenny warned, "from that big Navy alumni section in the sky, rooting for you to fall flat on your can. Why do you hate it now, Lee?"

"The Army, I don't," he said uncomfortably. "The Pentagon, I do." He kissed her good-bye. "Get a new dress. We'll go."

He crossed the Potomac, spent a half-hour in the juvenile files of Metropolitan Police Headquarters, and drove to the grimy, tree-shaded block on 14th Street Northwest where Ellsworth's secretary lived in a red sandstone apartment building. There he parked under a scrawny elm, checked a cigarette-sized tape recorder in his inside pocket, turned up the sensitivity, and tested the switch. He walked up a concrete path cluttered with cigarette butts and roller skates. In the entrance foyer he found the woman's name: Mrs. Sherry Pace. Under it was scrawled: & Son. He pressed the buzzer, waited, and pressed it again. A strident young voice cracked out: "Yeah?"

"Colonel Frost, from the Pentagon, to see your mother," Lee announced. Silence, and explanations from above: she wasn't home, she'd be home that afternoon. How about coming back later? No, Lee would rather wait upstairs, if it would be OK. It wasn't, from the tone, but persistence won and finally the buzzer sounded.

The lobby was done in the imitation marble of the early Thirties and the elevator needed paint. On one of its walls was a decal: AMERICA, LOVE IT OR LEAVE IT, but busy hands and a penknife had made it AMERICA . . . LEAVE IT. During the ascent he smelled fried liver, pork chops, and someone's Saturday chicken. At the fourth floor a screaming argument drowned out the creaks and groans of the ancient cables. The fracas rose to a climax and then faded down the shaft as he passed. The car stopped with a jolt at the sixth floor, a foot too low. He slid open the gate, took a giant step, and walked down tattered carpeting to the end of the hall.

A sullen, sallow youth opened the door. He had luminous brown eyes, like his mother's, but bloodshot, and a mass of black curling hair. He had a case of mainline sniffles and he was not happy with the visit.

"You Jordie?" Lee Frost asked, sticking out his hand. Surprised, the boy took it. He had a shake like a limp mackerel. The dark eyes narrowed.

"Yeah. Like I said, see, she won't be home till later. Whyn't you—"

"She won't mind if I wait," Lee cut in, moving past him toward the living room. He noted that off the hallway were two rooms with unmade beds. From the mother's chamber floated cheap perfume and from the boy's the smell of incense. The kid's juvenile record and the running nose put him past marijuana into smack, but the incense

133

meant pot nonetheless. Maybe he had fallen on bad times.

Lee looked around the living room. Sherry Pace had lived there for twelve years, he knew. He knew also that the furniture, though shabby now like everything else, had come from a better time and a better place and that she owned it. Her latest Security questionnaire had shown that she drew $150-a-month alimony and support from Jordie's father. She made $785 a month at the Pentagon and paid $53 a month to the Pentagon Credit Union for her two-year-old Mustang, which Jordie had last month borrowed and almost wrecked. She was presumably paying a lawyer for Jordie's last drug-bust and still owed a bail-bond broker $275 for his bail.

"Where it she, Jordie?" Lee asked.

"Pentagon. Workin'."

Lee doubted that Ellsworth kept his office open Saturday mornings, Israeli deal or not. "She works *Saturdays, too*?"

"Is it Saturday? Oh. Saturday she works for a lawyer, or a doctor, or something." Jordie's limpid brown eyes lay on him, beautiful, if calculating. Lee placed him, in a few years, as a pimp, a pusher, or a bartender studding bored housewives from a neighborhood cocktail lounge. Jordie weighed his presence: "How come you know my name? You a friend of hers?"

He probably had Lee figured as Mom's new shack-up and was wondering if he could hit him for a ten.

"I know her from work," Lee said, sitting in an overstuffed chair stained with hair oil at the back. "Don't you work, son?"

"I'm a student," said Jordie, collapsing into the couch across from Lee.

"It's summer vacation," sighed Lee, "and besides, you've dropped out."

The boy tensed. "Look," he demanded again, "I asked you once, how'd you know my name?"

"From Juvenile Record Section, Metropolitan Police, maybe," said Lee. "Or from your parole officer?"

"Goddamn it," blazed the boy, "you said you were a Colonel! You're just a goddamn pig!"

"No," smiled Lee. "I'm really a Colonel. And I really

134

know your mother from work. Why's she need to work Saturdays, too?"

"It's none of your fucking business. Sir."

Lee shrugged. "Just wondering why you didn't help her out, that's all. You know, get a job in a filling station or something."

The lazy eyes turned hard. "She makes enough."

"I mean, you got a thirty-dollar-a-day arm, son. You used to shoplift, at least. But you haven't been busted for *that* for three months. You ought to get back with it, Jordie. Jesus, you could contribute *something!*"

The front door opened and Lee heard Mrs. Pace's throaty voice: "You up, Sweetie?" She stood frozen in the doorway. Her son flashed Lee a look of pure hate. "Some guy from the Pentagon I shoulda never let in!" Her eyes widened for an instant, and then she smiled, understanding all: Lee had not reported her for the memo; *ergo,* he was here for his reward. Rising politely, he flicked on the tape recorder in his inside pocket. Nothing he got on tape without warning her would be admissable, but it might be protection if she hollered foul.

She offered him coffee. When he suggested that it would be better that they talk alone, she smiled conspiratorially. Jordie called her to his bedroom, presumably to break the news that Lee was some sort of military J. Edgar Hoover, but she knew that anyway and hardly gave him a chance. Jordie slammed from the apartment and when his mother reappeared it was in a diaphanous negligee that took five years off her body and, despite Lee's amusement, aroused his stored desire. She had enveloped herself in the fragrance he had scented in the hall. She asked if it was too early to offer him a drink. She had no Scotch, having killed a bottle last night to celebrate his kindness, but there was bourbon, or would he like a martini?

"A little early, Mrs. Pace."

"Not really, Colonel," she said companionably, pouring herself a shot of Jim Beam and settling on the couch with him. Her eyes were shining and her lips were moist. *"I* need one. *I'm* in shock, you being here. And call me

Sherry. Cheers! You could have knocked me over with a feather!"

"I imagine," smiled Lee. There was a short period of silence, while they beamed into each other's eyes. She was a beautiful woman, really, considering the mileage, and he had damn well better watch himself. "So you live here all alone, with Jordie. No boy friends?" .

"None right now." The smile became a painted one: there seemed nothing to say. She got up suddenly, moved to a clutter of amplifiers and a record player encased in an unpainted plywood cabinet: God, she moved like a tiger; she was killing him. Distastefully, she peered at the uppermost record. "Kids," she said helplessly. "Rock, as loud as your ears can stand! Say, do you like Josh White? 'St. James Infirmary'?"

He nodded, and she put it on. She returned to the couch and patted the space beside her. "Colonel—" she began, "Oh, that's ridic!" She regarded him wide-eyed over the top of her glass. "What's your first name?"

"Lee."

"Sit here, Lee. The damn light's shining in my eyes, and . . ."

"The light shining in your eyes may be appropriate, Sherry."

She didn't get it. "Jordie's *gone,* Lee. I probably won't see him until—"

"What's he doing, Sherry? Stealing hubcaps?"

She understood instantly, and her face sagged, older and harried behind the makeup. "I see," she said hoarsely. "And all you were trying to do yesterday was to catch me off balance?"

"No, Sherry." He told her about the leak to Congressman Weintraub. She simply refused to believe him. People left restricted stuff all *over* the damn place, and his Spooks never found it half the time, and to try to tell her that simply because she had left one little memo in her basket it had ended up in the hands of an anti-Pentagon Congressman was too much to swallow. "I mean, you're saying the place is full of spies, or something!"

He pointed out that the whole security of the Pentagon was built on the assumption that it was indeed full of spies; anybody who bet that it wasn't took her own chances. In her case, the gamble had failed and even if it turned out that she had only been careless, her boss intended to can her.

"Oh, God, does *he* know?"

"I spent half the night with him." He began to drive a wedge. "He said that somebody might have got to you. Because financially you're in trouble?"

"The son-of-a-bitch!"

Lee suggested that perhaps to Ellsworth, a woman trying to keep her son in heroin was hardly a likely person to favor with a top-secret clearance, and maybe Ellsworth was right. She lit a cigarette. "Maybe so," she said harshly. "On the other hand, I've worked in that goddamn place for twenty years—"

"Your son was never in trouble until this spring, though. April eighth, to be exact, when he was released on $2,500 bail on a burglary charge. A month later he was up for simple possession. And then shoplifting. You owe the bail-bond broker and you owe for your car. And he still has a $30-a-day habit, according to his probation officer's report."

"He's kicking it."

"Good," Lee said mildly. "Still, it's not impossible that somebody approached you." He shifted ground. "Sherry, could I get that drink?"

She nodded, without moving, and he went to the kitchen and poured a light shot of bourbon over ice, drowning it in water. He brought it back and this time he sat on the couch. She was drawn into a knot of hostility, thin-lipped and angry. "Listen, Sherry, I *did* stick my neck out for you yesterday. I spent the afternoon with SecDef himself, trying to explain why I hadn't made a report."

"Sorry," she said distantly.

"My own fault. And I'm willing to go another step. If you'll tell me who bought that memo, I'll do everything I can to protect you."

She snorted. "If I was going to *sell* that thing, would I leave it all night on my desk?"

He reminded her that she might have left it out for a secret pick-up; it might even have been on its way back to her. She had no comment, so he got up, draining his glass. "I'd like you to be in my office first thing Monday morning. Would you object to a lie-detector test?"

She looked frightened, but said: "I guess not. Do they work?"

He assured her that they worked, left the apartment, and walked back to his car. He glanced across the street. The battered van, painted "Johnny's Electrical Repairs," which Maxon had parked the night before, sat locked and apparently deserted. Lee knew that inside, monitoring Sherry's phone-bug, sat a Counterintelligence agent from Holabird who had just photographed him leaving the apartment, to prove, if necessary, that he had actually interrogated the suspect. A little further down the street, busy polishing a Honda 350, squatted Liebholtz. Jordie was watching the motorcycle longingly. Lee climbed into his car and started it.

He had dropped the bomb. If the woman was shaken enough to phone an accomplice, the panel truck would pick up the call; if Lee had panicked her into physically running to someone, Liebholtz should be able to tail her through traffic whether she went by bus or in her own car. Assuming Jordie didn't steal his bike.

Passing Dupont Circle, he headed west to the Peace League. It was not his crazy curiosity over the Ban Doc picture that impelled him, either, and now he admitted it to himself. It was the girl Laurie, whose last name he did not even know.

The League office on the top floor of the church was crowded with long-haired men half his age, college students waiting outside Reverend Scott's office for draft-counseling, parade marshals gathered around a huge city map. An elfish young man with a scarlet headband binding straw-colored hair held forth: "*Don't* use force on anybody. Don't fuck with the Weathermen. You see bricks or bats or too many hardhats in one spot, call the pigs. If there's action, bend the line of march away from it. We'll have our own medics; anybody gets hurt, call them or tell the pigs. It isn't only the freaks and trashers will

138

want to get the main body involved, Justice will want it too. Screw 'em! If the Army rousts us chant 'walk,' like Chicago. *Nobody* runs. There'll be little kids to protect on this march. Let's fuck the Weathermen and Justice too and just keep 'em moving, right? And we'll have another beautiful thing."

They would have, thought Lee, a beautiful thing if they would turn en masse on the Weathermen, swamp them in sheer numbers, strip them of weapons, helmets, boots, padding, and clothes, and dump them into the nearest body of water. Most protesters laughed at them as masochists on a dismal trip, but all reserved judgment and none ever thought of his final solution.

The girl was not around, and the excitement he had felt all morning fled and left him lonely. Then Scott's office door opened and she appeared, arms full of mimeographed handouts. Her eyes met his and her tanned, oval face glowed. There was a current between them, all right; he felt that he had known her forever. What a woman she would have made for Rick, he thought, and then forgot Rick in the longing to have her himself.

"Wow!" she said, "Johnny-on-the-Spot! We were just talking about you. Why are you fucking-up the march permit?"

"I'm not," he said.

"Well, you better do something or this town's going to have one constipated bridge!"

He stepped past her into Scott's office. The minister was hanging up his phone angrily. He looked up at Lee but made no move to shake hands.

"I thought," Scott said bitterly, "you were with us on crossing Arlington Memorial Bridge."

"Personally, given the goddamn demonstration, I am. Why?"

"The Department of Justice, if you'll excuse the expression, says you've asked them to turn down the permit."

"That's not true."

Scott handed him a polite letter from the Department of Justice, refusing the permit because the Defense Department requested that the bridge be closed next Saturday. Lee, perceiving Picket Aspen's hand, asked for a copy. Scott called Laurie in to make it.

"I'll try to track this down," Lee promised Scott, watching her leave—God, what a trim little ass she had. "But now I'd like you to tell me something." He asked Scott what he knew of a film on the alleged massacre they had talked of. The minister regarded him for a moment from beneath his bushy brows.

"There *is* such a film," Scott said finally.

"Where?"

"I can't say. I wouldn't if I could."

"I think it was faked," said Lee.

"I wish I did."

Lee told him that he had seen a frame, enlarged, of a GI shooting a woman. He asked Scott if he didn't want the GI—if he was a GI—punished.

"I don't think he would be punished," said Scott.

"Why not?"

"That film," murmured Scott, "was shot in combat, as an Army training movie."

"A *training* movie?"

"On gas warfare," Scott explained.

Lee's voice rose. "The *Army* puts out a movie to train U.S. infantrymen to slaughter women? Reverend, are you out of your mind?"

"That isn't what I said. What about scenes shot by Army combat-cameramen? With troops on a regular search-and-destroy mission, one that got out of hand? You ought to hear the stories these kids bring back, and the Army tries to hide them."

"We tried men for Mylai," Lee muttered, knowing it was the wrong thing to say.

The Reverend Scott pointed out bitterly that the Army had done its damnedest to bury Mylai, and that if it hadn't been for the most providential circumstances, would have succeeded. "This one may be the worst of all. The film's said to be Army property, and I think if you could find it, you'd destroy it."

"Thanks, Reverend," Lee said tightly.

"Maybe not *you*, Colonel. But I think your superiors would."

"And, Reverend," exploded Lee, *"I* think you're full of shit!" He whirled and left the office. From an ancient copy-machine outside, Laurie was extracting the letter he wanted. She looked up into his face, and the look cut through twenty years. "What's wrong?" she asked.

"That silly bastard. He lives in a cocoon."

"He's not a silly bastard, Lee." So she had bothered, from correspondence files or from Scott, to find out his first name. She began to cover the machine. "He doesn't trust the military, and the reason you're up-tight is because you know he's right. He likes *you,* though. He told me about your son."

"If he liked me, he'd shut up about my son. Did he turn on a Joan Baez ballad, or just feed it to you cold?"

She put out her hand and touched his arm. "Look, I'm through. Would you drive me home?" Her skin was flushed, her eyes held his own unwaveringly. He saw the danger and charged ahead.

"Come on," he said harshly, and they left.

Her last name was Sands: Laurie Sands. She was from Long Island, and her father was a doctor, and her mother a professional artist. Something of her mother's color sense must have entered her psyche, for she vibrated to hues like the strings of a guitar. Grays and pastels seemed to depress her, and she became moody driving through the grime of northwest Washington, but when they reached Rock Creek Parkway, her spirits lifted and she pointed out that the woolly clouds looked like sheep grazing across the deep-blue sky scrubbed by last night's rain. But nature had compensated, he learned when he turned on the radio; she was absolutely tone-deaf.

He learned other things, too, for he did not drive her home, not then. They went to the boat, unsnapped the tarp, and while he sanded the lazarette, she tied her shirt-tail and stretched out on a cockpit seat to get the sun on her belly. By the time he had sanded off the old varnish, a breeze was tickling the river and *Misty* was tugging at the leash and eager to go. So instead of varnishing, he winched up the main, cast off, and caught a cat's-paw

141

of the afternoon southeasterly. He bent on the big, light jenny and they glided in state past the Pentagon, first boat out of the mooring on the first breath of air. *Misty* whispered upstream and Laurie, clinging to a shroud, leaned far outboard with one foot braced on the leeward rail and the other tracing a ripple in the water with a calloused toe. Her slim body made a glorious golden silhouette against the afternoon sun, which threw bronze glints from the tips of her hair. She glanced back at him at the tiller, flicking locks from her face with stubby fingers. She had sailed Long Island Sound all her life: she moved like a cat on the tender boat. Her even teeth were parted in joy at being on the water again, but when she looked at him her eyes fell grave. His longing to touch her must have shown in his face, for she swung inboard, moved to the cockpit seat under his arm, and pressed herself close.

He knew that she was his if he wanted her, and felt a tug of apprehension. There were things to say: he was twenty years older than she, it could lead nowhere. She might be hurt, or he, or Jenny. Jenny must never know. He began, huskily, to warn her: "Laurie?"

She looked up at him soberly, and he felt foolish, for all the wisdom she needed was in the look. "What?" she asked.

"Skip it." They ghosted into the slip on the dying gasp of the breeze, and he wanted her so much that he very nearly took her into *Misty*'s tiny cabin (how many girls, he wondered, had Rick had there?). But there were slip-neighbors too close, washing down their boats. A doughty little Pentagon Navy captain whom he and Rick had raced glanced appreciatively at Laurie, with a glint of new respect for Lee. The old bastard threw out his monkey-chest, leered, preened, and did everything but whistle. His presence was enough to send them off, so they tarpaulined the cockpit and he drove her home. Her hand lay lightly on his knee. His passion rose with every block; he felt twenty again.

He parked opposite American University, a conservative school, she claimed, turned-on since Kent. Its dormitory windows were hung with posters of Che and Viet Cong banners. She lived in a converted Georgian manor

142

across the street from the campus. Her own flat on the ground floor might have been a diplomat's study in the building's younger days. Her roommate, thank God, was North at a Women's Lib meeting. She could not find the key under the carpeting outside where she always left it. She frowned, listened, and tried the door. It opened.

A slim young man with cheerful blue eyes and a drooping moustache, on the floor chording a guitar, got up as they entered. A companion-piece, bearded and not as clean-looking, slumbered on a sleeping bag.

"Laurie Sands?" the guitarist asked.

Laurie nodded, resignedly. "Did Switchboard send you?"

"Right. Can you handle us?"

"It depends on what you mean by 'handle,' " Laurie shrugged. "Put you up, yes."

She drew Lee into an alcove almost filled with a queen-sized bed behind beaded strings. The walls were papered with posters, dominated by a huge yellow sticker: MAKE LOVE NOT WAR. She tossed her pocketbook on the bed and faced him apologetically. "I'm sorry, Lee. We expect eighty thousand, and they have to stay somewhere."

"Way it goes," he said tightly. The kid outside had made him feel forty-six again.

"But I'll go with you, anywhere," she offered. "I'd climb in that sack right now, if you wanted. And send those characters out on the street."

"I could give them a dollar to go see a movie," said Lee bitterly. "No, Laurie, I'll see you tomorrow." He took her in his arms quite gently, meaning only to stake his claim with a good-bye kiss, but suddenly she was clinging to him, vibrant body close, and he felt youthful flesh molding to his own hard frame. The supple back bent beneath him and the bed was very much there. He would have taken her then had not the long-haired freeloader (who could not have cared less what went on in the alcove) struck a sour chord and reminded him that they were not alone. He was of a generation that demanded privacy for sex, and so he left. Knotted inside, he climbed into his car.

He had not in the whole afternoon mentioned a word to

143

her of the Ban Doc photo. He was glad he had not, "Duty, Honor, and Country" be damned. But the moment he was in his apartment he looked up General Morris Greenberg's home number and asked him if the Chemical Corps had commissioned a training film on gas warfare in the field.

"We commission them all the time," Greenberg said. "You must have seen some."

"Lately, General? Using combat footage?"

"That I couldn't say," Greenberg mumbled. Lee detected uncertainty in his voice. "I told you before, Colonel, it's against cease-fire policy to use gas. Why do you ask?"

He did not really know Greenberg, and to mention evidence of a massacre to a strange general officer was to risk a courtmartial later for not reporting the facts up the chain of command, if the rumors turned out to be true. Lee told him simply that there was a story in radical Washington circles that GIs had used tear gas on civilians in a hamlet in Vietnam. Greenberg pressed him for details, but Lee minimized the story as gossip.

Until he had the facts, there was no use shaking the poor guy unnecessarily. Greenberg seemed to know nothing and fear the very light of day if it concerned CBW. Lee hung up and began to get ready for Lucius Hardy's party.

General Lucius Hardy's home lay five miles from the Pentagon in a cul-de-sac in Colonial Village, a residential development running only slightly to seed. Though the place was well away from any Army post, the architect had recognized his potential clientele and the style was late-American Army, circa light-colonel. Hardy had bought it during a previous Pentagon tour, as a hedge against inflation, and had rented it to other Service families when duty had called him to Japan, Vietnam, and Fort Holabird. Like most Regular officers in the Pentagon, he considered his Virginia property the best investment he had ever made. It carried itself when he was elsewhere and, innocent of financial training, he was more at ease owning real estate than stocks. Unless inflation forced them to Mexico he would retire here, near the Fort Myer PX, the Army-Navy Club, and Bolling Field, too, for the free military travel he and his wife, Skeeter, would have for the rest of their lives.

Lee parked and slid from behind the wheel. As he walked around the car to help Jenny out, he caught a whiff of the Potomac, miles away, reminding him of the girl sunning in the cockpit. It brought tomorrow closer and he almost forgot why he was standing oustide the car door. Jenny looked at him curiously: "Lee?"

"Sorry," he said, remarking that she looked lovely in her new dress, and she did, relatively, so that was no lie, and she accepted it.

They were the first to arrive. Skeeter Hardy met them at the door. She was a tiny woman with short sandy hair turning gray, wise eyes, a button-nose, and skin leathery from too much tennis in the tropics. She had always been too masculine for Lee's taste, but that was characteristic of women left too long in charge of families while their husbands served overseas. She was not ordinarily demonstrative, but when she saw Jenny she hugged her closely (a sparrow trying to envelope a pigeon). She shepherded Jenny to the kitchen to help with hors d'oeuvres and he drifted through the still-empty house looking for his boss.

Like the homes of most of Lee's friends, Hardy's was half personal museum. The first saber Lucius had bought, fresh from the Point, was crossed over the mantel with a ceremonial one presented by the King of Greece as a memento of Hardy's pre-Papadopoulos sympathy for the monarch. The affection had evaporated when the Pentagon line changed, as it always must, to one of support for the ruling junta. Under the crossed sabers hung a plaque with the sphinx of the Military Intelligence Corps, farewell gift of a G-2 office in Toyko. Autographed photos of politicians, General Ridgway (complete with polished grenades strapped to his shoulders), foreign admirals, Generalissimo Franco, and Big Minh lined the hallway from living room to den. To Hardy's credit, he had never seen any more reason to remove the signed photo of President Diem from his hall than the ceremonial sword of the deposed Greek monarch from the mantel. In a glass wall-case was a display of Union and Confederate small arms. In another glittered an exhibit of Hardy's medals (DSC, Silver Star, and Purple Heart, rampant in a gaggle of lesser campaign ribbons). The case (standard, as advertised in *The Army Green Book* for "achievers" at $39.98) was flanked by two photos of Army football teams (Lee was in one, as a scrawny yearling end). The pictures, spilling into the den, were dominated by an AP photo of Lucius twenty-five years younger as a stubbled captain in a jeep in France.

In her thirty-year career as a souvenir hunter, Skeeter Hardy, sponsored by the U.S. taxpayer, had become eclectic. A monolithic carved cabinet from Hong Kong, chests from Japan, rugs from Istanbul, camel-saddle seats from Cairo, a massive polished table and tall Spanish chairs from Madrid, all testified to Lucius Hardy's success as a paradiplomat and superspy, to Skeeter's acumen, and to the generous overseas shipping allowance for household effects of Regular officers. None of it would have disgraced the Watergate apartment of a millionaire Cabinet Secretary. There was not a Black Forest cuckoo clock in sight, and if the Hardys had ever owned a piece of PX modern, it had been dumped by the time he made major.

Tonight the cases and medals were freshly polished and the sabers over the mantel gleamed. A black enlisted man from Fort Myer, hired and white-coated for the evening, was setting up the bar in the den with Guantanamo Bay Officer's Club liquor. Neat ranks of $1.50-a-quart Johnny Walker flown in by the Air Force marched along the bartop. But Lee ignored it and for some reason—the girl, or their first party since Rick, or sheer perversity—found himself asking for a "Skeeter Special." The Special was a lethal martini invented twenty years before by Hardy at Fort Riley, frozen solid and then thawed back into life, a process that seemed to increase its fire-power tenfold. He was on his second when Lucius Hardy, cinching his tie, strolled in and eyed Lee's drink.

"What the hell, lad?"

"Just felt like it, Daddy," said Lee. "It's free, right?"

Hardy shrugged and, ignoring his bartender, poured himself a Scotch-and-water. He lifted it in the age-old toast of Napoleon's cavalry, delivered in flawless French: "To beautiful women and fine horses, and to those who mount them." They clinked glasses. "Picket Aspen," announced Hardy, "is coming."

"Is he crashing, or did you invite him?"

"I invited him," Hardy said simply, "because I want you to get back into his graces. Kiss his ass, polish his twinkly toes, but whatever it is, smooth it over. He's shooting you down in General and Flag Officers' Mess, in front of the rest of my class. Savvy?"

Lee swirled his drink. Studying the whirlpool it made, he thought of the girl's stubby toe tracing a tiny wake along the Potomac, saw her slim waist and trim hips and tight, youthful breasts and the curve of her golden cheek. He almost lost his train of thought. "You got me?" demanded Hardy again.

"I'm not going to brown-nose Picket."

"Oh, yes you are. Listen, we all kiss butt, we'll do it to the day we retire, and maybe afterward."

Lee told him of the Justice Department's letter to the Reverend Scott, and that he suspected Picket of bypassing them and forcing Justice to write it. Hardy agreed but waved his hand impatiently. "I'm not sure he's wrong, and as for trying to interfere with our show, I'll try to take care of that. *You* can't. You're still a buckassed Colonel, and sometimes I think you forget it. You were B.J. as a plebe, and damn near impossible as a yearling—"

The door-chimes sounded and Lucius Hardy moved off to meet his next arrivals. The house began to fill with generals from Hardy's class, a few Intelligence Corps colonels who had worked with Lee, some ONI and Defense Intelligence types, and retired G-2 officers working up the Potomac at Langley with the CIA. Most were West Pointers.

The club had met, the members more secure here than ever at a civilian party. Thirty years ago most of the men in the room had met on the Hudson, in the toughest crucible they would ever know. They had all followed precisely the same curriculum (with the exception of an elective language), worn the same bellhop uniforms, marched always to the sound of the same drummer or suffered for breaking step. Inside each graduate, of course, was a personality crying to be heard. Anyone with the guts and brains to get through the Point had to be an individual, and that was their mutual tragedy. The West Pointer's image obscured the man inside. Movies, television, fiction too, painted him in black-and-white and distorted him further. Lee himself, two years junior to most of the men there, had only since his son's death moved away from the group to evaluate it objectively, as Rick, he suspected, had tried to evaluate him.

Now he sat back, studying the crowd. The mold on the Hudson had stamped out not lead soldiers, but men both good and bad, and impressed them (and himself, he imagined) with some characteristics quite admirable along with those currently so reviled. They were loyal but clannish. Admiral Nelson had called his wardroom a "Band of Brothers," and it applied to Army officers too. They would cut a classmate to ribbons among themselves but close ranks against press, public, or politicians who sought to harm a Regular. They distrusted civilians. After three decades in the Service, they rejected, when they could, department stores for PXs and supermarkets for military commissaries, where Uncle Sam presumably was looking out for their interests. The fliers had a motto: "The Air Force Looks Out for Its Own," and it applied to the Army and Navy as well. Dying in a field-hospital or rotting as a POW, you knew that your classmate and his wife would be there to steady your own.

The men here had learned a code of honor at the Point. Most of them still subscribed to it when they could and would rather give a straightforward answer or keep silent than to dissemble. Like cadets who had missed bed-check they might even turn themselves in or volunteer information against their best interests, unless it tarnished the shield of their Service. But the code had loosened in a major war and two minor ones and now there were few among them who would not cut orders, when they could, for a fast tour of duty into a fire-zone to draw an income-tax exemption or combat pay, or who had not slipped a

Swiss watch or a Leica in a courier pouch through Customs, or accepted a medal he did not earn.

They were inwardly awed by the entrepreneurs they met in industry, wondering how a man could risk his family's security on the success of a design or the award of a contract, or even how civilians ineligible for officers' club liquor could make ends meet. Most preferred physical risk to financial. On retirement, even the generals among them—unless they were lucky enough to be hired by the arms industry—preferred jobs as math teachers or military-school instructors to higher paid but less secure work as salesmen. None had ever missed a salary check or had to worry about being fired. No War College course in Industrial Relations or the Inflationary Effect of a Rising Military Economy could give them a real feel for the problems of a parts-manufacturer trying to meet a payroll or a doctor trying to pay his income tax: their own taxes had for years been withheld at source.

They considered themselves apolitical, and were, most of them, more interested in who was someday slated for Chief of Staff than in the local elections of whatever community the Army had dropped them into. Nationally, they were ten-to-one Republicans or Southern Conservative Democrats. (It was odd, Lee thought, how a system of Congressional appointments, meant to assure West Point a class of plebes numerically reflecting the distribution of population, should result thirty years later in a group of generals predominantly from the South and 99 and 44 /100 percent white as Ivory Snow.)

The life narrowed intelligent men and, despite their travels, made them insular. The new climate of civilian hostility had angered them all. They had graduated from the Point in the darkest days of World War II, as saviors, and there were few among them who had not suffered wounds for their country. Now, no one cared, and they huddled head-to-head, rumps to the storm, against gales of scorn that took no notice of their patriotism, loyalty, and courage. They were vilified by eggheads who did not seem to realize that war was a normal condition of mankind and that, anyway, they were public servants and not politicians and had nothing to do with policy. Dark forces

149

were abroad, flaunting enemy flags, and there seemed to be nothing that anyone could do about it. To speak before a Kiwanis Club or an American Legion chapter and sit down to an ovation was gratifying but redundant, almost a form of group masturbation, and to venture a lecture on a college campus, where the damn fools needed all the military realism they could get, was to risk being booed or worse. A world in which youth considered the red, white, and blue as simply another collection of colors angered and frightened them. Most of them wished that their sons would follow them to the Point (God knew they were needed; Army couldn't even field a decent football team) and that their daughters would marry Regular. But their offspring seldom listened, and maybe their kids were instinctively right. A movement was afoot that made the men here unsure. They ascribed student unrest to International Communism and could not understand, after all the years, why the FBI, CIA, or they themselves had found no better proof of subsidies from Moscow or Americans taking guerrilla training on the steppes. They were exquisitely attuned to the cries of anguish from the Left, and, while predicting that the screams would trigger an avalanche from the Right, hoped that their fears were wrong. Most had disliked Hitler's brand of Facism almost as much as they hated Communism. They found it secretly hard to advise their sons and daughters on how to deal with the future. If the howls for disarmament didn't fade, a military man in another thirty years might be as obsolete as a village vicar. Who knew where personal security lay?

Lee spotted the guest of honor, General Harkin Blanding, a solid, pleasant officer with a wide, sincere mouth and a rugged smile. Blanding was the last in a line of briefing officers who had first persuaded Kennedy to expand Eisenhower's nine-hundred-troop contingent in Vietnam to twenty-five thousand (to test Green Beret techniques and jungle weapons), conned Johnson into exploding the commitment to half a million (to intimidate a foe who did not care if he lived or died), and convinced Nixon that the way out of Southeast Asia was the way into Cambodia. He was retiring next week in triumph, the expert who had more than any one man steered the President into Operation Total Victory and the Fish Hook and Parrot's Beak campaigns. It was on the Total Victory invasion that Rick, slithering down a muddy paddy-ditch, had crawled over a mine, but Lee found no difficulty in being affable to the general. Technically, there was nothing to criticize, the military logic of Cambodia having been unassailable. Lee had idolized the general in Beast Barracks thirty years ago; he remembered him as a carefree, iconoclastic cadet-officer and brilliant scholar. Blanding had developed into an expert briefing officer, of whom there were never enough. Lee imagined him in the quiet womb of the National Military Command Center, pointer in hand before the sweeping kidney-shaped table, prodding the President to action and consigning Rick to hell. *"Mr. President, the possibility of Chinese intervention is zero. The risk to you, sir, is domestic, political only."* (Thus lifting the JCS off the hook when the shit hit the fan.) *"Militarily, 'Total Victory' will succeed."*

A silent flourish and rattle of drums and Blanding, quiet, self-assured, would have retreated from his charts and the huge wall map. West Point had kicked off. Now let the woolly-headed Harvard, Yale, and Berkeley alumni from the State Department, or HEW, or Interior do their worst. Blanding had lit a bright beacon for the President on a dark night, as the Academy had trained him to do. No wonder the Man had chosen to follow it without a glance at flickering candles in shakier hands.

Lee congratulated the general on his retirement. Blanding's lined, honest face grew sad. Thailand, Burma, India would be next. "I almost hate to miss it. You guys from '45, you're going all the way."

Lee nodded, and returned to the bar, where he had another of Skeeter's Specials, wondering where, for him, lay "all the way." He was coming to dislike combat and to hate those who honestly expected (and thus showed their desire for) a comfortable little series of wars that would assure them their next stars. (Preferably *justified* wars, like Korea: Vietnam was bad; there were men in this very room who would disavow Vietnam, sometimes aloud.) "Peace is our profession," said SAC, and meant

151

it, so long as just enough of a threat remained to keep appropriations coming and promotions on schedule.

And the threat was always there, perfectly valid, perfectly salable: Marshal Grechko, ribbons from clavicle to belly-button, briefing Brezhnev in the Kremlin: quilt-jacketed counterparts in Peking warning Chairman Mao. They were all in the same business, and Lee was in it too; they should have an international association like physicists or astronomers and exchange professional hints on how best to influence their respective heads of state. They had built their separate juggernauts and were trapped unhappily in them now, unerringly guiding them toward collision, the Russian and Chinese machines navigated by men as sane and skillful as Blanding and Hardy and Aspen, who was approaching him now at the bar. The sum of all their collective rational decisions was leading them all toward the final insanity, with the only cries of warning coming from beneath the wheels of the biggest and most powerful juggernaut of them all, from kids of half the age of the men in this room, and apparently twice the vision. The machine creaked onward, the victims shrieked and pounded at its sides; you could hear them, but nobody here dared try to stop the monster and dismount while the other machines still rolled. "Shit," he mumbled into his innocent glass.

"You called, Colonel?" General Picket Aspen asked from shoulder-height, beside him at the bar. The waspish smile was cold and false, but Picket was no worse than the rest: more honest than he himself, who agonized and did nothing.

"You talked to your friend the Red Reverend lately?" Aspen asked.

Hardy had told Lee to stay clear, but he plunged ahead, fortified with gin. "Today," he said. "Why try to close the bridge? They've got enough parade marshals to maintain order themselves, as long as they can cross to the Pentagon."

"The way to handle them," Aspen said softly, "is at the bridge. And not with parade marshals, but with Regulars. Like MacArthur and the bonus marchers."

"Commanded from a white horse?" demanded Lee.

152

"General, these aren't beat-down veterans after sympathy! This is *now!* They think half the country's behind them! If we let them do their thing, they'll go home. If you try to put a cork on it, you'll have a confrontation at the bridge that'll make the Kent State murders look like a tea party."

"Murders?" Aspen said softly, raising his eyebrows. "Murders, Colonel?"

"They *were* murders. Only this time it won't be a bunch of half-assed Ohio Guardsmen. It'll be Old Guard Regulars a mile from your own damn Center!"

Lucius Hardy appeared from nowhere. His eyes were narrowed, a danger signal, but his voice stayed smooth. "Picket," Hardy said, "you're hearing my own party line, from Intelligence, not Lee's own feelings. You've got fifty States to take care of. Let *us* handle our own front yard. OK? Now how about a drink?"

"No drink right now," Picket said tightly. "And as for the bridge, I may have to go to the Chief of Staff, but *'Ils ne passeront pas.'*"

Aspen drifted into the living room, and Hardy glared at Lee. "Goddamn it, Lee, I told you—" A phone rang from a corner of the den and Hardy stepped past the bar to answer it. Lee heard him above the chatter: "Hello, Morrie. What can I do for you?"

General Morris Greenberg? Odd, but nothing he cared to puzzle out now. Lee floated euphorically to the patio, where a few gray-haired couples were dancing to the Hardy hi-fi. He found Jenny struggling, like a well-trained Navy junior and a good Army wife, to follow General Scorchy Blain, Chief of Army Chaplains. The general had slipped from the wagon again. His eyes were bleary and his dancing dangerous. Lee cut in. Jenny, full of Scotch herself, was after all the years and recent tonnage still light in his arms.

"That *Scorchy!*" she marveled. "Did you know he was *drunk* when he won that medal?"

Lee nodded, surprised that Scorchy had admitted it. In '51, the chaplain had been caught on the lines and pinned down in a sandbagged company C.P. near the Chosin Reservoir, under fire of a mortar behind a nearby peak.

Expecting an attack by a regiment of the Fourth Chinese Field Army, he had fallen to his knees and begun to shout prayers for the salvation of the doomed men around him. The company commander, to tranquilize him before he panicked his troops, had passed him a bottle of bourbon. Somewhere through the bourbon, Scorchy had cursed vilely, as rumor had it, grabbed a half-dozen grenades, and lurched up the hill. Warming his Texas-League arm, he had tossed three strikes on the Gook battery, cleaning them out.

"A great inspiration," Lee told Jenny, "praise the Lord and pass the ammunition."

"He wants to send us a letter about Rick," Jenny said, "signed by the *President!*"

"And edged in black?" Lee said gently. "To hang on the wall? No."

Jenny agreed. "But we ought to have some of *your* things on the wall, Lee. Your saber and the DSC, anyway."

Lee told her that when he needed an ad, he would buy space in *The Army-Navy Journal.* Then, as a good West Pointer should, he danced with his hostess, Skeeter, tiny in his arms after Jenny. She threw back her head and addressed him from a foot below. "Lee," she said, "I think Jenny's ready to come back to life. She's going to lose that weight."

"I hope so."

"It's up to you to help her. Will you?"

He promised, of course, and danced with Jenny again, but when he took her home he found himself worried that she would want to make love (she seemed so warm and alive that he was sure of it) and he was afraid that, despite their months of abstinence, he would find himself incapable, with her flab and his alcohol and the vision of Laurie intruding. Lurching around the bathroom, trying to brush his teeth, he was haunted by a sense that something in the evening was askew. Hardy's call from General Greenberg! Maybe it was an I.C.C.—"I can't come" —but it had come too late in the evening for even a last-minute apology. And why would Lucius invite a CBW general to an Intelligence Corps gathering anyway?

Greenberg was no classmate, nor even a West Point graduate.

He gargled, tried to fend off tomorrow's hangover with preventive aspirin, and wove into the bedroom. Mercifully, Jenny drifted off. He climbed into his bed as gratefully as if it were a foxhole in a fire-area. His last thoughts, before he slipped into restless, alcoholic sleep, were of Laurie and of tomorrow.

Chapter Six

Marty Lumpert, wearing GI boots and bell-bottoms, parked Handlemann's Volkswagen bus among buildings gutted by fire in the Washington riots. He moved up the grimy street clutching the work-print and original of Poma's film. Years after the flames, the neighborhood still smelled of burned wood and garbage. Great supermarket store windows were boarded and a new A&P had no windows at all but was brick from sidewalk to roof. A hot breeze swirled dust and ashes before him as he turned up Rand Alley. A gray-faced Negro sat hunched, one doorway short of the address he was looking for, drinking his Sunday breakfast from a pint bottle of flavored gin. Seeing Marty, he beckoned with his head. "You got a cigarette, man?" Marty gave him one and stepped into the next entrance.

The building, which may once have been a storehouse, seemed closed. On its doors was smeared the shibboleth that may have saved its life: SOUL BROTHER, and below it *Burn, Baby, Burn!* In pencil over the doorbell was the legend: New Age Film Processing: 8 and 16 Millimeter. Ulysses Studio. He pressed the button. In a few moments, with a clattering of bolts, the door opened and a long-haired, sulky young Oriental faced him.

"Harry Wong?" Marty asked.

"Yeah?"

Marty told him that he was from the *Underground Clarion* and gave him a note from Handlemann. The young man glanced at it reluctantly, then motioned him in, rebolted the door, and led him up creaking stairs into an enormous loft. A half-circle of movie lights was drawn up before a giant oil drum. Skeletal oil derricks rose on a backdrop of painted flames; a camera was zeroed in on the drum. A movie slate leaned against the tripod: Production:

156

Scene 42. Crossing the loft, the Oriental called impatiently: "He's OK, kids, let's go!"

From a room off the studio strode a nude Negress with coarse features but a proud body, so beautiful that it was almost a caricature. Following her, eyes glazed, apparently zonked out of his gourd, was a naked young white with a hooked nose and the longest penis Marty had ever seen. Bringing up the rear came a bored, frizzle-haired cameraman, exposure meter dangling from his neck, and a slim black with a gold tooth and a British accent, very fag. "From the top, then, kiddies," said the black. Marty, following the Oriental reluctantly from the loft, caught a last glance of the Negress spread-eagle herself, back to the oil drum, while the impassive cameraman hit the scene with a blaze of light and the hook-nosed hero, erecting as if on signal, sidled up to her, searching foggily for chalkmarked footprints on the floor.

"Jesus," breathed Marty. He had known that the lab processed pornography, but no one had told him, or Poma either, that they shot it too. Suddenly the precious rolls of film he carried seemed ridiculously hazarded. "Does Handlemann know you *shoot* here?"

Wong shrugged. "I guess so. I advertise for talent in his rag. Why?"

"I don't know," Marty muttered indecisively. Wong led him into the lab, past a monstrous, dripping, stainless-steel machine that creaked and groaned and clacked as it ate colorful tendons of tautly stretched film. Marty had a sudden vision of the whole gigantic device disappearing under the blows of the Metropolitan Vice Squad. He felt his cool deserting him. Handlemann should have made this trip himself, or Poma, even, as the only one qualified to judge the lab's ability. Suppose they wrecked the original in printing it? It was another indication, he thought bitterly, of the sloppy way Handlemann and the rest of the screwed-up radicals did things—all on a wing and a prayer.

He began to question Wong, trying to sound like an expert. As always, when excited, he started in a rush and talked too much. This film, he pointed out, was historic: a man had risked his life and freedom to help shoot the

157

footage and steal it afterward. To chance losing it in a police raid aimed at the piece of shit being shot outside was like risking the Mona Lisa in a pub during a dart tournament. "No offense, you understand, but you do dig, don't you?"

"I dig," Wong said tightly. "The Mona Lisa, huh? Well, maybe you better bag-ass out of here with your fucking original and your fucking work-print and go see Kodak or Sun Dial Labs or Guggenheim, over on 17th! Why don't you try *them*, Fat Boy?"

He slammed shut the notebook he had opened to log in the film. Marty moved to the window, thinking. In the alley below, the alcoholic Negro had left his niche, crossed the street, and was looking up at the building. He saw Marty and nodded.

"He a lookout?" Marty asked Wong. "That black in the alley?"

"No," said Wong acidly. "We leave him there for color, like the MGM lion."

The place seemed suddenly secure. "OK," said Marty. "How much?"

"Hundred bucks a print," said Wong. "As agreed. Cash. In advance." He opened the work-print can and pulled out a few feet, scanning it against the light from the window. "Army stuff? Who cut this?"

"Me, maybe?"

"Bullshit. You don't know a hot-splice from a lap-dissolve."

"Sergei Eisenstein," proposed Marty.

Wong eyed him balefully. "Thanks," he grunted. "Tell whoever it is he can dub on Wednesday."

Marty counted out Handlemann's bills and got a receipt. As he crossed the loft, he could see the white man humped over the barrel, haunches pumping furiously. The cameraman, on the floor, was shooting straight up at his face.

"Cut, Sweetie," called the gold-toothed director. "Hold everything, kids; reverse shot." As the cameraman scrambled to his feet, the director glanced at Marty. "Say, Mon, hold up. I'm from Central Casting. Thirty bucks, tomorrow at ten, and we don't show the face?"

Cheeks flaming, Marty shook his head and clattered down the stairs into the hot sunlight. By the time he was back at Handlemann's, he had as usual thought too late of a dozen answers for the offer. One of them he chose for June ("Who wants to be the prick on the cutting room floor?"). She didn't believe him and said she didn't even believe the story of the studio, trying to trick him into promising to take her along when he picked up the prints. That night at dinner, in the commune kitchen, he told Poma the set-up and saw him go tense with fear. Poma blew up at Handlemann, who claimed that the place had been there for years and that Wong must have the vice pigs all paid off, but Handlemann's confidence didn't seem to help. That night Marty, who had to drop two reds before he could sleep, dreamed of Poma's film, chewed and digested in the big steel machine, dropping in great bloody chunks on the floor of the loft.

Lee dressed without waking Jenny and scrawled her a note that he was driving down to his father's farm (true, and she would appreciate his not waking her to ask her to go). He added that afterward he was varnishing the boat (false, and he felt momentarily guilty, but the anticipation of the girl's golden skin and the curve of her cheek and the clear hazel eyes soon cured that).

So, hypocritically, he flashed first down Shirley Memorial Highway toward Fredericksburg, past Fort Belvoir, over Occoquan Creek, turning right on a rutted Prince William County road until he regained the stream. He paralleled a dusty whitewashed fence and paused at an open gate marked COTTON FROST, MAJ. USA RET. He leaned from the car door, picked up his father's Sunday paper, and jounced up the driveway.

The house lay in shabby splendor on a rise. It was always about to be painted, and the screen doors on the front porch fixed, but the old man had lived in government quarters too long to feel responsible for his surroundings. Lee's father might haul out brushes and buckets, but Cynthia, his current mistress, would tap the first beer can before Cotton could open the paint, and that would

159

be the end of it for the day. (Rick had been going to do the painting for him, but the draft call and all of the hearings had come up first, and then he was in and it was too late.)

Lee's father was peering under the hood of his new Cadillac. He straightened painfully, bending backward to ease his spine. His face was bright red from his morning beer, but his years in the Philippines had conditioned him to heat and his forehead was not even damp with sweat. He was as tall as Lee and as broad in the shoulders. In the months since his grandson's death he had aged, and his trim belly had slipped and his jowls grown loose, but he still bore himself somehow as a giant among pygmies.

He was a remarkable man at sixty-six, the only one Lee had known who had lived two lives, one after the other. For the true Cotton Frost, the warm and gentle soldier Lee had worshiped as a child, had died, somehow, with Lee's mother in a dependent's ward at Letterman Army Hospital when Lee was sixteen, to be reborn (after an hour of hysterical grief) as this second soldier, diamond-hard. Or maybe the mild and friendly one had been the false father, the apparent affection for Lee only a façade held together by love for the mother. Would the real Cotton Frost stand up? From the day of his mother's funeral there had been nothing left of the first father for Lee—only the memory of close, happy rides on an old Harley motorcycle through eucalyptus on the post trails above Fort Scott, and of fishing off the Golden Gate, and of his father marching, a tall square-shouldered buck-sergeant in the files of the glittering Regular Army ranks at Retreat. Nobody ever marched like the old Regulars any more, not even West Point cadets; parade grounds were no longer as velvety, the evening sun never as golden, no drums anywhere could throb with so deep and visceral a beat.

Cotton Frost, having died inside, had left Lee with an aunt and entered cynically into a strange second life as a gambler in uniform with no fear at all. In Germany, under Bradley, his heroics had won him a battlefield commission. He might have kept it after the war, on his brains and ability, but he said he was tired of officers' mess bullshit and reverted to master-sergeant. Before Pearl Harbor he had not even written when he heard that Lee had made the Point from the ranks, not proud of him or jealous or happy or unhappy, simply dead to emotion from the day Lee's mother had died, as drained of real affection for Lee as for the long line of Army wives, WACs, and, finally, the slatternly flotsam of northern Virginia who still tried to replace the woman he loved.

Lee joined his father at the opened hood of the Cadillac. The old man glanced at him wordlessly. Lee smelled the beer on his breath, and it was only ten A.M.

"Goddamn oil-pump seal," Cotton Frost announced. "A six-thousand-dollar car and a ten-cent seal on the oil pump." He wiped his hands on his trousers and slammed down the hood. "Well! I thought you'd been transferred or something. Back to Vietnam, or Thailand, or wherever. I mean, for all I knew. Don't you have a phone in that fancy apartment?"

Lee, puzzled, raised his eyebrows. "I didn't know you cared," he said. "If so, the phone works both ways." He handed the old man the morning paper and followed him through the tattered screen door, across the disheveled front porch, through the rugless, moldy living room where, if you wished, you could stare at a giant new television as purple-skinned Senators and red-uniformed Angels languidly fought it out on a diamond with an orange turf.

"You like that color scheme, Dad?" Lee asked, "or are you trying to drive Cynthia back home?"

"Set's gone blooey," said his father, who could fix anything and could probably have repaired it himself if he got his nose out of a beer can long enough. He winked at Lee and said softly, "But you know, about Cynthia, maybe you got something there?"

The old man stumbled on a dog-dish half full of food, spilling it. They passed through a kitchen cluttered with dirty dishes and selected the back porch as more fly-proof than the front. The old man sat down with a sigh, brushing a wild lock from his forehead. He had as much hair as when Lee was a child; more, really, for he had let the great mop go crazy last year, trying to shame Rick into cutting his own; that failing, and now that his grandson was gone, he had apparently decided to flaunt it in his memory forever. Now it grew as crazily as his fields spilling down to the creek below. For a while they sat in silence. They seldom had anything to say. Rick, quiet, humorous, and introspective, had filled some void in his grandfather's life, perhaps the vacuum left when Cotton Frost had cast out Lee. Maybe the old man had rejected Lee because he found in him unbearable traces of the mother, memories Rick had not evoked. Tough shit, Lee thought savagely: wear your hair long and beat your chest if you want; I'm Rick's father, and it hurt me more than you. A hundred yards below, where the Occoquan glittered through thick brush as it slid toward the Potomac, a chorus of frogs began to croak.

"Cynthia!" bellowed Cotton Frost suddenly in his first-sergeant voice, "front and center! My son, the Army Colonel, has arrived!"

Lee found two Burgies in the battered porch refrigerator, gave his father one and sat down to sip the other. It cut his thirst and calmed his nerves, and he began to feel that he could make it through the mandatory hour. Cynthia padded out in bare feet, breasts bobbling, wearing a print housedress, a hard-eyed woman no older than Jenny and twenty years younger than Cotton. "We didn't expect you, Lee," she complained, popping a beer can for herself. "I mean, you didn't call or anything."

She was the widow of a warrant officer. Lee knew that she was on her way out and found it easy to hide his dislike of her, because to show it to Cotton would perversely only prolong her stay. Besides, she would simply be replaced by another, older bat. It was incredible, at his father's age, how he kept mistresses flowing through his life.

"If you'd called," Cynthia said, "I'd have cleaned things up. But you never call and you hardly ever come."

"Get off his back, Cyn," growled his father. "He's *right* not to hang out here too much. He's practically got his star, and people talk. The CID might hear."

"Oh, Christ," breathed Lee. His connection with the Army's Civil Investigative Division had begun twenty years before, when he was thrown into the Intelligence Corps

162

after he had banged up his knee at Inchon and could no longer jump. After Intelligence School he had returned to Korea and passed through Seoul as a major. He had found that his father, top-kick in the local Eighth Army Headquarters, was a storm-center of local rumor. Cotton was deep in the black market, draining EM clubs, selling U.S. scrip for *wan,* smuggling Japanese radios, and living with the daughter of the wealthiest heroin merchant in town. Lee had no responsibility to the local CID office, but the signs of danger had been clear. "Dad," he had warned, "retire. Pick up your chips and go! Otherwise I, personally, will investigate this crap and get you twenty years in Leavenworth!"

Sergeant-Major Cotton Frost had gone into a remarkable act, pointing out that he had whelped an ingrate, and given thirty years to the Army. The local MP detachment was rotten to the core and breeding graft itself, and there were generals in Seoul deeper in the trough than he was. "Go pick on some goddamn Pointer," he had thundered, "and let your father, the peon, alone." Then, finally, he had chuckled and that very week retired safely on his pension (as a major, too, from his commission in World War II), dragging his fortune behind him—some estimated a quarter-million. And not so much as a company punishment on his record, either, a living proof to his peers in the Soldiers' Home that Army crime, properly conducted and terminated in time, could pay.

It had not been until a few years ago, when the ranking Sergeant-Major of the Army and no less than an ex-Provost Marshal had been accused of graft in Senate chambers, that Cotton had spoken of it again. "Son, maybe you saved my ass." But even then there was a twinkle in his eyes, and Lee knew that the warning in Seoul had been unnecessary. His father had been ready to quit and would not have cared anyway if the applecart spilled and he'd lost every cent and his pension besides.

Cynthia stirred restlessly, unnerved by the silence between them. She asked Lee if he would like a sandwich and went in to see if they had fresh bread. When she was safely in the kitchen, Cotton murmured: "Poor old Cyn. Got to unload her."

"Why?"

"She's smelled out the loot. She figures she's in, now that Rick's gone. Who'll I leave it to?"

Lee spread his hands. "Leave it to her. She's not the greatest housekeeper, but she's lasted."

"What about you and Jenny?" asked his father. "I could start right now—three grand a year—a gift—and avoid some inheritance taxes?"

The old man wanted him to say, "We could use it" (and they could), or at least, "Whatever you want." Lee crumpled his empty beer can and said nothing, instead. Slyly, his father said, "Of course, you wouldn't want it. It's dirty money."

That wasn't the reason. The reason lay thirty years back, in an ancient frame Army house on Sergeants' Row in San Francisco's Presidio, with the company commander's wife packing his mother's clothes for Army Relief and his Aunt Goldie sniffling over the china, and his father, for the third day, ice-cold and distant, hanging up the phone and telling him, without a tremor, "Orders are orders, Lee. And there's no dependent travel to the Philippines until things ease up. So I can't take you."

"They won't ease up! There's going to be a war, you say so yourself. They cancel orders, all the time! Ask Major Field, or hell, Dad, the *chaplain! She just died,* for God's sake!"

Silence, and then his father had said: "She just died, and I have to get away, I can't stand it, and you still need a woman around, and your Aunt Goldie is it." So Lee had known, and his world had crashed, but still, he hadn't refrained from putting the question to him: "You *asked* for orders?"

His father—the new one, three days old—had not even denied it. Well, the honesty was a plus. The old man's affection for Rick, too, had shown that he had not entirely turned to stone. But Lee was not now about to buy off his father's guilt for any three thousand a year, or the quarter-million, either. "Save it; you'll live forever."

"I'm leaving it to you, Lee. Hell, you must have figured that."

"Well, I don't accept it."

164

"All right, you goddamn cadet, pass it on to the orphanage in Seoul. The will's written." The old man glared into space, and for the first time in thirty years Lee felt a tug of affection for him. "What brought this on?" he wanted to know. His voice sounded hoarse in his own ears.

"Your mother."

"My *mother?*"

"I talk to her," said Cotton simply. Lee stared at him, a dismal knot forming in his chest. "I talk to her," the old man announced, "down there in the evening." He nodded toward the rushes, let his eyes wander to the north, and spotted the curving arc of a contrail against the summer blue. "B-52?" he wondered.

Lee, whose own eyes at long distances were almost perfect (and should anyway have been better than those of a sixty-six-year-old man who had just shown his first flash of senility), had to squint to identify it. By God, it was. He shook his head in wonder. "Incredible!"

"Cigarettes, and whiskey, and wild, wild women," his father explained. "You think I'm nuts, but I *do* talk to her."

"Knock it off!" Lee said sharply. "Christ!"

"OK," the old man shrugged. "How's Jenny?"

"Better, I think."

"Not well enough to come down here, though. My only daughter-in-law," he observed wryly, "doesn't like me."

He was wrong. Jenny was fascinated, as all women were, by the old stud. Lee told him so. "She just doesn't like Cynthia."

"Who likes Cynthia?" the old man muttered, following the plane. "Look at that! I told him he should have gone Air Force."

"Rick? Why?"

"He'd have been better off than as a fucking medical corpsman! My God, half of them are screaming homos and the other half end up dead!"

"He was a medic because he was a conscientious objector, not because he wanted to be a hero! Can you see him dropping napalm?"

The old man looked into his eyes. For the first time

since the wild hour of his mother's death, Lee saw tears in them. "I can't," Cotton Frost said quietly, "see *him* at all."

Lee ate a ham sandwich soggy with tired lettuce and rancid with old butter. Then he drove off to find the girl.

Outside her flat he smelled the paint. The door was open and he walked in. The floor was covered with poster paper and everyone but Laurie was painting signs for Saturday. He stepped carefully to where she sat at a flimsy table, composing slogans. Two new arrivals, unsmiling young men unlike the first two, were busy with Day-Glo paint and a stencil. Four rolled sleeping-bags were stacked out of the way against a wall; from one protruded a football shoulder-pad. Next to the bags lay two motorcycle helmets with plexiglass face masks. He prodded one with his toe.

"You putting up the headbangers, too?" he asked Laurie quietly.

"No," she said, "they came down from Penn State on a bike."

"Wearing shoulder-pads?"

She looked troubled but defiant. "If they're Weathermen, the marshals will handle them. Damn it, the *pigs* wear helmets and gas masks and carry clubs! Your construction apes wear tin hats and use ax handles! These kids have more to protect in their skulls than the people who want to beat them in!"

"Some of them do," he conceded, "but not the ones that have to wear the hats."

"Mister," offered one of the new travelers, looking up from his work, "you make bad vibes."

"Tough shit," said Lee. He began to wander about the room, inspecting the drying slogans: WAR IS GOOD FOR BUSINESS: INVEST A SON; BUY GM STOCK FOR A PIECE OF THE ACTION; YOU ARE A MEMBER OF AN ENDANGERED SPECIES; COMBAT IS A RELIGIOUS EXPERIENCE: THERE ARE NO ATHEISTS IN FOXHOLES; THE PENTAGON SUCKS.

"No offense, Colonel," grinned Laurie, putting away

her pencil and stepping over the placards to join him. "We all have our own point of view."

Laurie's roommate, a thin blonde with uncertain hands and distrustful eyes, was back from her trip North to whatever women's-liberation front she had visited. She looked up from the sign she was painting. *"Colonel?"* she gasped, in the sudden chill. "Oh, now, Laurie, look . . ."

"Actually, Fraulein," Lee snapped at the blonde, "I am no Colonel. I am a Field-Marshal in the Vest Cherman Army. Ven I finish with Fraulein Sands, I am coming back to question *you!"*

He clicked his heels, tossed a Nazi salute, and led Laurie out. Descending the mottled stone steps, she giggled. "You know, I think she'd like that? A good, solid Nazi?"

"Fine," muttered Lee. "Because if you give the right people the right encouragement, this country just might grow a few of its own."

"Believe me," she said softly, "it already has."

He stopped short at the foot of the stairs. "Laurie," he said quietly, "you're a sweet girl. I haven't even touched you yet, hardly—"

"You've touched me," she said firmly, "more than you think."

His pulse began to pound but he went on doggedly. "Before we get involved," he insisted, "you've got to quit handing me that Commie *Underground Clarion* crap!"

"Look," she flared, "this is Sunday. The sky is blue, the grass is green, the cherry blossoms are in bloom. If we're going to fight, I'd just as soon be in there composing 'Commie' slogans! And I will! A special one. For outside the Pentagon, at the height of the festivities. Borne aloft by a half-dozen Weathermen. A Colonel's leaf or an eagle or whatever tin toy you wear. Rampant on a thirty-by-thirty Viet Cong flag."

"What'll it say?" he wanted to know.

"Colonel Frost sucks!" she exploded.

She turned and started up the stairs. He could not let her go and grabbed her arm. She glared and tried to twist away. Suddenly she relaxed, then tore loose, giggled, and vaulted the iron fence to the old mansion's tiny front-yard. She stooped to study a bed of tired geraniums. She had the roundest, most perfect hips and the firmest legs and tiniest waist he had ever seen, beneath iron-taut Levi's. She picked two blossoms and he lifted her back over the fence: a hundred-fifteen pounds, he guessed, not nearly so fragile as she looked. (God, he wouldn't try to hoist Jenny without a forklift.) She smiled up at him and stuck a white flower behind his ear and a red one behind her own.

"That's for peace," she said quietly. "Not Peace forever, with a capital. Just peace between us, for this afternoon. Lower-case peace."

"The lower the better." He opened the car door for her. "I'm a dirty old man."

She looked up into his eyes. She was not smiling. "No," she said. "You're young and clean. I don't see how, but I think you are. And the peace is any way you want it."

He floated around the car and got in. Weightless as an astronaut, he pulled away from the curb and headed for the boat.

Lucius Hardy sat at a table in the canopied shade of the wide Army-Navy Club porch, watching Skeeter flit about the tennis courts below. He was waiting for General Morris Greenberg. He wondered what the dumpy Chemical Warfare Chief had on his mind. Hardy was mostly free of the anti-Semitism of his West Point generation, and liked Greenberg, whom he had known in Occupation days at Wiesbaden. He thought of him more as a technician than as a general officer, and attributed his unmilitary volatility and various fears to a lifetime of guilt at his unsavory specialty.

The porch creaked behind him and Greenberg, flustered and hot, sat down across the table. He was all wrong, in an aloha shirt and white slacks too tight over his belt, which was buckled with a Western horseshoe. "Thanks for coming, Lucius," Greenberg said, signaling a waiter. "Bloody Mary, or what?"

Hardy nodded and Greenberg filled out the chit, handed it to the white-coated steward, then sat back, wiping his face. He beamed at Hardy for being there, and then frowned at himself for asking him. "I hate to bother you on a Sunday."

Hardy told him that it had been no sweat, that they would probably have come down anyway, that he intended a round of golf later, if it didn't rain, that Skeeter was playing tennis now. Greenberg jumped as if jabbed, half-arose, spotted Skeeter on the court, and waved wildly, although she was in a hot rally and obviously could not see him. "Lovely girl," he commented (Skeeter was pushing fifty). "Wish I could get Bunny out there. Or me, even, for that matter."

Hardy suddenly remembered that a little of Greenberg went a long way. He abandoned a plan to talk him into the round of golf; he could move faster alone, and Morrie looked as if he had not played in years. They lifted their drinks. *"Prosit,"* said Greenberg, happily, remembering the Wiesbaden Field Officers' Club. Hardy clinked his glass and asked him what was on his mind.

"Two things," said Greenberg. "One's my own problem, the other's mutual." He told him that news of the bubonic plague at Da Nang had leaked to one Michael O'Hare, a young microbiologist who had developed an improved plague serum at Fort Detrick. "What the hell do I tell him, Lucius?"

Hardy rubbed his jaw thoughtfully. In 1968 the accidental gassing of six thousand sheep at the Army's Dugway Proving Ground in Utah had sparked Congressman McCarthy of New York into writing an anti-CBW book, prompting the President into announcing (the day before publication) a "No First-Use Policy" on biological weapons. There had been much hot wind generated along the Potomac for a cut in appropriations for Detrick and Edgewood Arsenal. Hardy himself had had to launch a CBW campaign on Greenberg's behalf. He had based his pitch on "secret" information that the U.S.S.R. was continuing to stockpile offensive bacteriological weapons and that the Chinese, having demonstrated to the satisfaction of half of Asia that the U.S. had used germ warfare in Korea, were experimenting with their own serum-resistant strains of plague, anthrax, and botulism. Hardy justified his warning as probably true, bacteriological warfare being, as everyone knew, the poor man's answer to nuclear warheads. Most of CBW's appropriations had survived, but Greenberg, who took Hardy's Intelligence estimates quite literally, had himself, with the Administration's tacit approval, diverted them into the development of hardier offensive strains. The defensive serums, vaccines, and antitoxins could come later, as they always did, once the lethal cultures had proved themselves. But later would be too late; there was none of O'Hare's vaccine available, and Greenberg was out of funds.

"I wish to hell we'd spent that money right," blurted Greenberg now.

"You did," Hardy assured him automatically. "Policy is still *Assured Destruction Against a Greater-than-Expected Threat,* and don't ever forget it." In his own mind it was simply bad luck that a medieval plague had caught the U.S. Army with its pants down. Anyway, there had been no GI cases to speak of; it was the poor Slopes in the hootches who were catching hell. (But that would be no comfort to the bleeding hearts, so the Pentagon had no intention of letting the public know that the impact of the U.S. Army on Vietnamese sanitation had produced the first epidemic of Black Death in seventy years.)

"This O'Hare, now," asked Hardy. "How long can you hold the son-of-a-bitch off?"

Not for long, Greenberg decided. He was a hot-headed young genius who had quit in a rage when he discovered that a botulism antitoxin he had developed had been tested on a volunteer before he considered it ready.

"That's interesting," murmured Hardy. "Had his *antiplague* vaccine been tested when he quit?"

"No."

"Suppose," Hardy conjectured, "some volunteer had died from that? Or from testing with plague, afterward?"

"Nobody did. It's ninety-six percent effective and a hundred percent safe."

"Does he *know* that?"

"No, but he presumes it, since he wasn't told differently."

"Well, do you ever spread the news, when you lose a volunteer?"

Greenberg protested that they had never lost one, and Hardy pointed out that O'Hare would hardly expect them to broadcast the news to civilians, if they did. "Right?"

"But damn it, Lucius, we *didn't* lose one!"

"I said *suppose,* Morrie! You're not stupid."

Greenberg didn't like the idea, not at all. "Lucius, it'll tear him apart! I just can't tell him *that!*"

"Can't you, Morrie? Think about it." Hardy sipped his drink. "Now, what's our *mutual* problem?"

Greenberg rubbed his eyes tiredly. "Your man Frost." His voice dropped, although there was no one else on the porch. "I think he knows. Ban Doc?"

Hardy stared at him. "Jesus, Morrie, I already told you! Some hippie broad gave him a picture of it. I showed it to you!"

"You said he thought it was a fake, though."

"Well, what makes you think he doesn't?"

Morrie chewed at his lips furiously. Hardy had a faint memory of him, similarly shaken, in Germany. They had driven down to Dachau for the regular tour of the camp. It was after the bodies had been removed, but there had not been enough time or Clorox to erase the faint reek of death from the chambers. They were looking at pictures of the mess the first troops had found when Greenberg had almost collapsed. Up to that time he had been a calm and contained little chemical officer; from that day on he had become a nervous, rabbity nail-chewer with his heart and his fears on his sleeve. Hardy studied him narrowly, now, wondering why it had affected him more than the rest. There had been other Jewish officers on the staff. Hell, you didn't have to be Jewish to feel the rage; it had rocked them all. Perhaps Greenberg had been more sensitive because the work had been done with gas.

"Lucius," Greenberg murmured now, so softly that Hardy had to lean forward to hear him, "it's been six weeks since Poma deserted. You and I've known about Ban Doc for a month. It's *misprision* that we didn't take action immediately. I mean, right then!"

Hardy sat back, angry. "All right, then we're already in violation. So don't sweat it."

"But why did we do it? Damn it, it's the Chemical Corps that would have suffered, not G-2! It would have hurt me worse than you! The damn movie team was along because *we* requested the training film, and I *still* wanted to buck it upstairs and take whatever licks were coming! Why didn't we, Lucius?"

"In the national interest?" suggested Hardy. "For the good of the Army?"

"That isn't good enough," Greenberg said heatedly. "We could get six years!"

Hardy sat back, thinking. If Greenberg had been more stable, he might even have leveled with him. But to entrust even a hint of Operation Strangle to this nervous little officer was unthinkable, at least until the Man decided yes or no.

"Keep the faith, Morrie. That's all I can say."

"But what about Frost?"

"I told you, I don't think Frost believes it at all," Hardy insisted. "He thinks that photo was posed in the field. Anyway, I took him off it. I told you that, too."

Greenberg, with the air of a man laying down an ace, whispered: "Then why did he call me last night, Lucius? Tell me that?"

Hardy stared at him *"Last* night? He was at our house last night. At a party." Damn, why had he said that? Greenberg and his warm, bubbly wife (whom neither he nor Skeeter had seen in years) had never even been in their home, after all the time together in Germany. And Greenberg, when he called last night, must have heard the party background in the den. Irritated because he had to explain, he said: "A party for G-2 types. Farewell to General Blanding."

Greenberg's moist lips slid into a grin, just a little too wide. "Sure, Lucius. G-2. I figured Frost was there. No, I mean *before* the party, he called. Last evening."

"Well, what did he say?" Hardy asked uncomfortably.

Greenberg told him, and Hardy's anger rose. Why the hell couldn't Lee leave it alone, before he found out too much? But hiding his displeasure, he said serenely: "That

172

doesn't mean a thing. He just had a last thought, that's all. He found out it was Army film, you knew that on Friday. He deduced from the gas mask that it was some kid hamming it up, pretending to shoot the woman during a Chemical Corps training film. It doesn't follow that he's sniffing out a massacre, does it? He's never heard of Poma."

Greenberg looked relieved. "I guess you're right."

"He'll probably come around tomorrow and tell me about it himself," said Hardy.

"Probably," admitted Greenberg. "He seems like a very conscientious officer."

"He is," Hardy assured him. Greenberg winced visibly. Hardy patted the chubby arm. "Not conscientious enough to lower the boom, Morrie; I don't mean that. Even if he knew."

"You sure?"

Hardy hesitated. Lee had changed. But loyalty was loyalty. "He was my plebe on the Plain," he said heartily. They had another drink and by the time Greenberg left, thunder was growling to the south. Hardy gave him time to get out of the building and moved to the phone at the entrance. He dialed Frost's home, and got Jenny.

"He's at his father's or working on the boat. Unless it's raining down there."

He hung up quickly and left to pry his wife from the tennis court, mid-set. While she was showering sullenly, he paused in the bar to pay his respects to a table dominated by the Army Chief of Staff, hiding his impatience well. But when he pulled away from the parking lot he nicked a fender for the first time in years.

"Stop and leave your name," demanded Skeeter.

It was raining in big, solid splats on his windshield. "Screw it," he growled, afraid he would miss Frost.

"My!" marveled Skeeter. She was thirty years an Army wife. Almost singlehandedly she had herded through adolescence two stubborn sons who towered above her now. She feared no one, but she knew her husband. She shut up and said no more.

Chapter Seven

When Lee Frost and Laurie reached the boat, the afternoon had already become sultry and the cumulus clouds to the north were heavy anvils hanging over the Potomac. He had intended to sail upriver under the Arlington Bridge and to anchor windward of Memorial Island, where the afternoon would be cool with grassy breezes from the Virginia shore. But by the time they got the tarp off the cockpit, it was whipping from their hands in violent gusts. To cast off and try it would have been fun; reefed-down, *Misty* would have flown northward with a bone in her teeth, but a wet, crazy ride up a frothing river was not the kind of excitement either had in mind, so he took the key from its hiding place in the lazarette and unlocked the hatch and they slipped into the tiny cabin. Then he slammed the hatch shut as the first drops slapped down hard.

The cabin was a dark cuddy, really not a cabin at all, not big enough for Lee (or Rick) to stand erect in, but he and his son had slept in it for two weeks on a cruise of the Potomac, gunkholing all the way to Point Lookout and Chesapeake Bay. Lee found forgotten beer cans from that trip and popped them open. A brass kerosene lamp hung on gimbals at the head of the bunks. Lee had kept it polished and full of fuel. Why, he didn't know: he never came below except to get brushes or paint or change to work clothes. Now he set a flame dancing against the gloom and cracked the portholes for air. He sat back, beer can in hand, watching Laurie as she poked around in everything, like a child in a new treehouse.

"She's just beautiful, below," she breathed. "Everything's brass!"

"Rick didn't like chrome. Jack London decor or nothing."

"I thought this was just a sail-locker. Why didn't you show me yesterday?"

"It seemed kind of, well, precipitous."

She grinned. "The way I throw myself at you, that's very sweet."

"My whole generation's up-tight."

"Yes," she agreed, "it is." She went back to her inspection, running her hands over a mahogany binocular-rack that Rick had turned out in his grandfather's workshop. "All this varnish, the little galley, it's like an infant yacht! But the *work!*"

He shrugged. "He didn't mind work."

"It's work to keep her up, and you do that."

"I don't keep her up worth a damn." He took a deep swig. "I'm selling her."

She stared at him. "The *hell* you are!" Not a question, an order.

"Keeping her is stupid," he explained. "I never sail her."

She kneeled on the bunk, brushed back the long hair flickering bronze in the lantern light. It was a gesture he was beginning to love. She looked gravely into his face. "We sailed her yesterday. Why *not* sail her more?"

Because, he wanted to say, it's no fun sailing alone, and my wife, if I could get her out of the goddamned apartment, would probably sink her cold. Instead he shrugged. "All a matter of what you like to do. I like handball and squash."

"What you like to do is sail, and your wife won't sail, and you're too proud to say it," she decided. "Keep her."

"My wife?"

"*Misty.* You now have a crew."

"I noticed," he said softly. "A very lovely and competent crew."

"An agile crew."

His heart was beginning to hammer. He kept his eyes on hers but his hands off her body. "Young, and supple," he said hoarsely.

"A truly fabulous crew," she whispered.

"A fabulous screw? Oh, the hell with it!" He crushed the beer can and let it fall to the cabin sole. "Games!

Come here!" A crash of thunder sounded, very close, and a quick gust of wind hurled rain through the tiny port above her, beading her cheeks with drops of gold; she did not even flinch. Instead, with a liquid motion, she slid down the bunk alongside him. "I thought," she said in a low voice, "you'd never ask." Her stubby fingers plucked at the buttons on his shirt, her tight little stomach thrust against his loins. Her hands slipped inside his shirt. He fumbled at the ridiculous, masochistic belt buckle she wore and peeled her Levi's over firm tanned thighs and rounded calves. He slithered, with her help, from his slacks and shorts; he ripped off her shirt and she his. She wore no bra, to his surprise; the firm, round breasts had fooled him—too good to be true. For a moment, at arm's length, he regarded her body, flawless from calloused toes to the tip of her silken head. He ran a finger along her thigh. "You are a fine Swiss watch," he said, feasting his eyes.

"A joke? Or an old song? Gruen!" she remembered, from somewhere. "'I gave her a gorgeous Gruen!'"

"That's from the Forties, or are you a witch?" He held her close, kissing her deeply; her tongue dodged and teased and finally she bit, almost too hard: "I'm a white female witch, five-feet-five inches, twenty-four, several previous convictions, on probation," she confessed, "in the arms of a satyr." Her fingers trailed up his leg, softly, and stopped, pressing tenderly. And so he took her, gently at first, with her firm legs grasping at his waist and her head thrashing wildly in the bronze lake of hair on his son's sleeping-bag; gently, then harder, feeling the power to torture her forever, as he pleased, loving the moans and cries, not even feeling the nails tearing at his back until, as she arched, he knew that he could hold back no longer, not one moment longer, but he did, and so help him, when he released the flow, it was to a peal of thunder and a blue-white flash that must have split the Potomac wide.

They lay for a long moment. There were tears on her cheeks; she was half-laughing, half-sobbing. "Can you *always* do that? The thunder?"

"I'm Thor," he said.

176

"You're—"

"Shut up," he commanded, "or I'll start a typhoon."

He lay back exhausted; he was asleep in seconds. When he awakened, a shaft of golden sunlight was sweeping in a great clockwise arc on the side of the cabin. *Misty* was rocking in her slip to the last swells of the squall. The girl lay beside him, studying his face.

"Hi, Thor," she said. She bounced to her knees, peered out the port and announced that they could sail now; he had cleared the air and the wind was upstream. "We could run up to that island," she speculated, "or . . ." She leered at him, evilly, and he felt the power again in his loins. *"Or . . ."*

"The 'or' sounds good," he said, but warned: "This isn't a precedent. I'm forty-six."

"You keep *saying* that," she protested, "and I don't give a damn!" She reached out and touched his bare shoulder, where he had taken the shrapnel, lying helpless on the torn knee, at Inchon. It made him uncomfortable, and when she asked if it was a war wound, he answered brusquely: "Yeah. Why?"

"From Korea, or Vietnam, or whatever?"

"Whatever," he said. "About this 'or' . . ."

"Korea?"

He nodded. "I've been telling you, I'm just a beat-up old soldier—"

"Don't hand me that *Across the River* shit. OK?" Her clear young eyes hardened. "And *then* you went to Nam?"

"Doesn't everybody?"

"Why? *Really* why? And please don't say 'because it was the only war we had.' "

"Well, it was."

"I'm growing very fond of you, Lee," she said soberly. "You're beautiful. But you're a damn fool."

"What gives you the background to say that?" he demanded, suddenly angry. "Four years at American U? Or your vast experience elsewhere?"

"It's self-evident," she said simply. "I'm twenty-four and I already know that it's stupid to make a career of being a target. You're forty-six and you think it's just great!"

177

The days when he thought it was great were long past, but he was not going to admit it to her. "Groovy's the word," he said. "Not great."

"But for Christ's sake, *why?*"

He had not thought of "why" since Rick had asked years ago why he had ever enlisted. Lee had fought to join, battled his aunt; fought his father, too, in the Philippines, who had not really cared but backed his sister-in-law as a matter of policy. On the eve of his eighteenth birthday Lee had rocketed down to the Presidio parade ground, a lanky adolescent in corduroy pants and a high-school letterman's sweater, to watch Retreat. Sitting astride his father's battered motorcycle, he had affected an air of nonchalance, which probably had fooled no one, since everyone knew he was signing up. The drums had throbbed. Lieutenant Foley, West Pointer and hero of a thousand daydreams, had swung by with his dad's old platoon, saber flashing, and passed him a wink. (Lee remembered a quick adolescent fantasy: the lieutenant pinned down, wounded by a Nazi machine gun, and Lee slithering toward him, butt-down, using the terrain: "Hello, Lieutenant." "Hello, Frost. You come to help, or draw more fire?" "I came to ask about those corporal's stripes, sir. . . . Where'd they hit you?") *Tomorrow,* in *one more day,* he would be one of them, and then, if America would just get into the war, where it belonged, and *if the war would just last long enough* . . . It hadn't, for he had gambled and gone to the Point, and missed it, all but a few months on Okinawa, when it was almost over.

"*Why,* Lee?" she demanded. "Of all the things you might have done—"

"I joined," he said, "for a different war."

"Are there different wars?"

"Yes, Virginia," he said bitterly. "There are different wars."

"But why'd you *stay* in?"

"Because I missed the one I joined for."

"And did you ever find it?"

"No," he admitted. "I didn't."

He turned away impatiently, his passion dead, ready to settle for the sail, after all, or something to eat in Georgetown. He was mired in the swamp of life-as-it-was and she was pelting him with childish questions from the landscaped prospect of life-as-it-ought-to-be.

"Then *why?*" she persisted.

"Man is an animal," he told her. "Face it."

"You malign animals."

"A flawed animal?" he suggested, a theory of Rick's.

Someone knocked suddenly on the bow. "Ahoy, on the *Misty?*" It sounded like Hardy's voice. Lee sat bolt upright, cracking his head on a beam as the voice rose: "Lee?" There was another imperious, startling tapping from the forepeak; a class ring on the side of the hull, Lee decided. He had a quick memory of the same rap on a door in Beast Barracks, equally galvanizing, equally ominous.

"Stay put," he muttered. "My boss." He yanked on his pants and popped out of the cabin. General Lucius Hardy, in golfing slacks, had hauled in the bow and was getting ready to board; to preclude this, Lee slammed the hatch and scrambled forward, ready to vault to the dock. Inhospitably, he said: "I was just securing. Can't varnish, rain and all. What's up, Lucius?"

Lucius was not pleased. "Can I come aboard a minute? Something I want to talk to you about."

"Yes sir," said Lee, hoping that another quick squall would not suggest shelter below. He held out a hand, helped the general aboard, and led him aft to the cockpit. The seats were wet, and the flotation pillows out of reach with Laurie below. To keep the general's pants dry, they perched on the cockpit combing. Hardy regarded Lee curiously. He seemed suddenly to have had second thoughts or to have forgotten what he came for.

"I'd offer you a beer," Lee said lamely, to break the silence, "but I'm out."

"No beer, thanks," said the general. Another long silence. Lee asked if Skeeter was with him. Yes, she was in the car, not having wanted to get her sandals wet. Hardy, once talking, seemed to have made a decision. "Why'd you call Greenberg last night?"

"I got curious."

"I told you to stay off that thing."

179

"Well, it may have started as a training film, and—"

"I don't want to discuss it. That is a direct order, Lee; stay off it."

"Well, who's *on* it, Lucius?"

"I don't want to discuss it. I told you."

"Then it may not be a *lawful* order, am I right?"

Hardy stiffened. His face grew white. *Misty* strained at her lines and her jib-halyard began to slap the mast as a rear-guard gust from the fleeing storm made the rigging sing. The general stood abruptly, looking down at Lee.

"I am reading you, Colonel," he said slowly, "loud and clear." He dropped his voice strangely, as if afraid of being overheard. "But my advice to you, Lee, is still to stand down! Is that clear?"

"It's clear, sir," said Lee. "The reason isn't."

"Damn shame," said Hardy and abruptly left. Lee watched him march rigidly up the dock. He went below, puzzled and disturbed. Laurie waited, nude, cross-legged on the bunk, studying an old *Guide to Inland Waterways*. She slid it back with Rick's books on the tiny fiddled shelf.

"You never introduced us," she protested. "Are you ashamed of me?"

"Not you," he said. "The General. Sex-offender. Record long as your arm."

"Offend *me,*" she suggested, and flowed into his arms again.

Lucius Hardy climbed into his car in the marina parking lot. He slammed the door viciously. Skeeter looked at him, wide-eyed. "Wasn't he there?"

"He was there." Hardy drummed the steering wheel for a moment. "Tell me, Skeeter. Does Jenny ever discuss her sex life?"

She had never been a gossip. "Oh, come *on!*" She saw his jaw tense and changed her mind. "Yes. Last night. In short, since Rick, there ain't none." She stared at him. "Has he got a woman down there?"

"A woman," said Hardy, starting the car, "or a wildcat. You ought to see his back."

180

"Jenny will," groaned Skeeter. "Oh, God! Did you tell him?"

"No," he said. "Let the son-of-a-bitch fry."

He roared from the lot. He hit nothing this time, but when he got home he sat for an hour in his den, staring blindly at the pictures on the walls and sipping Scotch, and when Skeeter called him for dinner he ate hardly anything at all.

Chapter Eight

The Aerodyne–L.A. complex sprawled vastly at the seaward edge of a pool of tan smog that ebbed and flooded against the ocean breezes. Until afternoon westerlies swept away the airborne garbage, it seeped into factory air-conditioning and seemed to Bull Collins to leave an acrid odor on every scrap of paper and to rise even from the office carpets along executive row. Bull lounged in the sanctum of the Director of Military Sales, dabbing at his eyes and longing for the relatively clean air of Washington. Above Sonny's desk, an oil painting of the Old Man, cruising now in Mexico, smiled cynically down on his only issue. Sonny, pushing fifty now himself and heavy in the jowls where the Old Man was lean and taut, always seemed diminished by the portrait, but apparently lacked the guts to shit-can it while his father lived. Now he glanced nervously up from the top-secret memo Bull had lifted. "How the hell did you get this?"

"Anything for Aerodyne, Sonny." Bull did not like his immediate boss and loved to risk calling him Sonny, although another Aerodyne sales-rep who had tried it had ended up running a company office on a dingy back-street in Athens. "How I got it's a long story. But Admiral Strickland alerted me. I think we owe him a job."

Sonny seemed uncomfortable. "Don't commit us. Even if we win."

"Aye-aye, sir," Bull said companionably. He could always go to the Old Man in a pinch; right now, he wanted Sonny squarely in his corner against Hound Dog Cassell and Engineering. "We *won't* win unless I hand that proposal in tomorrow. Modified."

Sonny looked distressed. "Bull, I think you have to back down. Ask Air Force Evaluation for a five-day extension—"

"They won't grant it. General Dynamics would be all over them, screaming favoritism."

"Then submit it as is or Hound Dog will quit. We can't afford that."

"Well," Bull suggested, "can you afford it if *I* quit?"

"Aw, now look—"

"While your dad's away?"

"Don't twist my arm, goddamn it," blazed Sonny.

"Well, can you?"

"It would be embarrassing," Sonny conceded. "But I doubt if he'd fire *me*."

Bull was not so sure. For years the Old Man had watched him and his son approach battle for the vice-presidency of sales, held now by a good-natured relic of the company's days of fabric skins and spruce wingspars. Sonny was ahead not because his father was president— the Old Man hated nepotism—but because the son had chained himself to L.A. headquarters, fighting the Old Man's political skirmishes, and because Bull's last divorce had been messy enough to alienate the board of directors. But the vice-presidency still dangled before both as a prize, and Bull suspected that this was what the Old Man had plotted all along.

"Besides," Sonny continued, "you're not about to quit."

He was right, of course. Bull would stick, as much to frustrate Sonny as to capture the twenty-thousand-dollar bonus the Old Man had promised if the proposal won. Sonny's reluctance to pressure Cassell now might mean that secretly he hoped Aerodyne's baby would die in the Pentagon womb. Bull moved to the window, thinking. Past the factory's bleak green buildings, government-built in World War II and sold to the company for a song, lay the deserted concrete runway of the Culver City airport, which had drawn the Old Man to locate here in the first place. Between factory buildings and landing-field lay acres of parking space, empty except for a few dozen cars outside Cassell's working area. Bull's company car, with the stewardess who waited for him, was parked in the Old Man's spot. A young company guard lounged at the passenger window, probably nursing a hard-on as he shot the breeze with the girl. Bull had a sudden premonition that she would entice him into the car. Instead, the guard opened the door, the girl got out, fine legs shimmering and smile flashing, and the two disappeared into the parking-lot's security shack.

Bull chuckled. Damn! Coffee or something hotter? Behind him Sonny said: "What's so funny?"

"Just thinking how empty the parking lot is. And the airstrip. Remember how it was with the Skyshark contract?"

"Well, it's Sunday; never on Sunday, as they say."

"*Even* on Sunday we used to have four thousand cars in there, overtime, graveyard, night-and-day, half of them new T-Birds. What do sheetmetal workers do in this town now? What do engineers do? Sell soap?"

"OK, *OK!*"

"You're going to lose them *all*. You've got an obligation—"

"Obligation?" Sonny's porcine eyes flashed. "Listen, there isn't a goddamn aeronautical engineer here now, and never has been, who wouldn't leave us for twenty bucks a week more at Lockheed or Boeing. Don't ever forget it!"

"All right," Bull said reasonably, "so if Hound Dog leaves, so what?"

"Hound Dog's an exception! He doesn't care about money, just getting it done right, like the Old Man." He jerked his head toward the portrait. "If Hound Dog says he won't change it and submit it quick-and-dirty, then he won't, and we'll have to submit it as is. I'm damned if I'll force him. The Old Man'd kill me. Is that clear?"

"Sure, Sonny," grinned Bull. "Explain how we lost the bid when he gets back, OK?"

Sonny looked miserable. "Well, Jesus, I don't know what to do!"

"Offer Hound Dog a bonus for his team. Hound Dog cares about his *team!* Tell him if he'll submit it modified, right or wrong, you'll give everybody a five-per-cent raise, except the idiot who screwed up the weight-and-balance."

"The budget won't support it. Neither will my dad. Because suppose we lose the contract anyway?"

"Then you lay them off," explained Bull.

Sonny shook his head. "I've got a better idea. I won't

184

take a stand at all. I'll leave the office and won't answer the phone at home. Sell Cassell as hard as you want. Hell, you can sell anything!"

"You're too kind."

"The Old Man thinks you can," Sonny said, with some bitterness. "OK, if you talk Cassell into it, fine. And if he wants to quit, I can still calm him down and we'll get him back."

Bull wondered if he seriously expected him to act as fall-guy, or if he was kidding. But Sonny was a humorless man, and apparently meant it. "Sure," Bull said affably. "You're a great executive, Sonny." He glanced at the fierce portrait above the desk and the timorous man beneath it. "You know, sometimes I think you were strained through a sheet."

Sonny half-rose in his chair: "I'll mention that remark when he gets back!"

"I doubt it," smiled Bull. He closed the door gently behind him and headed for the domain of Hound Dog Cassell.

Hound Dog had lodged his proposal group in the Whale Tank, named for a Gargantuan Aerodyne cargo plane that had never got past the wooden mock-up state. The building loomed massively in the afternoon haze between administration and the airstrip. It was a hangar-like structure painted the same shade of government-green as the rest of the Aerodyne-L.A. complex, a tone identical to that at Hughes, McDonnell-Douglas, North American, Boeing, or Lockheed, so that an engineer job-jumping from one corporation to another could sometimes forget just where he was.

Inside the hangar, the resident whale, a mammoth construction of pine and plywood, had been abandoned by Aerodyne and the Air Force at budgetary low-tide in the fiscal cuts of '70. The beast was quite dead, but its carcass, long ago stripped of laminated skin by Lilliputian carpenters, stretched centrally the length of a football field. Its ribs and backbone were still surrounded by scaffolding. Presumably, if Bull won the AFX contract for Aerodyne,

185

the skeleton would be hauled away and its cavernous tomb would come to life again.

The whole area was under tight security, more against industrial spies from General Dynamics than lurking agents of the Reds. The guard saluted the golden company identification badge that ranked Bull at department-head level and passed him into the vast interior. He walked down the length of the abandoned carcass toward a glare of flourescent light where Hound Dog's draftsmen, engineers, cost-analysts, and programmers were breaking camp. Some had been sleeping by their drawing-boards for weeks. He heard Hound Dog's strident voice echoing over a hand-held bull-horn and saw his scarecrow figure addressing his troops from the mezzanine. While he talked, his men rolled sleeping-bags, covered drafting-boards, knocked down wooden cots, and drifted wearily toward the exits.

Hound Dog's words were tight with affection. He did not, he explained, want to see even one of the crazy bastards coming to work on Monday or Tuesday: "Go home, get drunk, screw the old lady, meet your kids. And get some sleep."

Bull climbed the stairs and followed him to his bleak office. Hound Dog's eyes were red and tired, his iron-gray hair sprouted ludicrously, he had a faint stubble of silver on his jaw, the vertical lines in his face had deepened, and he looked more like Don Quixote with a slipstick than ever. He regarded Bull without enthusiasm. "You here to pick it up?"

Bull nodded. Hound Dog hoisted a leather-bound folder the size of the L.A. phonebook from his desk and held it out. Bull did not take it. "Cockpit modifications in there?" he demanded.

"No. As I told you, they're not valid."

"Valid or invalid, I want them in there. When we get the contract, we'll submit for restudy. And charge 'em."

"No."

"It isn't my fault you screwed-up, Hound Dog."

"It isn't?" Hound Dog's eyes bulged, a sign of impending explosion. But his voice remained low. "When you spring a cockpit change forty-eight hours before the dead-

186

line? And a young aeronautical engineer, after a hundred hours at his desk *this* week and God knows how little sleep *last* week makes a mistake in weight-and-balance, and—"

"Who was he, incidentally?"

"A perfectly competent, well-trained man miscalculates because he's been given forty-eight hours to do a four-day job, and it isn't your fault? You're out of your fucking mind!"

"Put in the mods, Hound Dog," Bull said evenly.

"Bullshit!"

"Call Sonny," suggested Bull.

Hound Dog, seamed face flaming and eyes popping, fumbled for his phone. He dialed a number, waited, dialed it again. Finally he asked the company operator to connect him with Sonny's home. He waited again and slammed down the receiver. "I can't get him."

"*I* got him. He says submit it modified, right or wrong; we'll pick up the pieces later." He looked at his watch. "Got to catch the 6:15, so let me have the changes."

"Or what?"

"Or fight it out with Sonny, I don't care. *I* don't care if you quit."

"Apparently he doesn't, either."

"Apparently not."

"That son-of-a-bitch! Twenty years! All right, I'll quit!"

"OK. Where are the changes?"

"In the safe. Those I keep for the Old Man when he comes back. He can decide whether we should have defrauded the government."

Bull picked up the bulky proposal. He hefted it speculatively. "Ten pounds, fifteen?"

"You selling it by the pound?"

"How many man-hours, Hound Dog? A quarter-million? Half a million, maybe?"

"You'll miss your frigging plane," muttered Hound Dog.

"How many men, Hound Dog?" Bull persisted. "How many kids didn't get to go camping with Daddy this summer? How many pissed-off wives? How many divorces in this here proposal, my friend? Ten, fifteen?"

"You're breaking my heart."

"How many of your designers are you going to throw out of work when General Dynamics wins? Just because you got to protect your repuation?"

Hound Dog smiled, suddenly and sweetly. "But Bull, my reputation's all I got. No wife, no kids, no mama-san, no papa-san. I don't have the Congressional Medal. I'm not even the world's greatest cocksman. All I got's the reputation, Bull. A hairy-assed engineer."

"Sure," said Bull. *"You'll* always have a job. Here, or somewhere. What about the others? Where are they going? You seen the Unemployment Insurance lines? Around the block with defense engineers!"

That got him. The silly bastards, Bull Collins reflected, had to be reminded that the world outside had turned cold. They had been sucking off the public tit for so long that they couldn't believe the nipple was running dry. The American taxpayer, soaked almost twice for his military establishment compared to what the Soviet citizen was for his (and thirty-five times what the Chinaman was) was turning from pigeon to dove. The "defense" industry still supported directly one out of five American engineers and blue-collar workers, one out of ten scientists, and, directly or indirectly, kept food on the table of one out of seven wage-earners. But if the Pentagon didn't stir up a fight or the threat of one somewhere (and soon), California was doomed. "It's the last contract in sight," Collins warned, "but *I* don't care. Let 'em starve; they're yours, not mine."

Hound Dog fiddled with a plastic model of the Skyshark on his desk. He had built that plane, and loved it, and now the last of the line was getting away. He looked up. "In forty-eight hours we can submit it right."

"We don't have forty-eight hours! Does General Dynamics need forty-eight hours?"

"Are they modifying their cockpit?"

"You're damn right they are," lied Bull. "You think they weren't told?"

Hound Dog wavered. "Suppose somebody on Air Force Evaluation or Source Selection runs a weight-and-balance check? It'll cast a stigma on our whole damn design."

"I'll handle Evaluation," promised Bull. "And Source

Selection is three generals, an admiral, and a NASA adviser that thinks a slipstick comes in a jockstrap. There won't be a real engineer gets a shot at this for six months. Jesus, you talk like they were going to test-fly it tomorrow!"

Hound Dog drummed his desk, paced the floor, rubbed his jaw, and finally asked if Bull thought he could borrow the proposal back long enough next week to slip into it corrected pages for the ones in the safe. Bull doubted privately that he could get back a sealed proposal once submitted, but right now he would promise anything to get the cockpit changes out of the safe and into his dispatch case. "My God, Hound Dog, you've done it again! Of course I can!"

Hound Dog dialed the combination, jerked out a dozen blueprints smelling of processing, and handed them reluctantly to Bull. "These you burn when you get the corrected pages. Right?"

"Sure," promised Bull. He stuffed them into his dispatch case along with the proposal itself. "If I had time, I'd buy you a drink."

"I'll buy my own drinks," Hound Dog growled. "Just sell the package."

Bull started for the door and snapped his fingers. "I forgot. I talked Sonny into a five-per-cent raise for your whole damn team."

"You did?" Hound Dog exclaimed. He looked suspicious. "I wonder why?"

"Precedent. I want to make sure I get my bonus."

Hound Dog bought it. "Jesus," he beamed, "is it official?"

"You can announce it," Bull said cheerfully from the door. "Announce it loud and clear."

Let Sonny straighten that one out with the Old Man, he thought gleefully, at about the time he himself brought back the award in triumph. He imagined an oaken door on executive row: Robert E. "Bull" Collins, Major, USMCR (CMH), Vice-President, Sales. Seventy-five thousand a year and options, a secretary plucked from Sunset Strip, and a Bigelow carpet asshole-deep to a tall giraffe. A long way from jungle-rot, fighter-pilot piles, and flame over Buckner Bay, and from the pain of watching squadron-mates ten years later, when they should have learned caution, creamed on Korean mountainsides. He had suffered as much as any man in his country's holy causes, but things were getting better all the time.

When Lee found Jenny's Danish pastry in the cupboard as he was rummaging for the sugar bowl, Jenny, washing the dishes, winced.

"Well," she said blushing, "you know my secret." She flashed him, tentatively, the new, rubber smile. "Take one."

He shook his head and replaced the package. He carried his coffee to his easy chair by the TV and switched on the news. He shifted in his seat: his back felt sunburned. Perhaps, since they hadn't left the slip or even the cabin today, it was scorched from yesterday's sail with the girl. In a moment Jenny was behind him, running her finger along his sideburn. "Lee? I'm sorry about the coffeecake."

"It's *your* weight," he shrugged. (Her heart, too, and her goddamned cholesterol and blood sugar and all the other things they had warned her of, but he had learned that to dwell on that was stupid; it only made her nibble more.)

"I lost two pounds this week," she bragged, settling onto the couch.

It didn't show. "I thought so," he lied. "Good for you."

His mind wandered as she discussed a new diet in *Good Housekeeping,* his attention riveting finally on a girl in a commercial who became Laurie as she ran toward him in slow-motion, lithe as a deer, and he was the lover she was rushing toward in long, graceful strides. He could even smell the meadow she pranced through. He almost reached out to take her into his arms.

He arose, stretching and easing his smarting back. "Hitting the sack," he explained. "Got to go to Edgewood tomorrow." He stripped to his shorts and brushed his teeth. Jenny waddled in and they were turning back the spread when the phone rang. She answered and handed it to him. "Lucius Hardy, Lee."

"Yes sir?" Lee answered formally, sitting on the bed.

Hardy spoke harshly, as if he were addressing a POW or a larcenous supply officer. "Don't know why I'm warning you, Colonel. I ought to let you hang yourself. But things are rough enough on Jenny already."

"I don't get you, General."

"If I were you, Lochinvar, I'd check for clawmarks before I started flashing that beautiful torso around. You read me?"

Lee tensed. *Son-of-a-bitch!* Hardy could have told him *that* at the boat. "I understand, sir," he said. "It may be a little late, but thank you."

"Don't thank me. Thank Skeeter."

There was a brutal click. Lee sat for a moment, gathering his courage, before he got up, turning to Jenny. She was standing at the window, looking out, fiddling with the air-conditioner. He tried to decide if her stance was rigid, or only seemed so, if her shoulders were taut or his guilt only made them appear to be.

She swung back, chin up, and her eyes met his. They were bright, tearless, but unreadable. He smiled dubiously, feeling like an idiot.

"What did he want?" she asked.

He made a decision to lie. If it was the easy way out, he could rationalize it later. "He wanted me to bug that woman's apartment. The typist. Ellsworth's secretary."

"And he was too late because you already had?"

He nodded. His lips felt dry and an ache began behind his eyes. "First thing I did."

She climbed into bed. "He should have known that, shouldn't he? I mean, doesn't he read Dick Tracy?"

He grunted noncommittally, still wondering if she had spotted the scratches, which seemed to smart more, now that he knew what they were. She picked up *Rise and Fall*. If Lucius had spotted them so quickly, they must be foot-long welts, or worse, but apparently she had missed them. She turned to him, and suddenly he was not so sure that she had missed them at all. "When you left yesterday, you

191

were going to 'bang' her, as you so delicately put it. You didn't tell me how she was."

"The typist? You didn't ask."

"I forgot. Now I'm all on pins and needles."

He climbed cautiously between the sheets, careful not to expose his back. "You bang one secretary, you've banged them all."

"Yes," she smiled, "I guess if you do, you have. Did you?"

He studied her narrowly. Her face was innocent. "You aren't serious?" he asked carefully.

"Of course not," she said offhandedly. "Who knows better than I how celibate you are?"

"Well," he said tersely, "I've had help."

Her eyes filled with tears. "Damn you, that's not fair. You know what Gerstel says!"

Gerstel was her psychiatrist at Walter Reed Medical Center, a bright-eyed, birdlike young major who talked too much. "Colonel, face it. Rick was conceived illegitimately. Jenny interprets his death as a punishment on her. She wants to punish you, too. Her partner in crime, you know?"

"In crime? Gerstel, Rick was born in 1950, not 1850! We didn't consider a roll in the hay a crime!"

"Not consciously. And not you, maybe, at all. But her." Thus, according to Gerstel, her frigidity since Rick's death; thus, wrapping it all in a neat package, her obesity, sublimating her sexual drive at the same time she cooled his own. Now Lee seized on Gerstel gratefully. "That fag shrink!"

"That fag shrink has probably saved me from suicide!"

"Oh, come on! He wasn't talking about you cutting your wrists. He was talking about your eating too much. And you still do that."

"Suicide's suicide. If I die, I die, and he's helping me not to."

"How? Hell, you're stronger than he is. And a hell of a lot smarter. And probably less neurotic. Why's he in the Army? In love with his uniform, or blowing the poor damn GIs they give him to fiddle with? If he knew his ass from his elbow, he'd be outside getting rich."

"Maybe," Jenny proposed viciously, "I should go to a civilian at fifty bucks an hour."

"You couldn't do worse than him at any price!"

"And *you* couldn't do worse than that Pentagon whore, and she's going to use you! Wait 'til she quotes you *her* price!"

He stared into angry, tearful eyes, stroked the bloated cheek, once so perfectly curved, and felt a surge of affection. "What kind of idiot do you think I am?"

"A horny idiot," she said, beginning to cry in earnest. "Because of me, I guess. Lee, *did* you?"

If it was his back, he would have to tell her that she suspected the wrong woman on the wrong day. He hated evading her, and doubted that he could carry off a real lie; after twenty-one years together, he didn't want to try. "What brought this on?"

"Sitting in front of TV, while I was talking, you were smiling kind of, well, the way you can smile. You haven't smiled at *me* like that for a year!"

He was relieved, but guilty, too, for he hadn't *felt* like smiling at her for a year, and couldn't fake it. He kissed her lightly. "I promise, Jenny, I give you my word, I never laid a hand on her." Not precisely a lie, that, not a lie at all. Besides, he was saving her agony. "My God, I may have to file Security charges against that woman! You think I'd lay a hand on *her?*"

She grinned through the tears. "Look, Ma, no hands?"

"No hands, no feet, no nothing." He kissed her again and suddenly, for the first time since the Army's telegram on Rick, she seemed to respond, or was she faking it? For a moment his passions glowed, and then he went dead.

"Pooped," he mumbled finally. "Good night, honey." He turned out the light, and when he felt that she slept, he got up quickly and padded to the bathroom to check his bare back in the mirror. Laurie had clawed him, all right; the sight and memory of it warmed his blood. It would be a week before he could go shirtless. He ordinarily slept barechested in shorts, a holdover from enlisted days, but now he drew on a T-shirt: he could always claim a cough.

Jenny must have got up too, sometime during the night, for when he slipped from bed in the morning to make his

193

coffee, he found the Danish pastry eaten, the wrapping stuffed into the garbage, and crumbs on the sink.

He wondered if after all she *had* seen his back last night. Without waking her, he dressed and went to work.

Chapter Nine

When Lee reached his office Monday morning he found the transcript of Sherry Pace's phone calls, taped in the van across the street from her apartment, typed neatly by Thelma and lying on his desk. He inspected the sheets, double-spaced and legal-sized, over his coffee. The first call was just after his visit.

> *SATURDAY, 4 AUGUST*
> *10:37 Outgoing, dial to 628-4200 (Number registered to Marriott Twin Bridges Motor Hotel, Arlington, Va.).*
> *Recipient: Good morning. Marriott Twin Bridges.*
> *Female Originator: Mr. Collins, in 217E?*
> *Recipient: Thank you. (Eight rings follow.) I'm sorry, there's no answer. (Call terminated.)*

Collins? There were obviously a lot of Collinses, but a good one to start with might be the Marine who rubbed her neck when otherwise unoccupied. His pulse began to drum. It was time to find out just how far the old-time ace had climbed in rank. He drew a worn Navy Register from his bookcase, leafed to the Marine section, and looked in vain for a Collins with both the Congressional Medal and the "NA" designator, which meant wings. Thoughtfully, he slid the book back in. Well, no one had actually told him that the beefy flier in civvies was still in the Service; he had simply assumed it from the Congressional Medal lapel pin and the proprietary way he had been floating around the Brass Ring. Maybe Pentagon officers should be encouraged to go back to wearing uniforms, to separate the sheep from the goats. He continued his search through Service directories, finally finding a Robert E. Collins,

Major, USMCR (Retired), CMH, in a register of reserve personnel. So the florid satyr, if he had legitimate business at all in the Pentagon, represented not the Corps but something else.

He called Security Review. The Clearance Clerk told him that one Robert E. "Bull" Collins, retired from his country's battles, held a top-secret clearance and had represented Aerodyne-LA in the Pentagon for almost fifteen years.

Aerodyne rang a bell, too, as the company Congressman Ab Dennes had predicted would benefit most from the leak of the Israeli-Greek plane deal. It was probably parochial to distrust Collins more as a civilian than as a regular Marine officer, but not unfair at all to suspect him if he had a company interest in leaking the memo, especially since Sherry had apparently phoned him only minutes after Lee had left her apartment Saturday. He scanned the rest of the transcript: six more calls to the Marriott, one every hour on Saturday, no answers. On Sunday, an outgoing call from Jordie, who discussed with a friend a stolen tape deck from a '68 Merc, bennies, reds, hash, shit, and speed. Interesting for later, if they had to put muscle on Mama, but he continued down the page through a dozen more unanswered calls from the woman to Collins, until he found the last, at eight P.M. last night. There was no answer then, either, only word from the desk clerk that Mr. Collins was in California, but usually returned by early Monday morning.

He glanced at the clock. Sherry was already five minutes late for her lie-detector test. He had Thelma call her at home, and her son reported that she had already left, and now he began really to worry. He wanted the woman to contact Collins, but only by home or office phone, both already tapped. If she had decided to visit the Aerodyne rep in his unbugged room at the Marriott, they had missed their chance to hear what passed between them, even though Leibholtz would presumably tail her there on his motorbike.

Homer Troy bustled in with a photo of his newest obscene mural, found in the basement ladies' room not a hundred yards from the office door. "Good, Homer, stay

196

on it," Lee said distractedly. Finally he left for the Marriott himself. He swung into the parking lot opposite a row of varicolored doors fronting on a veranda, and checked to see that it contained 217E. He saw Liebholtz's Honda parked nearby, and then spotted the fox-eyed agent moving soft-drink cases near a Coke machine, trying to pass as a vendor. Lee parked and picked a newspaper from the seat, pretending to read it until Liebholtz noticed him. The sergeant wandered over, dragging a crate of empties, and paused to light a cigarette.

"217E?" Lee said quietly, without looking at him.

"The Colonel's fantastic," marveled Liebholtz, between his teeth.

"Fantastic," Lee agreed, "but a little late. Go get a cup of coffee, and I'll cover for a while. And bug his room first chance you get. With imagination, too, OK?"

Leibholtz lifted the crate to his shoulder and left the lot. Lee, who would have given a month's pay to overhear the conversation upstairs, settled down and waited for Sherry Pace to leave.

Bull Collins had had no choice but to let Sherry Pace into his room. She sat on the bed and faced him as he glanced at the work-piled hotel desk and tried to arrange his priorities. He had to insert the modifications into the proposal and to deliver it to Air Force Evaluation by high noon, then to contact a girl he knew on the House Armed Services Committee staff and try to find out why Congressman Weintraub had been so ungrateful as not to release the Israeli-Greek plane deal over the weekend, after Bull had risked his ass to make sure he found out about it. But first he had obviously to deal with the frightened woman sitting tensely on the bed. When she told him that the memo had been discovered on her desk by Frost's Spook Patrol, he felt a twinge of guilt: he should have at least hidden it under her blotter. But when she told him of Frost's visit to her apartment Saturday, the guilt turned to rage. The damn-fool Congressman had apparently turned the memo in, like a Boy Scout, and Security was in full cry. He wondered if she had been followed. He moved to the closed Venetian blind, pulled up a slat, and peered down into the parking lot. There was no one there but a soft-drink salesman, and he was leaving with a crate of empties.

"Why'd you come here?" he demanded. "You know damn well I didn't lift your memo!"

"If you didn't, why do you care if I came here or not?" He restrained an impulse to slam his fist into the caked makeup. She smelled like a distillery, her eyes were red, he began to wonder how he had ever gotten it up to lay her in the first place. He explained that of all times for a factory rep to be involved in a Security investigation, this was the worst. "I'm submitting a proposal today!" He waved his hand at the jumbled desk. "I've spent a year bird-dogging this! Suppose they suspend my clearance, say? Even for a week? Christ, nobody in Evaluation or Selection or Review will give me the time of day without a top-secret!" He had another thought. He lifted the pile of phone messages, accumulated through the weekend. "They keep copies of these at the front desk. Suppose he starts sniffing around here? You must have called a dozen times!"

She told him that she had been scared. "I got to thinking, who'd steal it? Who even knew about it? Well, you knew, because I told you!"

"Did you tell *him* that?"

"You got to be kidding! They'd be shooting me now! But he saw you hanging over my shoulder Wednesday, while I was typing it. Didn't he?"

Bull had forgotten that. "Jesus! He probably thinks I *did* take it!" He thought for a moment. "Does he know you spent Thursday night here?"

She said that she hadn't thought it was any of Frost's business, and he agreed. "Sherry?"

"Yeah?"

"I'm asking you now. *Don't* tell him."

She shrugged. "If you didn't take it, what difference does it make?"

He took a deep breath and told her that he was married.

"You said you were divorced," she reminded him, without much interest.

He mustered his most embarrassed smile. "Guys must

198

tell you that all the time, don't they? I mean, a girl with a build like yours, and face? I was hot for you, I still am, and hell, you know . . ." He gave himself a jealous wife, not essentially unlike his last, and a fictional son who worshiped him. "He's only ten. He's delicate, Sherry, health-wise. Leukemia! We don't mention it, but he needs his mother, and he needs me, even if I am back East most of the time trying to earn enough for his treatments. He just couldn't stand up to a divorce. If Thursday night came out in the papers, and it would, don't kid yourself, with a Congressional leak and all—you told me some Congressman got hold of that memo—hell, it'd be all over the Coast. I'd lose my job—"

"Look, Bull," she said heatedly, "I'm sorry about your little boy. But you've been catting it up around the Pentagon for fifteen years that *I* know of, so don't try to turn *me* into a home-wrecker. If you say you didn't take the memo, OK, but I've probably *lost* my job already, and I got a kid, too, in and out of trouble all the time, and I want to know what to do!"

Bull studied his hands, looked her straight in the eye, and announced virtuously that she should tell the truth.

"The whole truth?" she prodded.

"Well, anything that applies."

"But you don't apply?"

"Of course not."

"That figures," she said, standing up. "Thanks, Bull. You've been a great help."

"Any time," he said.

"Like tonight?" she asked suddenly.

He looked pained. "Jesus, Sherry, I have to go back to L.A."

"To see your son?"

"Well," he said cautiously, sensing a sharper brain than he had suspected, "on business, primarily. But I'll probably see him, too."

"That's sweet." She smiled and half-opened the door. "One thing. I got a date with Colonel Frost for a lie-detector test this morning."

"A *lie-detector* test?"

She nodded. "Suppose he asks me if I saw you again

after he noticed you drooling over my shoulder Wednesday? And *I* say, no, I haven't seen you. Will that show?"

Bull felt his heart settle heavily. His whole being protested against the injustice of it. He had no answer. She stepped closer and looked up into his face. "Will that show, Bull? *Or blow up the goddamn machine?*"

He drew her gently inside and closed the door. "You got a lawyer?" he asked dismally.

"There," she said comfortably, patting his cheek. "That wasn't so hard, was it? I *knew* behind that rugged chest you had a heart of gold." She sat down, crossed her legs, and indicated the phone companionably. "Whoever Aerodyne wants to use is jake by me. Hey, you got a drink?"

Lee Frost stiffened when he saw the special Pentagon visitor's sticker on the fast-moving Lincoln Continental swerving into the parking lot. The car glided into a nearby space. The driver was Charles Brewster Hammond, III, ex-JAG colonel, currently the most expensive civilian specialist on military law in Washington. Ex-Colonel Hammond slid from the front seat, fierce-eyed and lion-maned. Like many men who had served too long in uniform, his taste in civilian clothes was execrable; unlike most, he was sloppy about it too. His Palm Beach suit was crumpled and his pink-and-yellow tie awry. He loped up the steps with his briefcase swinging and tapped at the door of 217E, disarranging his tie further as he waited, as part of the image, Lee guessed, of a sort of Clarence Darrow among warriors.

Lee, watching from his car, knew that there would be no lie-detector test for Sherry Pace this morning, if ever. Seething, he noted the time and left for his office. He was so sure that the woman would not show up that he canceled the use of the interrogation room, freeing it for Homer Troy, who thought he had his sex-fiend in the person of a pimply, bucktoothed young civil-service janitor.

Lee set into motion the whole machinery of Army Counterintelligence and Civil Analysis in a search for items to add to the Security dossier of Bull Collins. Before he could begin to read it, Hammond arrived with Sherry Pace. Collins, of course, had evaporated. Lee seated them and ordered them coffee. He had tangled with Hammond before, in the case of an Air Force clerk alleged to have raped a Pentagon typist after hours. He expected no good to come of the present meeting, and he was right.

Hammond, who explained that he now represented Sherry Pace but didn't mention Collins, wanted to discuss the lie-detector test. "What she hasn't explained is what you intend to do with the results."

Lee didn't answer. He pressed the button on his intercom. "Thelma, bring your pad." Thelma arrived with her steno-book. "Mrs. Pace," he said to Sherry, "for the record, I'm asking you to take a polygraph because a top-secret document was found at night unlocked on your desk. You agreed to do so Saturday. Do you now object?"

Sherry Pace, sitting back, inspected her fingernails and remained mute. "Obviously," said Hammond, "she objects."

"OK," said Lee. "I just wanted it on the record that she was offered a chance to clear herself. Obviously, you don't trust her veracity, or you wouldn't—"

"You have no right to draw that conclusion," Hammond snapped, "and I think you know it. Actually, she wanted to take it. I told her that if she insisted, she'd have to find another lawyer."

"And I want to stay with Mr. Hammond, Colonel," Sherry said, flashing a dazzling smile. She was crocked, Lee observed, to the eyeballs. "I'd like to take your test, I really would. But it isn't every day a poor little GS-6 gets a chance to be represented by Mr. Hammond."

"It *is* remarkable," agreed Lee. "I wonder how you lucked-out?"

Hammond flushed: "That's none of your business, Colonel, if you don't mind my saying so."

"You see," Sherry went on, "I figure you're going to stick either me or my loyal, courageous boss with this, and dear Mr. Ellsworth would maybe grab Hammond if I didn't, so—"

"Well, Counselor," Lee cut in, "was there anything else?"

Hammond looked surprised. "Yes, What are your intentions? Are you dropping this, or what?"

"Beats me."

"Well, is she suspended? Is she working today? Or what?"

Lee spread his hands. "How would I know?" Something occurred to him and he eased open his top drawer a few inches, glancing down surreptitiously. A small oscilloscope had been installed years before by a suspicious predecessor, to pick up minute emissions if anyone operated a tape recorder in the vicinity. Hammond was the sort of tricky bastard who would try to tape every word, but the line across the scope was unruffled. Lee slid the drawer closed and smiled placidly across the desk. "I'm not her boss."

"You could still yank her Security."

"It's an idea. She handles some pretty hot material up there. Should I?"

Hammond had spent twenty years in the Army. Lee watched, amused, as the ex-officer battled the successful new advocate. "That's your decision, not mine," Hammond said uncomfortably.

"Will I get sued if I do?"

Inside, Hammond the lawyer triumphed over the soldier, but barely. "You might very well get sued," he said, without conviction.

"Then I better not suspend it, right?"

Hammond looked as if he would prefer to stick around and worry the point, so Lee, to keep him off balance, stood up quickly. "I'm sorry, Mr. Hammond. I have an appointment at Edgewood Arsenal." Hammond hesitated, picked up his briefcase and followed his client out the door. Lee snatched the phone and called Ellsworth. A new girl answered. Within seconds Ellsworth was on the line, as if he had dreaded the call.

"You making any progress, Colonel?"

"No. What are you going to do about Mrs. Pace?"

"It's done. She's canned. Papers forwarded to Personnel. Let her fight it out with the Civilian Review Board."

202

"That's very decisive," Lee told him. "Well, if events should conspire to make you change your mind, change the combination to your office vaults, too."

"Why should I change my mind?"

"She's got a lawyer," Lee said.

"A *lawyer,* for Christ's sake?"

"Charles Brewster Hammond, III," Lee said comfortably. *"The* Charles Hammond."

"Jesus! Look, damn it. I *have* to can her, don't I?"

"You're the boss," Lee informed him happily. He hung up and caught a helicopter for the Army Chemical Center.

In the kitchen of their rickety 1900 home clinging to a shaded hillside in Catonsville, outside Baltimore, Michael O'Hare, Ph.D. in microbiology, towered over the squirming table of seven males he had spawned. Finding no room at the scarred oaken antique as usual ("screwed himself right out of a seat," his wife, Toolie, liked to put it), he stood at the lead-topped sink to spoon his breakfast eggs. He watched Toolie, blond, rawboned, with short wild hair and Roland Park arrogance in every move, force-feed his youngest replica, a choleric two-year-old wriggling lockjawed in a high-chair. The noise-level, which she ignored completely, was impressive.

"So are you girded?" she wanted to know.

He had told her last night that he intended to see General Greenberg one more time today, and then start screaming plague. "Girded," he answered, "and loined."

"Loined, you are," she agreed. She noted an opening in her victim's face, poked a spoonful of oatmeal into it, and leered triumphantly. "But are you really ready if they get you turned down on next year's grant? Do we feed from Mama's golden trough, finally? How do we eat?"

"I don't see how the Pentagon could ace me out of an HEW grant," he said uncertainly.

"You don't pay the slimy machinations of our government the proper respect."

"The *what?*" She had been an English major at Goucher College. She was given now, when he was home, to verbosity, probably because the rest of her day was spent in a series of one-syllable shouts.

Number Two son, nine, exploded at some private joke with a mouthful of milk, showering Number Four. Her own prey, Number Seven, gaped at his brother's feat. Expertly she exploited the hole again, inserted the spoon, and pried upward, scraping the last of the oatmeal off on the roof of his mouth. "That'll hold the little son-of-a-bitch," she drawled, arising.

"Son-of-a-bitch," crowed Number Five, the first intelligible words he had spoken in weeks. She beamed down at him and pinched his cheek, leaving a welt an inch wide. He blushed modestly and overturned his plate.

"What's scheduled for today?" Mike asked companionably. His own disciplined and unhappy childhood in the Franciscan orphanage had operated in reverse, filling him with a love for the chaos he found at home, but he was fascinated by the distractions she dreamed up to keep it in bounds during summer vacations. Yesterday's lunch, he believed, had been backyard *tacos* in honor of Marijuana Harvest Day and Sun Dance Festival in Tuxpan, Sinaloa; the previous afternoon had been a bird-watching hike triggered by (she swore to it) the first annual meeting of the International Friends of the Condor in Castaic, California.

"Somebody's birthday, or something, I think," she muttered, clearing the mess on the table. He moved to a large wall calendar, on which the plan of her day was plotted for weeks in advance. He studied her neat, finishing-school script. "Who's H. Fiedeldy Dop?"

"*Doctor* H. Fiedeldy Dop," she told him, "noted Amsterdam pediatrician."

"What did he do?"

"Translated Spock into Dutch."

"Ice cream and cake?" he wondered. "Party hats?"

"It's probably not really his birthday," she admitted. "We're burning him in effigy as a gesture of sympathy to Holland."

He put down his coffee and kissed her good-bye on the back of her neck as she bent over the sink. "*Nil carborendum illegitimum,*" he intoned. Rotten Franciscan

Latin was his defense against superior education. "Don't let the bastards grind you down!"

"Don't you, either," she warned. "Make waves, but don't blow the grant, and don't be too rough on poor Greenberg."

General Morris Greenberg had been the only officer at Detrick that she liked. To her, Morrie was no more responsible for his position than if he had been a child: he was simply a product of his times. Her husband, of course, was another matter, a rational being, and she had never accepted his involvement in germ warfare, "defensive" or not.

He pushed open the sagging kitchen screen door. She had turned out to be right; you could not trust the Army. He headed down the rickety steps to do battle with it once more.

Chapter Ten

Lee Frost was not a hunter, at least not of animals, but Lucius Hardy had once dragged him to Edgewood Arsenal in deer season and he had killed his first buck. Now, thrashing northeast of Baltimore toward the ten thousand lush acres between the Gunpowder and Bush rivers, he decided that if he were a huntsman this would be the post he would most like to command.

Through the stately forest of the Chemical Warfare Center bounded a herd of nine hundred royal deer, half-tame beneficiaries of tight Security regulations, which protected them from civilian sportsmen. (Until they had to scatter under an annual hail of military fire during hunting season.) Squirrels and rabbits hopped everywhere, wild turkeys clucked along the trails, quail crooned over green meadows, pheasants whirred underfoot, mallards drummed along the shores of the embracing rivers, safe from all but Army guns. It was a manicured forest primeval, a royal park. The waters of the Gunpowder and Bush were alive with fish. For security reasons, the Provost Marshal issued on-post hunting and fishing permits only to the military (and to their guests, a boon to chemical officers courting Baltimore tycoons or Washington politicians). When herds and flocks suffered under Army enthusiasm, the base Rod-and-Gun Club could restock, confident that no strangers would benefit.

Of all the game preserves in history, including those of the British crown, Lee imagined Edgewood Arsenal to be most poacher-proof. Local citizens tempted to hazard the chain-link fence and MPs on the land side or the armed patrolboats churning the Chesapeake could easily see on Carroll's Island and Grace's Quarters the vast concentric circles of the toxic grid where nerve gases were tested in the open air, and which even the game had learned to avoid. Lee was sure that no sane hunter had set illegal foot on the Gunpowder Reservation since World War I, when Army Ordnance had first erected sheds in the quiet groves to fill artillery shells with chlorine. (The ancient structures were still in use, leased by American Cynamid, the Bata Shoe Company of Baltimore, and the Humphrey Chemical Corporation, none of which, the Chemical Corps would swear, had any operational connection with the Chemical Center, but had simply located where they were because the rent was cheap.)

The chopper churned over a fringe of trees and slanted downward toward a single alabaster runway set in an emerald field bordered by modern laboratories. Lee dismissed the helicopter, asking the pilot to return at five. A sedan Thelma had arranged awaited him at the strip. His driver was a stubby, cheerful private, who reached over the back seat to open the rear door and invited him in with a touch of friendly superiority. He wore dark glasses. Lee told him to take him to the Army Environmental Hygiene Agency, a Chemical Corps euphemism, he imagined, for something quite different. The cameraman Alioto, whom Congressman Weintraub claimed had been at Ban Doc and whom Lee intended to catch unawares, was supposed to be filming a technical movie there.

The driver lost his grin. *"That* fuckin' place," he muttered.

"What's wrong with 'that fuckin' place'?" Lee inquired.

The driver turned to Lee and took off his glasses. His eyes were bloodshot, the corners filled with some sort of ointment. He had been a volunteer in the building they were heading for. "But I won't sign no more releases, and they can't send me overseas until my eyes clear up, so now I'm a hack driver."

Edgewood's chemical-warfare volunteers, unlike the Fort Detrick conscientious objectors, who were civilians supplied for biological experiments by the elders of the Seventh Day Adventist Church, were soldiers. Lee had often wondered what would impel an enlisted man in his right mind to volunteer body and brain like a white rat:

patriotism, masochism, a way to get off a platoon sergeant's shitlist, a laudatory entry in his 201 file. He asked this one why he had come.

"Man, it sounds like good duty when you're, you know, in a infantry company. Ping-pong all day, good chow, three-day passes every week, you're the prize bull. And, you know, when you're *here,* you ain't *there."*

"There" meant Vietnam. Lee wished that Rick had somehow got it into his mind to volunteer, but that was ridiculous—he would never have contributed to gas warfare, not in a million years. "Well," Lee observed with some satisfaction, "it caught up with you, didn't it?"

"Man, did it ever! I first get here, they're on this, you know, LSD-25 bit? We ain't going to kill the enemy, just blow their minds a skosh? Great! Free trips, drop a little acid and get paid for it, man! OK, then they find out it eats away the brains of people, just like it did the rats, that ain't so encouraging, not that these volunteers got any brains, but let's fall back and regroup; let's try out a little crying juice, dig?" He replaced his dark glasses and swung away from the airstrip. "OK, they sit you in this cell behind a window and they're taking your picture for the movies and then, wow, they hit you with this new tear gas, it's like they threw acid in your fucking face. Doctors up the ass: 'OK, son, it's only temporary, don't wet your pants, best medical care in the world; now how'd you like to participate in our BZ program?'"

Lee stiffened, jolted to the core of his Security-consciousness. BZ was belladonna in an oily aerosol spray, as secret a psychedelic weapon as the Army possessed. Even with his own sources of information, he had not known that they were trying it already on human volunteers.

The kid rambled on: " 'Bullshit, Doctor,' I tell him, 'you just lost me! LSD, OK, but you ain't scrambling *my* marbles with something the *heads* ain't even tried. Send me back to the grunts—' "

"Has it occurred to you," Lee cut in sharply, "that you're sitting there hanging yourself by the balls." *BZ?* Christ, I wouldn't mention that to my wife!"

208

"I guess you wouldn't," chuckled the private. "But I don't think I got to worry. One, the dispatcher said you're a Colonel, right?"

"Yes."

"So you probably know all about BZ. Two, how the hell they going to courtmartial me when *they're* the ones fucked up my head in the first place? Best way to handle a loudmouth like me is to give me a Section Eight so nobody outside'll believe me anyway. Right, Colonel?"

Lee stared at the back of his head, speechless. They pulled into a curving drive and stopped before a modern, gleaming lab labeled: Wesley C. Cox Building. Numbly, Lee got out. He looked down at the beaming driver.

"You're quite a soldier," Lee admitted. "I think you'll go far."

"Yes sir, if you say so," the boy agreed. "See you don't sign anything in there, and don't push any, you know, buttons?"

Lee shook his head admiringly, and entered the building.

Congressman Cyrus Weintraub sat talking on his phone in the grimiest office his Chairman had been able to find for him in the Old House Office Building. His bird-eyed secretary, shaken at the enormous mail, placed a new batch of letters and telegrams on his desk. Cy wedged the telephone between neck and shoulder and ruffled through them, trying to estimate their number. Twenty, thirty? A week's mail in a day! On the other end of the line, one of his favorite supporters allowed her voice to soar another octave. "So, Cy, what are you going to do?"

"I don't know, Bea, but something. I'll look into it now. Your son's not the only one, believe me. Selective Service's gone ape, maybe. Meanwhile, don't be a Jewish mother, OK?"

"Listen, I *am* a Jewish mother, and I ran my fat *tail* off for you, and so did Larry himself, and I know damn well you're on the Armed Services Committee, and there's got to be something you can do. So do it! He's in pre-med, he's not studying Sanskrit literature, and that board has no *right!*"

Weintraub hung up, puzzled. Something very strange was happening in New York City. Since ten A.M., when he had arrived at his dismal office, he had been plagued with calls. Men he had known at NYU, some of them still eligible for the draft, were phoning long-distance, asking what he or they had done to antagonize Selective Service. Two civilian employees of the Naval Reserve Center on the fringe of his district had demanded that he check out a rumor that the facility was being deactivated. A crank phoned long-distance to call him a Red. Now his light was flashing again.

"Mr. Green's on two," reported his secretary.

His heart sank. *"Howard* Green?"

"Who else?"

He wiped his forehead. God, it was hot. His air-conditioning had been failing for weeks, but House Building Maintenance seemed always to be working somewhere else. "Hello, Howard," he said desolately.

Mr. Green had a problem. Well, no problem, really, it had to be more like a mistake. As Cy knew, he had won a garment contract for military fatigues from the Army Materiel Command. He had thereupon hired half the unemployed on the Lower East Side, and now the Army wanted him to hold up production until it could audit his books. "Audit my books, fine, Cy. But hold up production? What's with 'hold up production'? Who pays the help?"

Cy didn't know, but promised to call back. Mr. Green thought that would be nice. "Like by five? I mean, if I got to start pink-slipping your constituents, I got to know today."

A commander from the Navy's Congressional Liaison Office was announced, and Cy Weintraub finally had someone to bully: "What the hell's going on?"

"I looked into it, sir," said the commander, a square-jawed officer with a dimpled chin who looked more like a male Madison Avenue model than a fighting man. "Fund-wise, it's an operational necessity."

" 'Fund-wise'? 'Operational necessity'? Why *my* district? Who decided?"

"SecDef, sir." The commander was looking at him with faintly veiled amusement. Cy felt like slamming his pen-set at the square, handsome jaw. "It's all a matter of appropriations, sir. Can't get blood out of a turnip. And sometimes those who try hardest to effect military economies, well . . ." His voice trailed off.

"Well *what?*" Weintraub said tersely.

"They come to realize that their districts have more equity in the military establishments than they thought, you know what I mean, sir? But by then, of course, it's too late."

"We'll see how late," Weintraub growled. He asked how many other Reserve bases were being deactivated, and when the commander didn't know, requested a list of every Naval Reserve Training Center in the continental United States, a run-down on their expenditures for the past five years, a compilation of their civilian payrolls by grade, the number of Reservists who drilled at each, and topped it off with a request that the commander obtain from the Labor Department certified unemployment statistics for each Congressional district that held one. The officer hardly flinched.

"Aye-aye, sir. And when would you like this?"

"There's a Committee meeting tomorrow at two. I'd like to present an argument then."

That shook the bastard, Weintraub noted with satisfaction. He dismissed him while he was still screaming, and was attacking the stack of mail when his secretary showed Chairman Ab Dennes in. Dennes had never visited the office of his most junior Committee member before, and didn't even sit down, but simply grinned at the mail on the desk.

"My goodness, Cy! Where I come from, can't hardly enough people write to give me that much mail in a month. And them that could, they're so happy, I never hardly hear from them."

"I bet you don't," said Weintraub grimly.

Dennes suggested that Cy's mail might fall off if he spent less time worrying about the Greeks getting U.S. jets and more time worrying about New York getting military contracts. "Pork-barreling, if you'll excuse the expression, son. You decide what to do with your little old top-secret memo?"

"I'm bringing it up in Committee, and the majority can decide," said Cy.

"Sure, son," agreed Dennes. " 'Course, it'll leak out that you cost the Israeli Air Force a quarter of a billion dollars worth of airplanes, but I don't reckon you care that much about the Jewish vote, when you got all those principles at stake. You're right. Let the majority decide."

Cy watched him waddle through the door and angrily attacked the mail, but in a few minutes he gave up. There were two Committee members he could depend on and another three he could at least confide in. He decided to go and try to organize his revolt.

Michael O'Hare arrived for his showdown with General Morris Greenberg just before lunch, having stopped to check measle cultures at his Bethesda lab before he went to the Pentagon. He found the general looking tired and shadowed with strain. A crew was installing a new window in his office. Greenberg used the glaziers to postpone conversation about the Da Nang plague, even picked the Executive Dining Room rather than the General and Flag Officer's Lounge in case Mike lost his temper during lunch. But when finally they returned to the office, the repair crew was gone and Mike knew that he had him cornered. He bored in mercilessly.

"Again, Morrie! Are you going to use my vaccine?"

"We can't inoculate the whole population, without admitting the plague!"

"Then admit it! Jesus, the *Army* doesn't spread it! Rats spread it!"

"And we're killing the rats," said Greenberg. "Quietly."

Mike found his temper going. "That's great thinking, General!"

"I told you," Greenberg said gently, his nervous mouth working, " 'Morrie.' Not 'General.' "

"When you think like a general and talk like a general, then to me you're 'General,' " Mike burst out. "You're sure no goddamn scientist!"

212

Greenberg flinched. Mike was instantly sorry. As a rookie on the Baltimore police force, he had once backhanded a teen-ager who spat at him. The same flood of shame tightened his throat now. Years ago at the Detrick Officers' Club, waiting for their wives to join them after work, Greenberg had told him of a daughter and her kidney disease, and how it defeated his plans to take a doctorate. "Army medical care, Mike; we couldn't have done without it, and it kept her alive until, hell, after Korea, and then it was too late to go back and try to compete with kids like you. . . ."

Now Mike, redfaced, backpedaled. "You're a damn good chemist, Morrie, I didn't mean that at all!"

Greenberg shrugged. "You were right. Hell, you know more about *Pasteurella pestis* than I do about the whole field. I'm no scientist to a scientist and no general to a general. On the other hand, I love the lab, and I love the Army; it gave my daughter a good five years." He became suddenly brisk. "Well, what happens when we *don't* use your vaccine in Vietnam?"

Mike was ready for that. He pointed out that, Black Plague being Black Plague, there were TV talk shows he could get on. There was a World Health Symposium at the UN next week that would be glad to have him on a panel. The medical editor of *The New York Times* might be interested in knowing why the Army wouldn't use a safe and effective vaccine to inoculate a population it had evacuated, resettled, moved, rousted, and jostled for five years.

Greenberg studied him for a moment, then unlocked a drawer and pulled out a report. His hand was trembling. "Mike, I didn't want to show you this."

Mike took it. On its cover was the enigmatic shield of Fort Detrick, an arrow pointing downward. Mike recognized it as the laboratory journal, typed up, he had begun on his plague serums. Despite the rage in which he had quit, he had very nearly stayed to complete the work on plague. He considered it the most important he had done.

"Page twelve," Greenberg said hoarsely.

Mike found the page. At the bottom was a paragraph

encircled in red. His heart began to pound. *"Symptoms:* At 1130 hours on first day, after vaccination with Culture 57, but before the challenge dose, Volunteer E.T.G., 23-year-old male, complained of severe headache. By 1330 hours volunteer had developed high temperature. Breathing accelerated to 80 respirations per minute. A cough developed." Mike's temples began to pound. He read on. "Sputum showed blood. Severe edema. E.T.G. was treated at 1400 hours and thereafter with massive doses of streptomycin, aureomycin, and chloramphenicol, but course of disease was fulminating, involving left upper lobe of chest and finally both lobes. (See Roentgenogram, Annex A.) E.T.G. died at 0347 hours second day. *Autopsy Report:* Microscopic examination of lung tissue showed viable strains of surviving *Pasteurella pestis,* apparently introduced intravenously when vaccine was administered. *Cause of Death:* Pneumonic plague. No further volunteers were inoculated."

Mike's legs began to quiver. Greenberg poured him a glass of water from a pitcher on his desk. Mike gulped it down. The general, his mouth twisted strangely, said in a strangled voice: "I hated to tell you, Mike."

Blindly Mike arose. He stared at Greenberg, then lurched from the office. He was driving dazedly home to Catonsville when he realized that, had it not been for his fit of temper at Detrick, he would have inoculated himself, as he always did, before allowing the vaccine to be tested on the poor damn Seventh Day Adventist.

Whoever he was! He hadn't even asked the name of the man he had murdered! He stopped at the first road-house on the Washington–Baltimore Pike, tried to reach Greenberg, and failed. He shoved into the bar, and by the time he stumbled up the steps of the rickety house on the hillside the boys were asleep and it took all of Toolie's sinewy strength to get him up the stairs and into bed.

He had a better night than General Morris Greenberg, who was flown as main attraction to an American Ordnance Association dinner in Chicago to speak on "Our Silent Weapons." Greenberg stayed bravely sober for his talk and forgot his whole train of thought between anthrax bombs and Q fever sprays. He stuttered, mumbled, and sat down mortified, to thin applause and embarrassed smiles.

Chapter Eleven

Lee Frost moved through the gleaming corridors of the Wesley C. Cox Army Environmental Hygiene Building, searching for the test ward where Alioto was supposed to be filming. He passed a decontamination station crammed with stainless-steel tubs, then an eye-ear-and-nose examining room, a physical-test facility in which volunteers, apparently wired for sound, were slogging toward nowhere on treadmills. He noted a psychotherapy division with its doors ominously closed and the windowed door of a glittering operating room, ready for emergencies and complete with hissing sterilizers, manned by a bored, green-gowned Army nurse. If he were overcome, as his driver had implied, by a team of mad scientists and given a brain-transplant, it would at least be a sanitary one.

When he reached the test ward he found a technician playing solitaire at a console in its center, under a row of closed-circuit TV screens. The room was surrounded by jungle-green glassed cubicles, each with padded walls and floors, containing a bunk, a padded chair and toilet seat, a padded table, and a soldier. Most of the volunteers in the cubicles were sleeping, but one was doing pushups, and in another cell a young man with a scarecrow frame twisted happily to unheard music. Closeups of the cells were duplicated on the TV screens above the technician, who glanced up, stirred himself, and flicked a switch. Music from the scarecrow's cubicle blasted through the room.

"Gabriel," the technician said to no one in particular, "you OK, man?"

The soldier stopped, giggled, and waved, not toward the glass, which was apparently one-way, but toward the TV lens in his wall. "Crazy, man!"

"You can say that again," the technician said, making

a note and flicking off Gabriel's sound. He saw Lee. "Colonel Frost?"

Lee nodded and the technician led him across the room toward a cubicle larger than the rest. Inside, a three-man movie team was filming five volunteers who were trying to reassemble M-16 rifles. Cleaning kits, oily rags, and ramrods were scattered everywhere; a soldier dropped his weapon. Lee flinched as it bounced, but the GI only snickered.

The cameraman straightened from his eyepiece. Alioto was a redheaded bear of a man with a handlebar moustache and an intricate pattern of alcoholic capillaries lacing his cheeks. "Eighteen minutes already and a thousand feet of film. You zonked-out fuckers aren't going to make it today."

Lee was jolted. If field-stripping an M-16 took eighteen minutes, the bloodless war promised by CBW might last a hundred years. He introduced himself to Alioto, who had not been told he was coming: "Colonel Lee Frost. Intelligence. I wondered if I might have a few words with you alone?"

The "Intelligence" jolted the sergeant more than the rank. He was scared of Ban Doc, or heavy with some other guilt. Lee put him at ease. He had heard of the sergeant's work, he said, and wondered if he could estimate the cost of a training film for G-2 Reserve officers.

Alioto lost the hostile look in his eyes. He was through for the day, he said, and the Colonel wouldn't believe how good it would be to discuss a sane project after the asshole assignment he found himself on now. Lee suggested somewhere off the base, where they could get a cool brew. The sergeant's eyes lit up like a neon beer sign and he did not even wait to help his assistants break the set.

Leaving the cubicle, Lee glanced at the volunteers trying to clean up the mess, as volatile and disjointed as fifth-graders let out for recess. Whatever they had been gassed with—LSD or BZ or something even newer—they were certainly meat on the table for a thinking enemy, but he wondered if an enemy, or even a friend, would be safe confronted by a giggling Army of children, equipped

217

with grenades, tanks, and nuclear rockets, whose minds had just been blown.

It might be CBW's idea of humanitarian warfare, but he didn't like it at all.

Marty Lumpert led his black sharpshooter up the creaking stairs of the *Underground Clarion,* meeting June outside her darkroom on the second floor. She was inspecting a dripping print at a dingy airshaft window. It was a shot of the Washington Monument, with a peace symbol hovering over it like a halo. Across the bottom was scrawled simply: *Saturday.* He introduced Dewey Dupays, who looked at her outstretched hand for a good three seconds before he unbent sufficiently to shake it.

"Where's Horace Greeley?" Marty asked, to break the tension.

"Upstairs sulking." June had refused to shoot the Arlington Memorial Bridge until the Justice Department gave them a permit to use it. "He'd run it Friday, and if they had it closed off, half the rally would think we were supposed to cross. It'd be murder!"

Marty agreed. They continued up the stairs, Dewey inspecting the posters at each landing, looking for Panthers. They entered Handlemann's office, where the wolfish redhead sat under a huge poster of Bobby Seale, fist up in the Black Power salute. Unmollified, Dewey wandered around and let Marty present his case for him.

"Canada?" Handlemann reflected. "You don't want to go to Cuba?"

"Canada, that's right, man," Dewey said. He was leafing through a pile of last week's *Clarions* stranded on a battered chair. He gazed with admiration at the insert that told of his shot at the Pentagon, stacked a dozen copies, and put them under his arm.

"You got wheels?" Handlemann asked.

"Yeah."

"Then why come to me? Just head North."

Dewey smiled at his civilian ignorance. He would need cover, and contacts. He was in the Marine Corps, to start with; he wasn't one of your goddamn Army grunts. He was an expert marksman. The Green Machine had money invested in him, and would go into gear like a plantation owner after a runaway stud. "I'm JCS Security Force, too. I know that NMCC from the Rooshin hotline to the coffee-machine, so they ain't going to sit back—"

"NMCC?" Handlemann asked, alert. "National Military Command Center?"

"Look, Dewey," Marty said, "you got delusions of grandeur. You're still just a frigging private, you know."

"Listen, fat-boy," Dewey said harshly, "they's a lieutenant down there would follow me to *Hong Kong,* personally. I need names, addresses, the whole bit, man, the minute I head that Olds North. And bread, specially bread."

"Bread. I see." Handlemann, chewing his lip, reflected so long on the stubby private that Marty grew uncomfortable and even Dewey shifted on his feet. "Well, what's so fuckin' funny about going to Canada? I want out, man!"

Handlemann ignored that. "A guard at the NMCC?"

"Honor guard," Dewey said impatiently. "Like the British Grenadiers. 'You men all been chose from combat troops, Army, Navy, Air Force, Marines. You got courage, loyalty, marksmanship, appearance. Now get your ass humpin.' Shine them shoes, rub that brass, tote that bale, whole mother-fuckin' *world* is watchin' you.' "

Handlemann smiled absently. "Where do you actually work? What do you actually do?"

"Red," Marty said uncomfortably, "he wants money and addresses. An interview he doesn't need, or a pat on the ass!"

"Look, Clausewitz," Handlemann said, "why don't you go downstairs? June's in the darkroom. Maybe she's got time for a fast screw on the layout table. OK?"

Marty leaned across the desk. "OK, you half-assed scarecrow! You pull another crack like that, and you'll be taking your own damn pictures!"

"Does she know that?"

"She's about to!" Marty started out. "Come on, Dewey. This son-of-a-bitch won't help you!"

"No, Dewey, wait." Handlemann grinned. "When you

get ready to go, I got some addresses. I know a minister in Niagara and another chick in Toronto'll blow your mind, and not just your mind, either. But first, I got an idea."

Marty jerked his head toward the door. "His last idea got you a half-inch in a paper a Mongolian idiot wouldn't wipe his ass on! If it'd bombed any worse, you'd be climbing the walls in an Army cell!"

"This is better," Handlemann said complacently. "And it's worth a few bucks."

"Well, I ain't hardly got the dough to get past Baltimore now." Dewey seated himself on Handlemann's desk, flicked open a switchblade knife, and began to clean his fingernails. "You got my un-dee-vided attention, brother, so go, man, go."

There was nothing Marty could do. He decided that when he finished helping Poma with the film, he was splitting, even if he had to desert, and June was splitting too. He found her closing the darkroom. He disentangled Sunshine from a roll of curling negative. The little girl kissed him and dodged under the sink, teasing. He told June his plans, half-expecting her to refuse. Instead, when he had captured Sunshine and stood up, she said, "I'm with you, soldier."

To find that she would risk her future and Sunshine's with his own put him into such a haze of glory that he paid no real attention when Dewey came down, smiling secretly, and told him that he had decided not to go until after the demonstration. Marty was so proud, happy, and relieved over June that he didn't care to know why.

At the Gas House outside Edgewood's gates, Tony Alioto, Army cameraman, led Lee Frost to a table a few feet from the bar, apologizing for the bleakness of the place but promising more action before nightfall than the Rocker Club in Tokyo. Lee ordered a bourbon and beer for both of them, to get things moving as quickly as possible. He told Alioto that he was looking for someone with combat-camera experience to make a film on field interrogation of suspected agents.

"You're looking at him, sir."

"So I've heard. Can I screen your last combat footage?"

Alioto tossed down his bourbon, drew swiftly on his beer, and played with his glass. He called for the bartender and ordered them both another round. Not three minutes had passed since the first. "Colonel, no offense, could I see your G-2 card?"

Lee passed him his identification. It seemed to satisfy him. "My *last* film, sir, you wouldn't want to see it if you could."

"Why not?"

"If you ever did, you'd have to hang a good infantry officer and a platoon full of gung-ho combat men. You ever hear of Ban Doc?"

Lee's heart leaped. "Of course," he said quietly. "And hold down your voice."

"I was there," Alioto said in a low tone.

"What happened, anyway?" Lee asked carefully.

"Well, you know. Candy Rawlins, he was the company commander, kind of body-hungry, and they were using gas to flush them out of the hootches. They'd come out puking, *supposed* to be Charlie, and rubbing their eyes. You couldn't tell Papa-san from Mama-san, and somebody shot a kid, maybe by mistake, and then the shit really hit the fan. I guess Killer didn't want any witnesses. I quit filming, but my men didn't, and that big, crazy Lieutenant we had, he kept on grinding away with his Eyemo, close-up, with a 25-millimeter lens. Bad scene, Colonel. Hell, *you* know all about it."

"Yes. Where's the film?"

"The *film?*" Alioto stared at him. "Jesus, sir, you know about the film!"

"I heard something," Lee said quickly. "Burned in a chopper crash?"

"Swiped!"

"*Swiped?*"

Alioto nodded lugubriously. "Secret fucking film. Chemical *warfare* fucking film. Swiped!"

"That's right. Swiped, by what's-his-name?"

"Lieutenant Christopher E. Poma, Army of the United States!" spat Alioto.

221

"Yes. P-O-M-A, right?"

The sergeant nodded. "Took that film. 'Thank you, Sergeant, here's a list of shots we still need, you're a better director than I am anyway, G-2 has to see this,' he says. 'They won't *want* to see it,' I tell him, but I didn't have to worry about that, because you never did see it, did you? Or Poma, either!"

"Or Poma, either," agreed Lee. They commiserated agonizingly about an Army from which Lieutenants deserted and which had to bribe recruits in basic training with Brownie-points. Then it was time for Lee to leave. Alioto drove him back to the Edgewood airstrip.

The helicopter flailed skyward from the Center's lethal game preserve like a startled dove. Lee's last glimpse of the sergeant showed him lurching toward his car. He hoped to see him no more until he got him somehow onto a witness stand, but first there was Poma to find. Passing the tan pool of smoke over Baltimore, he had the copter land at Fort Holabird. When he left, it was dusk and the pilot was sulking like an untipped taxi driver, but Lee had an inch-thick dossier on Second Lieutenant Christopher Poma, Army of the U.S., betrayer of his country's special confidence and trust.

Chapter Twelve

Michael O'Hare awakened with his mind clear, as if switched on when his eyelids opened. He instantly recalled Greenberg's disclosure that a volunteer had died of his vaccine, and in fact remembered last night's hazy trip home. Before he even saw a priest, he had to call Greenberg for the name of his victim's next-of-kin, though he had no idea, once he did contact the family, exactly what he would say. He swung his feet out of the bed and sat with throbbing temples, listening.

The house was quieter than it had been since Son Number One was born. Toolie came in bearing coffee. She had taken the boys to her mother's in Roland Park, to get them out of his hair. "You were awfully drunk last night," she said, sitting on the side of the bed, "but are you sure of what you said?"

"I even know the poor bastard's initials: 'E.T.G.'"

He called the Pentagon to get General Greenberg and he finally gave up, sure that Morrie was trying to avoid him.

"He knows what you're after," Toolie decided, "and he's not going to tell you."

"Why not? The Army's not liable."

"Maybe there is no 'E.T.G.'!"

"Thanks," he said softly, "but you're wrong."

Downstairs the grandfather clock rumbled, rattled, and chimed reluctantly. Ten o'clock. He had to get moving.

"He's lying," she blazed, "and you better believe it!"

"He wouldn't do that." He reminded her that she had liked Morrie. Out of all the Army at Detrick she had trusted him alone.

"I *did* like him," she admitted. "But he's been in thirty years. He's like a good cop turned rotten, you told me yourself about *them!*" She was a cool Baltimore aristocrat

223

taught never to cry, but now her voice began to tremble. "You don't *make* lab mistakes! There's some other reason they're not using the vaccine, and they'd rather wreck your life than tell you what it is!"

While she went to fix breakfast, he called Greenberg again, and this time the dumpy clerk in his outer office put him through. Morrie sounded terrible, but would not budge. "I'm sorry, Mike, it's confidential information."

"Who's spoken to his family? Who told them what we were trying to do? Have you?"

There was a long silence. "As a matter of fact," said Greenberg, "I have."

"That, I *don't* believe! *What was his name?*" There was a click. Mike knew that the general, as a source, was shut off for good. In a blind rage, he pawed through a scuffed leather shaving kit in which he kept his relics: Saint Chris medals from the Fathers at the orphanage, rosaries, two merit badges, an old Marine dog-tag, Korean campaign ribbons. Finally he found his Fort Detrick civilian ID card, which he had neglected to turn in when he left the place in his momumental tantrum. It had expired last year, but that was a minor matter. He found, too, his red immunological button for biological hot-areas and restricted pass for his old domain in Building J. The main gate would be no problem, either, because their battered station wagon, purchased at Detrick, still bore a scratched and tattered Base windshield sticker.

His year on Baltimore's finest had taught him that breaking-and-entering was a difficult crime to prevent. An intelligent human animal who knew the terrain and what he was looking for was a hard organism to keep from his goal, if he was willing to risk enough.

He slipped the ID cards into his pocket, noting that his hand was shaking. He wished that the boys were home. Noisy or not, their recklessness and physical courage was catching. Downstairs, at the strangely empty kitchen table, he told Toolie only that he was going to check some lab reports today and of course she assumed he meant at Bethesda and not Fort Detrick. He kissed her good-bye and squeaked down the crazy steps. Within an hour he was rolling through the sleepy town of Frederick toward the bleak buildings of its largest industrial plant, the Bacteriological Warfare Center at Fort Detrick. He passed the restored glove shop of Barbara Frietchie where, according to Whittier, the white-haired woman, wrapped in her country's flag, had tested her luck against Confederate Gray. He drove toward the guarded gates to test his own against the Union Blue.

Lee Frost laid the photo of Lieutenant Christopher Poma, deserter, dead-center on his desk. The young man was smiling placidly. He had blond hair and widely spaced eyes and despite his name, which seemed Italian, there was a Slavic slant to his high cheekbones and a Scandinavian firmness in his lips. Lee studied the picture until he was sure that he would recognize him anywhere, clean-shaven, bearded, or moustached. He already knew more about Poma's post-adolescent life than he did about his own son's.

He stared into the clear young eyes, trying to put himself into the place of an unblooded, noncombat lieutenant who had just had the shock of his life, but had remained cool enough throughout it to film a bloody massacre. He would become an instant, angry maverick, distrusting the Army from platoon to Pentagon. What would the moves be? First, he would have to get the film out of Division and Corps. But both had probably been busy in a frantic and apparently successful attempt to plug other leaks of Ban Doc to the correspondents. So that part must have been easy: the last threat to secrecy would seem to be a young lieutenant in charge of an official Army camera crew. It would be easy for an officer on TDY to con a chopper out of Corps. Even to get past Army in Saigon would be simple, for no one there would have yet been alerted, news of civilian massacres historically having a hard row to hoe up the chain of command.

From Saigon on, Poma's track was easy to follow without guesswork. It was recorded in Poma's file by agents of the 18th Military Police in Saigon, who had been only a step behind him. With his Priority I orders as a combat-camera officer, he had no trouble climbing aboard a

225

MATS C-133 for Tokyo, where he had reported to Headquarters, U.S. Army, Japan, which had cheerfully handed him a Work Order to Kodak Tokyo. There he had personally nursed fifteen thousand feet of secret Ektachrome film through the lab at government expense, letting no technicians near it. With film in hand, he had departed on a Pan American military charter for Travis Air Force Base, California, thirteen hours ahead of a frantic TWX from the Saigon MPs, sparked by his chief cameraman, who had had second thoughts about his lieutenant's sentiments. From Travis, an hour before the time stamped on the federal warrant for his arrest, Poma had floated serenely from government jurisdiction on a Blue Air Force shuttle-bus to San Francisco. The last official eyes to light on him had been those of the Air Force bus driver, who described him as somewhat unshaven for an officer, tired, and unwilling to let go of his briefcase even to put it on the rack above his seat, but otherwise unremarkable, relaxed, and happy.

Lee found himself smiling at his prey. The picture returned the smile with calm amusement. OK, you crazy bastard, Lee promised, you're tangling with the prime Army expert on your own generation. I'm shagging a girl your age, I had a kid hardly younger than you, and I remember backward too well myself. Where would *I* have gone?

Despite his qualifications, Lee simply didn't know. He supposed he should drop the whole massacre. He wondered how many Army agents were searching for the lieutenant already, how much General Lucius Hardy really knew of the missing film, whether risking the anger of his boss was worth the satisfaction of running the case to earth. Lucius knew about the slaughter, obviously, and was only hiding it from him to protect his future, but why was he concealing it from the Inspector General, anyway? It was risky and dishonorable. Above all, it seemed unintelligent, and Hardy was never that. It was as if the universe had shifted its center.

Impatiently, he put aside the file on Poma. He began to read the material developed in the last three days by the Intelligence-School agents from Holabird who were tailing General Greenberg's clerk, Lumpert. The more he read the more he appreciated his own Sergeant Liebholtz and even the irritating, obsequious Maxon. One of the students shadowing Lumpert had lost his trail twice on a bus, apparently afraid to blow his cover by getting off at the same stop. The other unhatched operative suggested that Lumpert's best friend was a black Marine who lunched with him in a Pentagon courtyard, but after three days he had not determined the man's name or even where in the building he worked. The instructor-agent himself had developed no contact with Lumpert, apparently content to supervise his students from the Street Folk Coffeehouse on Dupont Circle, where he had diverted his attention from his assignment long enough to finger two draft dodgers for the FBI and a Navy deserter for the District Shore Patrol.

The only hard information that the three had dredged up was that Lumpert was apparently shacking up with a female photographer in a house on Q Street, and that a lanky redheaded male and assorted hippies lived there too.

Well, there were probably lots of lanky redheads along Q Street, but Handlemann was certainly the first who came to mind. Lee did not even need to call Fort Holabird for his file. It was so in demand that Counterintelligence Analysis Division on the Pentagon's third floor kept a copy handy. When it arrived, Lee checked his last-known address. It was the house Lumpert was using.

So the dumpy little clerk, Lumpert, who had looked so innocently into his face when he had denied reading the paper at all, had *Underground Clarion* contacts! He was probably writing its scientific column, or working in its photo lab. Even if he were not, he was undoubtedly the source of the leak that had put the shot through his own general's window on the front page of last week's issue.

Proving it might be a job. He visited Greenberg's office immediately, not planning to shut Lumpert off from classified material officially, for that would flush the quarry, but simpy to warn Greenberg to keep important information out of his hands until they moved in on him. He did not see Lumpert, and the general, according to his gray-haired receptionist, was out to lunch, so there was nothing he could do about it now. He would warn Greenberg this afternoon unofficially, and leave the chubby clerk staked out for further study.

Distastefully, he tossed aside the reports of the Holabird agents. If Liebholtz were not busy with the Collins case, and Maxon with Sherry Pace's phone-tap, he would have put them on Lumpert, and they would wrap it up in a day. He shoved back his chair, overcome by his crowded desk. There was simply too much: Congressman Dennes and Secretary Royce and Lucius Hardy would be bugging him about the top-secret memo today, sure as hell, an unread file on Bull Collins was growing like a cancer in his "pending" basket, and there was Major Homer Troy and his lurking perverts, to say nothing of the long-standing mysteries of who was running numbers to janitorial help in the basement and the unknown agronomist who tried continually to grow pot in the courtyard. On top of everything else, he had to rewrite the Pentagon Security Plan for the peace demonstration Saturday. He wondered how many transient Weathermen crowded Laurie's apartment now, and thought of the handsome young guitarist on her floor, and it took an almost physical effort to get back to his work.

Perversely, perhaps because Hardy had forbidden him to touch it, the massacre tugged at him hardest. He wondered if Poma were across the Potomac. It was after all here in Washington, not New York or San Francisco or Hollywood, but under the Pentagon's nose that every hippie in town seemed to be carrying a memento of the moment of truth in Ban Doc. The four-by-five blow-up had surfaced here, and he knew of it coming to light nowhere else. The Reverend Scott claimed knowledge of the film. Hell, evidence of the massacre had been the push that Handlemann needed to get the peace rally retargeted to the Pentagon, so Handlemann had seen the enlargement too, yet had not run it in the *Clarion,* which was interesting. He was saving it, or didn't want to have to explain where he got it. Handlemann might well have contact with Poma.

Lee moved to the huge District of Columbia map

228

covering his office wall. He felt a tingle of excitement, as if the pieces might fall into place. He inserted a pin at Handlemann's address, another at the Peace League, where, conceivably, someone had shown the blow-up to Reverend Scott and given a print to Laurie, a third at the *Underground Clarion* office, which had a photo lab. He could cover all three pins with the palm of his hand.

Lee was struck with the jarring notion that it all tied in with the shot and with Lumpert. Lumpert lived with Handlemann. If Handlemann had contact with Poma, maybe Lumpert had contact with Poma too. Perhaps the general's clerk, despite his harmless manner, had played a more active part in the shot into Greenberg's office than that of a random leak. Maybe the slug had not, after all, been intended for the Israelis' helicopter. Maybe Handlemann had arranged it, and Lumpert had cooperated, trying to show the press before the rally that CBW was not in fact extinct.

Whatever the pins signified, Lumpert and the house on Q Street were the keys to Poma and the film, although he couldn't grasp why. Thought failing, he decided to act. He told Thelma he would be gone for the rest of the day, went to his car, and headed across the Potomac for a stint of old-fashioned cloak-and-dagger work outside the house on Q Street.

He felt as if he were cutting school, and wondered if he would see Laurie.

At the Fort Detrick gate, Mike O'Hare discovered that nothing had changed in a year. As he slowed for the sentry-box he noticed that even the hopeless lone picket from FLAG, the "Frederick League Against Germ Warfare," still padded her beat in her death's-head mask. Through some symbiosis, overcoming the rage of her fellow townspeople and the lofty scorn of her federal government, she had been permitted to move herself and her signs into the shade of the servicemen's bus stop ouiside the entrance.

The sentry, a white-hatted MP wearing a holster creaking with polish, frowned at the state of his windshield sticker but hardly glanced at his ID card, failed to notice the date of expiration, and waved him through. An industrial-safety campaign was apparently under way, and a huge billboard formerly advertising government bonds now read PLAY SAFE FOR DETRICK, but nothing else seemed to have changed. He drove past the new Army Medical Research Lab, a jewel among Detrick's shabby World War II buildings. From the number of cars parked outside, it seemed to have survived the President's public revulsion at germ warfare. He could doubtless find a file on "E.T.G." inside, but resisted the temptation to try. The administrators there, unlike the working personnel in J-Lab, were idle enough to ask questions, and he would be sure to meet some former colleagues who would welcome him back to the ranks of scientific outcasts. He wanted no conversations at all.

He drove under an ugly checkered watertower. It dominated the base and the whole town of Frederick more loftily than the Revolutionary church-spires the Chamber of Commerce so admired. He passed the old wooden laboratories, piped front and rear to keep their inner "hot-labs" at a lower pressure than the atmosphere. The Frederick League Against Germ Warfare, to the discomfiture of the Army, the mayor, and the town council, periodically predicted that an epidemic of Venezuelan encephalomyelitis, breakbone fever, or airborne plague would rage through the community if someone dropped a test tube inside. Establishing an air-barrier, a draft against which microbes could not swim, theoretically solved the problem, or at least quieted the radicals. Boy-Scout tours, Little-League sponsorship, and classroom talks by Army officers helped even more than the pipes outside the labs, and a local civilian payroll of three thousand did not hurt.

He cruised past the Naval Bacteriological Unit, with which the U.S. Fleet kept its foot in the door of germ warfare, noting that the Army had so far unbent as to actually paint the peeling walls, or perhaps the Navy commander had finally lost patience and piped all hands on deck with chipping hammers and brushes. He drove past an immaculate row of animal houses, where germ-free cattle, white mice, rabbits, and monkeys lived in luxury and ignorance of their fate. Finally, pulse racing, he slowed. Across the street was J-Lab, the nondescript, heavily guarded structure that for so long had been his second home.

He had timed his arrival for lunch, hoping to meet a minimum of personnel. Most of J-Lab's parking spaces were empty, including the important one belonging to his successor, Chief of the Communicable Disease Section. It was now or never. He parked in a visitor's spot, pinned on the red immunological badge with shaky fingers. He clipped the J-Lab pass, bearing his picture, to his right lapel. He crossed the street and stood for the first time in a year before a door labeled: J-LAB. TERTIARY BARRIER. He prayed that the building guards had been rotated since he left, and opened the door.

Before the Security counter sat a craggy guard of the General Services Administration. He had never seen him before. Mike scrawled an approximation of his signature illegibly in the log, giving as his title "Microbiological Saftey Inspector, Laboratory Hazards Section," and as his purpose, "Informal Inspection." He hoped that the guard would not be overimpressed and call his superior. But he had hit the proper note. The man, a hard-eyed individual he judged to be a veteran of some police force, glanced at his badge, his face, checked his ID card, and touched a button under his counter. A buzzer sounded and the steel door opened. It was labeled: SECONDARY BARRIER: TO CLEAN CORRIDOR. Mike passed in.

So far, so good. He moved briskly along the Clean Corridor, passing another PLAY SAFE FOR DETRICK sign and, unable to resist a glance into his old office, glimpsed his former secretary eating lunch at her desk, lost in her union paper, the *Government Standard*. He moved past animal cabinets from which fluffy white rabbits, uncontaminated but ready, munched their food and watched him reflectively. A technician in a white gown shuffled past and nodded briefly, as if Mike were someone he should know. The quicker he could get his head into the anonymity of a ventilated hood, the safer he would be.

He was nearing his goal, the Contaminated Area in the heart of the lab. He pushed through a swinging door to Clean Change, a locker-room with benches and clothing racks. There was no one in it, but he noticed that two lockers inside were hung with street-clothes, which meant that there were technicians ignoring their lunch-hour and working in Contaminated. A bad break, but the place would be even more crowded after lunch, so it was now or never. He stripped to the skin, hung his clothes in an empty locker, picked freshly sterilized lab-trousers and a smock from a stack and plastic boots, which he tied at his calves, from a pile in the corner. With relief, he pulled on a ventilated personnel hood. For the first time he felt safe from discovery. He moved to an airtight door marked: CONTAMINATED AREA: ARE YOU PROPERLY DRESSED?

Below the sign was a stainless-steel wheel, which he spun, unlocking thick lugs. A blast of air whistled from the Clean Room behind him into the evacuated airlock. He stepped inside, spun the wheel again, and turned slowly, like a model in a futuristic fashion show, before a battery of ultraviolet lights, a last effort at sterilization so that no random strains could enter the inner lab. He swung open the other airlock door and stepped into Contaminated.

The area was divided into Animal Challenge and Human Challenge. A technician was standing at one wall, halfway down a long line of animal-handling safety cabinets. The cabinets were transparent plexiglass, and in each was a rhesus monkey, but it was not the animals you first noticed. For each cabinet, loaded through a tiny airlock with syringes and bottled cultures, was pierced with two armholes, and stretched across the holes were arm-length rubber gloves, hopefully air-tight. Technicians exposing an animal inside a cabinet would insert their hands into the gloves and, working through the armholes, inject the beast with disease viruses, animal and human each safe from contact with the other. In this area it was the animal that must remain sterile from accidental infection until he was challenged with disease. To protect him, the air pressure inside the cabinets was kept higher than that outside, so that from idle cabinets the arm-length gauntlets, blown full of air from behind, always groped in a ghastly row like the gloves of a troop of knights caught in a quagmire.

The technician across the room was injecting a monkey with some challenge dose (perhaps they were still working on plague), stroking him treacherously with one hand and palming the syringe in the other. Potential victims down the row of cabinets saw Mike passing behind him and glowered, frowned, and gyrated, but the man was too intent on his prey to notice. Mike eased across the room to the door marked HUMAN CHALLENGE and glanced through the viewing window.

Human Challenge was empty except for the volunteers in the glassed isolation cubicles, which for the first time struck Mike as remarkably like the animal cabinets behind him. An Army medical corpsman was reading a volunteer's self-administered blood pressure on a gauge outside the patient's cubicle. Mike hesitated. Just inside, behind the record desk, lay his goal, the file cabinet where the original journals on his plague vaccine lay: they could not be removed except during the biannual airing out, when they were burned. Even the paper on which they were written was by regulation considered contaminated, the information in them daily transcribed over an intercom to his typist in the outer office.

Standing at the entrance, he felt trapped, fore-and-aft. There was nothing to do but storm ahead. He took a deep breath and pushed through the swinging door, went quietly to the file, and eased open the top drawer. He ran a finger down the familiar indexes until he came to Run 57, his final plague vaccine. He skipped page after page of his own handwriting, devoted to entries on animal challenges, finally coming to his successor's.

Shakily, he found the case history of the first human volunteer. All at once the name leaped at him from the emergency form at the top of the file. *Edwin T. Girard, 183 Antioch Street, Fullerton, California.* He memorized name and address and was about to consign the folder back to limbo, when, spurred by a faint hope that he would find a mistake in technique rather than in the vaccine, he read on:

"Despite virility of challenge-dose as demonstrated in Rabbits 1647 to 1687 inclusive, E.T.G. reported no discomfort. Having exhibited no symptoms by Day 10, he was decontaminated and discharged at 1300 hours. *Conclusion:* A 50 ml injection of Run 57 *Pasteurella pestis* vaccine provided immunity to Volunteer E.T.G."

He almost yelled in relief. Q.E.D., he breathed, Q.E. goddamn D.! His temples began to pound. His first instinct was to throw off his disguise, demand to be taken to Greenberg, display the file, and throttle him, but he was so deliriously happy that he found himself forgiving him. God, he had to phone Toolie! No, first he had to get out of here! Undiscovered! And now!

As his guilt fled, the enormity of his danger dawned. He was a weak, lone bacillus that had penetrated a root-nerve of Army Security. The host animal was healthy, vaccinated and resistant. Its antibodies were ready to mass at the first hint of his presence. He almost dropped the file to run. He looked at the clock above the row of cubicles. It was five minutes to one. The lab would be filling. He had to move, and move fast. He replaced the journal by habit, started for the door, changed his mind and returned for it. Laboratory Hazard Regulations or not, this was one document that was leaving Contaminated, but quick.

He put it under his arm and moved swiftly through the door to Animal Challenge. The monkey-shooter was groping in glove-to-hand combat with one of his trapped charges, cursing steadily. Mike could hear the monkey screaming back. He moved into the airlock, slammed the door, stepped through into Postcontamination Change-and-Shower. He stripped and hurled the gown, hood, and boots into a hamper. He tossed the file through the shower to a bench on the other side. He stepped under the showerhead, which started automatically at the pressure of his feet. It would run, he knew, for five minutes, and he did not have five minutes. The hell with it. If the Army was worried about contaminating the outside world, wait until it saw tomorrow's paper.

He gave himself a few swipes of chlorhexemene from the soap spigot, stepped out, and reached for a towel. Suddenly a bell began to clang. He froze. A bright neon sign lit up. Paralyzed, he read: SMILE! YOUR PICTURE IS ABOUT TO BE TAKEN IN THE NUDE! YOU HAVE JUST VIOLATED THE FIVE-MINUTE SHOWER! PLAY SAFE FOR DETRICK!

A flashbulb flickered from above a lens set flush in the wall. There was a knock at the door of the drying room. The craggy GSA guard stuck his head around the corner, breathing hard from his run up the hall.

"Sorry, sir, I have to take your name. First offense?" He saw the folder on the bench and stiffened. "What's that? Look, Inspector, get on your goddamn clothes, and let's go."

Mike's knees began to tremble badly, but he got on his clothes, and went.

Chapter Thirteen

After the second phone call to General Greenberg from the frantic wife of the scientist O'Hare, Marty felt sorry for her, and grew curious too. He pretended that he had forgotten that the general was not taking calls and put her through. He eavesdropped but he could not piece the puzzle precisely together. Her husband, apparently, had been picked up at J-Lab in Detrick, where he had no right to be, and she wanted General Greenberg to get him out of Army custody. There was talk of a death among the volunteers, too. Not surprisingly, the general said he could do nothing for her husband, but shockingly, did not deny the fatality.

Marty tensed. A death from biological warfare would make a hell of a spread in the *Clarion*. If there had been one, it was the best-kept secret in CBW. Greenberg left for the day, shoulders slumped, face white, but still able to forgive Marty for allowing the phone call. Marty checked the Seventh Day Adventist file. It held the name of every conscientious objector who had volunteered at the Fort since the Army had agreed to substitute a term as a guinea-pig for a sentence as a soldier. No one had died. Along with the O'Hares's phone number, Marty tucked this jewel of information into his mind. Something stank. He still did not understand why his boss had not denied the death, but the Pentagon was becoming such a Byzantine palace that he seldom understood anything anyway. If he didn't cut loose soon, he would go out of his mind.

He left early himself. He checked his bus for his fat shadow, and saw no one suspicious. Just the same, he dodged through two alleys and a backyard before he entered Handlemann's through the basement window. As Chris Poma lounged in the kitchen drinking beer, Marty worked for an hour, studiously printing out the phonetic spelling for the chemical terms in the script, so that when Poma narrated it onto his sound track he would not stumble. Chris, now that the film was at the lab, had nothing to do, and was suffering more than when he was overworking.

He needed to get out of the house, that was the trouble. Marty offered to take him to the Aquarius, off Dupont Circle. *"Lonesome Cowboy* back-to-back with *Chelsea Girls,"* he read from the *Clarion.* "How about it?"

Poma crushed his beer can, studied it, dropped it into a wastebasket under one of Sunshine's finger-paintings. He was considering going. Marty tensed, scared that he had talked him into danger. He wished that he had learned to shut up, to overcome the feeling that if he didn't fill a void of silence, Chris would get bored. Hero-worship, he guessed, or some latent homosexuality. He had even discussed it with June, who was kind enough to decide that if Marty was a fag, she needed more homos and less heteros in her life.

"OK, Marty," Chris decided. "Let's go." They took great precautions. Marty went out the front door to draw off pursuit, while Chris crawled through the basement window. Marty drove Handlemann's van around the block, stopped and checked, and finally circled back and drove down P Street. He parked across from the back alley, spent a few minutes watching in his side-view mirror, and seeing no one suspicious, finally signaled Chris, who rode all the way to the Circle in the body of the van instead of the passenger seat. They saw the film. Leaving the little art-theater, with his confidence high, Chris insisted on buying a beer at the Anchor Bar next door.

Marty left Chris outside while he checked the action within. It was a cave of a place, with sawdust on the floor, popular with students from G.W. He saw no one suspicious, so he returned to the door for Chris, and led him to the booth in the farthest, darkest corner. It was next to the john, and smelled of urine, but they were used to that from cutting film in the third-floor room at Handlemann's. Marty bought a pitcher of beer at the bar and got two glasses and they drank to Warhol's movie on lesbianism and theirs on human sacrifice. They agreed that it had certain artistic merits of its own, for an Army training film.

Lee Frost watched Handlemann's house from an easy chair in the lobby of the Bagdad Hotel. The hotel had been many things since the Thirties: a quiet retreat, an apartment house, finally a warren of prostitution until it succumbed to amateur competition, free-love, and drugs. Now its lobby was a meeting place for elderly homosexuals and strung-out long-haired boys.

At 1615 hours a lithe brunette with a camera climbed Handlemann's steps, leading a little girl. An angular young man with frizzled hair and thick eyeglasses was next, lugging a projector. The little girl reappeared to play with a toy on the porch, and a stubby young man in blue jeans delivered a stack of newspapers, rubbing the child's head in passing. No one ever came out, and he never saw Handlemann or Lumpert, so he soon grew bored and walked to Dupont Circle.

He suddenly admitted to himself the real reason he was here. He stepped into a phone booth and called the Peace League. Laurie answered, and he asked her to come down to the Anchor for a beer. Maybe they could go to dinner and a movie afterward, or something.

"Or something," she agreed. He phoned Jenny. This time he lied outright and told her he was on a field interrogation. He met Laurie, flushed and happy, outside the Anchor, and led her to a booth in back.

"Are you hiding me again?" she wanted to know.

He *was* hiding her, of course, from a chance encounter with Handlemann or one of his own Holabird agents, which would have been embarrassing. He was about to admit that he was hiding her (from the young studs at the bar) when suddenly he saw Poma in the rear booth, laughing at something; looked dead into his eyes, in fact, and saw in the shadows of the booth the back of Lumpert's shaggy head. As always in crisis, he grew quiet: the reaction would come later. Politely, he sat Laurie down in the closest booth, returned to the bar, bought two beers, and carried them back to her, to give himself time to think and to get a better look at Poma. There was no doubt. He excused himself again, moved to the pay phone in front, and called the duty-sergeant at District Armed Forces Police. He told them who he was, who he had, and to get down quick.

He hung up and looked around, studying the terrain. He had done all he could, temporarily. At least he could block the front entrance, and he knew of none in the rear. A fat young man drinking beer at the end of the bar was trying to catch his eye. Lee recognized him as one of the Holabird student agents, apparently trying to tail Lumpert, and cluttering up a perfectly clean make. "Stay put," Lee growled between his teeth. He turned to go back to the booth and stiffened.

Lumpert, empty pitcher in hand, was heading toward the bar for a refill. If there was no escape for Poma in the back, there was no escape for Lee in front either. The clerk saw him and almost dropped the pitcher. Smiling cheerfully, Lee said: "How you doing, son? No more fire from the gravestones?"

"No sir," stuttered Lumpert. Then he spotted the fat agent and his whole posture changed. He glanced wide-eyed back at Lee and swung the pitcher, backhanded, from waist-height. If Lee had not caught its glitter in the neon light of a Michelob sign, it would have broken his jaw. He ducked the blow, which caught him on the side of the neck, avoided the next swing, saw Lumpert, flailing the pitcher, catch the agent in the temple and knock him from the barstool. Lee moved in, feinting a left and catching Lumpert's cheekbone with a sidehanded chop. The glasses flew from the clerk's face and Lee sunk another left into the soft belly. Lumpert dropped. Lee whirled, setting himself low for Poma.

The lieutenant, big and broad-shouldered, was already sliding from the booth. Lee pointed a forefinger at him and barked: "Hold it! Right where you are!" Instead, the boy charged for the entrance like a good fullback, low and hard, feet churning on the sawdust. Lee dropped a shoulder, got it into his chest, and the two crashed to the floor. Poma outweighed him by twenty pounds and Lee

239

was lugging twenty more years, but the boy seemed out of shape, with reflexes slow and a strange reluctance to punch. They thrashed in the sawdust before the bar. Lee caught flashes as they rolled: Lumpert groping for his glasses, bearded youngsters grinning from the barstools, Laurie biting her thumb, wide-eyed and astonished, the proprietress fumbling in her register for a coin to call the cops, her scrawny bartender frozen in fear. The fat agent, blood pouring from his temple, crawled to his knees. Poma arched, squirmed, and got halfway free. Lee, clinging to an ankle, jerked. As the lieutenant toppled, he threw on a hammerlock.

For a moment he thought he had won, but he looked up to find Lumpert squinting down at him, pitcher held high and peering for an opening like a nearsighted owl. Laurie leaped from the booth behind him. Swinging a beer-bottle viciously, she cracked it down on his forearm. Lumpert yelled in pain and dropped the pitcher. The Holabird agent lunged vaguely for his knees.

"Split!" Lee heard Poma grunt. "*You* dub it!"

Lumpert tore loose from the agent and ran for the rear. He slammed the door to the john as the agent lurched past. Lee heard the crash of glass, yanked Poma to his feet, shifted his hold to an armlock, and shoved him to the toilet.

They found the agent sitting on the toilet seat beneath a shattered window. Laurie was dabbing at his head with a paper towel. Blood, Lumpert's or his, was everywhere. Lee left them, his bad leg throbbing, and pushed the lieutenant into a booth, crowding beside him. "Dub *what*? Your film? Son, the MPs are on their way. Take your best shot! Tell me where that film is. I'll see it gets to the right people."

Poma shook his head. "No sir. Not in a million years!"

Laurie stood above them. "What film? What's going on, Lee?" She spotted Lumpert's glasses on the floor, picked them up, and put them in front of Poma. "Your friend's," she said. "I hope I didn't break his wrist."

"I'll take those," Lee said, pocketing them.

"Why, Lee? He couldn't see!"

"Good. Maybe he'll quit trying to brain my agents."

240

"I *thought* that pig in the john was yours," she blazed. "That's why I'm here, isn't it? I'm some sort of goddamn cover!"

"Don't be silly," Lee said, taking her hand.

It was ice-cold, and she drew it away. "Look, I saved your nice white teeth. I deserve an explanation! Or is it some fucking military secret?"

"It is now. When it isn't, you'll be the first to know."

"Unless you tell me what you got me into, I won't be around!"

A siren rose and fell and rose higher. The skinny bartender, emboldened by approaching authority, bustled to the table. He pointed a thumb toward the entrance. "Out! Allayou!"

"Good thinking," agreed Laurie. "Let him alone, Lee! Let's go."

Lee shook his head, showed the bartender his identification, and announced that Poma was under arrest. Laurie flushed angrily. "It was the other one that hit you! What did *he* do except try to get away?"

"Deserter," said Lee tersely.

"I didn't ask what he did *right*. What did he do *wrong?*"

"Come off it," demanded Lee. "You *picked* your side!"

"No," she said. "You picked it for me. So don't count on me. Don't count on me at all."

She slid from the booth and marched down the bar, trim hips flouting him, and there was nothing he could do but watch her go, short of releasing Poma and chasing after her.

He wanted her so badly that he very nearly did.

There was a chill to the night air of Colonial Village, and General Lucius Hardy lit a fire in the den and poured himself a Scotch. If Lee had been looking for praise, he had come to the wrong place. Hardy studied him as if deciding whether or not to offer him a drink. Finally he tossed an ice cube into a glass, sloshed in some liquor, and handed it to Lee as if he wished he had something cheaper.

"So," the general said acidly, "you captured the famous

241

Lieutenant Poma in hand-to-hand combat. Did the gentleman resist?"

"No."

Hardy took a putter from the corner and began to tap an imaginary golf ball around the den. "I told you, Lee, I didn't want you involved. To know of this massacre and not take action is very risky business."

"It sure is. So why didn't you act?"

The general looked up from the putter and evaluated him for a long moment. Suddenly he said: "How did you feel about Cambodia?"

Lee stared at him, amazed. "What's Cambodia got to do with it?"

"How'd you feel about it?"

Lee studied his drink. "Before Rick, or afterward?"

"Before."

"Military, fine. Internationally, it was a catastrophe. Just one more Hiroshima. And just one more hole in the old Army image."

"And *now* how do you feel?"

"Now?" Lee's voice shook. "Well, goddamn it, he could have got killed in Vietnam just as easily. If you're going to use every half-assed revolution you can find as a combat-training course, you got to expect to lose a few."

Hardy regarded him sadly. "That's what I figured you felt. OK, Lee. You found Poma. That was good work. Because believe me, we *have* been looking. Tomorrow's Wednesday, and the press probably won't have access to him. Then there's Thursday, Friday . . . I don't know. By next Monday, it may become clear to you why I haven't begun an official investigation on this. Or it may not. But I would like you to cease and desist, until then."

The temptation was to accept, to promise anything if he could regain Hardy's friendship. Lee moved to the photo of the 1942 Army team. Lucius had hardly changed physically, except for the gray hair, and yet there had been too many expedient decisions between cadet captain and lieutenant-general to ignore. Besides, something smelled. "Then it isn't entirely because I'm such a vulnerable target," he suggested. "There's something else?

It's not *entirely* because you want to see me wearing stars?"

Lucius flushed and tossed the putter back into the corner. "Nothing's entirely anything, ever! You talk like a bloody plebe. Just *forget the massacre!* If you don't have enough to do, I'll find you some more."

"The *massacre,*" Lee said softly, "is leaking out anyway. You know Weintraub got into a hearing in the War Room. You think *he* won't follow up, if I don't? Look, do you want us to find that film and spring it when we court-martial these maniacs, whoever they are, or do you want Walter Cronkite to spring it some night on CBS? Some night when we're bragging about body-counts?"

"What I *want,*" Hardy said, "is for you to drop it. Because if you don't, I'll drop you, and those stars will melt like a pair of snowflakes in hell."

"I'm sure they will," Lee said, "and I'm sorry. But I can't."

He finished the drink and left.

Jenny awakened, and he told her about Hardy, expecting static, but she squeezed his hand, smiled, and dropped off to sleep as if she didn't care. Maybe she had not grasped the fact that after all the dreary years she might never be a general's wife. In a while, he drifted off to sleep himself.

243

Phase III

OPERATION HOLOCAUST

Chapter One

To ease Pentagon-bound traffic the Defense Department staggers its working hours. One shift must arrive at six A.M., so even before dawn, a few lights flicker on in the bedrooms of Washington Highlands on the eastern bank of the Potomac, where Pentagon officers will catch an Air Force launch from Bolling Field for a cruise to the River Entrance. But the predawn lights march mostly in from the west, blazing first in a few restored farmhouses near Manassas and Bull Run, then moving toward the capital like the campfires of Beauregard and Johnston in hot pursuit of the Feds. A twinkling skirmish-line first assaults the colonial tracts of Walnut Hill, Balls Hill, Spring Hill, Swink's Mill, Idylwood, and the Country Club country (Country Club Grove, Country Club Manor, and Country Club Hills). Then lights blink on in the bedrooms of Annandale Acres and Holmes Run Park. They flash along the cul-de-sacs of Belvue Forest, Madison Manor, Braddock Acres, Glencarlyn, Parkglen, Green Valley, Park-fairfax, Virginia Highlands, and Beverly Hills (eastern branch). Inspired by the Pentagon warrior's desire to sleep in peace, local real-estate developers have created, on billboard and mortgage, enough dales, hills, knolls, heights, hollows, parks, acres, valleys, and glens to enchant half the elves in the Black Forest.

Pentagon home-buyers are not really fooled by the visions of the salesmen, most of whom are retired military men. They suspect that the price of Camelot is high. They see that the hills are flat, the dales nude, that the shoulder-to-shoulder manors already need paint. Everyone knows that the true Pentagon lords live at the Watergate in Washington and the real squires in plain McLean, Virginia. But the rustic addresses will look good on cookout invitations, and when a retired general tells you that landscaping is just around the corner, it is impolite to doubt him. Besides, Pentagon arteries clog in the morning no matter where you live, and the traffic is even worse on the bridges from the District side of the river.

Lee Frost, living within sight of the building and having established eight A.M. as the beginning of his working day, seldom arose before seven. But this morning he awakened early from a dream of the cruise with Rick down the Potomac. For a while he listened to the drone of their faulty clock-radio and to Jenny's breathing (she was even beginning to breathe fat, somehow, although he couldn't explain it). Finally he decided to arrive early at his office and try to catch up on the work.

Entering the crawling traffic at dawn, swinging left down Columbia Pike past Arlington Cemetery, he found that it was still only five-thirty. Already South Parking was filling. By nine A.M. there would be ten thousand vehicles in the lots, and the last of their drivers would have a mile to walk from car to office. He could hardly bear at this hour to think of his own jammed desk, so he continued around the Pentagon to the marina on Columbia Island. *Misty* lay dripping with dew. He stepped aboard, unlocked the hatch, and slid below.

He sat on Rick's bunk. He decided to start trying to sell the boat. Laurie was wrong to urge him to keep it, and anyway, from the set of her shoulders last evening, he would never see her aboard again. He would pin up a FOR SALE notice today on the Concourse bulletin board in the Pentagon and next week, after the rally, perhaps run an ad in *The Washington Post*. He began sliding the drawers from under Rick's bunk to see how much work there would be in cleaning her cabin. He pulled out a blue Scandinavian Airlines pamphlet, thumbed through Norwegian fjords, Danish farms, Stockholm statuary, finally Uppsala University, where Rick, threatened by the draft, had almost fled to finish his graduate work in anthropology.

Lee crumpled the pamphlet, suddenly sick. Damn it, it was too late for remorse now, and besides, he had only said that if Rick were sincere, he would demonstrate his convictions better as a federal prisoner than a federal fugitive. Not one more word had he said, and besides, Rick was old enough to make his own decisions, had been making them for years.

Savagely, he attacked the drawer again. Jammed between a Chesapeake tide-table and a greasy engine-manual, he found the beginning of Rick's unfinished graduate thesis, "The Errant Gene." He had never asked to read it, but now he tried to follow the penciled interlineations and the drunken lines from Rick's crazy portable.

His son began with *War and Peace:* "The aim of war is murder; the methods of war are spying, treachery, and their encouragement." (Well, Rick, no shit! I never would have believed it. And what has Tolstoy got to do with anthropology?) Then Darwin: ". . . the finest young men are taken by the conscription. Shorter and feebler men, with poor constitutions, are left at home, and consequently have a much better chance of propagating their kind . . ."

More to the anthropological mark, that. He read further, as Rick took over from the masters: "The purpose of this paper is to outline how a search might be made of the anthropological time-spectrum, to locate that errant gene in man which permits him, almost alone among fauna, to destroy his own species. To find the first mad ancestor who bore the gene might not be as difficult as it sounds."

Rick and Laurie sang the same note. Again he reflected that it was too bad that his son had not found her. *"Ramapithecus,* last ape in our line, was peaceful," he learned. "So the fatal flaw lies somewhere between *Australopithecus,* son of *Ramapithecus,* and me. But only one hundred thousand male ancestors stand between us. If they materialized in single file, I could walk the line in a day. Only the nearest ten thousand of them are *Homo sapiens* of my own genus, species, and brain capacity. If every single one of my *Homo-sapiens* forefathers was queued outside a Senator ballgame (where the whole family section will extend for only one hundred seats, one hundred rows deep), I could start at the gate and walk to my first thinking ancestor in half an hour. More importantly, it would take me less than a minute to reach a progenitor contemporary with the outcast Middle-East Semite named Jesus, perhaps mythical, perhaps not, who possibly first recognized the flaw in our genus and who, without sufficient anthropological data, tried unsuccessfully to remove it with spiritual surgery.

"So we have not even been *trying* to cure the disease of murder, legalized or illegal, for very long . . ."

With a sinking feeling, Lee realized that this was all that there was, all that there would ever be. Lee had left it aboard, a false start, perhaps, and taken the fat green binders, rich with research material, back to George Washington with him. None had turned up in his personal effects. They must be somewhere. He would never have taken them into the Army with him, for they represented two years of work and besides were too bulky. Lee wondered if he had left them with some girl, or in the apartment he and Handlemann had shared near the campus. If so, Handlemann might still have them. Lee discovered that he wanted them very badly.

He folded the pages on which Rick had sweated, closed the hatch, and headed for work.

At nine, Lee had a call from Picket Aspen's Civil Disturbance Center, requesting him to report for an emergency briefing. He met Lucius Hardy outside, tight-lipped and angry, and learned that the Secretary of Defense had awarded Aspen responsibility for handling the demonstration if it marched on the Pentagon. Hardy's glacial calm showed that he felt Lee's handling of the Israeli-Greek memo had lost them the ball. Firing for effect inside, Picket Aspen had coffee served and then made them wait at his long table under the lighted map before he joined them from the glassed cubicle in which he had been checking the national blood pressure.

Lee noted the other guests at Aspen's kaffee klatsch. The colonel commanding Fort Myer garrison had been invited, the Commander of the Old Guard, 1st Battalion,

Third Infantry, a brigadier from the 80th Army Reserve Division, a light-colonel commanding the District Armed Forces Police, the Chief U. S. Marshal, a clerk from the Pentagon branch of the Federal Court, and Lieutenant-Colonel Chip Bolen from Public Affairs, wearing his ribbons and command-pilot wings and one of his sincerest smiles. All seemed fascinated by the plastic map towering over Aspen. It had been glowing in its normal green, violet, and amber lights, but now it flickered into ruddier activity as the country, having breakfasted, lurched into another day. Boston began to pulse red and Lee could hear a great clatter from the teletype machines lining the walls. He wondered if the new American revolution had just started or if a Panther headquarters had merely opened up on the Boston police.

Aspen briefed them on how he intended to hold Arlington Bridge, if the demonstrators were foolish enough to try to cross. Because they would never reach the building, he refused to discuss Lee's Military Contingency Plan for the Pentagon, set up long ago, and handed out his own Operational Orders instead. Lee wondered why he and Hardy had even been asked to the briefing. He suggested that there might be more demonstrators than the Justice Department estimated. Aspen only shrugged. Lee sat back, worried. He was sure that rivulets of marchers (certainly the trashing element and any Weathermen left after the bridge) would somehow bypass the span if they didn't storm it, and if they arrived angry, he had better be ready. Aspen wasn't that stupid, though; he had something in mind, although he wouldn't admit it.

Gas! Choppers and gas, he would bet his life on it—and not CN, either; CS, for the demonstrators would never forget that. General Hardy was shaking his head, leafing through Aspen's Op Orders. "Picket," the general warned, "I don't like your thin red line. Suppose Lee's right? Suppose there aren't just twenty thousand? Suppose it's more like sixty or seventy?"

"They can only come across a thousand at a time," Aspen pointed out. "Remember Horatio."

"Who?" Hardy asked incredulously, getting up to leave.

"I think he means Horatius, sir," remarked Lee, picking up his own copy. "But General Aspen?"

"Yeah, Frost?"

"Horatius had to swim home." He followed Lucius Hardy out the guarded door.

Chapter Two

A prematurely cool air mass slithered southward along the Middle Atlantic Coast, bringing an early touch of autumn to Washington and a snap to the gait of the government workers. It was a very good scene on Dupont Circle, and getting better all the time. George Washington University, Georgetown, and American U began to swarm with bearded young men and long-haired girls, twelve-string guitars, acne and acid, knapsacks and bedrolls. Hondas by the hundreds snarled along the street and Day-Glo vans were thick. Suddenly you could pick up a joint on a street corner for the asking, or a Marighella booklet on guerrilla tactics, or a dozen RDs for a dollar. Metropolitan Narcotics gave up. *The Quicksilver Times* estimated ten thousand new people in town, with three days still to go; ·Handlemann's *Clarion,* not due on the street until Friday, reset its type and made it fifty thousand, just to be safe. The Switchboard worked quietly and quickly, placing the homeless in crashpads. Telephones in the Peace League, quiet since draft calls had fallen off a year ago, began to jingle continually, as it dawned on even the least aware that years from the last Moratorium, U.S. troops still sweltered and died in Vietnam. The Free Clinic went on three full shifts, treating trips and epileptics and delivering two destitute young ladies who had misjudged their times. Everyone there agreed that babies, mothers, weather, and the Movement's rising tide were beautiful.

The rumor that a deserter had been captured in a fight in the Anchor Bar had little impact on the freaks in the Circle, but along Q Street so many people had seen the blow-up from the Ban Doc film that Poma had become an unseen folk-hero. Today he became a political prisoner. Switchboard developed its version of the bust. *The Quicksilver Times* scooped the *Clarion,* which could only put out a quick mimeographed pamphlet protesting Army brutality. A fund for Poma's defense was begun at GW, and by noon it had collected a hundred dollars. In the Free Clinic, where Marty Lumpert had appeared briefly trying to get his arm set, then panicked and split before anyone could really help him, the rumor was that the Anchor still swarmed with agents. At the Peace League Laurie ruefully admitted that she had contributed to Poma's capture, not taking refuge, either, in the obvious fact that she had not flashed on the truth until after the act. She was absolved by even the two militants among her houseguests, although not by Handlemann, with whom they had made contact. Handlemann claimed that she was old enough to know that if you played with pigs, you would get pig-shit on your feet, and that Frost, whom he said he knew well, was the trickiest agent in the Establishment's employ.

Only those who lived in Handlemann's pad knew where the film was. On the Street, the consensus was that the Army had won again and captured it. Handlemann was sure that Poma was rocketing around some interrogation room under Army truncheons and that he would shortly break and that then the FBI, CIA, CID, Metropolitan Vice Squad, and Colonel Lee Frost would all swoop down on the New Age Lab and confiscate the film. He was afraid to go near the place, setting great store by his freedom until Saturday. He was afraid to panic Wong uselessly, too, since the Chinaman would destroy the film, so he seemed to put the whole problem into the hands of fate to concentrate on the rally and attendant festivities.

No one knew where Marty Lumpert had fled when he left the Free Clinic with his wrist in a crude splint, over the protests of the resident medical student. June was frantic when she heard that he was hurt and without his glasses. She stormed into Handlemann's office and demanded that he send the staff out looking for him, Tom-Tom, Chute, Sue, everyone.

"I can't," said Handlemann. "Try the film lab."

"Why?"

"That chick that broke his arm. She said the last thing Poma told him was to dub the film. He's queer for Poma, he'll try it."

"And if I go down to find him, I suppose I may as well pick up the film?" she said sarcastically.

"As a matter of fact, yes."

"I figured." He handed her the spare keys to the van and told her where Marty and Poma had parked it. "And if Marty's there, don't bring him back here!"

"Just the film. Find *him* a nice soft gutter?"

"That's right, love."

"And if I get picked up," she said softly, "don't call you, you'll call me?"

"Call the ACLU."

"You're sweet, Red," she smiled. "You'd have made Sunshine a wonderful father."

On the way down the stairs she suddenly faced Dewey Dupays on the dark landing, a jet-black shadow with white teeth. He carried a cardboard box on his shoulder and as they met they played a polite dance, right, left, right. He ended up laughing and shook the box, listening. "What's in there?" she wanted to know.

He seemed to find the question funny, but only said: "Any word from that fat little dude?"

"He's not fat, he's not little, and no," she said coldly.

"Oo-ie," he chortled, continuing up the stairs. "Mind yo' tongue, Dewey-stud. Oo-ie, oo-ie, oo-ie . . ." She heard a mighty oath from Handlemann as he stumbled into the office. "Dewey, you stupid son-of-a-bitch! Be *careful!*"

She decided that Dewey was strung out on pot, or speed, or on the strange excitement that Handlemann seemed to generate in people. Until they really knew him.

Sergeant Fred Liebholtz reported to Lee Frost that his subject, Bull Collins, had enplaned again for California and that he had bugged his room at the Marriott and alerted Army Counterintelligence in the L.A. Federal Building to pick him up at L.A. International and tail him until he returned to Washington. Now was there anything else the Colonel wanted?

There was: to find the massacre film or Marty Lumpert, or both. They went to work together and discovered the New Age Film Lab without moving from the office, by induction, deduction, and considerable luck. Since Poma had told Lumpert to dub the missing film, then Lumpert must know where it was being processed. If he knew where it was, maybe he had delivered it there. Lee went through the amateurish reports of the Holabird agents and had Liebholtz plant a red pin on the wall map at every point to which Lumpert had been tailed, or, if lost, last seen. He had gone nowhere but to the Pentagon, to Handlemann's, to the *Clarion* office, or to the Anchor except last Sunday, when he had driven the *Clarion* van to an intersection in northeast Washington. Here, in unconscious luck, Lumpert had made a traffic light and left the agent stewing in a line of halted cars. Discouraging, but if he had delivered the film to a lab in the past six days, this had to be the trip, and they need only find the lab.

Lee and Leibholtz found a half-dozen movie labs in the Washington phone book, and got another half-dozen unlisted porno ones from Metropolitan Vice. He eliminated all but those with northeast addresses. One, the New Age Processing Lab (8 and 16 mm.) seemed to share a home with the Ulysses Studio, which had a familiar underground sound to Lee. He and Liebholtz spent half an hour leafing through the office file of the *Clarion*. Liebholtz finally stumbled on Ulysses between an ad placed by a fun-loving hetero couple looking for a switcheroo and a swinging chick looking for a ride to Oregon. *Male and Fm. Models Wanted for Art Films. Auditions Mon-Fri Ulysses Studio 2319 Rand Alley NE.*

All roads seemed to lead to or from Handlemann and the *Clarion*. A pin placed at 2319 Rand NE was within a half-dozen blocks of Lumpert's lucky traffic light. To make sure of his ground, Lee had Liebholtz check the studio out with Vice.

"Harry Wong, *et al*," reported the sergeant to Lee, reading from notes. "Wong is a male Oriental American citizen five-feet-seven inches and so on, and so on . . . No known felony convictions . . . Produces porno films . . . Negro and white models . . . Charged with obscene material through the mails April 12, 1969, charge dismissed lack of evidence . . . Frequents Dupont Circle, but no narcotics arrests. Stuff like that there, Colonel."

Lee got a hurry call to report to Hardy's office. He told Liebholtz to check out Wong with Holabird and Pentagon Civil Analysis for subversive activity. "Then stake out his lab for Lumpert. But don't take Lumpert unless he's carrying film. And if you do take him, you're arresting him only for one day AWOL and assaulting a superior officer."

"There goes the Colonel bragging again," sighed Liebholtz, "but you're certainly superior to some I've seen."

In Lucius Hardy's office Lee found General Greenberg looking like a sickly candidate for Walter Reed Medical Center. Hardy was running a tape recorder backward in a garble of Donald Duck jargon. "Lee," he said, "the voice you are about to hear may be your sniper."

"Jesus!" exclaimed Lee. "Who?"

"An angry young Ph.D. who quit Detrick with a hard-on because he felt CBW took unnecessary risks with a botulism antitoxin? Erratic, hot-tempered? How would that grab you?"

"A scientist? Could he shoot?"

"Ex-Marine," said Hardy simply. "And an ex-cop, too."

That wasn't enough, obviously, and he asked Hardy what the scientist's motive was supposed to have been.

Hardy nodded to Greenberg, who rambled uncertainly through an involved story of one Michael O'Hare, Ph.D., who wavered in and out of focus for Lee, and the story made a certain sense, but not enough, since the motive for the shot didn't seem to exist until after the shot was fired. He pointed this out, and Hardy said: "He was just as erratic before he was told that a volunteer died. And just as angry that his vaccine wasn't being used in Da Nang."

"So when General Greenberg set this erratic mind at ease by falsely claiming his vaccine killed a man, then what did O'Hare do?" Lee asked sardonically.

"Don't be insubordinate!" Hardy said heavily. "Telling him *that* was my idea, anyway, not Morrie's. What he did was psychotic. He drove to Detrick and busted into the most securely guarded agency of the U.S. Army this side of Fort Knox."

Lee suggested charitably that no Security was perfect.

257

"Who would know better than you?" observed Hardy. "Anyway, he found the file he was looking for."

"So now he knows he was lied to." Lee watched Hardy narrowly. He began to get the drift. "He doesn't sound insane to me."

"Would *you* penetrate a contaminated CBW lab?" Hardy wanted to know.

"He wasn't even current on his shots," mumbled Greenberg.

"Well, go ahead," Lee snorted, feeling as if he had stumbled into a madhouse himself, "then what?"

"Listen to this, from Fort Detrick Security when they questioned him," said Hardy, flipping on the recorder.

"—matter of curiosity, what have you got against General Greenberg?"

"I'll kill the son-of-a-bitch!"

"But why? You haven't explained why?"

"He'll tell you why. I swear by all that's holy. I'll kill him. I'll kill him for this!"

"OK," Lee agreed. "I'll find out where he was when the shot was fired. That ought to be easy if he's running a lab at the National Institute."

Hardy shook his head. "It won't be. He's lying about it." He turned on the recorder again, and Lee heard O'Hare report that he had worked all day in his laboratory last Wednesday, and had eaten in the cafeteria. Hardy turned off the machine. "But his assistant reports that he left at ten for home and didn't come back all day."

The sound of his ex-colleague's voice had almost finished off Greenberg and he left, looking even sicker. As the door closed on him, Lee turned to Hardy: "What's going on? Charge him with penetrating Detrick, if you have to. Personally, I think he was damn near justified. But *don't* hold him as a murder suspect! That's a lot of crap!"

"He's not much of a suspect," admitted Hardy, "but he's all you've got."

"He's all *you've* got."

"It's your case."

"Well, I'm not going to harass him for a shot he never fired!"

"You don't *know* he didn't fire it."

"I don't know *you* didn't fire it. Am I harassing you?"

"More than you think, Lee, more than you think."

"I think you want him held for murder, because otherwise he'd make bail and be out screaming plague in Da Nang, and why aren't they vaccinating them?"

"True, true," Hardy smiled. "That's the chance you take when you rave about killing generals, I guess."

"So the longer we hold him, the more he raves, and who would even listen to him if he *did* get out? You never mentioned that!"

" 'Right on,' Lee, as your friends across the river say." Lee nodded. "Well, sir, I guess it's time."

"For what?"

"To get yourself another boy." Lee spun and headed for the door.

"Lee!" Hardy's voice cracked out like a rifle shot. Lee turned. The general was rounding the desk, offering his hand. "Come on, Lee! It's been too long."

Lee's throat tightened, but he refused the hand. "I'm sorry, Lucius, I just won't do it."

Hardy smiled. "I didn't really expect you to, I guess. Not on that evidence." But there was more, he said, that he hadn't wanted Greenberg to know, not liking to divulge Intelligence methods. He'd had Holabird tap O'Hare's home phone the moment the report of his arrest had come in. "Guess who contacted his wife?"

"Who?"

"Greenberg's clerk!"

"Lumpert?" gasped Lee. "When?"

"Midnight."

"Where from?"

"Pay phone, in Washington."

"What did he say?"

"That he had information on her husband, and he'd call back. It's all on tape at Holabird. You want to listen?"

"No. I want to talk to the wife."

"I thought you would." He gave Lee an address in Catonsville, and said, comfortably, "So we'll call it a preliminary investigation for assault with intent to kill, OK?" He picked up his phone and told his secretary to get him the Pentagon branch of the Federal District Court. As Lee moved to the door, Hardy asked: "How's that clawed-up back of yours?"

"OK," Lee said uncomfortably.

"Jenny ever notice?"

"No. And thanks. I'd forgotten all about it."

"I wouldn't, Colonel," Hardy said paternally. "That would be ungrateful, and we can't have that."

Chapter Three

Congressman Cy Weintraub sat at the foot of the long Committee table, wondering if anyone besides him was listening to his expert witness attacking the MIRV Program. Cy glanced up the table at Dennes, presiding at the center. Something today had brought out the best in the old bastard, who had been fighting Cy's efforts to bring his young expert before the Committee for months. Cy wondered if it was the secret memo on the Israeli-Greek plane deal, still ticking like an unexploded bomb in his own briefcase, that had brought on the Chairman's quiescent mood, or whether it could be the absence of reporters and TV cameras, barred from this testimony, that had calmed him. To the eye, Dennes was as intimidating as ever, slumped wetly behind his microphone, but he had not once set the famous alarm clock with which he limited opposition debate, and those few token witnesses from State and HEW that the doves had collected had been allowed to speak all morning with hardly a lash from the old man's tongue.

Doctor Manning Carroll, a dark, stolid young man who worked with Sternglass in Radiation Physics at the University of Pittsburgh, reached the summation of his report from the last Hanford Symposium, and his scientific monotone rose to something like emotion.

"Gentlemen," he said, face glowing with sincerity, "thirty-four thousand infants *still* die each year from fallout incurred *before* the 1963 ban on atmospheric testing." He paused for effect. Channing, a New Jersey Congressman, was scribbling notes for a speech. Haloway of Massachusetts dozed. Martin of South Dakota, on whom Cy could usually rely, had a plane to catch for Rapid City and was covertly glancing at his watch.

A desperate note entered Carroll's voice. "I have shown a rise of one percent in actual over expected infant deaths downwind of the Trinity test of a *small* Alamogordo weapon in 1945. A hundred such would have killed every infant born since 1950 in Texas, Arkansas, Alabama, Louisiana, Mississippi, Georgia, and both Carolinas!"

Dennes picked up his gavel, and Carroll's words began to race. "The Russians know from their *own* infant-mortality tables that even if we exterminated them and they did not retaliate, our *own* fallout would extinguish the next U.S. generation. And they know *we* know it. Where is the credibility of—"

"Doctor Carroll?" Ab Dennes drawled politely.

"Where is the credibility of Multiple Independent Reentry Vehicles—"

"Doctor Carroll!" Dennes called more sharply, tapping the gavel.

"Where is—"

"Carroll!" The gavel crashed. The young man subsided in shock. "Motion for adjournment?" Dennes asked.

"Mr. Chairman," Cy said swiftly, "I have another matter—"

"Well, I move that we adjourn," said Martin of South Dakota.

"I second," mumbled Haloway of Massachusetts, coming to life.

"Wait a minute!" exploded Weintraub. "I have an urgent matter of surplus sales! I want it brought up today!"

"Adjourned," said Dennes, pushing back his chair. "Until one P.M. tomorrow."

Cy Weintraub slammed his chair away from the table, strode center stage as the room cleared. "Goddam it, Ab," he sputtered, "I warned you. I'll give it to the press!"

"What's that you'll give?" Ab smiled. "That egghead's wet-dreams?"

"That egghead's wet-dreams," Cy said, "are already known to the JCS and the Administration, which has apparently decided to button-up rather than cause any more defense unemployment. I'm talking about the Israeli jets, which is something we can still handle."

"There's so *much* you young fellows want to leak," sighed Dennes. "I forgot all about them jets, I swear I did. Just one man I want you to talk to first. Young Jewish pilot. You ever learn Hebrew? I mean, from your folks or anybody?"

"Did you learn Swahili from your Mammy?" snapped Cy. "Hell no, I don't speak Hebrew!"

"That's all right. He speaks English, kind of fancy. But if you understand that boy-scientist you just crammed down our throats you'll understand this Jewish fellow just fine."

"It won't do any good."

"I'll tell you what," offered Dennes, "if it don't, I'll release that plane deal myself. Fair enough?"

"*I'll* release it. I'm still releasing that memo."

"Why? I can get it declassified. You'd get prosecuted, maybe, lose a lot of Jewish votes, too. Why sink yourself for nothing?"

They had reached the door. A Congressional page handed a note to Weintraub. On it was a list of phone numbers. All were code 212, New York. All were urgent. And leading the list was the number of Howard Green, clothing manufacturer, campaign angel, and would-be maker of Army fatigues. Cy's secretary had encircled that one twice, in red.

"When can I send this throttle-jockey?" urged Dennes.

"Hell, I don't care," Cy said despondently. "It looks like I'll be in my office half the night."

"Looks like I'll be in mine 'til the day I die," Dennes chuckled. "Best you don't forget it."

At two P.M. Sergeant George Maxon, watching from a one-way window recessed in a dent in the plumbing van parked outside Sherry Pace's apartment, observed with some admiration the professional nonchalance of a really good car thief. It was a civil matter, not military, and he would never have done anything further than to phone the Metropolitan Police and report it when he had time, had it not been for the fact that the thief was the teen-ager who had almost caught him last week bugging his mother's apartment.

The kid had wandered out of the building, kicking idle dirt, and headed up the opposite sidewalk from Maxon. Maxon would have ignored him had it not been for his choice of sidewalk position, which Maxon recognized, from a stint as an MP working with the Tokyo police, as that of a car thief who wanted to check ignition keys while seeming to wander aimlessly down a residential street.

So when Jordie Pace stopped, stretched, climbed into a Plymouth Barracuda, and pulled out of the parking space after a suspicious delay, Maxon was not in the least surprised.

Maxon had an instant decision to make. His safer course was to stay precisely where he was, since the phone in the apartment was bugged with a transmitter good for only a few hundred yards, and if he moved he might miss a call. He wished that he had instant communications with the colonel, or even Liebholtz, but he did not. He tried to judge what Frost or Liebholtz would have done. The answer was unclear, so he chose valor over discretion and began to tail the car, which was traveling most staidly down the street.

He followed it halfway through Washington, and when it was suddenly ditched in a private garage, where an accomplice was waiting, he called Metropolitan Auto Theft from a nearby gas station. He was back at his post outside the Pace apartment in fifteen minutes, manning the van's receiver. He did not have to wait long for results. Sherry Pace, who had been quietly boozing at home while she awaited her civil-service hearing, had not had a noteworthy call for two days. Now the Metropolitan Juvenile Detail commanded her presence at the station. Before she could leave, Jordie got his official two-minute call through. He complained that it was all a joke, he had thought it was a friend's car; the only reason they had been stripping it was for extra laughs. Mama did not laugh. In a low, frantic tirade she quoted his record, which Maxon found impressive. They would throw away the key on the kid. He

264

hadn't liked the little bastard on sight, but now he felt queasy about it all. They hung up.

Sherry Pace appeared quickly at the apartment entrance, buttoning a frilly blouse and running unsteadily to her own car. With the apartment empty, there would be no more telephone traffic, so he let her get a block away and began to tail her.

He did not know precisely what he had stirred up, or whether Colonel Frost would be proud or angry. He had a long imaginary conversation with the colonel, which resolved nothing since Frost was not present and his own arguments sounded one-sided. He took refuge in something the colonel had once said: "When in doubt, throw the bomb."

From the desperate look on the mother's face when she parked and ran into the station, he had certainly done that.

Lee found the O'Hare home clinging precariously to a shady hill above a narrow street. The house was rickety, Victorian, all knees and elbows. It stared down, astonished, from under an oak at horseless vehicles wandering past below. Lee climbed cracked stone steps, avoiding skates, baseball gloves, and plastic toy rifles. Two little boys played mumbletypeg without much interest on the gray wooden porch, and another swung listlessly on a knotted rope from the oak in the yard. Somewhere inside he could hear two more arguing.

Toolie O'Hare was lean, blonde, and ice-cold. She shooed a tiny replica of the other children out of the living room and slid closed old-fashioned paneled doors. She had been crying but she was over that, steel-taut in her anger. She brushed a stray hair out of her eyes. "All right, Colonel, what's going on? He's a Reserve officer! He was cleared secret once! That used to be *his* lab! He had a good reason for being there!"

He told her that he was not here to discuss Security, but to find out where her husband had been at noon last Wednesday.

Her head snapped up like a startled doe's, and he real-

265

ized with surprise that he had hit a nerve. "I'd rather not go into Wednesday," she said, "or any other day."

He sat opposite her and looked into her eyes. "I think you'd better. He's under suspicion of having tried to kill General Greenberg."

"Having *what?*"

He repeated himself. Her face grew impassive, as if a gate had clanged down. "I see, Colonel. The Security charge isn't enough to keep him quiet, so you've dreamed up something else. Well, it's none of your **goddam**ned business where he was last Wednesday."

"I'm sorry you won't cooperate."

She flashed him a smile of icy brilliance. **"I didn't** say *that,* Colonel. I shall, I shall! Attempted *murder!* My very own husband, a *murderer!* You never know, do you? But in this case, we just might be wrong. Shall we go have a look at something?" She led him to the kitchen, where the mumbletypeggers were now raiding the refrigerator. She ignored them and walked to the wall-calendar. She pointed to last Wednesday. "You'll note," she said, "that while most of the other days are taken up with childish fun and games, last Wednesday was reserved for more adult pursuits."

He saw a female biological symbol playfully entwined with a male one. Scrawled across the daily square was a note: "Kids to mother's by 11 for *sure.*" Two numbers stood in a corner of the square. "Now, the top one's my rectal temperature. Under it, as I'm sure you've guessed, is the number of days since my last period of ovulation."

"Look, damn it, I'm just trying to check his story," he said, feeling the color rising in his face.

She ignored him. "See, Mike works weekends quite often, so he feels justified—"

"OK, OK, I get the picture!"

"Justified in celebrating the end of the drought, so to speak. Even on a weekday. A sort of unfertility rite, a 'nooner,' as you'd probably put it. We're nothing if not Catholic around here, and—"

"I *told* you," he growled, "I understand."

She looked suddenly stricken. "But however shall I prove it in court?"

266

"Frankly," he offered weakly, "that's what I was going to ask."

"Well, let's think. If *you* don't perjure yourself, I can prove that the calendar was here when you came. And if my mother doesn't lie, I can prove that the kids were dropped on time. Since Mike's a government scientist, you wouldn't have any cameras in our bedroom, would you, so we could prove we were actually screwing?"

"I'm just trying to do my job," he said.

She smiled again, diamond-hard. "I'm glad, sir. I'll sleep better tonight, knowing that my Army realizes how we till our humble acres, how our children pass the time, and how we breed."

"OK," he cut in sharply. "Don't lose that calendar."

"It goes in a vault," she said tightly. "You never know who's dropping around."

"That's wise." He watched her face. "Because your husband claims he worked all day Wednesday."

"He *says* he worked all day."

"What?"

The ice melted and her eyes filled with tears. "Oh, God! Of *course* he would! You wouldn't understand that, would you?"

"I just might," Lee said softly.

"Then let him come home to us!" She whirled and ran back to the front of the house. He slammed out through the screen door, stumbled over a basket of puppies, and moved down the creaking back steps to his car. His shirt was soggy with sweat.

He would tell Hardy about the calendar, but it would be useless, of course. Hardy would never admit until it suited him that he had no case, and the more O'Hare ranted, the easier Hardy would find it to keep him quiet.

As he drove home, a sharp pain tore at his stomach. He wondered if he was finally getting an ulcer. At Holabird, he picked up the tapes of the tap on O'Hare's phone. He listened to Lumpert's voice: *"I have information on your husband, but I haven't time to talk. I'll call back."* He wondered what Lumpert's interest, or the *Clarion*'s, was, in O'Hare or Mrs. O'Hare. He called his office and told Thelma that he had decided to stop off at the Peace

League to offer Reverend Scott some Army walkie-talkies to help the rally marshals at the Monument Saturday. Driving on into Washington he told himself that he was trying to frustrate Aspen and prevent a confrontation at the bridge, but what he really wanted was to see Laurie, and the knowledge did not help the pain in his stomach at all.

Marty Lumpert checked with Wong from a pay phone in a busy Negro supermarket a few blocks from the lab. The Chinaman told him that his girl was there with the script for dubbing and that the lab seemed safe. Marty had slept painfully in an all-night movie, doped and restless, waking intermittently to watch John Wayne's quick-frozen valor as a U.S. Marine. He had eaten a greasy egg in a White Castle, was almost broke and hungry again. Before he was tempted to steal, he left the supermarket and headed for the lab, squinting in the sudden sunlight. When he turned up Rand Alley, the alcoholic Negro on watch outside did not recognize him without his glasses, giving him hope of at least temporarily evading capture. Then the black flashed a grin and asked for a cigarette. Marty gave him one and pressed the button in the shabby door.

He found June sitting against the wall in the studio, staring at a living tableau under the movie lights. The white, stoned as before, was performing more-or-less happy cunnilingus on the squirming Negress, who still seemed bored. The West Indian director seemed to have abdicated to the fat little cameraman, who darted in and out, selecting his own angles and working without even a tripod. June arose and hugged Marty, frightened at his half-splintered wrist and the dark, vicious lines running from a slash on his forearm up to his elbow. Wong hurried them back to a crude sound studio in the rear of the place, where the script had been set on a lectern in front of a screen.

Narration turned out to be a job for a professional, and one with keen eyesight, too. The words had to be

268

keyed exactly to the picture, and Marty found that if he watched the screen, he lost his place in the script, and if he tried to follow the script, the room lights came on within seconds and the Chinaman's voice came over an intercom: "Cut!"

He was starting again for the fifth time when a buzzer sounded. Wong leaped for the window, looked down, and yelled: "Fuzz! Get your asses out!" Wong jumped back to the projector, spun the reel and removed it, tore the sound track from its console, and tossed it into a bin marked BURN. He was about to hurl the film in too when Marty grabbed it.

"All right, take it," barked Wong, "but split!" They passed through the studio as the female lead, trying to zip the pants of her stoned white co-star, gave up and headed for an exit at the far end of the loft. The director was gone. The stubby cameraman tore his magazine loose and followed the girl. Marty led June down the creaking steps behind them and they found themselves in the alley, fifty feet from the front entrance. Beyond it, he thought he recognized the young agent with foxy eyes who had been in Greenberg's office the day of the shot. He was strolling toward them down the alley.

"It's the Army," Marty grunted, and they broke for the main street. They had a good start and only a few yards to go to reach the van. June slid behind the wheel and Marty tossed the film in back and dived in beside her, yelping in agony as he banged his arm on the door. She lurched out in a squeal of tires. Before they had gone a block, Marty heard the high-pitched whine of a heavy Honda in pursuit. He twisted in his seat. It was the colonel's agent, and gaining fast. He felt with his foot for the brake, past the gearshift, over June's ankle. "Brace yourself!" he warned. He jammed down hard and the van bucked to a stop. From behind, there was the shriek of a skidding tire, and a solid jolt. He heard a shout from a pedestrian, glimpsed June's face, white and terrified, and peered back. *"Now* drive," he told her.

She looked at him strangely but started the engine, which had stalled, jammed the van into gear, and pulled away. He turned. Behind them, growing more blurred in his vision as they sped off, lay the twisted motorcycle. Beside it sprawled a rag-doll figure. A pedestrian kneeled beside it, looking after them.

He felt himself coming apart, fought for control of his tongue, and failed. "Well," he blurted, his voice high, "you can't make an omelet without—"

"Shut up!" June shouted. "You aren't Handlemann, so shut up!"

He looked away, ashamed to let her see his face. His eyes were smarting, his throat was rigid, and he was afraid that he was going to cry.

Red Handlemann dangled a long leg over the arm of Reverend Chuck Scott's office couch. He smiled patronizingly when Lee offered the walkie-talkies, but did not object when Scott accepted them, although he volunteered that if the rally took a notion to march on the Pentagon, a few walkie-talkies were not going to make that much difference.

"They better," promised Lee, "or you're going to have some busted heads."

Handlemann smiled. "You know, you sound like Spiro Agnew. I think your own *son* had you wrong."

Lee's aching gut twisted. "I'm glad to hear you say that, you screwed-up son-of-a-bitch." He started for the door and paused. "Incidentally, since you mention Rick, have you got the research on his thesis? Big green notebooks, looseleaf, thick? They never turned up with his stuff."

Handlemann shook his head. "I've changed pads, as you've probably learned. And I'm a screwed-up son-of-a-bitch, you know. Maybe I overlooked them."

"Or maybe you'll want a master's in anthropology some day," suggested Lee. He strode out, slamming the door behind him. Laurie was typing at her desk in the empty office. Their eyes met. The moment froze. In the church below, someone struck an organ note. A Good Humor truck chimed faintly through the open window. His anger left him.

"Laurie," he said, "I didn't ask you down to that bar last night for cover, or anything else, except to be with you. It just happened."

She seemed to waver. "Maybe so, but it did happen. Do you know what I *did* to that poor little guy?"

"No."

"I broke his arm!"

He almost asked her how she knew, but stopped in time. He would find Lumpert himself; he refused to try to use her. She answered her phone, looked surprised, and handed him the receiver. "Your office, Lee." He spoke to Thelma, tensed, and slammed down the phone. He told Laurie what had happened to Liebholtz. "Broken leg, fractured skull! He's in a coma! My best agent," he said, "and a damn good friend! And that 'poor little guy,' as you call him, did it, or his girl did."

She was shocked. "I'm sorry, Lee."

"New ballgame, Laurie," he said tersely. "I want to find where you heard that you broke Lumpert's arm, who treated him, and when."

Distrust flashed back into her eyes. "No way, Lee."

"I could play games, I could go to the Free Clinic; that's where he must have gone. I'm asking you, instead."

"I never doubted your straightforwardness," she said coolly. "It's your priorities that screw you up."

"It's hit-and-run! They left him there! Hell, he might die!"

"I don't condone it. I just don't know their side of it."

"And you don't trust me?" he asked bitterly.

"I trust you, but not your reflexes. Somebody rang a bell, and you're salivating. You're too damn conditioned. It's inhuman! I don't trust your training, and I don't trust your background, and if you still want me, you better shake it loose. Put it that way."

"I'll put it *this* way," he said, leveling a finger at her. His stomach began to ache again. "You obstruct me on *this* case, and you just may end up on more than probation! You believe *that?*"

"Sure," she said, her eyes growing moist. "That's just what I've been saying! Now—" Her voice broke. "Now, let me get my typing done."

He spun on his heel and left. By the time he reached his car his stomach was churning so badly that he thought he would throw up.

Chapter Four

Aerodyne-LA was too sophisticated to jar its workers' nerves with a factory whistle like an Ohio steel mill. Industrial Relations had long ago piped classical music into the engineering spaces and sent country-western echoing through the clangorous hangars for the ex-Texas dirt farmers who crawled over half-assembled aircraft. Quitting time on the assembly lines was signaled with a bell and announced in the wall-to-wall executive offices with quiet chimes, which always reminded Bull Collins of dinner-call in an aircraft carrier's wardroom. At bay in the Old Man's office, he heard the chimes now, but reflected that neither Hound Dog nor Sonny nor the Old Man seemed ready to leave without another chew at his ample ass.

Hound Dog Cassell, hayrick hair bristling, took a nip: "He promised he could get those changes inserted! If he can't, they'll be using our proposal for scrap paper for the next ten years!"

Sonny saw an opening: "It'll be the most expensive scrap paper in history. Dad, he got Hound Dog to tell his team you were *raising their salaries!*"

The Old Man had been hunched behind his carved teak desk, content to let his son and Hound Dog work him over, but this hit home. "Why in the name of God," he rumbled from under the storm-cloud brows, "would he do a stupid thing like that?"

"Because he doesn't give a damn!" Sonny offered brutally. "The same reason he tangled with this Pentagon broad! He's getting us a corporate image like a Las Vegas whorehouse!"

Bull wished that he had Sherry Pace within strangling distance. Whatever had stirred her up today, she had tried to go right to the top, phoning long distance, first to him, and then striving actually to get through to the Old Man himself. Bull had no desire to learn what her problem was. She would have a hell of a time finding him if he kept his real name off the passenger manifest flying East, and if he avoided his room at the Marriott when he got there. He would live in the Statler, perhaps, until he could correct Aerodyne's proposal, and then escape for a month's vacation until the award came through. Skiing in Chile might be good.

"Damn it, Dad," Sonny bored in, his fat face setting into lines of doom. "I think it's time to make a move. Don't forget, he lost the TFX. Let's not lose this one too."

Bull decided to ignore the jackel and go for the Old Man's jugular. "I think," he said calmly, "Sonny's right. You ought to can me, pay me a year's salary as per contract, and let me go to General Dynamics. It wouldn't take long for somebody here to learn the ropes in Washington. Sonny himself, say, could figure out the Pentagon in five years or so, easy. Like, who to see on the Air Force Evaluation Team, who'll take tips on the stock market, who'll turn you in if you offer to buy him a drink."

"Just a damn minute," exploded Sonny. "We're talking about you, not me!"

Bull looked him up and down. "I think you'd get along with the military real well, Sonny, with your war record and all. Especially when they realize how much Aerodyne needed you right here to make all those airplanes. Good for the corporate image, too, staying here to help Daddy. Hell, *everybody* couldn't be a hero."

That wounded Sonny but amused the Old Man. "Bull, you're one of a kind. If I fire you, it'll be for cause. No year's salary. And Fort Worth wouldn't touch you. Nobody would. You could maybe sell Canadian gold-mining issues to widows and orphans but nobody else in aerospace would hire you. You play *too* dirty. I think you better stay right here."

Junior sagged. Hound Dog shook his head in disappointment. The Old Man's eyes twinkled, but there was a threat behind them, and Bull read it accurately: *Screw whoever you want, but win: one more strike, and out.* The trouble was, the old bastard was right about General Dynamics, Boeing, and all the rest. At fifty, with his reputation as a cocksman and boozer, no other company would touch him.

Well, there was nothing to do but try to pry loose the proposal long enough to make the changes. He had been in worse spots, and with empty tanks, over Guadal and Bougainville. He glanced at the errata sheets that Cassell had given him. "You guys sharpen your pencils?" he asked innocently. "You think you finally got it straight?"

For a moment Bull thought that the rawboned engineer would swing on him, so he winked at the Old Man, picked up his briefcase quickly, and left for the airport in a company taxi. Here, he failed to perceive the Army Counterintelligence agent who had followed him since his arrival yesterday and who noted that he did not use a company credit card but paid cash for his ticket and gave a false name to the ticket clerk.

Collins boarded the jet for Dulles. He flew First Class, as always. When the stewardess recognized the tiny lapel ribbon of the Congressional Medal of Honor, he told her he was the Commandant of the Marine Corps. By Albuquerque she was "Angel" and he had her Washington phone number; by Dallas he had conned her out of a third extra drink; and by St. Louis he suspected that he had the night's hotel problem solved. He fell into a deep and blameless sleep.

Sergeant George Maxon dumped the eight-hour typewritten transcript of Sherry Pace's calls onto Lee's desk, and asked that he be taken off the woman and put onto the Lumpert case. Liebholtz was always riding him, he said, but he missed him and wanted a crack at the little bastard who had tried to kill him. Lee, scanning the sheets, shook his head. "I need you on this." Sherry Pace had made a half-dozen frantic phone calls when Maxon's call had got her son arrested: first to her lawyer, Hammond, whom she hadn't reached, then to Collins at the Marriott, unsuccessfully, finally to Aerodyne in Los Angeles, where she had demanded to speak to the president himself. "And tell him if Collins doesn't call me back by midnight, they've built their last government airplane!"

"Was I right to start all that?" Maxon asked anxiously.

"You sure were." He had a TWX on his desk from Los Angeles Counterintelligence: Collins was bound for Dulles, traveling under an alias, probably to avoid Sherry Pace if she tried to call various airlines for his arrival time. Maybe Lee could help her. He phoned her apartment and told her that he was the night clerk at the Marriott and had noticed her messages for Mr. Collins. "He just called from L.A. He asked our courtesy car to meet him at Dulles. So he'll be in shortly."

She sounded drunk: "Save the gas. I'll meet him myself."

"Why, thank you, Ma'am. TWA Flight 74, arriving at 8:43."

He phoned Jenny and told her to eat without him. He had Maxon load the office Minox with the fastest film they had, and they raced toward Dulles under a full yellow moon through the moist, dark hills of Virginia. Lee rolled down the passenger window, breathed in the smell of the trees, and ached for Laurie.

They reached the terminal fifteen minutes before the arrival time of Flight 74. They went swiftly to the docks at which the elephantine FAA airport buses dumped arriving passengers. Sherry Pace had not yet appeared. Lee hoped that she was sober enough to make it in time, but there was nothing they could do about that, so they sat down to wait.

Congressman Cy Weintraub hung up from the last call from his beleaguered constituency and faced the slim, tanned Israeli pilot Dennes had sent to snow him. It was going to be hard to explain to this happy warrior, only a few years older than himself, why he was ready to slip a knife into the back of a Zionist Buying Commission. For an eternity the two sat smiling in awkward silence. "Well," Cy said finally, "what can I do for you, Colonel Sharett?"

The flier looked puzzled. "Why, I don't know! Didn't *you* call for *me?*"

"No. Congressman Dennes said he was sending you down to see me, because I'm releasing the facts on the F-111s. He thought you'd talk me out of it."

The Israeli looked at him, startled. "Try to talk— Not my cup of tea, Congressman. I surely can't interfere. Do you know what my Wing would do to me? You must be joking!"

Cy looked into the pilot's brown eyes. They were absolutely sincere. "Why, that old bastard," he murmured. "I can hear his wheels turning now: 'If I get those two Jew-boys together, that Colonel will have him volunteering another hundred planes!' "

"Don't like Dennes myself," Sharett said, eyes glinting angrily. "Awfully sorry, Mr. Weintraub. Sticky, but I'm glad you understood. I shan't bother you further."

Cy got up and slung his coat over his shoulder, starting to turn out his office light. "You had dinner, Colonel?"

"No, Mr. Weintraub."

"Cy," smiled Weintraub.

"Chaim, here," said the flier. They went to O'Donnell's Grill for seafood. Which was probably, Cy reflected as they slid into a booth, precisely what the old son-of-a-bitch had had in mind.

Bull Collins awakened as the plane jerked to a stop. For a moment he had trouble remembering where he was and what plane he was on: Red-Eye Special, Seattle Milk-Run, Coast Executive, or National to Cape Kennedy. The bump of the FAA shuttle-bus against the fuselage told him that he was at Dulles International.

He was crumpled and unshaven and wished that he could simply go to his room at the Marriott and sleep for a week, alone, but the Marriott was out because of the damn Pace woman and besides he had an obligation to the Corps to show the stewardess, younger by twenty-five years, what an old-time Marine general, genuine or not, could do in the sack. She had buckteeth, denoting passion, but piano legs, which meant a lack of whip in the ass. Well, active witch or passive angel, it was all for free, and any port in a storm.

She had to sign in at Crew Operations, and he told her to meet him outside the terminal when he had rented a car. He stifled a yawn as he dragged himself across the lobby. He had a moment of despair. He had been here so many times, over so many years, and through so many other airline terminals, and ahead of him stretched an infinity of others: El Paso, La Guardia, Kennedy, Midway, LAX. Dizzy, he stopped, leaned against a chair until the spell passed, and then dragged himself to the Hertz counter. He was not as old as he felt, damn it, and the night was warm, so he asked for a convertible. He was signing it out when he decided that whoever was standing behind him in line had a broken bottle of bourbon in his suitcase. He turned and his heart thumped.

Sherry Pace was staring up at him with a twisted grin and half-focused eyes. "Hello, Bull," she said thickly, "I get you fired out there?"

"You didn't even come close," he lied. "Why'd you try?"

She told him that she had got mad when he wouldn't return her calls to Los Angeles. Her son was in jail, and she needed money. She wasn't mad any more, and what should she do?

"Call Hammond," he said in a low voice. "He costs enough. Maybe he'll have an idea."

"I did. He's out of town. And I have an idea all my own. I'll drive you in and we'll talk about it."

"I have a better idea," he said, glancing around for the stewardess. "I'll drive myself in, and we'll never talk about it again."

She moved closer. God, she was snockered! "Bull, I need a thousand dollars!"

"So do I."

"Your company will pay you back!"

"*Sure* they will." He was getting jumpier. The stewardess was due any moment. "Look, I haven't got it, and if I had, I wouldn't give it to you."

"All right," she said, voice rising virtuously, "tomorrow morning, bright and early, I am going to make a full confession. I am going to Colonel what's-his-name, Frost, and I am going to tell him—"

"Hold it down, Sherry!"

"I am going to tell him how you took me to your room—"

278

"Shut up!"

"And screwed me, and conned me out of top-secret information—"

A businessman at the counter looked at them with amusement. From the adjoining Avis booth a girl flashed them a glance of contempt. A group of youngsters with knapsacks, arriving for Saturday's rally, slapped past in sandals and snickered.

"And I'm going to tell him," she blurted, "how and *when* I figure you snagged that memo! Now, how's *that* grab you?"

"Pipe *down.*"

"A grand, Bull. Just a thousand. My boy's in jail!"

"Who carries a thousand dollars?"

"Write me a check."

"Won't that look great?" he scoffed. "Then you'd really have us by the balls!"

"Write it," she insisted, "or I'll call Frost now. Bring cash tomorrow and you get it back."

Something in her boozy eyes told him that she was ready to cut loose. He envisioned airport security guards converging as she screamed and clawed at his face. Everyone at Hertz, Avis, and National Car Rental was listening now. He drew her to an empty Information booth. He could lay the whole problem on Hammond's lap tomorrow, before she could cash the check or even get to Frost. He whipped out his checkbook and wrote it. She squinted at it carefully, folded it, and stuck it into her bra.

"If you want it back," she said, "meet me at that Arlington First National branch in the Pentagon concourse. By ten."

"Noon," he begged. He would need time to reach Hammond.

"My son's in a cell," she said, "with *criminals!* Ten o'clock, or Frost will have this by eleven!"

"You're a sweet kid, Sherry," muttered Bull.

"I like you, too, Bull," she smiled. She swept toward the door. He slipped his checkbook back into his pocket and strolled out to meet the stewardess. He found her finally in a crowd of crew-members waiting for a Hilton bus. He took her hand possessively and was leading her away when he heard the squeal of a tortured tire at the curb. Sherry Pace leaned from her car.

"Hello, honey," she giggled to the girl. "Hello, Bull. 'Bull'? Shit! Anybody ever tell you you're a lousy lay?"

She chortled and pulled away, narrowly missing the Hilton bus and peeling rubber on her take-off. The stewardess stared after her. "Who was that?" she demanded. "Why'd she call you 'Bull'?"

"Nickname," Bull said briefly, very tired. "Let's go."

She hesitated. "Some other time, OK, General?" She saluted like a marionette and was gone with her flight-crew. Burning with a dull anger, he found the convertible and put the top down. He started through the damp Virginia night, wondering how Sherry Pace had known he was arriving in the first place. He decided that Sonny had got her phone number from the Old Man's secretary and his flight number from the company driver and called to alert her out of pure malice.

Some day, some way, he would hang Sonny by the balls.

Reading a newspaper while the shoeshine boy slapped at his feet, Lee Frost watched Bull Collins leave the terminal to pick up his car. Maxon, leaning casually on the Avis counter as he pretended to study a rate schedule, clicked one last picture from the hip and strolled to the stand. Lee paid the shoeshine boy and moved away, reminding Maxon that the light had been poor and that he must be sure to have the Pentagon lab force-develop the negatives. He had handled the tiny camera like a good instructor in surveillance techniques at Fort Holabird, and Lee took him to dinner in the terminal restaurant, congratulating him on his technique.

For the first time since he had known him, Maxon quit posing. "When you're number two," he said, referring to his injured partner, "you try harder."

They toasted Liebholtz and ordered dinner. Maxon was getting over his habit of judging everything he said by its effect on Lee, and it was good to feel that he still had an agent he could relax with. He told him to be on Sherry Pace's tail bright and early, for it was obvious that she couldn't use a personal check for bail and would have to cash it first, and they would want to know where to subpoena the check for evidence.

When they were finished, Lee sat back, full of steak. It had been a long week, and it still had a long way to go, but most of the pressure from above had been on the F-111 memo, and it was nice to see the light of day at least on that. They decided to have a beer for the road.

In the Hertz convertible, Bull Collins bored swiftly through the moist night along Dulles Access Road toward Arlington. The highway, split with a grass divider, was a federal boondoggle like Dulles Airport itself, intended for much more traffic than it would ever see, so it was empty and smooth enough to give him a chance to diffuse his anger and unrein the car. As he hit eighty-five, the slipstream whipping his thinning hair seemed almost tropical. He was flashing through hills a good five miles from the Potomac, but the riverine dampness and orange moonlight brought him back to eager nights searching for kills over Henderson Field, with the terrible jungle shadow of Guadalcanal stretching south and the Straits a golden platter below.

As he tore past Dolley Madison Highway toward Pimmit Hills, he caught the faint wail of a car horn to his left. It rose in volume and pitch, and when it dropped and grew thinner he slowed, listening. His ears had always been keen, and when the honking did not stop, he made a U-turn over the grass island and headed back. The horn was somewhere off to his right, now much louder. Suddenly in the beam of his headlights he caught a pair of dark furrows where a Washington-bound car had sloughed across the divider and plowed into the dark, thick underbrush. The horn croaked, stopped, started again, and died as the battery gave out, and then there was nothing but the thrum of crickets in the bush.

He got out and walked slowly along the track the rolling car had bulldozed through the trees. At some point along the crumbled lane he realized that the car might be Sherry Pace's. When he reached it his heart was pound-

281

ing wildly. The auto had landed upright, and a dark figure sat jammed against the steering wheel. He approached more closely. He had no flashlight, but moonlight streamed down on what had been her face. Her skullcase was crushed and the features sagged, but there was no doubt that it was she and none at all that she was dead. *Who's a lousy lay now?* he thought vindictively. Though he had seen too much of death to be overly shaken, he hesitated. Finally he took a deep breath, reached through her window, slipped his hand under a bra slimy with blood, and drew out his soaking check.

At his car, he touched a match to it and found it dry enough to burn. He made a U-turn back to the Washington-bound lane and, feeling a faint twinge of conscience, stopped at a phone booth in the first filling station he came to. Though he gave the precise location of the wreck, and the officer should have been grateful, he chose to become threatening when Bull refused to give his name.

Bull hung up on the outraged voice and continued to the Marriott. It looked as though, finally, he could rest undisturbed in his own bed. But then, he reflected, he had always been a lucky sort of bastard, after all.

Lee Frost awakened late, to the sound of rhythmic thumping. It was almost eight o'clock, and sunlight had haloed each slat of the bedroom Venetian blind with a fringe of fuzzy gold. The thumping was coming from the living room. He peered in.

Jenny, haunches wobbling, was jogging before their TV set in step with a taut athlete in skintight pants. The lamp over Lee's chair danced sympathetically, the TV screen shivered, Rick's photo on the mantel quivered. Hoping that sound-proofing saved the people downstairs, he moved to the bathroom. This morning she had Scotch-taped two photos of herself to the mirror: one, slim and pretty, taken with their son on the Army-Navy Club tennis courts, the other, fat and puffy, shot by an Army photographer as she danced with Chaplain Scorchy Blain at General Hardy's party. Similar pairs were stuck in the mirror above her dressing table. He moved to the kitchenette for coffee, patting her encouragingly on her bouncing tail, and found two more pictures plastered to the refrigerator door.

At breakfast she had coffee and only one egg and announced that she had lost another two pounds in the last three days, was going to play tennis with Skeeter Hardy, and that she wanted to help him work on the boat. It was exercise, and if they did sell it, they would get more if they cleaned up below.

He agreed, wondering what had finally set the old Jenny beneath the lard to thrashing toward the surface. He felt vaguely guilty. The fat somehow excused Laurie, and now that Jenny was trying to shed it he should forget the girl. But all that was academic anyway; he might as well forget her—she was lost.

Jenny laid a letter on the table. It was Scorchy's masterful announcement that they had lost a son, indeed signed by the President, indeed edged in black. He began to read it, angry and disturbed: *We should like in this inadequate way to express our condolences, indeed, our grief . . ."* Grief, yet. Horse-hockey! He jammed it back into the envelope. "That goddamn sky-pilot, I *told* him—"

"I asked him to send it, Lee."

He looked at her, amazed. If she wanted to frame it, it would be too much. "Why, for God's sake?"

"For your father." She told him that she hadn't wanted to bother Lee, but Cotton had been calling for two days. Something was wrong. "Mentally. I think you should drive down and see him tonight. And show him the letter. Give it to him, if he wants it."

"Why?"

She flushed, avoiding his eyes. "Well, he *rambles.*"

"He's crocked half the time."

"He never rambled!"

That was true, or had been until Lee's last visit, with the talk about his mother. His father could be sarcastic, brittle, sullen, morose, but always, when drunk, less talkative than when he lapsed into sobriety. "What's he rambling about?" he asked dully.

"Rick. As if he were alive, like your mother, and living down there with him. He doesn't want you to sell the boat. And he wants you to bring down Rick's typewriter."

Lee winced. He had dealt with Cotton Frost as a runaway father, a satyr, an embezzler, a black-marketeer, and an alcoholic. Cotton, insane, was something else again.

"Well, I'm selling the boat, and he can't have the typewriter."

"Why?"

"It's the only one we've got, and I'm used to it."

"And Rick used it?" She smiled at him more tenderly than she had in months.

"OK," he said tightly. "I'm still keeping it. The letter, I'll give him."

He found his office in its usual morning chaos. Thelma had checked on Liebholtz at Walter Reed. He was slipping in and out of consciousness. The dozen Army walkie-talkies were on their way to the Peace League, and Picket Aspen had heard about it, which meant that Picket had his own sources of intelligence somewhere, working at cross-purposes. Picket phoned to predict that the Army would never see them again and slammed down his phone in a rage before Lee could explain.

Lee, waiting to hear from Maxon when Sherry Pace tried to cash Collins' check, read Major Homer Troy's latest theory on "The Passionate Prince of the Ladies' Latrines." He was finishing the dissertation when General Lucius Hardy called him to the Office of the Secretary of Defense. Not wanting to be caught with his pants down again, Lee phoned Security Review and had the clerk of the Top-Secret Board cancel the clearances of Sherry Pace, GS-6, and Robert "Bull" Collins, of Aerodyne Corporation. The clerk squeaked and howled in protest: he needed notice in writing, with justification, in quadruplicate. Lee replied that the phone call was notice, the eagles on his shoulders justification, and that he would get it in quadruplicate when the rat-race eased for one day. Flushed with triumph at having got on the trail of the stolen memo, he cinched his tie and checked his newly shined shoes. He turned down a call from Maxon, impatient to explain to the powers that had hounded him that no matter what else was going wrong, at least "The Case of the Purloined Memo" was wrapped up and neatly tied. He hopped onto an escalator and soared to the Brass Ring.

Marty Lumpert awakened lying on a dirty floor in an evil-smelling sleeping-bag soaked with his own sweat. It took him a long moment to get his bearings, but finally he separated fact from the delirium of the night before and remembered that he was in the dressing room off the chapel of Reverend Scott's First Unitarian Church. He had never been to the Peace League offices on the top floor, and had been carefully prevented from going there last night, but he could hear even at this early hour the footsteps—hobnailed, sandaled, bare—up and down the creaking wooden stair that led to it. An organist was practicing for a funeral in the chapel, and the deadly chords sent him into a deep depression.

He was alone in the room. June had found the sleeping-bag in the rear of the van, apparently forgotten by Handlemann when he traveled to some demonstration, and had taken it when they abandoned the vehicle. When finally they hid here to bed for the night, June had insisted that he sleep in it alone, afraid that she would hurt his arm if she tried to squeeze in beside him. For herself she had found an old raincoat of Scott's in the closet with his vestment, and bundled in that next to Marty on the floor.

His arm ached from wrist to elbow, and the fever, which had broken once, was on him again. June had sometime last night found a dozen reds for him, and it had only been them that kept him from going out of his gourd with pain. Logically, sooner or later, the wrist must be set and cast, but the risk of going to a city clinic or even trying to find a private doctor was too great. Whatever he did further about the wrist, it could not be until they were safely rid of the film.

With his good left arm he felt along the side of the sleeping-bag. The flat round film-cans were there, reassuringly. They had to be gotten to Handlemann before the colonel tracked him down, or the police found June. Panic struck him. June was out in the world, somewhere, exposed and looking for medical help, or getting them food, or turning herself in for hit-and-run. She had begged him all night to let her do that, even though it was he who had spilled the agent (or killed him, suppose that?).

The organ left off its doleful mourning and began to climb exultantly, but only plunged him into darker despair. If June were picked up, he did not care to survive. Painfully, he began to inch from the bag, protecting his arm.

Someone tapped and entered. In the dim light from the window above a shabby writing desk, he could see that it was a woman, but it was not June. He squinted nearsightedly up at her face, not believing his eyes.

The girl was utterly beautiful, but she was the girl from the Anchor Bar, and in his fevered mind, completely lethal. "What the hell," he mumbled, "are *you* doing here?"

"Lumpert," she said, "I'm sorry."

"You going to arrest me? You got a gun in your bra?"

"I was with him in the Anchor," she admitted, "but if he was there to pick you up, I didn't know it!"

"Oh, hell no!" He struggled clear of the bag, gauging his strength and the distance to the door. "Look, if you haven't got a gun, you better stand clear. Or maybe you have another bottle? You still have one arm to go!" She came closer, touched the wrist. He drew it away and said: "You didn't know he was a pig? That's bullshit, girl! He's the top Army agent in the whole frigging Pentagon!"

"I knew that," she said dully. "How bad is it?"

He wondered if she had spotted the film by the sleeping bag. "If you're so damn sympathetic, why'd you swing that bottle?"

"You were going to smash his face."

"I sure was. I wish I had."

"Then I'm not sorry I swung. I like his face. But I'm sorry I broke your wrist."

"Where'd you hear it was broken?" he demanded.

"Free Clinic."

"That strung-out medic talks too much."

"He knows me."

"Then he talks *way* too much. What are you, a WAC, or a civilian agent, or a goddamn Washington policewoman?"

"My parole officer would get a blast out of that. I'm Chuck Scott's secretary, upstairs."

"The Movement's got more leaks than the Pentagon," Marty said sardonically, wincing at a sudden pain. "We're doomed."

"You'll be doomed if somebody doesn't look at your wrist."

He felt suddenly faint. She sensed it and threw an arm

287

around his waist, helping to ease him back down to the bag. Her hip was firm against his own. It felt good, but he wanted another RD, and was afraid to dig into his pocket for one, with her around, and afraid that she would steal the film if he fainted. He wanted June, but was afraid to ask where she was: if the girl was an informer, it was stupid to let her know that he was not alone. He felt himself slipping fast.

"Wait," she said softly, "I'll get you something."

He hung on long enough to slide the film-cans under the sleeping-bag and then he slid off into unconsciousness.

Laurie met the long-haired brunette as she left the room. She had seen her often at rallies and demonstrations, carrying a child in a back-sling, a photographer for the underground press. She was without the child but carried two cellophane-wrapped sandwiches and take-out coffee from a nearby café. Laurie told her she had found Lumpert and that she was the one who had injured him.

The black eyes widened: "My God, does that colonel come here?"

"Upstairs. Never down here."

"Suppose he raids it?"

"They can't raid a church. Or can they? Anyway I think you're safe down here."

The girl studied her carefully and apparently decided to trust her. She asked her to go to Handlemann's and tell him to come to the church if he wanted his film. "And would you bring back my little girl? We're going to split when we can."

Laurie promised that she would. She had spent a miserable night in her cold bed in her flat's alcove, listening to the murmur of the radicals planning God knew what for Saturday, and weighing their reckless mindlessness against Lee's cold questions about Lumpert and how she had known about his arm.

If he couldn't see why she wouldn't turn fink, then he wasn't the man she had thought. She could fight him so much better if she could just keep them out of bed.

General Lucius Hardy watched Lee Frost leave the office of the Secretary of Defense. He was proud of his protégé but dubious about the speed with which he had canceled Collins' clearance. Aerodyne had too much clout with the Administration to push their representative around so contemptuously. He listened as Secretary Royce called Chairman Ab Dennes of House Armed Services to tell him that the leak on the Israeli-Greek plane-deal seemed to be stopped at the Pentagon, the culprit plainly unearthed, and what was he doing to plug Weintraub at his own end of the sewer?

He seemed satisfied with the answer. He hung up the phone, looked across the Potomac toward the White House, and said: "Lucius, the President wants to postpone your briefing until Sunday."

Lucius Hardy tried to hide his dismay. JCS, uneasy in political situations, had hoped to have a firm go-ahead for Operation Strangle before the rally. Lucius toyed with telling Royce about the Ban Doc massacre film hanging over their heads like an anvil on a thread, and of O'Hare's crazy threats to expose the absence of plague vaccine at Da Nang, but decided against it. Royce was the President's man, not the Pentagon's, and to panic him would only frighten the President as well. There was nothing to do but hope that the anti-war demonstration fell flat on its ass. Royce seemed to read his mind. "Don't worry, Lucius, a few thousand kids with no political base aren't going to take His eye off the ball."

Hardy was not so sure and suggested that it would depend on how many demonstrators showed up, how stirred up they got, and whether any of them got themselves hurt. Royce seemed undismayed. "Doesn't Newton's First Law say every action has an equal and opposite reaction?"

"Third," said Hardy.

"Well, it's a political law too. If they get violent enough Saturday, the mood of this whole country by Sunday might be to take 'em out and shoot 'em, and let's get on with the war."

Maybe so, Hardy reflected, as he left the office and passed the gleaming plaques in the Hall of Heroes.

Royce's hopes seemed reasonable, but he wished that they had the Ban Doc film safely in hand, that there was some way to suspend until Monday the write of *habeas corpus* in the case of Michael O'Hare, and to temporarily amend the First Amendment as it applied to Congressman Weintraub as well.

Chapter Six

Bull Collins jiggled impatiently in a chair in a cubicle of the Air Force Evaluation Team's office space. The walls around him were covered with framed lithographs of experimental aircraft, from the old Bell X-1 to the X-15. Jet models hung from the ceiling and crowded the desk of the tweedy colonel who had longed for the cockpit change and caused all the trouble with the home office in the first place. The officer, who smoked a pipe and wore a British sports jacket straight from Kowloon via MATS, looked more like a teacher than a military test-pilot. He congratulated Bull on arriving in the nick of time. The Aerodyne proposal lay on his desk, yanked from under the noses of the Team's engineers just as they were beginning to check the weight-and-balance figures. Bull wanted to snatch it up, insert Hound Dog's changes, and head for his Andean ski-resort. But he sensed that first he must allow the colonel to wallow righteously, like a reluctant professor deciding to let a student retake an exam. And the colonel had something else in mind, too, a familiar question Bull read instantly somewhere behind the twinkling green eyes: what's in all this for me, and when?

From his brutal experience with Admiral Niles Strickland, Bull had learned that military honor was easily bruised. He knew the colonel's history, as he knew the record of every other member of the Air Force Evaluation Team. The man was a dazzling product of the Test-Pilot Training Program. He had flown half the experimental aircraft that Edwards Test Center had evaluated in the past fifteen years, but had never had a combat command larger than a bomber crew.

The Air Force did not demand of its officers all of the professional ticket-punches that the Army required en route to general, but still the colonel must know that he was as overspecialized as a mastodon, and just as incapable of survival in the struggle for stars. He was forty-two, probably longing to get back to flying, and obviously favored Aerodyne's proposal over General Dynamics' already, or else he would not have dropped Bull the hint for a cockpit change.

And he would never have risked giving Aerodyne a chance to change a proposal after submission date unless he liked the plane already, or wanted something from the company. If he liked it, he had probably already wedded himself to it in secret conference, had staked his professional reputation on it (they all did, emotionally, like children who wanted a new toy), and was fighting the good battle for Aerodyne right now. But if he wanted something from the company, that was even better. Bull felt suddenly more secure. "You had a chance to study it?" he offered, nodding at the proposal.

"Great airplane," the colonel said blandly. "But confidentially, General Dynamics comes in eight hundred pounds lighter and around a hundred Gs a copy cheaper."

That in itself was a leak to be treasured. Bull explained that when he corrected the weight-and-balance figures they might find that he had solved the weight problem, and that concerning cost-estimate, everyone knew that General Dynamics would bid low to buy in. "One thing about us, Colonel, you can trust our cost-analysis people right down the line."

"Bullshit, Collins," grinned the colonel.

OK, thought Bull, we all buy in and wait to get rescued later, but they couldn't blame him for trying. He dropped the subject, affected a dreamy smile, and took up a matter predictably closer to the colonel's heart. "You know, Colonel, when our design's accepted, and the prototype's coming off the line, I wish I could be young enough to fly her. What a bird! You ever feel that way about a plane you've ramrodded?"

He had phrased it right this time. The colonel drew on his pipe with a faraway look, saying, "You never know. That's a long time off. Assuming you even win the contract." He looked Bull squarely in the eyes. "I'll probably be retired by then."

"As you say, Colonel, you never know. Hell, you might even be test-flying for Aerodyne." That was the place to leave it, and Bull did, his hands itching for the proposal and his feet longing for the sweeping Chilean snow. The colonel's secretary, a trim little WAF, jiggled in. She had a vacant, puzzled expression but a bouncy ass. *That* was one he would like to bang, anytime at all. She glanced at him curiously and turned to her boss. "Colonel," she said, "I typed the receipt for Mr. Collins, but when I called Security Review there was some kind of snag!"

"Security?" Bull chuckled, hiding a clammy premonition. "Jesus, Baby-san, I practically wrote this proposal! Colonel, I don't need an act of Congress to borrow it back for a couple of hours?"

"Well, Bull," smiled the colonel, "not an act of Congress, just a plain old clearance. I'll nail it down." He moved to the outer office, where Bull could not listen in. There was a great dialing of phones and a half-audible monotone, which Bull strained unsuccessfully to hear. The colonel returned, apologetic but nowhere near as warm. "No more top secret, secret, or confidential! If I were you, Bull, I'd trot my ass down to Security and find out why. It might be a little hard to sell a top-secret airplane if nobody's allowed to talk to you about it."

Bull lurched to his feet. A murderous rage began to throb in his throat, his heart began to pound, too hard and too fast. He was dizzy again, as he had been in the terminal last night. "I know just where to go, Colonel," he said thickly. "Will you give me an hour?"

The colonel looked at the clock on his wall. "Bull, they'll be crawling all over me. They've checked General Dynamics' figures; they'll want to start on yours!"

"An hour," pleaded Bull. "Just one goddamn hour!"

The colonel nodded and Bull left, moving very swiftly, for Lee Frost's office in the basement.

Lee stood in his office before the huge detailed chart of the Pentagon. He finished briefing his short, pock-marked civilian guard-chief, along with two uniformed GSA captains, four lieutenants, and a half-dozen sergeants of the Special General Services Administration Task Force from across the river. The latter were huge men, well over six feet and two hundred pounds, who wore lead-impregnated black gloves stuck into their belts. With the U.S. Marshals who could be spared from General Picket Aspen's heroic defense of Arlington Bridge, along with the Joint Chiefs of Staff crack Security force and some MPs, these would be the troops with which he must defend the Pentagon itself from strays who crossed the river.

He stepped away from the map, afraid to ask if there were any questions. The GSA guards, and even their officers, were an unimaginative lot, starting at minuscule pay and working their way up to not much better. Their main amusement during their long, boring days seemed to be in senseless bull-sessions, and he was afraid that they would anticipate some obscure problem on Satur-day, bring it up now, and want to gnaw on it here for the rest of the afternoon. He dismissed them, to their disappointment, and they filed out.

Bull Collins, choleric and grim, walked in behind Thelma. Lee did not offer him coffee or a seat. The big man glowered down at him. "OK, Colonel, what the hell's the idea?"

Lee regarded him coldly. "You were always here on military sufferance and it just ran out. I've already passed the word to bar you from the building." He smiled. "You've got Hammond trying to get your girl Sherry Pace back in; maybe you better have him go to work for you."

Collins grinned suddenly. His guts were incredible. It was as if he could not imagine that anyone knew of his meeting last night with Sherry at the airport, or could unearth the check he had given her, or had the muscle Lee intended to exert to make her turn government witness.

"I'll get Hammond, all right," Collins agreed. "But right now, I need my clearance back. Aerodyne supported this Administration, Frost, and if I *don't* have it back in thirty minutes, you're going to be cleaning latrines on the cease-fire line."

"I see," said Lee. He pressed the key to his intercom and spoke to his Security chief. He told him he wanted Collins out of the building in ten minutes, with his desk inventoried and his ID cards canceled. "And I don't want to see him again." He grinned up at the big man, who was breathing hard. "That tell you how I feel about your latrines, Mr. Collins?"

Collins stepped closer. He seemed almost ready to swing. Lee hoped that he would. Although he outweighed him by a good thirty pounds, he looked slow. Lee very nearly rose to sink his fist into the beefy jaw, and the hell with the legal consequences. With an effort, he restrained himself. He sat back. "I wouldn't worry about your lousy Security clearance, Collins. What you want to worry about is a few years in the federal pen for a violation of the National Security Act. Because frankly, my friend, we've got you cold."

"I see," Collins said, his eyes distant. "And what do you mean by 'cold'?"

"You figure it out, Buster," said Lee. "Maybe I know more than you think."

"And maybe," Collins grinned suddenly, "I know something you don't know at all."

Lee's Security chief, redfaced and embarrassed, arrived to escort Collins from the Pentagon. As they left, Maxon burst in, back from the Pentagon photo lab. He tossed a roll of developed negatives on Lee's desk, looking as if he were about to break down. "I'm sorry, sir. And there's worse to tell you."

Lee held the roll to the light. It was absolutely transparent. He felt sick. "What happened?" he asked thickly.

Maxon lapsed uncharacteristically into profanity. "The lousy, fucking *work* order, sir! It's got to be in triplicate, and the stupid fucking clerk in their front office didn't type hard enough or something, and it's only the last carbon that goes to the guy that actually soups the film, and he didn't see the 'special processing,' and—"

"And he gave it normal development?" Lee barked, his throat tight. "That it?"

Maxon nodded, face aflame. "Yes sir."

"This goddamn place!" Lee thundered, slamming his fist on the desk. "OK! She cash Collins' check?"

Maxon licked his lips. He seemed to find trouble speaking.

Lee looked at him curiously, a strange dread tugging at him: *"Did she cash his check?"* he asked again.

"She's dead," Maxon blurted.

"She's *what?*"

"Killed! On the way back last night! He must have run her off the Dulles Access Road! I tried to get you, and you were with SecDef—"

Lee half-rose from his chair. "Did he get back his check?"

"The State Police never found it in the car," said Maxon, "and I couldn't either, and it wasn't in her clothes or on her body at the morgue!"

"Do they *know* who ran her off?" asked Lee.

"They don't know anybody did."

"They will," said Lee, reaching for the phone, "they sure as hell will now!"

Bull Collins stormed away from the civilian GSA guard, who had wordlessly escorted him to the rented convertible in North Parking. In five minutes he was in his room at the Marriott, dialing Aerodyne-LA. He informed the Old Man that if his top-secret clearance was not reinstated immediately, they were going to lose the AFX contract, and that it had probably been due to the devilish manipulation of his own son that it had been canceled in the first place.

Then he dialed Charles Brewster Hammond, III. "Counselor," he blurted, "you've lost one client, whether you know it or not, but you've gained another."

"What do you mean, Mr. Collins?"

"Sherry Pace was killed last night on the Dulles Road. But I've got somebody over at the Pentagon that needs a large kick in the balls, and I think you may be the one to do it. Shall I come over?"

Hammond invited him to his office, and Bull started for the door. He had a sudden ugly thought. He knew little of electronics, but he had a great distrust of his fellow man, especially Frost, and he had just admitted knowledge on the telephone of a death that he had no valid reason to suspect. He went back to the phone, unscrewed the earpiece and mouthpiece, inspected the instrument, and found nothing that seemed foreign. He put it all back together, and thought for a moment. Finally, starting at his closet, he began to feel under his shelves, his sink, his bedside table, behind the drawers. A garish Cubist reproduction of the Washington cherry trees hung over the desk. He took it down, and behind it found a flat recorder the size of a matchbox, which began to spin tiny reels at the sound of his breathing and stopped when he moved silently away.

"Son-of-a-bitch!" he marveled, gloating. He slipped it into his pocket and was combing his hair when he heard a knock at the door.

It was a sergeant of the Virginia State Police, whose office had just been informed by a reliable source that Mr. Collins might have been involved in an auto accident on the Dulles Road, and would he answer some questions here, and then take him to look at his rented car?

Bull Collins kept his face rigid. He knew very well who the reliable informant was, and therefore that he had been tailed, for possibly a week. He had a suspicion that it was not Sonny in California who had somehow alerted Sherry Pace to his arrival last night, but Colonel Lee Frost. His conscience clear, he admitted having been on the Dulles Road last night, expressed horror that a woman had been killed, but saw no reason to confess to knowing her. He took the officer to the parking lot below to let him inspect the convertible, offered him a drink at the Windjammer when he was finished, and was rather hurt when he refused. Then he headed for Hammond's office in Alexandria. If the Aerodyne proposal failed because he didn't get his clearance back in time, he might

297

lose a twenty-thousand-dollar bonus, but suddenly the prospect of shooting down Colonel Frost made it all worthwhile.

Chapter Seven

All day long in the dressing room off the chapel, Marty Lumpert had drifted in and out of consciousness. June hovered near and then finally Sunshine, whom she had somehow got delivered. Now that the three of them had it all together again, the chemical valences meshing and the bonds reunited, he felt better. A crippled minister he hadn't met lurched in on sticks to see him and very nearly insisted on calling a doctor, until Marty told him that he'd walk to Toronto first. He relaxed after that and dozed while Sunshine played with her violet duck and June, cross-legged at the head of the bag, massaged his temples, her fine features pensive.

Sometime in early evening he awakened to Handlemann's grating voice. His eyes burned. Handlemann sat at the writing table, drumming his fingers. June, a slender Modigliani in the slanting evening light from the window above the desk, looked down at the redhead coldly.

"It's perfect, Junie," Handlemann said, looking around at the room: "I didn't even know it was here."

"It's for Marty," June said.

Handlemann ignored her. "Even if they bust the League, they won't raid a chapel. And there's even a goddamn safe for the film!"

"No! I don't want your blood-tripping Weathermen friends stumbling over him, looking for Molotovs or whatever you have in mind!"

"Put the film in the safe," demanded Marty. "He's right!"

"First find out where he's going to show it," demanded June. "He won't tell me!"

Marty asked him, and he only shrugged. "Sell it back to the Army to finance the Revolution? Hold it as host-age for Poma's release? Print it frame-by-frame in the *Clarion* to raise circulation?"

"You're funny as hell," said June. "You're going to stir something up with that film that you won't be able to handle."

"That's my problem, isn't it? Not yours. In the meanwhile, if they pick up Clausewitz here, they'll get the film too."

"Let him put it in the safe!" Marty insisted again.

Handlemann left and returned with Laurie, who spun the combination, put in the film, and closed the vault. She refused to give him the combination and he flushed. "You mean Scott doesn't trust me after two marches and the Moratorium?"

"Not with the combination to his church safe," Laurie said dryly, "and not with the plans for the rally, if you want to know."

"Maybe he ought to let your pig-colonel plan it," suggested Handlemann.

"We'd be better off if he would," said Laurie. She stooped and felt Marty's forehead. Her hand was as cool as June's. He slept again and when he awakened it was dark outside and June had taken Sunshine for a walk. Dewey Dupays had arrived and there were cartons stacked in the corner, like those Handlemann had kept for mimeo stock in the *Clarion* office. On each, fuzzily, he could read PEACE MARCH. Dewey was hunched like a dark monk at the writing table, intent on something, and Handlemann was leaning over his shoulder.

Foggily, Marty tried to focus his eyes and his brain on what they were doing, but it all seemed too much trouble, and when he saw them place whatever it was in a carton and bury it part-way down the stack, he fell back to sleep. The next morning he had forgotten it, and though later would remember it dimly, he would never be sure whether it was something he had seen, or whether it had all been a dream after all.

Lee watched his father's farmhouse turn as usual from colonial magnificence to twentieth-century decadence in the last quarter-mile along the jarring road. As he climbed the stairs to the front porch, the columns, pink in the setting sun, lost their smoothness and became shoddy, flaking before his eyes.

Passing through the living room he stopped. The giant TV set had been shattered and slivers of glass from its immense eye still lay around it. "Cotton?" he called. "Cynthia?"

She appeared at the bedroom door, redeyed. For the first time he felt sympathy for her. The stony-faced old bat was apparently sticking, and if ever Cotton Frost needed help, it was now. He nodded at the broken glass. She shook her head. "He saw demonstrators on some talk-show; hippies, down for their rally. He thought about Rick, so he busted it. It's spooky, Lee! And a six-hundred-dollar set! Now, that isn't right!"

She said Cotton was down at the creek. Lee passed a long-unused outhouse still reeking richly under a swarm of bluebottles, skirted a sagging stable, and moved along a narrow path with weeds snatching at his pants. He reached the willows with the shine on his shoes gone, his shirt soaked, and dragging a cloud of mosquitoes. He thrashed upstream toward a fishing-hole where he and Rick and Cotton had cast in cooler seasons, and where Rick had liked to swim. Slapping at his neck, he broke from cover to find his father plumbing the bottom with a willow. The old man, impervious to mosquitoes after too much quinine in the Philippines or too much alcohol at home, simply nodded and said: "He wants his boat in here."

"Who?"

"Rick. He's going to live on his boat and work on his degree. So let's go have a beer and figure how we're going to get that big fucking boat up this little fucking creek."

Speechlessly, he followed his father back to the house. Cotton got him a beer but, instead of dropping to his moldly easy chair on the back porch, motioned him through the kitchen and led him down a hallway edged by torn wallpaper to the room Rick had used when he

301

visited the farm. In it was an olive-drab Army desk Cotton had somehow liberated when he retired. On the desk were the two green looseleaf anthropological notebooks Lee had been looking for. He was about to ask for them when Cotton said: "Thought he'd be here studying, but he'll be back."

"He's dead," Lee said bleakly.

Cotton ignored him. "Did you bring his typewriter?"

Lee glared at his father. His gut ached miserably. Through clenched teeth he said: "Get it straight, and get it straight now! He was reported KIA. Not MIA, not WIA! He's *kaput!* Finished!"

His father regarded him impassively. "He just went down to the crossroads for a pack of cigarettes!"

Lee grabbed the sinewy arm and steered him through the living room to the front porch. He jerked his thumb at the Cadillac. "How? There's your car."

Cotton's eyes were blank. "He walked."

"You want proof?" Lee pulled out the letter edged in black. "Read this!" His father took it and held it in a long golden slant from the sinking sun, squinting. Lee found his voice rising: "You get the message, Dad? Can you read it? You want me to read it *to* you? It's signed by the *President!* Genuine ink! *The President of the United States!*"

Cotton Frost looked up at him placidly. "Don't yell, boy. I can read." He finished the letter and handed it back. "Army shit."

"Keep it," said Lee.

"OK. He'll get a kick out of it."

Lee crumpled the beer can, hurled it at a pile of empties overflowing a GI can on the front lawn, and climbed into his car. As he started the engine the Old Man called: "You meet him on the road, tell him chop-chop, home by dark!"

Lee spun from the driveway onto the rutted road, almost slid into a ditch, and found himself searching the gloom ahead for the tall, easy figure of his son. Tears began to blur his vision. He pulled over and sat for a timeless moment. When he came back to earth he found himself slapping the wheel over and over, like an idiot child.

The air smelled of coming rain. He pulled himself together and drove home.

Chapter Eight

Lee Frost arose tired and jumpy after a miserable night. Jenny was up already, faithfully jogging with her TV athlete. He glanced out the window. Giant brushstrokes of golden cirrus hung to the east over the Virginia forests. With a spark of hope for rain tomorrow he fumbled through *The Washington Post* for a forecast.

"Increasingly cloudy with fifty-per-cent chance of precipitation by noon Saturday." The map below showed a front sliding across the Appalachians and already dangling a hook to the south to snag Richmond, Virginia. If it poured tomorrow evening, perhaps the rally would dissolve.

At the Pentagon he found his desk swamped with requests from the Secretary of the Air Force, Navy Deputy CNO (Air), and Air Force Procurement for an explanation of the cancellation of Collins' clearance. A California Senator and two Los Angeles Congressmen had called. He grimaced. With no pictures of Collins meeting Sherry Pace at the airport and the personal check from Collins lost somewhere, or destroyed, Lee had only his own testimony and Maxon's that the two had met at Dulles. He hoped that there was proof on Collins' rented car that the two had met on the road, as well, but he was at all costs going to keep Collins shut off from secret material if he had to accuse the son-of-a-bitch of murdering his own grandmother, proof or no proof at all.

Sergeant Liebholtz had bugged Collins' room at the Marriott but just how or where, Lee did not know. He called Walter Reed and found that he was often confused but sometimes lucid. He sent Maxon down for a bedside vigil and left for the Free Clinic near Dupont Circle, where he intended to spread bait for Marty Lumpert in case his injury drove him to seek help there, if he hadn't already.

The odds were poor. Lumpert was probably halfway to Saskatchewan, hugging the film of the Ban Doc massacre close to his pudgy body.

The abandoned store awaited sale for property taxes. Over its dusty window hung a sign: COMMUNITY FREE CLINIC. 24 HOURS. Someone had added in red beneath it: SPEED KILLS, and under that, BAD TRIP? WE RELATE. In its last commercial life the place had been a cheap drugstore with a lunchcounter. Now the counter had been turned into a freefood cache, where elderly loaves of bread, stale pastry, and damaged cans of food donated by nearby bakeries and groceries were stacked under the caution: *Don't be a Pig*. Sitting on the counter's stools, ignoring the food, was a line of shaggy young men and girls in bleached-out clothes waiting for examination or treatment.

Lee passed them and entered what had been the pharmacy in the rear. Two chubby girls comforted the restless victim of a bummer on an examining table. The young man on duty, whatever his qualifications, wore no sign of his competence, just blue jeans, sandals, and a scraggly black moustache. Lee told him that he was from Army Counterintelligence and he showed not the slightest surprise. "We busted?" he smiled, counting out tranquilizers for his patient. "Who's going to treat the casualties tomorrow?"

"You're not busted." Lee told him that one Martin Lumpert, who had a broken wrist or a broken arm, might arrive for treatment if he hadn't already, and that he was a deserter and to give him a message: "If he turns himself in within twenty-four hours, I'll charge him with AWOL instead of desertion. It could save him a year in Army prison. Tell him Colonel Frost told you that, OK?"

A chill had settled on the room, and even the tossing patient quieted and glared at him stonily. But the young

305

man studied him without hostility. "Frost? You *Rick's* father?"

Lee stiffened. "Yes. Why?"

"We went through Combat Medic school together. We went to the same company in Nam, and into Cambodia. He told me your line of work. You know how he got killed?"

"All I *want* to know. He crawled over a mine." The room was hot and smelled of sweat and faintly of blood, like a real aid station, which was what they were after, he guessed, with their eternal charade. Lee continued: "He was trying to get at a sapper who'd just lost half a leg."

The boy nodded, but his pale-blue eyes stayed on Lee's: "Did the Army tell you why we were there?"

"I heard," Lee said coldly, "there was a war on." He wanted to get into fresh air, away from this fetid, stinking imitation of revolution. But he found himself rooted. "All right, why was he there?"

"We took this so-called 'strong-point.' There were dead Slopes left in a paddy, two or three, depending on who you talked to. Battalion commander dropped down in a chopper and told us to get back to the company CP. 'Olly, olly, oxenfree.' Good day's work. Two dead Charlie, like I say, or three. If they *were* Charlie, of course." His voice rose. "Big deal, you know, another Battle of the Marne. But Shitty Smitty, he was our platoon leader, he decided we had to go back to look at the paddy."

"Why?" Lee asked tensely.

"Why?" The ex-medic stared. "Hell, Colonel, to find out if it was two or three! You know why! It's your fucking Army!"

Blindly Lee Frost moved through the waiting patients and back to the dirty street. It was cloudy and a gentle drizzle was beginning. It looked good for rain tomorrow, but he didn't even care.

Lee Frost found Congressman Cyrus Weintraub in a muggy little office in the Old House Building. The young Congressman regarded him suspiciously from beneath his heavy lids. He seemed tired and sour. "Did Dennes get you to come over?"

Lee reminded him that he was simply fulfilling a promise to report on the Ban Doc massacre and his interview with Alioto the cameraman. He told Weintraub that his constituent, Private Hackle, had been right: the massacre had indeed taken place. He described Poma's capture and mentioned the missing film. He promised to find it, and when he did, to see that an official investigation was begun, regardless of pressure from above.

Weintraub pointed out that Lee's efforts so far seemed merely to have landed Poma, the only witness who had tried to do anything about the massacre, in jail. "Where I'll probably join him tomorrow, because I'm releasing that memo this afternoon."

"Oh, no!" groaned Lee. He began to pace the room. He told Weintraub that one Bull Collins had stolen the memo and why he had sent it to him and the reasons he should not leak it. "If you do, you're doing nothing but knocking out his competition for him! He's trying to use you! Very possibly, he's a murderer! And if you oblige him, you're going to get clobbered!"

"We are not going to sell more airplanes to Greece," Weintraub said stonily. "At least not without a fight. Directly *or* indirectly. If this gives me a strange bedfellow, I can't help that. I told you once, I have to use what weapons I can."

Lee warned him that the Pentagon would accuse him of having instigated Collins to steal the memo in the first place. "And when I put the screws to him, he'll claim the same thing! The minute you release it, he's got a Congressman to share the blame with. 'He asked me to do it, he's on House Armed Services, I acted from principle, I thought he should know.' Let's not give him ammunition!"

For the first time Weintraub looked shaken. His secretary, a bright, birdy creature with a hooked nose, popped her head in and informed him that the wire-services were coming to his press conference and the networks wanted to start laying cable. He nodded, abstractedly, and asked Lee if his pitch had anything to do with tomorrow.

"It sure does," admitted Lee. "What'll your story do on

307

tonight's news? There are fifty thousand people ready to march on the Pentagon *now*."

"Good," blurted Weintraub. "Maybe it'll help. The '69 Moratorium kept us out of Jordan."

"It didn't keep us out of Cambodia, though," snorted Lee.

"It got us out sooner," said Weintraub. "Maybe tomorrow will keep us honest somewhere else."

Lee looked at him wonderingly. He visualized Weintraub fifteen years younger, in a schoolyard, trying to substitute brains for brawn and guts for weight, but always last chosen for a basketball game or a local gang-bang in the haunted house. Some men were born to be crucified.

"You'll start a riot at the Bridge," predicted Lee.

"Then clear the fucking Bridge!"

"Mr. Weintraub," Lee suggested heavily, "you can get yourself in just as much trouble if you leak it Monday, and maybe save a few lives. Or do you care?"

Weintraub's eyes flashed. "You're talking to a member of Congress, Colonel! Now get your ramrod ass out!"

Lee Frost left. For a long time Cy Weintraub stared into space. Abruptly, he walked to the door. "Marge, postpone the conference. Until Monday."

"OK, Cy," she said surprised. "Ab Dennes is on the phone."

"I bet he is," said Cy. "Tell him I'm out with the Israeli Air Force, getting drunk."

He left the office and went to look for Chaim.

Lee Frost returned to his desk to find the latest tape from Fort Holabird's tap of Toolie O'Hare's phone. He listened to interminable calls to her mother and her mother's lawyers, none of whom seemed to know how to proceed to free a civilian prisoner of the Army held temporarily in the psycho ward of a federal jail. He stopped the tape, startled, as he recognized Handlemann's nasal twang, introducing himself as Chairman of the Peace Rally Committee, with information about her husband. *"He was told he was responsible for a death at that germ factory at Detrick, wasn't he?"*

"What's the information?" she asked cautiously.

"Well, there was no such death."

She gasped and asked if he could prove it. He replied that his informant, Marty Lumpert, could, but was injured and hadn't been able to call again. *"Mrs. O'Hare, do you know any reason the Army lied to your husband?"*

"You're damn right I know!" She told Handlemann about the plague at Da Nang and her husband's vaccine. Her voice rose: *"If the vaccine's safe, why aren't they using it?"*

"Would you ask me that tomorrow at the rally? In front of a hundred thousand people?"

"There's nothing I'd rather ask."

Handlemann suggested that, knowing the Army, she should drop out of sight until then, and asked her to meet him at seven P.M. tomorrow at the Sylvan Theater under the Washington Monument. *"I'll be the redheaded scarecrow running the show."*

"I'll be the gaunt survivor of seven childbirths," Toolie O'Hare said, *"and wild horses couldn't keep me away."*

Lee visited Lucius Hardy's office and suggested that O'Hare be released, tonight. The general shook his head.

"He's in that psycho ward now screaming for a direct line to the White House, and everybody think he's nuts. If we let him out, he just may find a way. 'Not tonight, Josephine.' "

Lee watched him narrowly. "But Monday, we don't care if it all hangs out?"

"That's right."

"That doesn't make any sense." Hardy was hiding something. "You're trying to keep the White House calm this weekend, for some reason. And it isn't the peace rally, either."

"*Sure* it is, Lee," Hardy said smoothly. "I don't want the demonstrators mad enough to cross the river. I don't want you to have to draw blood on the Pentagon steps. You'd never make general, then. It's all for *you*, Mr. Dumbjohn!"

That was bullshit, and he told Hardy so, and the general only grinned, so there was no use trying to pry the real reason out of him. He would only get mad. Lee returned to his office and found ex-Colonel Charles Brewster Hammond, III, waiting for him, disheveled and sloppy, his white hair bristling and his eyebrows pawing his nose. Lee's stomach began to ache at the sight of him, but he was damned if he would show it. He seated the lawyer cheerfully. "OK, Mr. Hammond," he said, "make my day complete. You represent Collins now, I'll bet. And out in the open, where we can see too. You're here about his clearance. Or ex-clearance, I should say."

"Do you know he's liable to be fired? Do you know he's already lost a twenty-thousand-dollar bonus?"

"Good," yawned Lee. "Next time he conspires to steal a top-secret document maybe he'll be more careful who his accomplice is, God rest her soul. *De mortibus nil nisi bonum,* but she sure was stupid to tangle with that ape."

"One stroke of your pen," bellowed Hammond, ignoring him, "and he was through!"

"Got you there," Lee smiled. "It was by telephone. The paperwork's coming later."

"I can prove you made the call to Security Review!"

"I admit it," Lee offered. "I insist on the credit."

"Jesus, Frost," Hammond burst out, "you're an arrogant bastard!"

"That's not very lawyer-like," Lee commented. "If you're not careful, I'll bar *you* from the Pentagon too."

"How? Are you going to accuse me of murder?"

Lee felt his temper rising. "Mr. Hammond, your late client Sherry Pace met Bull Collins at 9:03 Wednesday night at Dulles. She shook him down for a check. She stuck it into her bra. She left first. He followed. Now, cut to the local Virginia State Police office. A sergeant gets a call from a male who refuses to identify himself. Your deceased client, for reasons unknown, has torn out a new highway through a couple of hundred yards of Virginia jungle and her car is wrapped up like a ball with her body inside. Collins' check is missing from the body at the morgue, also from the automobile. Why? I think it is missing because after he ran this poor damn idiot off the road, he went back and lifted it!" His voice had climbed, and he tried to temper it. "If suggesting this to a law-enforcement officer is an accusation of murder, then I accused him of murder. Is all that clear?"

Hammond sat back, seeming strangely satisfied. "You put it so succinctly," he murmured. "You should study law. Or maybe you shouldn't. All right, your contention is that he ran this woman off the road, so you canceled his Security clearance?"

"His Security clearance was on its way to being canceled," Lee said brusquely, "when he had to hire you to protect a woman who'd just 'lost' a top-secret memo. I just had to wait for more evidence."

"Until he killed the woman, you mean?"

Lee told him to put it any way he wanted, and rose, ending the discussion. "I'll never prove he killed her," he conceded, "but if he gets that clearance back, it'll be over my courtmartialed body."

Hammond agreed that it might very well be, and pointed out that there was the civil route to think of, too: Lee was not exempt from lawsuits. He snapped his fingers. "I almost forgot. We owe you a 'bug,' as you call it in the trade."

Lee's spirits sank. "A bug?"

"Little tape recorder," said Hammond. "Mr. Collins found it behind a picture in his room at the Marriott, kind of unimaginative place for a professional to put it. I'll have to keep it to show how you harassed him, but maybe after the trial, or suit, as the case may be, who knows? It's government property, I guess, and we ought to give it back."

He screwed a smile onto his seamed face and moved toward the door. Lee was struck by a thought. He slipped open the drawer in his desk and glanced at the oscilloscope installed by his predecessor. The ordinarily smooth, green line across its face was jiggling hysterically. As Hammond moved out of the room it resumed its normal undisturbed profile. He overcame an inclination to go after him, shake him down, and remove his hidden recorder, but he was too well acquainted with the laws of search and seizure to try. He had said nothing that he wouldn't stand behind in courtmartial, Security review, or civil suit, so the hell with him.

He called Maxon at Walter Reed. Leibholtz had awakened once, but was too vague to remember Collins' bug. Lee told Maxon he might as well quit trying. "He stuck it behind a goddamn picture!"

"A picture?" Maxon asked incredulously. "Liebholtz?"

Lee couldn't understand it either. Maybe he had been rushed, or maybe Hammond had been lying. But it had obviously been found, and whatever it had taped was lost. His spirits were not lifted when Thelma brought him the report of the Virginia State Police:

No damage observed on suspect's rented Hertz convertible when inspected at Marriott Motor Hotel 18 hours after accident. Investigating officer, who was same officer receiving anonymous report on location of accident, unable to determine if suspect's voice that of man who telephoned said report. No skid marks on Dulles Access Road eastbound indicating deceased's vehicle had in fact been forced from highway. Deceased's blood contained .18 per-cent alcohol by volume. Investigating officer concludes no evidence connecting Collins to accident #1013 (fatal).

312

How he was going to make his cancellation of Collins' clearance stick was all at once too grim a question to face, so he put it from his mind and began a last tour of the Security centers to deliver his revision of the Building Military Contingency Plan. He visited GSA Security's tiny control room, then the Army and Navy Security centers, and finally the Air Force Security Operations Room, where a magic empire of consoles, flashing lights, and electrostatic sensors had somehow been funded, to the envy of the other Services. Everywhere he went he quizzed the section chiefs to see that they were ready for tomorrow if the rally broke across the river.

Finally he arrived in Joint Chiefs of Staff country, on the outer ring of the second floor above the River Entrance. He would not be responsible tomorrow for Security here: it was in the hands of the JCS Special Security Force, an elite and unfriendly group quite sensitive to interference from Counterintelligence. But JCS Security would be responsible for a slice of Pentagon pie all the way from the River Entrance outside the National Command Center inward to the Hall of Heroes on the inner ring above the courtyard, a wedge-shaped segment of the total building that he could not afford to neglect, regardless of what the Table of Organization said. He flashed his NMCC striped identification card at the glittering sentry outside, signed in, and finally inserted the card itself in an electronic slot and passed into the Center.

It was the central cell in the cortex of the U.S. military Establishment. Its nucleus was the "Tank," a half-walled cubicle some seventy feet on a side, set precisely in the middle of the surrounding Center. The Tank itself contained nothing but a thirty-foot mahogany table, flanked by a dozen beige padded armchairs. Before each chair, built under the lip of the tabletop, was an intercom with five square buttons. Less comfortable seats arose in tiers behind the armchairs for personal aides squiring the titans below. Near one end of the table stood a lectern. The place was set up for a briefing, Lee noted. A map, shielded with a green shade, saying, WARNING: DO NOT UNCOVER, sat propped on an easel. A pad of paper and golden pen lay neatly before each seat.

The Tank, completely surrounded by glass, had a fish-bowl aspect that seemed comforting when real action erupted: the Joint Chiefs had lately valued it during the Bay of Pigs, Santo Domingo, and the crossing of the Cambodian border. It was reassuring to see one's silent staff outside the Tank, moving among the maze of consoles and computers, terminals of the Pentagon's worldwide communications system. But it was not so snug for secret briefings, so, although the Tank was completely soundproof and isolated from the electronic clattering and muted voices of the Center itself, tall automatic curtains on four sides could isolate it in seconds from the surrounding world.

Snuggled outside the windows of the Tank were long communication consoles manned by field-grade officers. When the curtains were left open, the operators were staring face-to-face at their chiefs inside the glass. Over the windows was a line of twenty-four-hour clocks, each set to the time zone of a Command for which that particular console was the nerve ending. The officers who worked below the clocks, visible representatives of staffs, which numbered, incredibly, ten thousand Army, Navy, or Air Force personnel for each of the Joint Chiefs, were flesh and blood synapses, screening out nonessentials and passing currents of information through the table's intercom to the men in the easy chairs inside. The clocks above the Tank showed NORAD time in Colorado Springs, SAC's time in Omaha, Pacific Fleet time in Hawaii. Beyond the consoles were computers, ranging the outer walls of the Center and connecting it to the Air Force's "Hole" in the basement, to Flag Plot, and to the Army War Room. Further out yet lay receptors from Goddard Space Center in Green Belt, Maryland, where space garbage could hopefully be distinguished from incoming warheads, and from Cape Kennedy, where stray astronauts could be similarly identified. Other receptors permitted the JCS to test its theories on the Blue and Red Teams of the Joint War Games Agency on D-Ring, its Cold War Division in the basement, the Army's Gaming Division in Bethesda, or the flesh-and-blood playing fields of Southeast Asia.

In an obscure corner sat a teletype, manned twenty-four

hours a day by qualified interpreters, who were almost the only civilians allowed in the Center. The keys were printed with both Western and Cyrillic letters, and their termini were in the Kremlin. The famous phone on the White House desk was for practical purposes a fiction, and the teletype, Lee knew, was the real hot-line to Moscow. It was tested faithfully from both ends at the beginning of each six-hour shift, the Americans playing the machine in English and the Russians thoughtfully accompanying in Russian. Otherwise, it was almost always silent.

The office of the Commander of the JCS Special Security Force was a small one, off the Center, crowded now with his troops. The commander, a slit-eyed professional Marine who looked as if he should be playing guard for the Packers, sat on his desk, swinging his feet. His deputy, a sinewy Army lieutenant, was briefing their men, a flashy collection of athletes dressed in trim gray-and-black tailormades rather than the uniforms of their parent services, Army, Navy, Air Force, or Marine.

The Marine captain nodded at Lee but did not bother to call the room to attention. "We're already briefed on tomorrow, Colonel, if that's what you wanted to know."

Lee waved his hand. "Don't fuss, go ahead, just forget I'm here."

"One thing tomorrow, Lieutenant," a stubby black volunteered, "I can't fall in with the troops on the steps; my boots are in the cobblers. Can I maybe have Post Number One?"

The lieutenant looked disgusted but made a change in the watch bill. "So much for tomorrow. Sunday, it'll be Presidential honors outside the NMCC, full duty section, Dress Alpha, white scarves. Do you think you can handle *that,* Dupays?"

"Got to," grinned the black. "I'm your token nigger."

"Then we're in bad shape," the lieutenant snorted. "Dismissed."

Lee joined the officers as the men filed out. He asked if the President was coming to the Pentagon Sunday. The captain regarded him like an S.S. palace guard confronted by a presumptuous Wehrmacht officer. "Could be."

" 'Could be,' *sir?*" suggested Lee.

"Sir," the captain flushed. "I reckoned you'd know. Your own boss is briefing him in the Tank."

It all tied in with the vibrations he had sensed from Hardy. He wondered if the two had any idea what was hidden behind the shade drawn over the map. If they did, they would never tell him. He made some suggestions for coordination tomorrow, which the captain did not deign to comment on.

Lee went back to his office, wishing the arrogant son-of-a-bitch were Army instead of Marine. Sometime during Vietnam the whole fabric of military life had started to unravel, and a pair of eagles on your shoulder meant no more than chevrons on your arm. Stars would be no better. He might just pick up his marbles and quit for a lake in Mexico or a Bahamian cay, and the hell with the dream of a seat at the long, polished table.

An hour after everyone else had left, he finished work and went home. The lone picket at the River Entrance flashed him a peace sign, and he waved back. Thunder groaned to the west. The front was arriving too soon and might pass too quickly to spoil the Rally.

If things went sufficiently wrong, and he was sure they would, the lonely picket would not be alone tomorrow.

Chapter Ten

Vollies of night rainshowers had raked Washington. A line of thunderheads hung ready for a new assault as first sunlight slanted through the dripping trees on the Capitol Mall. The image of the Washington Monument lay in its reflecting pool as straight and solid as the original towering above it, wobbling only when a waterbug skittered on the surface. The city was airless, breath drawn, as if waiting for a blow.

The Park police had given up during the night, for there were simply too many sleeping bodies sprawled under bushes and trees to try to clear them out. Showers had sent scores crawling under the abutments of the Rochambeau, 14th Street, Roosevelt, and Arlington Memorial bridges, where they were packed like cigarettes. The first Army convoy to cross Arlington Memorial from the Virginia side to set up a command post found sleepy demonstrators coming to life. They shared joints with the GIs, who were under the impression that the Rally had been canceled. A bearded demonstrator and his girl fed a tousle-haired private who had missed chow, and then wandered off as a sergeant put him to work.

The Pentagon, normally closed on Saturday, would have half of its military personnel on duty today, under Lee Frost's contingency plan. GSA security guards were checking ID cards at all entrances, and the military had been ordered not to arrive in civvies. By the time Lee himself slid into his parking space at the River Entrance, he had seen more uniforms around the building than since the days of World War II, but otherwise there were no visible changes in routine.

Reports began to flow into his office from across the Potomac. A sort of minor miracle of the loaves had been staged on the banks of the river near the Lincoln Me-

317

morial at dawn. Bread, collected by the Peace League, had been dispensed from the back of a two-ton truck. There was no trouble, but the U.S. Park police's crowd-estimate at the handout was from five to ten thousand. Lee flinched and went to tell Hardy.

The general had never been a spit-and-polish zealot, even as a cadet captain thirty years before. But hanging in his office now, apparently ready for Sunday, was a fresh uniform laden with ribbons, new jump-wings, and an un-marred, gleaming silver-and-blue combat-infantryman's badge. Under razorsharp trousers, a pair of glossy new shoes stood at attention. He had a pointer in his hand, and was striding up and down before a wall map of Southeast Asia, mumbling into the air.

"What time Sunday do you brief him, Lucius?" Lee asked woodenly.

"Who told you that?" growled Hardy.

"I read it in the *Underground Clarion.*"

"I'll bet," said Hardy. "What can I do for you?"

Lee told him of the unexpected size of the crowds ar-riving in Washington, and suggested that *one* thing he could have done, since Lee was responsible for Pentagon Security, was to have let him know that the President was visiting the Pentagon Sunday.

Hardy shrugged. "Sorry. But the Rally will be all over by Sunday. Anyway, the Secret Service gets him here, and JCS is responsible while he's being briefed. You're just pissed off you got left out."

"No. Just curious as to why."

Hardy studied him, slapping a calf with the pointer like a swagger stick, and finally decided to speak: "How do you feel about Communist cease-fire violations?"

"Oh, I'm for them, sir," Lee said acidly. "I *like* to see our grunts get ambushed, I'm *appalled* that we complain to the UN."

"Seriously, damn it!"

"Seriously, I think we should get our aching asses out."

"That's what I thought you thought, and one reason you were left out. But how would you like it if we snatched victory from the jaws of defeat?" He moved to his wall map, drew the tip of his pointer slowly from the Gulf of

318

Tonkin westward to Vientiane in Laos. "What would you think of that?"

Lee felt his palms grow damp. "Amphibious?"

"First Marine Division by sea, 101st and 82nd Airborne, by air, and ARVIN and the 1st Cav up by road from the south."

"Why not just drop the nuke on Hanoi?" Lee muttered. "Lucius, for God's sake, *why? Why now?*"

"Because the JCS wants a last crack at it. 'On, Brave Old Army Team.' Eighty-yard pass from the shadow of our own goal line." He pretended distress: "Lee, you're not *buying* it!"

"No," said Lee. "And neither will the President. He may be impetuous, but he's not nuts!"

"I think he will. Because I think the North Vietnamese are planning a trip south themselves. Don't you?"

"No," said Lee, "and neither do you."

"Intelligence from Dong Hoi—"

"Bullshit!"

"Aerial reconn—"

"Horse-hockey!"

"There's an eighty-per-cent increase in southbound coastal traffic!"

"Look, Lucius, I've been scaring politicians too long myself!"

"I think they're getting ready to mount an attack," Hardy announced virtuously. "Anyway, we don't know they *aren't.*"

"The country," warned Lee, "will come apart! And the Army with it, joint by joint."

"Well, I'll discount *you,*" Hardy observed comfortably. "You're not a good subject for this briefing. You're influenced by personal matters."

"Bull. I'm G-2 first and a bereaved father second."

"I wasn't talking about Rick," smiled Hardy. "I mean that hippie broad at the Peace League. How's your back, anyway?"

Lee slammed out and returned to his office. He scanned *The Washington Post* and found no mention of the Israeli-Greek deal. Maybe, after all, his visit to Weintraub had turned him off until after the Rally. He checked the *Un-*

derground Clarion for the Rally schedule, wishing he could contact Toolie O'Hare too, before she blew the whistle on the Da Nang plague in front of Handlemann's alleged hundred thousand protestors. Maybe he could get to the Rally this evening and cut her off at the pass.

Maxon phoned from Walter Reed Medical Center. He told Lee that he had been at Liebholtz's bed at dawn, when the nurses had told him he would be most coherent.

"I knew damn well," Maxon said loyally, "he wouldn't waste a bug behind a picture."

"It was a plant?"

"Yes sir. He figured if Collins found it he'd quit looking for more."

"Where's the other one?"

"Stuck inside the sideboard of Collins' bed."

"He remember how he got in?"

"Triple-A Yale master. I've got one."

"Go, man," breathed Lee. "Go!"

He hung up. Some you won, and some you lost, but Maxon was winning more for him all the time.

Sergeant George Maxon left the Medical Center and drove through Rock Creek Park. He had decided to park outside Collins' room until he saw him leave for breakfast, make his grab, and split with the bug. He drove past lines of thumb-trippers who had camped in the dripping underbrush with their girls, heading now for the action in town. Rock Creek Drive looked like a pilgrimage scene from a Robin Hood movie. He found himself envious of the freaks who had nothing to worry about but scoring on women, drugs, and food. He picked up a Christlike character with a sweet-faced girl, six-months' pregnant, who looked like a barefoot Virgin Mary in a Mother Hubbard. Like rabbits they were, he reflected, a bunch of frigging rabbits, all getting laid the first night in town, while he had found precisely one piece of tail his whole tour in Washington, and that from a WAC old enough to be his mother.

He warned the two that the town was full of narcs, and she kissed him for that when he dropped them at the Lincoln Memorial. She didn't smell half as badly as he'd have expected, after all night under a bush in the rain. A mixed group was splashing happily in the reflecting pool, bare-assed as the day they were born, and it took all his strength, fortified by a desire to please Colonel Frost, to continue on when a squad car arrived to bust them and expose all the lovely boobs and bottoms to the cheerful light of day.

He noted, crossing Arlington Memorial Bridge, that troops from the Old Guard had already set up barricades on the city side. He sped to the Marriott and parked where Liebholtz had told him to, so that he could see every bedroom door in the wing containing Collins' room. He climbed the stairs to the veranda and walked past. On the scarlet door of 217E was a sign: DO NOT DISTURB. Like all civilians, he was probably a lazy bastard, and might sleep all day, so Maxon went to the lobby, dialed his room, and when a deep voice answered he asked for a girl named Georgine. The receiver clicked down and he returned to his car to wait.

Collins was awake now, presumably angry, and possibly hungry. Maxon settled back to wait.

Lee looked up from the desk as Thelma led in the Navy captain who kept his ketch in the slip next to *Misty*'s. The doughty little sea-dog fixed twinkling monkey-eyes on Lee and waited until Thelma had left. He moved his chair closer, with a mischievous glint, as if he were about to tell a dirty story. He didn't want to be out of line, Lee should understand, but up in Flag Plot this morning, with nothing really to do, he had got to thinking about last night. "Did you spend the night on your boat, Colonel?"

Lee gaped at him. "No. Why?"

The captain looked concerned. He had been down to check his docklines in the storm and noticed lights in *Misty*'s cabin. He hadn't wanted to knock, of course (he winked), or call Lee at home (because his wife might have answered) but this morning he had begun to wonder (with all the filthy hippies in town) if it really was Lee and a girl, or some doped-up long-hair who'd broken aboard. "So I thought I'd come down and tell you."

Lee's spirits soared. It was Laurie, brought by the storm. It had to be; no one else knew where he hid the key. The lightning, first since the glorious afternoon squall had rocked the river for them, had brought her back, certain that he would go too, if not for her, to check the boat. And he had failed her, sleeping like a pig in the sterile apartment, all his mental receivers turned off, when they could have been together in the cabin lamplight while the rain slammed down and the thunder crashed.

"It was a friend of mine," he explained briefly. "I wasn't there."

The monkey-face screwed into a leer. "If I'd have known that, Colonel, I'd have boarded her myself!"

Lee got him out of the office, somehow, lunged for the phone, and called the Peace League.

Laurie answered, coldly. "Yes, Lee?" she said.

"Laurie," he pleaded, "I'm sorry about last night."

There was a moment of silence. "Last night?"

"I wasn't on your frequency, or I'd quit hoping, or I thought I'd never see you again, or something."

"I'm not sure what you're talking about," she said in a soft voice, "but I like the tone."

"Can you meet me there? At the boat?"

"Lee, today's a rat-race!"

"Here, too."

"Oh, the hell with it. When? Half an hour?"

"I'll be there." He hung up, his heart drumming wildly, told Thelma he would be back before lunch, and left for the marina.

Chapter Eleven

Bull Collins had eaten dinner the night before with Charles
Brewster Hammond, III, in the Saddle and Sirloin Room
of the Marriott, and then they had gone upstairs to the
Windjammer, where Bull had absorbed a half-dozen
Scotches-on-the-rocks as Hammond endlessly recollected
military men he had got sent to outer Siberia as he intended to do with Lee Frost. He had not hit the sack until
two, and when the phone rang beside his bed in the morning, he had groped for it blindly and hung up when he
found that it was a wrong number. He tried to sleep. He
could not. In the bathroom he found himself swaying before the mirror. His face was beet-red, the whites of his
eyes tinged with yellow. He would have to get out on the
squash court more in the Athletic Center; no, he had forgotten—even that was denied him until he squashed Frost
and re-entered the brotherhood-of-arms. He dressed and
wobbled unshaven out the door and into excruciating sunlight on the veranda. He went to the coffeeshop off the
lobby and jacked himself into a booth. Christ, he was getting fat.

He ordered coffee, changed his mind, left a dollar for
the waitress and slid out. What he needed was a drink.
The Windjammer was still closed, so he headed back for
his room.

Sergeant George Maxon had felt a thrill of fear when he
saw the size of the man who emerged from 217E. He
looked more like a retired and weary wrestler than an
aerospace salesman, as he dragged himself along the veranda, across the parking lot, and disappeared into the
lobby. Maxon waited long enough to make sure that Collins would not return for a forgotten handkerchief or a

wallet, moved swiftly to the red door, took a fast look around for a stray room-maid, and worked at the lock until he felt the tumblers slip. He stepped in and closed the door. The place was dark and evil-smelling after the rainwashed air outside. Papers, clothes, and suitcases were jumbled everywhere. The scent of whiskey and tobacco and after-shave lotion was heavy; a half-empty bottle of Chivas Regal sat on the desk.

He moved quickly to the rumpled bed and lay down on his back on the floor beside it. He began to feel inside the sideboard, starting at the head and inching his way toward the foot. Halfway down he felt the compact little recorder, sticky-backed to the wood. It was tightly adhered, so he shifted, stuck his head under the bed itself, and began to work the instrument free with his fingernails, afraid to damage the minute reels or the fragile tape.

He had it almost free when he heard heavy footsteps dragging down the row of doors outside. He froze in fear, then tore blindly at the bug, forgetting the risk of breaking it. He was trapped and terrified under the low box-springs. At last the recorder came loose with a jerk. He barked his knuckle on a spring. He dropped the bug, felt wildly until he found it, and slithered clear of the bed. He was rising to his feet when the door swung open and a huge figure shadowed the entrance.

"What the fuck!" Collins exclaimed, sliding the curtains wide. Maxon stood squinting in daylight. Collins seemed even bigger, close-up, florid and beefy, outweighing him by thirty pounds. The sergeant's training at Holabird had proved him no fighter, and he knew himself to be no talker, either, so he simply stood rooted, cringing under the bulging eyes.

"OK," Collins said, edging toward the phone, with a threatening finger extended. "Make a move for the door, and you're going to think the roof fell in!"

But he had to try. He could never face his colonel if he gave up the bug without a fight. Big men were slow, and so he charged in a mindless rush. He found that the man was not slow at all—he was very fast—and the roof did fall in. Maxon, clutching the recorder, found himself enveloped in the huge arms and overpowered with the smell of stale whiskey and sweat, and the man was squeezing him to death, suffocating him; he was caught in the arms of an animal, and the reddened eyes were bulging, bulging, bulging . . .

Suddenly the pressure eased. Collins' ruddy cheeks distended and a groan burst from the barrel-lungs. Collins stepped backward, pointed at his throat, shook his head pitifully, took a step toward the bed, clutched at his chest, and dropped to his knees like a felled tree.

Maxon yelped in fear, stepped to the open door, and began to yell for help.

The rain had begun again, pelting the boathouse on Columbia Island and frothing the basin as Lee drove onto the graveled marina lot. Two cars were parked in it. He stared through his sqeaking wipers at his father's polished Cadillac, at the head of the wharf, rain dancing on its roof. Now he understood everything. It had been Cotton, not Laurie, aboard last night. "Jesus," he breathed. The old boy seemed finally to have cracked. He had remembered where Rick had kept the boat key, perhaps, or forced entry: he could get into anything. A respectful distance from the Cadillac was a purple VW, and behind the wheel was Laurie. He pulled to the passenger side, braved the torrent, and plunked beside her into the seat.

Her hair was sodden and her T-shirt soaked, plastered against the swell of her breasts. She twisted in the seat and was in his arms, straining against him. They kissed crazily, as if it had been months instead of days. He felt her strong back arching under his hands. The rain cut them off from the world. If there had been room in back, he would have taken her then.

"I just went down to the boat, Lee," she said huskily, when they pulled apart, "and I heard somebody aboard."

"My dad." He told her why he had mistakenly called her, and she touched his cheek, liking the idea that he'd assumed she'd go to the boat in the storm. He explained Cotton's delusions and guessed that he was talking to his dead grandson now. Tears came to her eyes. "Don't grieve, Laurie, he's hard as nails. And right now," he promised, "I'm going down there and kick his senile ass off, and we are going to start another thunderstorm."

"Tomorrow, Lee," she smiled. "I have to get back." She drew his hand over and looked at his watch. She studied him for a moment, hazel eyes thoughtful. "I have to open a safe in the church."

He didn't understand. "A safe?"

"For that idiot Handlemann."

"Yeah?"

"Your film's in it."

His heart jumped. "Ban Doc?"

"Yes."

"Thank you," he said hoarsely, "for telling me that."

"I *love* you, I think. I have to trust you, don't I?"

He wanted to forget the film, never mention it again; it was unfair to risk her trust once more, but he forced himself to go ahead. He asked her why Handlemann wanted it now. "To show at the Rally?" he suggested.

She thought it over. "I guess so."

He told her that he knew what was on the film, almost scene by scene, from the cameraman Alioto. "It's worse than I thought, Laurie. And I'll get the murdering bastards if it costs me my career. And it'll *be* shown."

"Good."

"But not tonight, Laurie. Please. Not to a crowd like that."

She looked into his eyes. "So don't open the safe?" she asked.

The rain stopped suddenly. A lance of sunlight through the beaded windshield dappled her smooth, round forehead. He pressed it with his lips. "Oh, no," he refused. "Not again. Not *me*. You decide, Laurie. You're a big girl now."

She nodded gravely. "OK, Colonel, slide out. I'll tell Handlemann."

"The hell you will! I will!"

"*I* will! Hell, I won't go hide!" she grinned. "I'm a big girl now."

She meant it. He kissed her. "I'll see you tomorrow. Be careful!"

She left and he heard footsteps on the wharf. His father,

326

tall and erect, moved up the ramp and faced him. "Who was that, Lee?"

"A girl."

"You chipping off the old block?"

"I hope not," Lee said dryly. "You through with the boat?"

Cotton nodded. "I get drunk, I keep forgetting he's dead, I guess. I was going to take it down to the farm, but I couldn't even start the engine until I dried out the points. And then I was sober."

"Good."

"Never could have got her up the creek anyway," Cotton shrugged. "Stupid idea." He glanced at the sun. "Got to get back; Cynthia's probably having a shit-hemorrhage. Damn it, come down and see us next week."

"I'll try," promised Lee.

Cotton climbed into the car, rolled down the window, and said: "And *he wants his typewriter!*" He backed the Cadillac from the space and crunched off across the wet gravel. Lee sighed and returned to the Pentagon.

Sergeant George Maxon watched the ambulance pull from the Marriott parking lot. Through the rear window he could see the attendant adjusting the oxygen mask they had jammed on Collins' blue-tinged face. Even with the huge bulk safely on its way to Arlington Emergency, Maxon was still trembling as if he could somehow arise to point a finger at him. The Marriott manager, who had believed him when he identified himself as a passing guest, accepted a phony room number too, so he drove to the Pentagon.

Lee Frost tensed as his agent tossed the tiny recorder on his desk. Maxon seemed almost lethargic about it, so Lee rewound it and carefully set the tiny reels to playing. Garbage—squeaking springs, coughing fits, TV shows, and Collins singing in the shower—had activated the mike for days, but finally, as Lee's tension rose, they struck gold. Sometimes after a Wednesday-evening talk-show and before a Thursday-noon weather report, before Collins could legitimately have known of Sherry Pace's death, they heard him phone news of it to her lawyer: *"You've lost one client whether you know it or not. But you've gained another. . . . Sherry Pace was killed last night on the Dulles Road."* It was immediately followed, to sew things up neatly, by an interview in Collins' room with the Virginia State Trooper. On the tape, just after he had announced her death to Hammond, they heard him deny knowledge of it to the police.

"You may have proved a murder," Lee suggested.

A few hours ago Maxon would have glowed. Now he simply said, wearily, "I may have practically *committed* one," and asked to go to lunch.

Lee watched him leave the office. Some men were made for Intelligence, and some were not. He wondered if he was, himself. He worked until dusk, went home, and changed to civilian clothes. Then he left for the jam-packed Monument grounds to try to find Toolie O'Hare.

Chapter Twelve

Marty Lumpert awakened moaning for June in the room off the altar. He could sense from the light falling from the window that it was late afternoon. Handlemann and Ronnie Flieger, his hair haloed and his granny glasses glinting, waited at the vault.

Reverend Scott wheeled in. "Laurie's gone," he told Handlemann. Reluctantly he began to work the combination. "Why do you want that film now, anyway?"

"Ronnie's giving a little light-show at the rally," said Handlemann. "I'm the sound track."

Scott stopped. From the still he had seen, he was worried about controlling the crowd if they showed it, although he admitted that it had to be released somehow, and soon, before the Army found it. But if it was confiscated at the rally, how could they show it in the art-houses?

"That's our problem, it's our film," said Handlemann. "Now hurry up, Scotty!"

"It's Chris Poma's film!" Marty objected thickly from the floor. "You got to ask Chris!"

"Chris is in an Army stockade," Handlemann pointed out. "Go back to sleep, Clausewitz."

Reluctantly, Scott began again to spin the dials. Marty wished drowsily that Chris or June or someone who really cared were here, but it was all too much trouble to think about and he drifted back to sleep. He awakened again when he heard them leaving. Handlemann had hoisted one of his cartons to his shoulder, and Flieger carried the film. Marty's wrist ached in sharp, rising waves. He called for June, and no one answered. The church was very quiet now. Everyone seemed to have left the Peace League, too, for there were no footsteps on the stairs. He was going to miss the whole rally, film and all, but his arm throbbed so badly he didn't even care.

He wondered where June and Sunshine were, whether Handlemann had talked her into shooting the rally for the *Clarion,* whether they would really go to it without him. He raised himself to his elbow. On the writing table was a bottle. Thinking it was the rest of the reds the Free Clinic had given him, he crawled from the bag and lurched over. When he peered nearsightedly into it he could see that it held no pills at all, but some sort of oily liquid. He sniffed it curiously. Almonds? Oil of lavender? The odor was familiar, evoking fear. Nitroglycerin! As sensitive as the fulminate of mercury, most volatile of fuse primers, he had seen in the gas-shells at Pine Bluff Arsenal. But obtainable, where fulminate was not. Anyone stupid enough to do it could simply boil blasting dynamite and skim the surface.

"Jesus," he muttered. The pile of Handlemann's cartons seemed depleted, but he stumbled to it and looked into the top one. Nothing but rally pamphlets, which he couldn't even read without his glasses. He pulled off the top carton, one-handed and clumsy, and flinched as it fell to the floor, bracing the tottering stack with his body to keep it from falling too. He opened the flaps on the next carton down. There were no pamphlets in that one, just neatly stacked sections of lead pipe, lined like cordwood, alternating with cylinders of blasting dynamite, and an open box of cheap wristwatches.

He heard June's voice in the chapel outside, and Sunshine's piping answer to something her mother had said. He heard June, more clearly now: "Marty?"

"Still here," he yelled. "My God, June, look at this!"

He heard the slap of Sunshine's little sandals. The door burst open and the child was running across the room toward him, squinting up into the golden light, face flushed and smudged with chocolate, lips ready for a kiss. He reached out to embrace her, forgetting his arm, and jerked it out of her way in an instant of searing pain. It struck the bottle of nitro on the table and he stuck out his foot to break its fall. He felt it strike his toes and the world turned red and he was floating on a black

330

velvet pillow with Sunshine's baby face still before his eyes, and then there was no more.

Lee Frost showed his ID card to a harried policeman and parked at a wooden barricade near the Sylvan Theater bandstand under the loom of the Washington Monument. The throb of rock was overpowering. He looked up at the crowd. He felt rather old and very small and absolutely helpless. The fleeing light gilded a sea of young faces jamming the slope from the shadowed stage in the glen to the sunlit Monument at the top of the rise. The lawn was hidden under a whole nation of bodies, sitting, lying, loving. Hundreds cued for temporary johns set on the fringes and some did not cue at all. The hill was packed solidly from 14th Street to 17th Street and hordes still poured eastward from the Mall and wandered westward from the cherry trees and Tidal Basin. Giant loudspeakers boomed from the bandstand. Like the hiss of breakers on a gravel beach, a crowd-voice backed the thump of music. The mob was liquid: there would be sudden splashes of movement in the sea of sunlit faces as a marshal tossed a loaf into the ocean, then ripples would spread in a widening circle as neighbor passed the bread to neighbor. Over it all and into the glen drifted the pungent scent of pot.

Floodlights burst on suddenly in the darkening glade and Lee spotted Toolie O'Hare talking to Handlemann at the foot of the stage. He picked his way swiftly to the bandstand, sifting through a line of arm-banded marshals who let him pass without comment. He caught her starting up the steps, having to shout to be heard. "Mrs. O'Hare, could I talk to you?"

"No," she snapped. "Just listen."

"Your husband's going to be out by Monday!"

"You're damn right he is!" she yelled. Handlemann beckoned and she ran up the steps. The tall redhead moved center stage, holding up his hands for silence. It was minutes before the crowd grew quiet enough for him to be heard. When the residual roar had died, he introduced her, and she began.

"My husband is a scientist. He learned of an epidemic of Black Death in U.S. Army-occupied Vietnam. He has refused to be silent, so he's a political prisoner of the U.S. Army. And now I shall give you the details."

A sibilant, ominous breath passed up the darkening slope. Lee felt his stomach beginning to ache. Thunder rumbled distantly, and it started, too late, to rain again. No one moved at all.

General Lucius Hardy passed through clacking lines of teletypes and entered the silent glass Tank of the National Military Command Center. He pressed a button and the curtains slid closed, shutting him off from view of officers manning the consoles outside. He roamed the empty glass-walled room, checking to see that tomorrow's briefing was set. He uncovered his maps on the easel, checked their order, flicked a switch on the lectern, tapped the microphone, and tested his speaking voice.

"Mr. President," he said to the head of the vacant table, "and gentlemen," he nodded to the empty seats flanking it, "I'll begin with certified instances of penetration by NVA elements through the cease-fire line . . ."

He continued, feeling not in the least ridiculous. He had no idea how many politicians, State Department officers, and generals he had briefed in the past thirty years, but he had never been better prepared, and never so certain of success. He had the ball, was fading toward his own goalpost, and ready to throw the bomb. He stopped, poured himself a glass of water from an invisible pitcher —he would have his aide see to that—and sipped it coolly.

Lucius Hardy had a kaleidoscopic vision of the bad times that had earned him his place at the lectern. Choking dust on the Plain at the Point, the smell of fear, excrement, and diesel in the fog of the Ardennes, a thousand asskissing cocktail parties with Skeeter, from NATO to Saigon. His heart began to thump elatedly.

Son-of-a-bitch, my Sweet, he promised her silently, meet the next Army Chief of Staff.

When Toolie O'Hare finished and walked from the stage there was a moment of shocked silence and then a roar from the crowded slope, drowning the grumble of thunder from the west. Lee, soaked to the skin with rain, listened for the familiar howl he had heard in the Palace Grounds in Tokyo, during the riots of '51, the insensate baying of a mob on the verge of rampage. He did not hear it, and decided to return to the Pentagon. Threading his way through the rock performers behind the stage, he felt a jolt from somewhere to the north. It was not thunder, too sharp for that, more like a mortar shell or the secondary explosion from an ammo dump. When he reached the barricade at which he had parked, he found the policeman at his squad-car radio, head down, listening to a female dispatcher. The cop straightened, shaking his head. "Hell of a bang, Colonel, up in the Northwest. Church blew up, she says."

"Where?"

"That Peace League place on Decatur."

"Oh, God," moaned Lee, and raced for his car.

Lee Frost could get no closer than three blocks to the Peace League, the streets were so clogged with emergency vehicles. He parked double and trotted past fire engines, TV trucks, and ambulances, talked his way through police lines, and stopped, appalled. In the row of pleasant town-houses lay a gap like a missing tooth. Where the church had been was only a jumble of timbers and jagged chunks of sandstone. A minor fire crackled in the junk. A body lay nearby, under a tarp behind an ambulance. Lee approached the attendant, knees shaking. "Man or woman?"

The driver, a chocolate-brown youth with wavy hair, said coldly: "Woman, we think. There's a male in the ambulance, or what's left of one."

Lee lifted the tarp and dropped it again on a blackened corpse. There was no way to tell. He found a police lieutenant questioning a doctor who, at the time of the blast, had been dictating case histories while he gazed from his office window. "Anybody get out?" pleaded Lee.

The lieutenant answered: "Most of them had left for their goddamn rally. Unfortunately."

Lee asked him if he knew who had done it. The lieutenant had decided that maybe they had done it themselves; it was no church at all, it was a fucking powder-magazine. A fireman stumbled from the rubble with the mutilated body of a child. "They could have kept their *kids* out," complained the lieutenant, and asked the doctor to describe the last to leave.

The doctor dabbed at a cut from his own window. He had seen Reverend Scott wheeled out, watched them fold his chair, stow it in the car, and drive him away. Later a couple of Weatherman-types with crash-helmets had left. "And then a weirdo with glasses, carrying film or something, and a tall redheaded kid carrying a box."

"Handlemann," blurted Lee. "That crazy son-of-a-bitch!"

"That figures," the lieutenant agreed.

Lee could stand it no longer. "A girl from the League, Doctor? Medium-sized, long coppery hair, slim, beautiful figure, worked for Scott?"

"I've seen her," the doctor recalled, "but tonight, I don't know. They've been pouring in and out of there since five."

"Think, Doctor," begged Lee. "Going in? *Or* coming out?"

They were looking at him curiously. The doctor shook his head and said that he couldn't be sure. Lee whirled and jogged back to his car. If he couldn't find Laurie, if she were dead, he would pluck Handlemann from the mike, batter him to the footlights, strangle him in plain view, and let them demonstrate over that!

Lee had to abandon his car on the West Mall, for pedestrians arriving after dark had simply jammed the roads. When he jostled clear of the latecomers he found himself halfway up the Washington Monument slope. He stared.

Handlemann had picked the marble face of the Monument itself as a screen, and the audience had turned about to view it, facing up the rise. When Lee saw the great moving images hovering hundreds of feet above the flesh-packed incline, his first thought was that Laurie, alive now or dead, had been forced to open the safe to give him the film. The projector was somewhere in the ocean of spectators, but Handlemann was a tiny figure silhouetted at the microphone on the dark stage far below. Between him and Lee was a low, impenetrable wall of seated bodies, shoulder-to-shoulder, thousands deep. His instinct was to somehow kick his way through, but he knew that he was helpless. He could never force his way past the first spellbound rows without starting a riot. He could only wait until the crowd melted somehow, and then it might be too late. He looked up at the monument. The hush on the hill told him that the story of Ban Doc must be reaching its climax.

A third of the way up the towering shaft, in bright living color, stood a primitive Vietnamese village hootch, in a row of similar huts. A yellow vapor drifted down the dirt road past its door, and as Lee watched, a gas-masked GI twenty feet tall, wearing on his back a chemical disperser, lumbered to the entrance and began to slip from the harness.

Handlemann's voice echoed cheerfully from the glen: "Unlike the Expendable E-8 Gas-Launcher of the previous exercise, the M106 'Mity Mite' Disperser, manufactured originally by Buffalo Turbine as a sprayer for insecticides, can be used to force CN gas into any enclosure the enemy has chosen for cover."

The giant warrior, free of his harness, placed the disperser in the doorway, pointed its nozzle inside, yanked a starting lanyard, and stepped aside. When vapor began to billow from the door, he turned off the machine, slipped back into harness, and lurched to the next doorway. His place was taken by another masked GI with an M-16. Lee's heart began to sink. Damn, damn, damn, he moaned silently; what the hell had their platoon leader been thinking of?

"In the field," Handlemann droned meticulously, "you will find the Mity Mite useful in flushing troops from

335

sandbagged command posts, caves, and underground fortifications, but it may be efficient even against ordinary dwellings, where enemy strength is judged to be strong."

A ragged child ran from the hootch, saw the GI, stared at the mask, and ran back in. Lee heard a shocked murmur up the slope. His hands turned clammy. A woman appeared in the doorway, vomited, and straightened, blinded and rubbing her eyes. A second GI, with his weapon lowered, joined the first in the foreground.

"When the enemy has been exposed to the volume of lachrymator or nausea gases deliverable by Mity Mite, he will usually be found to be incapable of further resistance and may be handled by more conventional means."

The first GI looked at the second, who nodded and moved off down the road. The first stepped back, raised his M-16, and fired into the woman's stomach as the child clung to her thigh. His rifle bucked silently three times. The woman's eyes flew open in shock, her legs buckled, the child howled once, noiselessly, and the mother crumpled. For an instant the child gazed down at her and then smiled tentatively, squatted in the dirt, and began to pat her forehead. The GI looked down for a moment with vacant glass eyes, shook his head, and followed the other down the line of huts.

"For obvious reasons," Handlemann continued reasonably, as an odd, ominous groan swept up the slope, "personnel engaging in the exercises you have seen in this film must not remove their M28 Protective Masks, or—"

All at once he could no longer be heard above the strange, deadly mumble, so he quit. The picture continued. The camera drew back. The image on the lofty shaft became that of a lone GI, mask hanging loose, walking up a dusty village road, prodding at bodies with the muzzle of his weapon. The murmur swelled in waves, and all at once the projector was off, the footlights flashed on, and a semicircle of crash-helmeted bodyguards had formed on the stage around Handlemann. He faced the crowd, hair flaming red, arms upraised.

"Do we march on the bastards?" he screamed, "or do we crawl back home?"

A low, insistent chant started behind him on the stage

336

and spread across the crowds suddenly eddying below. *"March . . . March . . . March . . ."* Handlemann jumped from the stage into the first wave swirling past, one of his Weathermen handed him a carton, the rest dropped from the footlights to form around him, and the march was on in a roar.

Lee wanted the carton, and he wanted it fast. Under the roar he had heard the howl he had dreaded, of a mob turned animal. He did not know what Handlemann planned to do with the beast, but he knew one thing.

It would not be stopped at the Bridge.

From the Washington Monument, past Lincoln Memorial, to the Arlington Bridge at its foot, was less than fifteen hundred yards. Lee tried to cut from the flank to Handlemann at the point, and found himself in the flood of marchers splitting at the reflecting pool. He was suddenly tightroping along its edge, soaked with sweat, rain, and the splashing of those who had been forced into the water and were wading its length before trying to scramble back into the flow. If he did not reach Handlemann before the human river froze momentarily at the Bridge, he was afraid that he would never find him in the flood when it burst loose on the Pentagon approaches.

He glimpsed Reverend Scott on the left flank, trying to wave the marchers back from his chair. For a wild moment he thought that the girl wheeling Scott was Laurie, but it was not. He lost sight of them in the jam at the Bridge ramp. Overhead he heard the *chomp-a-chomp-a-chomp-a* of a low-flying chopper, and above it Picket Aspen's voice, booming ludicrous assurance: "I order you to disperse! My troops will open fire!" Then Lee was on the Bridge, swept past struggling knots of soldiers who hacked helplessly with rifle-butts at the unfeeling crowd, were jostled to the Bridge railings, were even picked up in the flow. Ahead he heard a rattle of bolts but, thank God, no firing: the troop commander, wisely, had dropped back to regroup, and he knew that was the last the fast-moving mob would hear from him. From the direction of the Pentagon he could hear Aspen's retreating helicopter, and he knew that gas was coming, and still he had not spotted Handlemann.

On the Virginia side, the vanguard began recklessly to jog. He stumbled once and a pink-cheeked, broad-shouldered youth wearing a shirt with a smeared red cross yanked at his arm and righted him, grinning. The pace grew faster, to a dead run, now that the cork at the Bridge had popped, and Lee could see the loom of the Pentagon, brightly lighted with emergency floods, a thousand yards ahead. Parade marshals, running too, pleaded: "Walk, walk, walk . . ." but no one could slow the pace.

They were at the Pentagon and he would never find Handlemann now, without help. Lee heard a clatter of bayonets. He cut left, toward the River Entrance, through marchers winded from their run. The chant had changed to: *"Get out, now! Get out, now!"* The swirl of the crowd was clockwise around the Pentagon, thank God, in the way he wanted to go, for he could never have breasted it. As it eddied around the building he worked his way toward the center. He caught a sudden flash of Handlemann's carrot-top, surrounded by the white helmets of his Weathermen, even glimpsed the carton again. Explosives, grenades, firearms? He fought to get at him, hurling men and girls aside, and then he lost sight of him. He would simply have to get help. He heard the drumming of choppers descending in a vortex around the building, the popping of E-8 gas-launchers from the steps, and he knew that it would not be long before he was blinded with gas. As he rounded the northeast corner he saw demonstrators overturning cars in Generals' Row. A detachment of gas-masked MPs, having fought its way down the steps to protect the vehicles, was retreating before it was swamped.

A chopper swept low, blades churning a minor typhoon that threw girls from their feet. Suddenly the whole of the River Entrance was shrouded in clouds of choking vapor. Billows of it writhed in the glaring floodlights and tore at eyes and set fire to sweaty skin and grabbed at guts. Demonstrators around him began to drop to their knees on the glistening pavement. Lee, gagging, sprinted for the JCS Security Platoon formed on the steps, grabbing for his wallet and ID card.

A great orange flash from inside the gaping bus entrance lit the low-lying clouds of gas. Lee felt a jolt through the marble steps. Retching, he abandoned the idea of sanctuary in the River Entrance and dashed for the Concourse door. Handlemann was the source of the explosion, and he wanted Handlemann more than air.

The explosion apparently had come from a contact charge, probably a bottle of nitro, tossed from the dim pavement onto the bus ramp. It had blown down the Concourse doors, closed for the demonstration, and dazed the elderly GSA guard nearest to the entrance. He was a potbellied veteran sitting on the floor propped against his desk. One of the crash-helmeted intruders, swiping at him with a ballbat in passing, had yelled something about the Hall of Heroes, and the guard's lieutenant, on the phone with the JCS Security Force, nodded to Lee.

"Says the bastards are already there, Colonel, tearing down the plaques. He's taking down everybody he's got."

Lee borrowed the groggy guard's gun and sprinted up the ramp, checking its cylinder as he ran. He was racing past the National Military Command Center when an Air Force major stumbled out, handkerchief to face, coughing. Lee skidded to a stop as a stream of teary-eyed Center personnel gathered around the unmanned sentry post. The sentry was inside with a maintenance man, someone said, trying to close off the ventilating system, which had apparently sucked in gas from the demonstration outside.

Lee started again for the Hall of Heroes, then stopped suddenly. He knew the Pentagon building plans. The NMCC contained an isolated, filtered-air system, for nuclear attack. If there was gas inside, it was not getting in from the riot. He soaked a handkerchief at a fountain, tied it around his nose and mouth, and shoved through the crowd waiting outside. The inner door was closed. He inserted his card into the electronic slot and stepped inside.

The Center seemed empty at first; teletypes clacking unheard and computer-tapes whirring unheeded. The JCS Security Force door was open. Inside he could see the stubby black sentry who had yesterday asked for Post Number One, donning a gas mask. Lee heard a feeble hissing and looked down at a burned-out tear-gas canister.

Gagging, he kicked it into the Tank. "Private," he yelled, "this isn't from the outside! Somebody tossed in grenades!"

The sentry glanced at him, nodded, and started out. Lee heard movement beyond the Tank. He tensed and skirted it, staying low. In the corner, intently watching the clattering keys of the Moscow hot-line, a rangy figure bent.

"Handlemann!" croaked Lee. "Get away from that!"

Handlemann turned, a gas-masked caricature with goggle-eyes. He swooped and came up with a short length of pipe. Lee cocked his weapon. "Drop that, you idiot!"

Instead, the young man advanced. Out of the corner of his eye, Lee caught a reflection on the glass wall of the Tank. It was the guard, automatic out, and stalking him, not Handlemann. The truth flashed, he whirled and fired, and the slug slammed the black into the computer, where he writhed to the floor. Lee kicked his automatic away and spun as Handlemann brought the lead pipe down in a crashing arc. He took the blow on his forearm, and as the pipe rose again, he fired. He caught Handlemann dead-center in the chest. The youth tore off his mask, fighting for air, and collapsed against a console. His red-veined eyes were fastened on Lee's. A stream of blood worked from his mouth: "Colonel?"

Lee dropped to his knees beside him. "Look," he cried, "I had to! Why'd you—"

"Out!" groaned Handlemann, pointing about the room. "Get out! Forty seconds!"

Lee glanced wildly around. Under every console, jammed into every switchboard he could see, were stubby lengths of lead pipe. "Jesus!" he blurted. He grabbed Handlemann under the shoulders. A sudden spasm wrenched the angry frame, he stiffened, quivered, and the life left him in a racking death-shudder. Lee turned. The stocky guard was inching for the door, gut-shot, and leaving a trail of blood. Lee dropped Handlemann, grabbed the Negro's arms, solid as oak boughs, and dragged him past the Tank. He was lead-heavy. For a hysterical moment Lee could not open the Center door, and when finally he crashed through, he found the passage full of JCS guards trying to get in.

"Get out!" he screamed. "Hit the dirt!"

He heaved the guard through, slammed the door, and dropped, cradling his head in his arms. For a moment he wondered if his heroics would make him a laughing-stock, and then it blew.

It blew beautifully, exactly as Handlemann might have wished, in a flash of rosy light. It blew down the door, leveled the Air Force's NORAD console, drove a V of shatterproof glass from the Tank halfway through the northern wall. It wrapped General Hardy's beautifully rendered map around the Blue Team Cold War console, atomized the lectern, and hurled his microphone through the switchboard from Goddard Space Center. It lifted the Moscow teletype from its foundations and deposited it in a jumble of twisted keys and sparking wires on the polished JCS table, which had been blown from the Tank clear into the Security Office. The message that had so intrigued Handlemann hung fluttering from the mess, in the airflow from a ruptured ventilating duct. The blast tossed Handlemann's body itself thirty feet across the Center, where it made things sticky for the Demolition Squad when they found it draped on the panel that displayed the disposition of the Navy's Poseidon Submarine Fleet.

It would have been a very satisfactory explosion from the viewpoint of the diversionary Weathermen forces trashing the Hall of Heroes, but they never got near the shambles to see it and in fact never learned if the plan had worked. They were captured in the Hall itself or hunted down one by one, lost in the Pentagon's web of rings and radials. The last one was flushed grinning from a basement laundry-chute at dawn, long after the bulk of the demonstrators outside had wandered home, and after the last victim of gas-convulsions has been picked up by ambulances cruising the lawns, and after the more violent or less lucky marchers had been hauled singing away to jail. Public Affairs clamped a gag into the whole explosion around the Tank, although Major Chip Bolen next morning ran an angry press tour through the Hall of Heroes, suggesting that in view of tight Pentagon budgetary limitations, the Medal-of-Honor plaques would have to be replaced by public subscription.

The Navy Explosive Ordnance Demolition team, which removed Handlemann's remains, found in his tattered pants a message he had typed and torn from the Moscow machine. The duty-interpreter had found the answer in the teletype. As Lee sat at his desk, briefing General Lucius Hardy on the film projected on the Monument shaft and the fall of Picket Aspen's Bridge, the Explosive team brought the TWXs in.

"'TELL SOVIET YOUTH THAT HEART OF PENTAGON PIERCED TONIGHT BY BROTHERS IN ARMS,'" Lee read aloud, "'ALL POWER TO THE PEOPLE.'" He looked at the reply, a charred teletype on which the interpreter had penciled English above the Cyrillic letters.

"I'm surprised they didn't answer by nuke," Hardy observed. "What's it say?"

"'DO NOT UNDERSTAND YOUR MESSAGE. SAY AGAIN.'"

"I wish he'd been able to read it," remarked Hardy.

"He didn't *have* to save my ass," Lee said softly. "I'm glad he *couldn't* read it."

"*I'm* glad," Hardy remarked, "the tricky bastards haven't got the clout to hit us. What a time!"

"Maybe you can work that into tomorrow's briefing," Lee suggested. "Change the scenario from the Gulf of Tonkin to the Gulf of Finland, and let's hit them first, just in case. After the Bridge, Picket Aspen's on the ropes. Press on, Lucius! You'll make Chief of Staff yet."

Hardy drummed his fingers on the arm of the couch. "The briefing's canceled."

"Why?" Lee wondered innocently. "Not on account of that little misunderstanding in the Tank? Nobody blew up the War Room, or the Hole, or Flag Plot, did they?"

"Not yet, but it makes you wonder about Security," Hardy remarked idly.

"Thanks, General," Lee said. "Why don't you brief him in the White House Map Room? Regular goddamn fortress, the White House. You could roll your stuff over in a wheeled suitcase, like a jewelry salesman."

Hardy got up and stretched nonchalantly. "No, Lee. Tonight's festivities have panicked our glorious leader, at least for this weekend. The stars are simply not propitious for a briefing. At least not on *that* part of the world. However . . . It's a big planet, and your boy Weintraub's about to be upstaged."

"What do you mean?"

"Didn't you hear about Syria?"

"I've been busy," Lee said grimly.

Hardy smiled and briefed him quickly. At 0035 Washington Time, a TWX had come into the Hole, confirmed by Flag Plot ten minutes later. Seventy Syrian tanks had crossed the Jordanian border. Israel was calling up Reserves. "Now, by Monday, when Weintraub leaks that memo, nobody will be looking, or if they are, any little thing we can do for Israel will sound great. *'When in trouble, when in doubt, run in circles, scream and shout.'* Sixth Fleet's got a carrier and a half-dozen cans leaving Naples right now, for Haifa."

"Oh, Jesus," moaned Lee, "are we going to try to sell *that* one?"

"We don't *sell* anything," Hardy said calmly. "When we find a threat, we call it as we see it."

"We see more of them all the time."

"And, having called it, we do as we're told. Like good soldiers anywhere. Now, can I have that film?"

Reluctantly, Lee got up. Every FBI and Counterintelligence agent at the Rally seemed to have converged on the projector when the crowd began to move. The machine had been demolished in the rush to grab the film, and the bushy-haired projectionist apparently arrested for inciting a riot, but the reel had finally gravitated to Lee's office. He took it from the vault.

"I'd like to handle it myself," he told Hardy.

"I'll handle it."

"When do we charge that platoon leader?" demanded Lee. "When do we get the GIs?"

"As soon as we find out who to charge," Hardy said.

"And when do we *try* them? Two years from now?"

Hardy slapped his hands down on Lee's desk and leaned across it. "Goddamn it, just *give* it to me! I'm tired of your bucking me every step!"

Lee handed him the film and he stalked out. Maxon

dragged in, bleary-eyed. He had found Lee's car in West Mall, but had no word of Laurie.

"Did you go to her apartment?" Lee asked pleadingly.

"Yes sir. It's staked out by the FBI. Nobody's been near it. She have some *Weathermen* there?"

"Maybe." He hid the panic in his voice. "What about the Peace League? You see the Arson Squad?"

"No more bodies, yet, but they aren't digging any more, either. Nobody's moving anything until it gets light."

Lee's phone rang. He sent Maxon home and answered it. It was the DeWitt Army Hospital anesthetist who had assisted in the removal of Dupays' spleen. The Negro was out of danger. "But, Colonel? Did somebody take a shot at the Pentagon tonight? From Arlington Cemetery?"

Lee tensed. "Why?"

"Going under, Dupay was talking like *he* did."

"Not tonight," said Lee. He called Hardy's office and suggested that now that they knew who had fired the shot, he get the attempted murder charges on O'Hare dropped before he ended up with a civil suit on his hands. He put down the phone. He suddenly made a note on his desk calendar that he had called Hardy, inserting the time of the call. He had never felt a need, in dealing with his mentor, to comply with the Pentagon precept of CYA— Cover Your Ass—but Lucius was changing before his eyes, and there was no use risking the accusation that he had not informed him immediately that the Greenberg case was solved.

He moved to the vault and took out the fine old Springfield. He had heard no static from the FBI and could probably safely keep it, but suddenly he discovered that he did not want it hanging over his mantel or anywhere else. Maybe tomorrow he would give it to Cotton, who sometimes hunted deer on the farm. He phoned Jenny to tell her that he was all right, but could not get home until afternoon.

Leaving the River Entrance, he returned the salute of the lonely GSA guard at the door and picked his way through empty CN canisters, pamphlets, abandoned sandals, and picket signs. A clean-up detail from Building Maintenance and a tow truck from the motor pool were

345

already at work, and the overturned vehicles had been righted. A half-dozen long-hairs were gathered on the banks below, bathing in the river, and chords from a guitarist drifted on the chill morning air with the faint scent of gas. *"Where have all the flowers gone, long time passing . . ."*

The faithful Pentagon picket wandered over. His placard was half-torn, and it must have been the biggest night of his life, for he was stoned and grinning broadly. Christ, thought Lee, with one dead, hundreds injured, and God knew how many jailed, they thought of it as a success. Maybe it was. The picket waved at him and asked: "You make the scene, Colonel?"

"Son," he said wearily, "I played second lead."

He drove to the Peace League and joined the firemen beginning to sort through the rubble.

Chapter Fourteen

By noon he was exhausted. The firemen and the Metropolitan Bomb Squad were still sifting through the jumble. They were confused by his presence, and if they had come up with anything, they were not telling him. He tried to find Scott in his rectory a block away. Scott was at the Post Office in Alexandria, which had been turned temporarily into a jail, trying to arrange bail for demonstrators. It gave Lee sudden hope, and he called the U.S. Marshal's office, wondering if Laurie had somehow been arrested. But her name was not on the list, and when he phoned Jenny at home, praying for some sort of message, there was no answer.

In a daze of fatigue, he drove toward the Arlington Bridge. The barricades were down, and there was no sign of the action of the night before, although the streets en route were packed with hippies leaving town. When he reached the Bridge he swung left instead of crossing it, and drove to the marina. He wandered down to the boat, and found the Navy captain chipping rust on an anchor chain. He asked him if anyone had been down to see him, and the captain leered and told him no. He was so pooped he thought of going aboard for a nap, but the thought of the empty cabin was too much, so he started back for the car.

All at once he saw the purple VW turning into the marina parking lot. He broke into a trot, and by the time Laurie had parked he was at the door.

"Hello, Colonel," she said, looking at him oddly. He slid in beside her, feasting his eyes on her face, but did not touch her.

"Laurie, where in the name of Christ have you been?"

"Long story," she said. "I read about the hassle in the Pentagon. They killed Handlemann?"

"I killed him," said Lee.

She was jolted. "You yourself? I mean, *personally?*"

He told her bitterly that Handlemann in effect killed himself, but left it to him to pull the trigger. "So that makes him a sort of folk-hero, I suppose. You can sing his praises loud and clear."

His voice had turned harsh, and she flared back that there were no heroes, not on her side, and certainly not on his: "And *I* didn't try to blow up your goddamn war machine; *he* did! Don't take it out on me!"

"Laurie," he said, "I'm sorry. I haven't had any sleep for forty hours. And I've been scared."

"Well, I have too. I got there just after the League blew up, and the little girl there, I'd met her, taken her to her mother, damn it, if it weren't for me she might not have even been there, and that poor kid Lumpert, I did that too. Oh, it's all such a fucking mess!"

"I was afraid you were dead."

"I wish I were!" She was close to tears. He took her hand but she pulled it away, and said, tightly: "I didn't get any sleep, either—you were right about those hard-hatted idiots we let stay with us; they were Weathermen or something. I slept in a room at American U, there are FBI crawling all over my apartment, and I'm on probation and I can't go home!"

"I can help, Laurie."

She didn't seem to hear him. "And Clancy, he's the kid with the guitar we put up, this is his Volks; he's about as violent as a puppy, and some U.S. Marshal beat the hell out of him and he's in the Alexandria jail and I can't get bail—"

"I'll get it, I've got it," offered Lee.

"You got it from the Army, and I won't take it, and neither would he! Did you see that *film?*"

"I saw it," said Lee. "How'd he get it out of the vault?" It had slipped from his tongue automatically, and now it was too late.

"Meaning?" she prodded coldly.

"Meaning nothing," he murmured. "Laurie, I don't care. You've been through hell, I don't want to—"

"Meaning *I* opened it, after I said I wouldn't? Well, Colonel, I didn't!"

"I believe you."

"Well, yes and no. Right?"

"Wrong!"

"It doesn't matter," she said. "And I'm glad you saw the film. I'm glad everybody saw it. What are you going to do about it?"

"Help prosecute them."

"From inside the Army? Or out?"

He looked into her hazel eyes. He would retire, and take her to Mexico, Portugal, anywhere out of the shadow of the great pile looming across the river. Jenny would simply have to get over it, as she was getting over Rick, have to make it back on her own.

"From inside, without me?" Laurie asked again. "Or out?"

He could not do it. "Inside," he said hoarsely.

"Why?"

"Nobody will ramrod it if I don't," he suggested. "They might not try them for years. Maybe that's it."

"No, Lee," she said, smiling. "That isn't it." She slipped from behind the wheel, moved to the seawall, looking down on the boats. He joined her there. A puff of wind flicked hair over her eyes, and she tossed it back with the gesture he loved. She looked up into his face and grinned. She seemed sixteen when she grinned, tired or not. "Have you thought of why we meet *here,* Lee?"

"The boat, I guess."

"Because you love it, and I was beginning to?"

His mouth felt dry. "Maybe."

"And *he* did?"

He licked his lips. "OK, Laurie, that's enough."

"And he'd have loved *me?* Is that it?"

"Shut up! That's *sick!*"

"That *is* it, Lee." She reached up, took his chin, and turned his face to hers. She kissed him. "It's not sick. It's sweet. But it isn't enough."

She went back to the car and slid behind the wheel. She tossed up her hand in a half-salute, still grinning, but he caught a flash of the tears in her eyes. She left in a shower of gravel. Wearily, he climbed into his own car and drove home.

He watched Jenny snuff out the tall candles and stack the dishes in the washer. He sipped the Mateus she had poured. In a week she had lost five pounds, and the emerald eyes and flawless skin were clear as ever. Beautiful, beneath it all, and on her way to beauty again. He felt stirrings, hot and demanding, and when she turned she sensed it, and when he led her to the bedroom her eyes were hot as his, and moist.

"So long, it's been," she whispered afterward. "So damn, everlasting long . . ."

He nodded, drowsily, full of sleep. He felt her slim fingers on the raking welts that still scarred his back. The emerald eyes looked into his own. "Healing?" she said softly.

He kissed her gently, and with gratitude. "Just about all healed up," he grinned, and slept.

OUTSTANDING BEST SELLERS FROM
WARNER PAPERBACK LIBRARY!

☐ **THE JESUS FACTOR** by Edwin Corley

The atom bomb doesn't work! You don't believe it?
You will when you read this novel of "Tremendous
suspense." —Publishers' Weekly   (66-680, $1.25)

☐ **THE ONLY WAR WE'VE GOT** by Derek Maitland

"Savagely funny is the obvious way to describe this
elaborate put-down of the whole Vietnam mess."
—Publishers' Weekly   (65-638, 95c)

☐ **E PLURIBUS BANG!** by David Lippincott

When the love-hungry wife of the president of the U.S.A.
seeks a more perfect union, it's time for E PLURIBUS
BANG! A novel of "hilarious and often biting wit."
—The New York Times   (65-709, 95c)

☐ **GOIN'** by Jack M. Bickham

At 40 (a **young** 40), Stan Pierce set out on a voyage
of discovery. Others, earlier, had gone looking for America. Stan was looking for himself.   (65-628, 95c)

☐ **MAGGOT** by Robert Flanagan

A ruthlessly honest novel of Marine Corps basic training, where the recruit is not a man but a **maggot**.
(66-741, $1.25)

EXCITING BOOKS FROM THE WORLD OF SPORTS!

☐ **THE 1972 OLYMPIC GUIDE** by John V. Grombach
All the triumph, pageantry and excitement of all the games ever held, making this the most comprehensive and authoritative work of its kind—a treasury of factual information as well as a colorful and dramatic story. FULLY ILLUSTRATED.   (66-799, $1.25)

☐ **OUT OF THEIR LEAGUE** by Dave Meggyesy

Dave Meggyesy, former star linebacker with the St. Louis Cardinals, reveals how a player can be hurt more in the locker room than on the field. "The roughest sports book ever written." **—LOOK MAGAZINE.**
                                                      (66-710, $1.25)

☐ **THE INCREDIBLE METS** by Maury Allen

Maury Allen tells the inside story of the New York Mets, their growth as a team, and how they won the 1969 World Series. FULLY ILLUSTRATED.   (64-301, 75c)

— —

If you are unable to obtain these books from your local dealer, they may be ordered directly from the publisher. Please allow 4 weeks for delivery.

WARNER PAPERBACK LIBRARY
P.O. Box 3
Farmingdale, New York 11735

Please send me the books I have checked.
I am enclosing payment plus 10c per copy to cover postage and handling.

Name ....

Address ....

City .... State .... Zip ....
_____ Please send me your free mail order catalog